New Garden's Hope by Jennifer Hudson Taylor
After Josiah Wall postpones their wedding a second time, Ruth Payne refuses to reset their wedding date. But everything Josiah has worked for means nothing without Ruth. He sets out to win her back, but it seems that each attempt is thwarted by disaster. Will their love and faith overcome their differences, or could this be the end he's always feared?

New Garden's Crossroads by Ann E. Schrock
Deborah Wall is thrilled to work for the Coffins in their home, a hub of the Underground Railroad. Nathaniel Fox has been dismissed from the Society of Friends and becomes a bounty hunter for runaway slaves. When an injury takes him to the Coffins' house, he tries Deborah's patience and challenges her beliefs. But, after accepting Christ and revealing his love for Deborah, will Nathaniel give up his worldly ways to join her?

New Garden's Inspiration by Claire Sanders
As an unwanted, poor relation, Leah Wall is surprised to discover that her Quaker uncle has arranged a marriage between her and widowed Caleb Whitaker. Leah agrees to the marriage and finds herself a wife in name only, caring for Caleb's children while he serves in the Union Army. Trying times are ahead for Leah, but she believes the Lord will make a way.

New Garden's Conversion by Susette Williams
Christian Jaidon Taylor is determined to plead his case with Quaker Catherine Wall and convince her that they are not as different as she thinks. Catherine promised her father that she would uphold the family tradition of marrying within their faith. As Jaidon begins to rethink his own spiritual walk in his endeavor to find love, Catherine tries to show him why their relationship would never work. But are they really *that* different?

THE QUAKERS OF NEW GARDEN

FOUR-IN-ONE COLLECTION

CLAIRE SANDERS
ANN E. SCHROCK
JENNIFER HUDSON TAYLOR
SUSETTE WILLIAMS

BARBOUR
PUBLISHING

New Garden's Hope © 2012 by Jennifer Hudson Taylor
New Garden's Crossroads © 2012 by Ann E. Schrock
New Garden's Inspiration © 2012 by Claire Sanders
New Garden's Conversion © 2012 by Susette Williams

Print ISBN 978-1-61626-643-1

eBook Editions:
Adobe Digital Edition (.epub) 978-1-60742-824-4
Kindle and MobiPocket Edition (.prc) 978-1-60742-825-1

All scripture quotations are taken from the King James Version of the Bible.

Cover design: Kirk DouPonce, DogEared Design

Published by Barbour Publishing, Inc., P.O. Box 719, Uhrichsville, Ohio 44683, www.barbourbooks.com

Our mission is to publish and distribute inspirational products offering exceptional value and biblical encouragement to the masses.

ecpa Member of the
Evangelical Christian
Publishers Association

Printed in the United States of America.

NEW GARDEN'S HOPE

by Jennifer Hudson Taylor

Dedication

To my husband and daughter, thank you for your loving support. To my Quaker ancestors who began at New Garden Meeting in Greensboro, North Carolina, thank you for inspiring this story. And finally, to my Lord, thank You for making all things possible.

Chapter 1

Josiah Wall looked as if he were about to propose, but he'd just done the opposite and postponed their wedding—again. Ruth Payne cringed as the empty void inside deepened.

He bent on one knee in front of her. She sat on a wooden swing, hanging from a large oak tree. Beneath the shade of a black wide-brimmed hat, his hazel eyes searched her face. She wondered if he could see the ache in her expression. Even though she'd known him all her life, right now he seemed like a distant stranger.

"Ruth, say something. . .please."

Josiah covered her hand where she gripped the rope, but his touch seared her, almost as much as his words. She jerked away and stood, slipping from his grasp. The swing swayed between them as his sensitive eyes blinked in surprise. Her gaze drifted to his brown locks around his ears and to his sideburns.

Her heart stammered through denial, anger, and then pure gut-wrenching pain. She wouldn't plead and cry like last time. She turned, clenching her teeth, and stared at her parents' white two-story house. Brown leaves tumbled in the breeze across the yard. The midmorning sun shimmered through shifting tree limbs in the crisp fall breeze.

"What is there to say?" Ruth asked, still avoiding his gaze. "The first time thee said it was because we needed our own home. Now that the new house is built, thee claims it must be after the presidential election. The only thing I can say is that I don't understand."

Ruth closed her eyes to shut out the threatening tears. She wouldn't humiliate herself again. Pride may be a sin, but she needed to preserve some of her self-respect, didn't she?

Josiah stood to his full height, at least a half-foot taller than she. He slipped his thumbs under his black suspenders. A robin swooped from the tree, flapping its wings. Josiah ducked and righted his hat.

"I was afraid thee wouldn't understand," he said. "But Ruth, I'm working with the Federalist movement, and it's imperative I give my full attention—at least through the 1808 election. I can't allow myself to be distracted by wedding plans."

Anger burst inside her. Ruth opened her eyes and whirled to face him. "We're not like the rest of the world. Quakers have simple lives. We have plain weddings and homes. Thee is making this much more complicated than it should be."

Ruth linked her trembling hands in front of her charcoal-colored dress. It contained pleats at the waist and long sleeves with white trimming. The drawstrings of her bonnet suddenly felt tight under her chin. She cleared her throat and leaned her palm against the bark of the tree trunk.

"It's only for a few months," Josiah said. "By then most of the house could be furnished. Right now it's too bare." He stepped around the swing and leaned close.

Ruth stepped back.

His eyes widened as he lifted a dark eyebrow. "Don't be angry," he said. "To prove my commitment, let's reschedule the date for the second month on the twelfth."

Ruth laughed. "Dates mean naught to thee. When that time comes, thee will only change it." His wounded expression pierced her, but she wouldn't take back the words. As far as she knew, they were true. "In fact I'm not even sure thee really loves me—if thee ever did."

"Of course I do!" Josiah stepped toward her but halted when she stiffened and leaned sideways. He gulped, his eyes pleading. "Be patient with me a little longer. I love thee, Ruth—even when we were children. I knew thee was meant for me that day in the school yard when I forgot my lunch and thee gave me an apple." He offered a handsome grin, but she managed to resist him by averting her gaze.

"Are none of these Federalists in thy group married?" Ruth laid a hand on her quivering stomach.

"Of course, but that's different. They're already settled. When thee becomes my bride, I intend to give thee all my attention. I want things to be perfect."

"Josiah," Ruth sighed. "I fear thee has some misguided notion about marriage. Either thee cannot love me or thee is afraid to make a commitment. Seek God and allow Him to show thee what to do. Right now I'll not agree to another date."

His mouth dropped open in disbelief. He touched the top of his hat, paced a few feet, and then came back. "What is thee saying? Is thee breaking our engagement? Ruth, don't do this. Please, I beg thee." Josiah's breath released in rapid gasps. His brows wrinkled and he rubbed his eyes as if they burned.

Ruth wanted to console him but feared she'd lose the tiny thread of self-control she still possessed. How many times could she allow him to do this? If he wasn't sure about his love for her, how could she be so selfish as to trap him into a lifetime of marriage? No. She couldn't do it. In spite of the pain it would cause, she'd sacrifice her own happiness to give him his.

"Josiah Wall, I release thee from our engagement."

⁓

The bell on the front door of the Wall Brothers Seed and Feed store rang, alerting Josiah to an arriving customer. He stopped stacking the new feed sacks he'd gotten in that morning and left the storeroom.

Matthew Payne, Ruth's father, strolled up to the counter. He had a healthy physique for a man of his age, with broad shoulders and a slightly bulging belly. Beneath his broad-brimmed hat, his gray hair was brushed to the side of his forehead.

"What can I do for thee?" Josiah tensed as he set his palms on the counter and forced a smile. Would Matthew Payne be angry he'd hurt Ruth by postponing the wedding again? Guilt sliced through his chest, causing him to take a deep breath. He hadn't meant to hurt her. He'd give anything to see her happy. That's why he worked so hard to make their future better.

"I was wondering if my cattle feed had come in yet?" His gray mustache moved with his lips as he spoke.

"It came in just this morning. If I remember correctly, ten feed sacks, right?" Josiah raised an eyebrow and rubbed his chin.

"That's right." Matthew Payne nodded and scratched his side-whiskers. He glanced at the parallel rows of goods on the wooden shelves. "I can't remember a day this store wasn't organized and immaculate. Thee and thy brothers have carried on and accomplished no small feat in thy father's shoes."

At the mention of his father, Josiah stiffened, his gut twisting like an angry tornado. Three years ago his father had turned fifty and couldn't stop talking of all the things he'd never gotten to do. As a lad he'd always wanted to be a seaman. Josiah used to enjoy the stories his father read to him about seafaring adventures. All those years sharing his father's love for ships and the sea, Josiah never imagined his father would one day disappear and choose such an adventurous life over his own family.

Josiah forced the unpleasant thoughts to the back of his mind, reminding himself that Matthew only meant it as a compliment. "I'm sure my brothers would agree in our thanks. I've always respected thy opinion—even more than my father's."

"I was looking forward to having thee as my son-in-law, Josiah, but Ruth returned from a long walk yesterday, weeping and saying the engagement is off."

She'd been crying? Hope lifted Josiah's heart. When she refused to set a new date, she'd appeared so calm that it frightened him. If she was upset, perhaps she wasn't serious about breaking their engagement. *Lord, please let that be the case.*

"I don't want to break the engagement. I asked to postpone it. I'd hoped for more time to make additional furnishings for the house and be able to give Ruth my all after the election."

Matthew nodded as he slipped his thumbs under his suspenders. "Son, thy reasons are sound and logical—for a man. Now a woman, she's going to think down a much different path. That's the main thing I've learned during all my years of marriage."

"I love Ruth, and I still want to spend the rest of my life with her. She says I don't love her, but that isn't true."

"Thee need not convince me, but her." Matthew's gray eyes pierced Josiah.

"I intend to try," Josiah said. "I was hoping Ruth might be in better humor today."

The elder man shook his head. "I can vouch thee might wait a few days for her good humor to return."

"I see." Josiah slouched against the counter, disappointed but thankful for the warning. "Thanks for letting me know." It would be disastrous to visit today and make things worse. He'd give Ruth time for her anger to subside, and then he'd try to reason with her again.

"Well I'd better get back to the farm to care for my cattle and livestock," Matthew said. "Now that Caleb is twelve, I plan to supervise the lad in fence mending this afternoon."

"Give my regards to everyone." Josiah pointed to the front of the store. "Did thee park the wagon out front or on the side?"

"In front. Shall I pull it around?"

"No." Josiah shook his head. "I'll bring the feed sacks out in a wheelbarrow." He stepped into the storeroom.

The bell rang. Josiah assumed it was Matthew leaving the store. Taking a deep breath, he closed his eyes, seeking a moment of peace. *Lord, I know that everything happens for a reason. It must have been Thy will for Matthew Payne to come in this morning and warn me about Ruth. Even though I long to try to mend things, I'll trust in Thy judgment. Give me strength to obey Thee.*

Josiah stacked the feed sacks in the wheelbarrow and rolled them from the storage room.

"Just the man I'm looking for," said a high-pitched female voice. Josiah looked up to see Sarah Goodson saunter toward him. Her blond curls framed her face beneath her white bonnet, her blue eyes sparkling in spite of her gray dress. Sarah's animated personality always outshone her plain appearance.

Dread pooled in Josiah's stomach. He'd better let her know he was with a customer, or he'd never break free to finish with Matthew.

"Good morning, Sarah Goodson. I need to load these feed sacks on Matthew Payne's wagon, and then I'll be right with thee."

"Oh! He passed me on the way out. I'm in no hurry. I only came to pick up some feed for the chickens."

Josiah moved on, but before he reached the door, footsteps rushed up behind him and a hand grabbed his arm. "Josiah Wall, I wanted to tell thee how sorry I am about thy breakup with Ruth."

"How does thee know?" Josiah's blood ran cold as he gulped in surprise.

News had always traveled around the community of New Garden at a fast pace, but this was unbelievable. Josiah gripped the handlebars so tight that his knuckles whitened on the wheelbarrow.

"She was in a very sour mood at the quilt meeting this morning, and when I asked her what was wrong, she told us— all of us."

Alarm spread through Josiah as a wave of fear prickled the skin along his arms. His anger faded to a dull ache that engulfed the back of his head, seizing his thoughts. Ruth was a private woman. If she'd shared the news with others in such a manner, this wasn't a small argument she needed to overcome, as he'd hoped. Ruth was serious. Their engagement was over.

Josiah's heart plummeted.

Chapter 2

Ruth slid the drapes aside and glanced at the sun-drenched landscape of faded grass the color of hay. The row of poplar trees along the narrow dirt road displayed an array of orange and golden leaves. It was a beautiful day for a long walk, but she couldn't bring herself to leave the house.

What if Josiah came by? Granted, she wouldn't agree to see him, but she couldn't help wondering what he was doing and thinking. Was he hurting as much as she? Or had he moved on with his life?

She sighed, leaning her forehead against the glass. It had been two whole days since she'd seen him. With her heart shattered, there were moments when her chest felt so heavy she could hardly breathe.

"Ruth, that's the third time thee has looked out the window in the past hour," her mother said. "If thee has changed thy mind, why not send Caleb to Josiah Wall with a letter?"

"I don't wanna get in the middle of their lover's quarrel." Caleb wrinkled his nose and eyebrows, his blue eyes glaring at her. "Besides I promised Father I'd finish mending the fence we started the other day."

"I haven't changed my mind," Ruth said, dropping the

14

drapes. "I need another project to keep me occupied."

"Well don't include me in any more of thy projects," Naomi said. "My arms are sore from scrubbing the floors yesterday." Her sister crossed her arms and rubbed them, her brown eyes surveying Ruth. "I've told thee before Josiah Wall loves thee. How can thee doubt him after all these years?" Her blond curls bounced as she shook her head in disbelief. "I don't understand."

"Well at fifteen I don't expect thee to understand. I love Josiah Wall, but he doesn't love me like a wife. He's in denial. I'd be selfish if I allowed him to wed me under such a falsehood, especially now that I've come to realize it." Her voice choked as tears pooled in her eyes. Ruth turned away, hating how her heart squeezed at the mention of him.

"I'm only three years younger than thee," Naomi said. "Old enough to judge Josiah's character. I don't understand why thee insists on torturing thyself this way."

"Girls are so strange," Caleb said, walking across the hardwood floor. "I'd rather be outside working."

"The attic hasn't been cleaned out in a while." Her mother's gentle voice echoed across the living room.

Wiping a few stray tears, Ruth nodded. "A good idea. I'll see to it."

Ruth climbed the stairs and walked down the long hallway to the half-size door at the end. She turned the brass knob. It creaked, and the bolt slid from its hold, allowing her to swing the door open. She peered into the dark hole, lifting the lantern to reveal a steep incline of narrow steps.

Gathering her skirts, Ruth ducked then plowed up the stairs. She came to a small room lit by only one rectangular window. It had been ages since she was here. She hoped no rats, bats, or spiders showed themselves. A rare shiver passed through her spine.

She shoved a hand on her hip and strode to the center of the attic, and then ducking her head, turned full circle. Dust littered all the boxes, discarded toys, and old furniture. Her gaze landed on two cedar chests by the window.

She bent to her knees in front of the large one and lifted the lid. The hinges groaned as they locked in place. A brown leather Bible lay on top of several quilts. The volume was so large and heavy she had to use both hands to lift it. She remembered seeing it years ago; her mother had since relied on a more recent Bible that was smaller and easier to carry.

Ruth hauled the book onto her lap and flipped open the cover to the inside. Various messages had been written in slanted cursive, along with a list of names in the Payne family, and dates extending back to the late 1600s to Sussex, England.

She sat on the floor so long reading her family history that her tailbone began to ache. She shifted to the side to ease her discomfort and caused the Bible to slide off her lap and thump to the floor. The edge of a piece of paper slipped out from the middle.

Ruth dug her fingers in the spot and shoved the stack of pages to the other side. She unfolded the thick brown paper, a handwritten recipe for gingerbread that required a measure of molasses, sour milk, vegetable oil, wheat flour, a dash of salt, and a tablespoon of ginger.

How long had this recipe been in her family? Ruth scraped her teeth over her bottom lip as she pondered what to do with it. The original was too important to remove from the family Bible. She would copy it, and if she had time, try it out this evening.

"Josiah!" Caleb called from below the attic window. "Wanna go fishing?"

Ruth paused, realizing Josiah must be walking toward the house. She leaned over the chest and scrambled to her knees to look outside. The lid slammed on her fingers where she gripped it for support. She yelped and bounced back. Her head slammed against a low beam. Pain sliced across her left temple as her legs crumbled beneath her. The voices below faded with her sight.

⁂

Josiah glanced up at the sound of a woman's scream. "Who was that?" He looked to Caleb for an answer.

"With two sisters in the house, there's no telling. One of them may have found a spider." Caleb shrugged, his mouth twisting in a grin as he followed Josiah's gaze.

"Caleb!" His mother hurried out of the house, clutching a cream-colored shawl. She breathed heavily, trying to catch her breath. "Go fetch the doctor. Ruth has taken a terrible fall and is unconscious."

The lad's blue eyes widened as he gulped.

"Go! Hurry!" Elizabeth Payne waved him away, her brows wrinkled in worry.

"Is there something I can do?" Josiah asked. He wanted to go see Ruth for himself, but he managed to keep his feet planted out of respect for her mother.

"I thank thee, Josiah Wall. Please, go find her father and her brother Elijah. I believe they are out in the pumpkin patch, loading a wagon for market."

She disappeared back into the house, where he assumed Naomi attended Ruth. Josiah ran past the swing on the oak tree to where orange pumpkins grew in long rows. The Payne's wooden wagon was half full from the harvest of four rows.

Over an hour later, Josiah paced the living room floor, his boots clicking a steady rhythm. He hoped they didn't kick him out, but he couldn't be still. His gut twisted in agonizing knots as he waited for news—any news. Voices echoed from upstairs, but he couldn't hear what they said. He rubbed his hand through his hair. His hat was somewhere around here. He was always losing the thing.

Footsteps sounded on the front porch. He rushed to open the door. Dr. Edwards, carrying a black bag, removed his hat. His plump form almost hid Caleb.

"Where are they?" Dr. Edwards asked, his brown eyes searching Josiah's.

"Upstairs." Josiah nodded toward the steps in the foyer, and the doctor rushed past him.

"Is she awake, yet?" Caleb asked.

"I haven't heard her voice." Josiah shook his head. "This is pure torture." He bit the knuckles of his fist as he paced the floor again. A discarded sewing basket lay on the couch with a threaded needle stuck in a shirt. He wondered if the work belonged to Ruth.

More footsteps sounded on the stairs. Josiah whirled and hurried to the foyer. Naomi followed her elder brother, Elijah. Grim expressions marred their faces.

"Mother asked me to offer thee some tea or coffee," Naomi said, looking up at Josiah. "I'm about to make a cup of coffee for Dr. Edwards."

"Has she awakened?" Josiah asked.

Naomi nodded, her eyes focused on the floor as she gripped her hands in front of her. Why wasn't she more happy? Why did she look so uncomfortable?

Behind him, Caleb breathed a sigh of relief.

"Did she say anything?" Josiah asked, stepping closer.

Naomi met his hesitant gaze then looked away. Confused, Josiah glanced at Elijah for an explanation. Two years Ruth's senior, he and Elijah had become close friends while growing up. But over the last year, Josiah had focused more of his attention on Ruth. At times Elijah seemed annoyed by it, but not today.

"She asked if thee was here." Elijah's blue eyes peered into his, an older version of Caleb's. "And she doesn't want to see thee." Elijah shook his head. His hair was a shade darker than Caleb's. "I'm sorry, my friend."

"May I at least stay until we hear a verdict from the doctor?"

"Of course." Naomi glanced up. "Mother said to make sure thee is comfortable. I think we could all use some coffee." She strode to the kitchen.

"Indeed." Josiah sighed, reeling from Ruth's rejection at such a time as this. When would she forgive him and get over his delaying their wedding? Would she have asked if he was here if she didn't care? Hope surged in his battered chest.

He joined the others in the kitchen. They all sat around the table while Naomi made a pot of coffee. The brewing pot smelled delicious. As he finished drinking his coffee, he heard Dr. Edward's voice in the foyer. He stood and followed the sound of the voices to the bottom of the stairs.

"It's a minor concussion, but she should be all right by this time tomorrow. Make sure she gets plenty of rest." Dr. Edwards turned from Matthew Payne, grabbed his hat, and headed for the front door.

"Thank thee," Ruth's father said, still standing on the bottom step. He rubbed his chin thoughtfully as Josiah approached with Ruth's siblings. He looked older, the wrinkles around his eyes more prominent. He met each gaze with lengthy silence.

"Here is thy coffee." Naomi handed a steaming cup on a small saucer to the doctor.

"That smells delicious." He nodded, gave her a grateful smile, and set his black bag on a table. He sipped the black brew as steam swirled around his bald head.

"Please have a seat and join us a bit longer." Matthew Payne gestured to the couch.

Dr. Edwards shook his head and sipped more coffee. He swallowed. "I appreciate the offer, but I have more stops I need to make."

"On that note, I'll be taking my leave as well," Josiah said. "Please tell Ruth that I was here, and I hope she recovers quickly."

"We will." Matthew slapped him on the shoulder. "Never fear. Ruth will come around eventually."

Josiah's heart thumped with optimism.

Chapter 3

The next morning Ruth woke with a searing headache. She touched the side of her temple and winced at the tender bruise. Thoughts of Josiah assailed her, and she groaned in embarrassment. If she hadn't been acting like a foolish schoolgirl upon his arrival, she wouldn't have lost her balance and hit her head like a simpleton. How could she face him in such humiliation? In her weakened state, she would have succumbed to his consolation and wept upon his shoulder like a lovesick fool.

Ruth washed from her basin and dressed. She pulled her hair up in a braided bun and opened the curtains in her room. Having a corner chamber afforded her two windows, one by her bed and the other in front of her writing desk. A fireplace with a simple mantel graced the opposite wall. The bottom half of her walls were taupe, while the upper half were adorned with pictures of various flowers she and Naomi had painted last summer.

Downstairs, the smell of biscuits, frying bacon, and fresh coffee made her mouth water. As she passed through the living room, her parents' low voices carried from the kitchen. A slight chill made her shiver, and she rubbed her arms. She noticed

Caleb's shirt where she'd carelessly left it on a chair. Thoughts of Josiah had distracted her when she'd mended the unfinished seam.

Ruth lifted the shirt to move it to a table so no one would sit upon the needle that poked out of it. Josiah's black hat lay discarded beneath. A sentimental wave of affection overflowed her heart and brought tears to her eyes. The back of her throat ached. Her fingers curled around the brim, and she hugged it against her chest. The familiar scent of his musk and soap drifted to her nose. She closed her eyes and basked in it, trying to ignore the nagging thought of never again hugging the real man as she now hugged his hat.

"Ruth, is that you?" her mother called from the kitchen.

Jerking to attention, Ruth tossed Josiah's hat on the chair. She took a deep breath, lifted her chin, and straightened her shoulders before entering the kitchen.

"Yes, Mother, it's me." She attempted a smile, but the muscles in her jaw and the throbbing at her temples intervened.

Her mother rose and came to her, a concerned expression wrinkling her dark brows. Gentle hands cupped Ruth's chin as her mother's brown eyes surveyed hers. "How is thee feeling this morning? Did thee sleep well?"

"Yes, and I had no dreams to interfere with my rest."

"What about the bump on thy head? Let me have a look."

Ruth tilted her head for her mother. When her fingers stroked the sore spot, Ruth winced.

"I'm sorry. It's still swollen." Elizabeth Payne bit her bottom lip.

Realizing her mother considered calling upon the doctor again, Ruth laid her hands on her shoulders. "I'm fine. Dr. Edwards said there would be swelling for a few days. Right now

I'd like some breakfast. I'm starving."

"I think a hearty appetite is a good sign." Her father's soothing and encouraging voice carried across the table, his own plate was half full. "Elizabeth, fix her a plate. Naomi, pour her a cup of coffee."

"I can do it," Ruth said, but her mother motioned to her usual chair.

"Ruth, what does thee have planned for the day?" her father asked.

"I found a gingerbread recipe in the old family Bible and thought I'd try it."

"Is that what thee was doing in the attic yesterday?" Her father sipped his coffee, staring at her over the cup's rim.

"I was supposed to be cleaning, but the trunk caught my attention. Mother, does thee know who the recipe came from?"

"Indeed." She nodded. Her brown, silver-streaked hair swayed as she laid down a steaming plate of bacon, eggs, and biscuits in front of Ruth. "It came from my great-great-grandmother and traveled all the way across the sea from England."

"How interesting!" Naomi set a warm cup of coffee next to Ruth's plate. "Did thee find anything else?"

"There's so much history written in the pages of that Bible, generations of our family, with names and dates. It's a treasure." Ruth picked up her coffee and sipped the strong brew. The liquid flowed down her throat and settled in her stomach, startling her awake.

"I want to help thee make the gingerbread," Naomi said.

"That's a good idea. I don't think Ruth should be up and about, doing too much today. Dr. Edwards said she should rest." Their mother glanced from Naomi to Ruth.

The side door opened, and Elijah and Caleb walked in, their shirtsleeves rolled up to their elbows. Elijah carried a pail of milk in each hand, and Caleb, a basket of brown eggs.

"The animals have been fed, and we already washed up outside," Elijah said. He glanced over at Ruth. "I saw Josiah walking up the driveway."

Ruth choked on a mouthful of eggs. Her mother rushed over and slapped her back. A tingle raced up her spine as she imagined seeing him in a few moments. She couldn't. She wasn't ready.

"Is thee all right, child?" Mother bent over her, but Ruth kept her gaze on her plate and shook her head as she covered her mouth.

"No, my head hurts. I believe I'll go lie down." Ruth rushed from the kitchen as a sturdy knock sounded on the front door. She paused on the stairs where Josiah couldn't see her and leaned against the wall, her hand on her trembling stomach. How was it possible that he could do this to her without even seeing him?

Ruth rested her head back and tried to ignore the pain lashing from her temple across her forehead. *Lord, please help me be strong so I can do what is best for Josiah.*

❧

Unable to leave, Josiah accepted breakfast and offered to assist the Payne men with their day's work. They said Ruth had gone to her chamber with a headache. He hated to think of her in pain, and he wanted to be as close to her as possible. His brother had offered to take care of the store, and so he was free. As he and Elijah each swung an ax outside Ruth's window, he couldn't help glancing up, hoping for a glimpse of her. A couple of times he thought he saw someone move the curtain aside but then wondered if he'd imagined it.

"It's exciting to know we'll soon be incorporated as a real town," Elijah said as he tossed two pieces of split wood on the pile. "I think it fitting to name the town after General Nathanael Greene. If it wasn't for him and the Patriots fighting for our freedom years ago, we'd still be under the British Crown. And us Quakers would have forfeited our lives in refusing to bow to a king's unfair demands."

"True." Josiah raised the ax over his shoulder and swung it in an arc, his breath gushing at the effort. A hearty satisfaction raced through his gut as the blade sliced through the oak with a jolting thud. One piece of wood tilted, and the other toppled over the stump, where his ax now lay buried.

"I like the name Greensborough," Elijah said. "It has an official ring to it." He paused, staring off into the distance.

"Have they sold all the lots around the courthouse?" Josiah asked, wiping his brow on his arm, his sleeve rolled up at the elbow.

"Yes, that's why I know it won't be long now before we're an official town." Elijah grinned and set another chunk of wood on the tree stump. "Our little New Garden community will benefit from the new people a town would draw. Folks are calling it New Garden's Hope. Has thee thought about relocating the store within the town limits?" Elijah raised a dark eyebrow.

"We'll stay right where we are—and we won't be building a separate residence in town. I won't allow all these changes to cloud my judgment on foolhardy decisions. The house I've built for thy sister is solid and not too far away when she has need to visit."

Elijah's grin faltered, and his eyes flickered before he looked away, rubbing the back of his head.

Josiah paused, recognizing his friend's hesitation to voice what was on his mind. "What? Thee might as well say it. Does thee think me naive to harbor hope that Ruth will change her mind?"

"I'm no fool, Josiah Wall. I know thee hasn't been out here helping me finish loading the pumpkin wagon and chopping firewood for fun. Thee hopes to see my sister and speak to her."

"I won't deny it. I've been worried about her injury, and while I take thy family's word for her condition, I'd feel better if I could see her." Josiah shoved his hands on his hips, paced a few feet away, and came back. "I need to talk to her. Help me. Please?" He rubbed his face. "Tell me, is she avoiding me?"

"I don't know for certain, but perhaps." Elijah averted his gaze. "I'm sorry, my friend."

A cool breeze lifted around them. Leaves fell from the trees and blew across the yard. Josiah lifted his face to the welcoming caress, realizing it felt similar to the hot summer day when Ruth had waved a fan in front of him.

The sound of Elijah splitting more wood jarred him to the present. "I figured she might be. If I could get her to talk to me, I'm sure I could convince her to change her mind. We belong together. Everyone knows it. I can't understand why she'd think differently just because I postponed the wedding."

"Does thee really think thee can change her mind?" Elijah picked up the wood he'd sliced and tossed it on the growing pile.

"I do." Josiah nodded. "She only needs to know how much I love her. It's all a misunderstanding."

Elijah nodded as he tilted the ax on the stump then leaned on the handle. "Why not stay for supper? I know my sister, and she doesn't like hiding out in confined spaces. After being in her chamber all day, I daresay she'll want to emerge for supper tonight."

"Is thee sure? It could be uncomfortable to the family to have me stay for supper, especially after breakfast. I don't want to overstay my welcome." Josiah flashed a grin at his friend.

"Thee is my friend as well as Ruth's. I may invite whomever I please to supper. My parents feel the same way, I assure thee." Elijah stepped back and lifted his ax. "Now let's finish splitting this wood before we lose more time. I'm working up a mighty big appetite."

"Agreed." Josiah felt the skin on his neck prickle. He had the sensation they were being watched. He glanced up to see a slender hand holding aside the lace curtains. The nerves in his stomach danced in glee. He recognized Ruth's blue gown but couldn't see her face. Feeling bold, he lifted a hand and offered a reconciling smile.

The curtain jerked closed, and the figure disappeared, leaving a black hole in the thin space in the middle, much like his aching heart as more pain burrowed deeper and deeper.

Chapter 4

Ruth's stomach grumbled as she finally left the sanctuary of her chamber. The smell of burning wood drifted to her senses from the living room, where her mother read a letter by the fire. The orange flames crackled in a gentle motion as a wave of heat warmed the atmosphere.

At the sound of Ruth's footsteps, Elizabeth Payne looked up and smiled. "How does thee feel? Get enough rest?"

"Yes." Ruth sat in a chair across from her mother and inhaled the scent of roast beef drifting from the kitchen. "Supper smells good."

"Naomi is finishing up the cooking so I can read the letter thy father brought home."

"Is it good news?" Ruth folded her hands in her lap, starved for conversation and company after lingering alone in her chamber all day with a headache.

"I think so." Her mother stacked the loose sheets of paper and folded them along the crease. "Cousin Dolley is coming for a visit."

Ruth leaned forward, excitement lifting her spirits. Even though Dolley was her father's age and his first cousin, she always told the best stories. She traveled all over the country and lived in Washington DC, where so much happened. It had been years since she'd last seen Dolley at Grandma's house in Virginia. Ruth wondered how much she'd changed.

"It appears that her husband, James, is stopping at the new town of Greensborough on his campaign trail." Mother shifted in her chair and, with a brilliant smile, reached out her hand. Ruth accepted her warm hand as her mother's eyes sparkled in the firelight. "Even though Cousin Dolley has chosen to leave the plain ways, we must welcome her with loving arms."

"I feel for her. She's endured so much ridicule for marrying outside the Quaker faith, but she's followed her heart. And her place is now by her husband's side," Ruth said, gazing into the fire as images of Josiah came to mind, the only man she could ever think of as her own husband.

"And just think how much influence she might have if James Madison is elected president. He'll make decisions regarding the laws that govern this great land. I can't help but think of our Dolley Madison as a modern-day Esther.

"Exactly! Why didn't I think of that?" Ruth squeezed her mother's hand. "Will they stay here?"

"Yes. Would thee mind sharing Naomi's chamber while they're here? I must make the same request of Elijah to share Caleb's room. Thy father and I will give James and Dolley the master chamber on the first floor. We must make room for their servants and traveling companions."

"Mother, I'm afraid we don't have enough space. They'll feel horribly cramped."

"My dear, we don't have any choice. There isn't an inn around here for miles. Tomorrow I'll write Dolley and ask her for the number of servants and guests who will be traveling with them."

"Since we never got around to trying out the gingerbread recipe, Naomi and I could make it for them." Ruth clasped her hands in front of her waist. "After all, they're part of the family, too. Dolley may want a copy for herself."

"I think that's a splendid idea." Mother folded the letter and tucked it in her pocket.

Footsteps sounded at the front door. Mother glanced at the foyer then back at Ruth. "Please, don't say anything about this to Josiah Wall," she whispered. "As a Federalist, his views differ from James Madison's, and I don't want any political arguments at the supper table."

"He's still here?" Ruth took a deep breath with her increasing pulse and tried to ignore the distress it caused her.

Her mother nodded as the door opened and men's voices carried on the cool air that instantly filled the room. Ruth shivered, but it had naught to do with the sudden draft and everything to do with the dark brown gaze that searched the room, landing on her like an owl that didn't miss a detail. Ruth broke from his luring gaze and pulled her shawl tight around her.

He started toward Ruth, but Mother's voice interrupted his charge. "Josiah Wall, I'm glad thee has decided to stay for supper."

"I thank thee for having me." He halted, awarding her mother with a handsome grin that began to thaw Ruth's insides. "I regret I must leave early. I've a meeting in town at eight o'clock."

Ruth's head swung up before she could check her behavior. At the motion he turned and caught her gaze. Warmth flickered in his eyes as his lips curled in a grin that threatened to fray her nerves. "I hope thee is feeling much better. I've been praying for thy recovery and looking forward to seeing thee."

"But thee is leaving early for a meeting?" she asked, wondering where he could be going.

"I've a meeting with the Federalists. We won't be holding so many meetings after the presidential election."

The temporary warmth inside her evaporated with her waning hopes. If it wasn't for this Federalist group that occupied Josiah's mind day and night, they might be married by now. A sharp pain sliced through her and dulled to a deep ache. He'd unknowingly given her confirmation in making her decision to break their engagement.

"Please excuse me." She stood. "I need to help Naomi in the kitchen." She stepped around him, but he grabbed her arm.

"Ruth, we need to talk. Please—"

She shrugged her arm away and met his gaze. "We've naught to say. Enjoy thy meeting. It's the path thee has chosen. I hope it gives thee all the love and support thee traded me for."

An eerie silence pierced the room, but Ruth didn't care. She needed to get away. Her heart pounded in her chest, but her lungs wouldn't open and give her air. She strode from the room, leaving him to stare after her.

"Josiah, I'm sorry." Her mother's voice echoed over the threshold.

Elijah spoke, but Ruth couldn't make out his words as she hurried down the hall. Footsteps stormed after her.

"Ruth, wait! What does thee mean?" Josiah asked.

A hand landed on her shoulder and whirled her around. She would have collapsed if he hadn't held both her arms steady. She gasped and finally caught her breath. Her head began to throb where her injury was still sore, and she lifted her hand to the area.

Josiah followed her action and touched the spot on her head. "It's still swollen. Thee should be in bed. Let me help thee. . .please." His voice gentled as his eyes searched her face.

"I'm fine. I missed lunch is all. I'm hungry."

"Then the last thing thee should be doing is helping thy sister in the kitchen. Sit down and rest." He touched his hand to her back as if he intended to lead her back to the living room.

"Don't touch me!" Ruth shoved him away and took a ragged breath. It was his fault she had this aching concussion. If he hadn't been outside the window, she wouldn't have lost her concentration or her balance. The man had a way of making her lose all reason and purpose. Feeling weak, she stepped back and leaned against the wall.

"Leave me be. Thee has made thy decision, and now thee must live with it."

He lifted her chin and looked into her eyes. "I don't know what decision thee believes I've made, but allow me to say this. I love thee, Ruth Payne. I asked to postpone our wedding, not break our engagement. This separation. . .this misunderstanding is killing me. I want things to go back to the way they were."

"That's the problem, Josiah Wall. I don't want things to be the way they were."

⚘

Still reeling from Ruth's cold rebuff, Josiah approached his friend's house and kicked a small stone with the toe of his boot. How could Ruth say that she didn't want things to be the way they were? Their relationship had been so perfect—practical— affectionate. The only thing that could have made it better would be marriage, to make it a permanent situation.

The cold air nipped his ears and face as he secured his

horse to a tree. He rubbed his hands and blew on them. His heart throbbed in denial as he pondered Ruth's uncharacteristic behavior. Right now the last place he wanted to be was this Federalist meeting. He couldn't muster his usual enthusiasm for the cause, and the election was around the corner, in only a fortnight. Yet he'd promised, so he would put in an appearance and slip out as soon as possible. He was hardly in a position to advise others if his own life continued to crumble around him.

"Josiah, how did the day go at the Payne farm?" Andrew called from the front porch, where a lit lantern hung above his head. Their younger brother, Samuel, stood on a lower step beside him.

"Confusing," Josiah answered with a sigh. "I don't know what has gotten into Ruth lately. I was sure I could convince her to change her mind if I had a chance to talk to her." He paused, looking up at them. "Thanks for working in the store."

"It was my turn. Samuel came in and helped this afternoon." He grabbed their younger brother on the shoulder. "We had a steady flow, so the day's profits were good."

Josiah nodded. He hadn't even thought about the store profits. Consumed with Ruth, he hadn't been able to concentrate on anything else. Only the grace of God had reminded him about tonight's meeting. Even though supper had been awkward after his heated exchange with Ruth and the tension between them at dinner, Josiah hadn't wanted to leave with things unresolved.

On three occasions he'd felt his cheeks warming when he tried to engage her in conversation, as if Ruth's blazing looks seared his skin. He touched a cold palm to his jaw. He'd taken fist shots that hadn't pained him as much.

"Sarah Goodson stopped by the store to see thee. I think she was quite disappointed thee wasn't there," Samuel said. "If things don't work out with Ruth, I'm sure Sarah would be happy to take her place."

"No one could take Ruth's place—ever." If the hard edge in his tone didn't give them a hint to drop the subject, his lack of presence would. Josiah climbed the steps and pushed past his brothers. He wasn't ready to admit defeat, regardless of what his brothers thought.

Inside, dense lanterns lit the parlor of George Osbourne's home. As the Federalist leader of their local group, George was deeply committed to their cause, and no doubt disappointed in Josiah's lack of participation of late. George had a way of making a fellow feel guilty for not doing his share. Josiah agreed to attend tonight only as a favor to his best friend. It wasn't that he didn't support the Federalist movement, but right now he had more pressing matters draining him.

For the next hour, he would try to concentrate on political issues. As he approached, George looked up from his conversation with Nathan Hyatt. They stood in front of the roaring flames in the fireplace, their elbows on the mantel's edge.

"Look who finally decided to show up." George uncrossed his booted feet and stepped toward Josiah with a pleased grin. They shook hands. Josiah greeted Nathan with another handshake.

The moderately sized room contained about fifteen men, and a few more stood in the foyer, talking under the brass chandelier. Additional light shone from two candelabras. The dark paneled walls increased the need for light.

"Looks like there's a good turnout," Josiah said.

"Yep." George nodded, a dark lock of hair falling over his forehead. "The numbers keep growing the closer we get to election, even among the Quakers. Did thee hear the latest news?" He raised a dark brow.

"No, I spent all day at the Payne farm."

"Rumor has it James Madison is coming through here on his campaign trail back to DC and plans to make a visit to the new town of Greensborough," George said in a low voice.

"We aren't incorporated as a town yet," Nathan said.

"But we will be," George said. "It's only a matter of time now. Mr. Mendenhall already drew up the streets on a map, and the new lots have been sold. Construction on the courthouse will soon begin."

"They're even building a new jail—with a whipping post." Nathan shook his head as if he didn't believe it. "Can we Quakers prevent the whipping post?"

"There isn't much we can do about it. Sounds like the others are doing what they please. They view discipline differently than we do," Josiah said.

"And slavery, don't forget about that," Nathan said.

"Gentleman, back to the topic at hand," George interrupted. "The point I intend to make tonight is that we be ready to welcome James Madison when he arrives—the Federalist way."

Chapter 5

Ruth wrapped her gray cloak around her as she sat between her mother and Naomi on the church bench. Men were lighting the fireplaces around the large sanctuary, eager to warm the chilly air. On the drive to New Garden Friends Meeting, white dew had layered the grass and bare tree branches lining the dirt road.

She loved attending New Garden every Sunday morning. It gave her a chance to see old school friends and distant family, and to worship in fellowship in the loving grace of God. This morning was the first time she'd ever felt apprehensive at the idea of attending meeting. Josiah would be here with his mother and brothers. Ruth thought highly of Pearl Wall and had looked forward to being her daughter-in-law. She prayed things wouldn't be awkward between them.

"Thee has hardly spoken all morning. Is thee all right?" Her mother whispered in her ear, her warm breath carrying in the frigid air like white smoke.

Ruth nodded, rubbing her gloved hands together to heat her fingers. She longed to go over and stand by the fire. But she remained on the hard bench, seated with the women, divided by a partition from the men, who sat on the other side of the room.

Families continued to arrive in a steady flow, filling up the benches and greeting each other with nods and smiles. Most of the women were garbed in plain dresses of black, gray, brown, or dark blue. Their bonnets covered their heads and shielded their expressions in shadow. The men wore brown or black pants, white shirts, black jackets, and the familiar round-brimmed hats.

Someone touched Ruth's shoulder. She turned. Pearl Wall smiled, her green eyes shining with warmth as she perched on the seat behind Ruth and swept a strand of silver hair beneath her white bonnet. No animosity or haughty judgment lingered in her demeanor.

"Good morning, Friend Ruth Payne. How has thee been lately? Josiah told me of the fall thee took. I worried about thee, but I knew thee would be in good hands with Dr. Edwards."

"I'm much better. I had a slight concussion, but the swelling is gone. And thee?" Ruth forced her gaze to meet Pearl's eyes, so she wouldn't be tempted to look around the sanctuary for Josiah.

"Same as usual. Although I'm looking forward to purchasing a few of thy father's pumpkins to bake some pies. It's Josiah and Samuel's favorite."

"What's my favorite?" Samuel paused in the aisle, his mischievous brown eyes full of youth and wit.

"Pumpkin pie," Ruth answered, grateful he wasn't Josiah.

"Not me, mine is cherry," Andrew said, walking up behind Samuel.

Ruth stiffened. Where was Josiah? He couldn't be far behind them. She allowed her gaze to drift to Andrew's tall frame.

"Good morning, Ruth Payne." Josiah walked up and stood beside Andrew. While they were of equal height, Josiah was thinner and his shoulders not quite as broad, since he spent more time in the store and Andrew worked hard at farming out in the fields. Had Josiah lost a bit of weight in the last few days? His eyes were bloodshot, and faint circles framed his dark brown eyes. She wished they were outside where the light was more telling.

"Good morning, Josiah." She clenched her teeth to keep from blurting out questions of concern. Their gazes crossed. His eyes were searching and penetrating, aching and soaking up every minute detail about him.

"The pastor is going up front. We'd better get seated," Andrew said, nodding toward the men's side. He and Samuel walked away, while Josiah lingered and stepped closer.

"Thee looks beautiful, Ruth." Josiah lowered his voice. Sadness lingered in his tone, piecing her heart like a double-edged sword. Doubt cast a spell in her mind, weaving a web of confusion as he strode away.

Pastor Gray stood and, with his hands folded, waited until all conversation faded. "Let's bow our heads to pray and let the Lord lead us."

Throughout their fellowship meeting, Ruth struggled to concentrate on her relationship with God. Raw pain sank her spirit deeper into despair. The last thing she'd wanted to do was hurt Josiah. If he truly loved her, why did he have such a hard time marrying her? Josiah was a decisive man who never acted on impulse. He planned every action. He would have given careful consideration to his decision to postpone their wedding a second time. Knowing this made his paltry excuses harder to bear.

Soon the meeting ended, and all the Friends filed out of church. Ruth kept her head down, avoiding eye contact. She didn't feel like engaging in pleasantries.

"Ruth Payne!" A man called her name, but she didn't recognize his voice. She took a deep breath, forced a smile, and spun around. Surprise lifted her mood as she watched Solomon Mendenhall take long strides toward her. He'd been away at the University of Chapel Hill for two years.

"I thank thee for giving me a moment," he said. He glanced at the members of her family who'd paused with her and nodded to each one in greeting. "A pleasure to see thee again, Matthew Payne, Elizabeth Payne, and Friends Naomi, Caleb, and Elijah."

"Welcome home." Ruth's father extended his hand with a wide smile, and Solomon shook it. "Is thee home for good, or is this only a short visit?"

"I'm home for good this time. I plan to set up an attorney's office in the new town of Greensborough." His bright blue eyes drifted to Ruth. "In fact, I wanted to ask if I may stop by for a visit sometime."

If Solomon had been looking at her mother and father when he asked the question, perhaps it wouldn't have felt so personal. But since he continued to stare at her as if he wanted her permission, Ruth's neck grew warm, and she felt her face flush.

"Thee is always welcome at the Payne home," Mother's voice said behind Ruth, rescuing her, and her mother laid gentle hands on her shoulders.

"We're going home to a big Sunday meal. Why don't thee invite thy family over? We'd enjoy thy company," Father said.

"My parents and sister have already accepted an invitation to my uncle's house. I would be the only one free to accept thy offer."

"Then come on over. I'd like to hear the news from Chapel

Hill. Elijah is intent on taking over the farm, but Caleb has a great interest in learning. I'd like to hear thy thoughts on the university there," Father said.

"I'd be delighted to help in any way I can," Solomon said. "I'll walk with thee to the buggy then grab my horse. I rode to meeting on horseback this morn."

"Thee brought thy stallion?" Ruth asked.

"Indeed. I thought he could use the exercise." He walked beside Ruth as they followed her parents. "Would thee like to see him?"

"Perhaps when we return home."

A motion caught her attention. She glanced to the right. Josiah paused before climbing aboard the buggy with his mother and brothers. He stared, his rigid back went slack, and he turned, but not before she witnessed the raw hurt in his dark brown eyes.

Guilt ripped through her. She knew he'd misinterpreted her walk with Solomon. She had no interest in anyone else, but would it do any good to try to convince him of it, now that their engagement was no more? Maybe it was better this way. She looked down at the grass and blinked back scorching tears.

❧

Josiah's gut clenched as Ruth walked by with Solomon Mendenhall, their arms a mere inch apart. When her gaze paused in Josiah's direction, her lips fell into a frown, and a tiny dimple formed on her chin. She crossed her arms over her middle and rubbed them—a sign of discomfort.

His head swam in a jealous rage as anger ripped through his battling chest. Torn by the desire to march over and interrupt them and the fear of upsetting Ruth, Josiah held back. If he caused a scene, winning her forgiveness might take even longer.

He stepped forward but pivoted on his foot, turning around in a circle. What should he do? He couldn't just stand by and watch Solomon take his place—especially now, when Ruth felt unloved.

At thirteen Solomon had started hanging around Ruth, teasing her, and walking her home from school. It was the first alarm Josiah had ever felt at the prospect of losing her to someone else. He'd always assumed they'd grow up and marry, until Solomon came along and shook up his confidence—then and now.

How could he have gotten so comfortable and sure of himself that he'd taken their relationship for granted? Wasn't Solomon supposed to be at that fancy law school in Chapel Hill? Perhaps Josiah could wait it out until the fellow returned to school and was no longer a threat. He didn't need a smooth-talking lady's man flattering Ruth.

"Does thee plan to stand there and gawk after Ruth Payne long after she's gone?" Samuel asked.

"I wonder when Solomon Mendenhall came back and how long he'll be here." Josiah rubbed his chin and shifted his weight from one foot to the other.

"Sarah Goodson was looking for thee after the meeting, but thee had already left the sanctuary." Samuel winked, a teasing expression on his face as he raised an eyebrow.

Josiah sighed in frustration and turned to walk away. He didn't need his brother's taunts right now.

"I thought thee might like to know—" Samuel's words chased him. "I heard Sarah telling Mother that Solomon is home for good. He graduated and plans to set up a law office in the new town of Greensborough."

"Is thee sure?" Josiah paused in midstride and closed his eyes.

"Yes." Samuel cleared his throat. "What will thee do?"

"I'm not sure." Josiah shook his head, glad his hat sheltered his eyes. He blinked several times, willing the sting away as he turned to face his brother. "Right now I'm going for a walk. Tell Mother I'll be home later."

Josiah didn't wait for a response. He set out with the cool breeze and kicked at the brown leaves tumbling onto his path. With no destination in mind, he let his feet carry him to the house he'd built for their marriage. He stood outside and surveyed the white two-story structure, a dream he'd envisioned for almost a year.

While everything on the outside looked finished, Josiah knew the rooms on the inside were bare and in need of furniture. He'd wanted everything to be perfect when he carried Ruth over the threshold. She'd worked so hard all her life. This was one gift he wanted to give her—without her having to work for it.

He slipped his hands inside his pockets and climbed the three steps to the wraparound front porch. He pulled out a key, inserted it into the lock, and turned the knob. The bolt slid and clicked into place.

The door opened on the newly oiled hinges without a sound. He stepped inside and sniffed the fresh scent of pinewood flooring. The empty foyer with the white-painted walls greeted him like a barren castle. His satisfaction of accomplishment vanished in the realization that it meant nothing without Ruth.

If she didn't come back to her senses and renew their engagement, he couldn't live here. The dream would be incomplete—a reflection of his failure—a constant reminder.

His booted heels clicking against the floor was the only

sound as he strolled into the living room then the dining room. Perhaps if he filled this house with the furniture they'd talked about making, and brought her back to see their dream had become reality, she'd realize how much he loved her, and she'd understand.

Josiah shrugged out of his black jacket and laid it on a counter in the kitchen. He'd start on the dining room furniture today. If he worked out back in the shade, no one would see him laboring on the Sabbath.

Hadn't the Lord used the analogy of going after a lost animal even on the Sabbath if it strayed? How could he do any less? His love had strayed under some misguided perception. All he needed to do was prove he still loved her and lure her back. What better way to do that than show an act of faith— provide a finished home, fully furnished, and ready for a new family—theirs?

Chapter 6

The sound of an entourage of carriages and the clip-clopping of horses traveled up the drive. A flutter of excitement spiraled through Ruth as she placed the last gingerbread cookie on a plate piled high for their guests.

"They're here!" Caleb called from the living room.

"I hardly can recall what Cousin Dolley even looks like," Naomi said as she bobbed up on her tiptoes and leaned out the kitchen window in anticipation.

"I daresay," Mother said, straightening her cap and adjusting her collar, "she won't recognize any of my children. Everyone is so grown up." She gestured to Ruth and Naomi. "Come, let's meet our cousins."

Ruth untied her apron, hung it on a peg, and followed them outside, where they joined her father and brothers. A black coach hitched to six proud horses, along with a brown buggy, rolled to a stop. Several horsemen surrounded the carriages like guardsmen.

"Whoa!" The coach driver pulled the reins and set the brake. The door opened and out stepped James Madison, Dolley's husband. His hair, which hung straight down his neck, was whiter than Ruth remembered. Although she knew him to be considerably older than Dolley, she hadn't expected him to have aged so much. Even from a distance of ten feet, James wore wrinkles around his eyes and mouth when he smiled. He turned to assist his wife.

A gloved hand slipped into his, and Dolley stepped out wearing a bright smile, a silver turban headpiece, and a royal-blue cloak. She rushed to Ruth's father, gripped his hands, and kissed his cheek.

"Dear cousin, it's so wonderful to see you again, and in such good health, I see," Dolly said. Ruth smiled as her father's face and neck darkened to match his nose, reddened by the biting cold.

"And thee, Dolley Madison." Father nodded, and his eyes lifted to her husband, who stood tall behind her. Dolley moved on to Mother while the two men greeted each other with a handshake.

She threw her arms around Mother, tears warming her dark eyes. Though Dolley and Father were first cousins by blood, it was Mother she wrote and confided to in her monthly letters.

"Elizabeth Payne, it has been too long." She squeezed Mother's hands and sighed. "Oh, we've much catching up to do."

"Indeed." Mother's white cap bobbed with her nod. "But first let's get thee into the house where it's warm. I know thee must be tired from traveling. Elijah and Caleb will see to the servants and thy luggage."

"But first let me greet them." Dolley clapped her hands once as she made her way down the line greeting Elijah, Caleb, Naomi, and then Ruth. She grabbed Ruth's hands in hers. "My, how you've grown. You were just a little girl the last time I saw you." She stepped back and looked Ruth up and down. "Now you're a young woman about to be married."

Ruth looked down at her feet, unable to hide the despondency that filled her. They hadn't had time to write Dolley with the news of her broken engagement. Now she wished they had.

"Ruth, what is it?" A very perceptive Dolley lifted her chin.

Ruth met Dolley's deep brown eyes, knowing she'd find wisdom and compassion, but now wasn't the time to unload her burdens. "We'll talk more once thee is settled in," she said.

"She's not marrying Josiah anymore," Caleb said. "But Solomon Mendenhall came to call the other day."

"Caleb, hush!" Ruth glared at her brother. "Dolley, I made some gingerbread cookies from an old family recipe I found in the attic. I'm sure they'll taste great with a warm cup of coffee."

James stepped beside Dolley and bowed to Ruth. "Good to see you again, young lady." He winked at Dolley. "You've grown into a stunning beauty."

Ruth's cheeks grew warm in spite of the freezing weather. A beauty she was not, nor did Quakers bow and curtsy to others, so she wasn't sure how to respond. She didn't want to offend him, so she glanced at Dolley for help.

Dolley grinned and looped her arm through her husband's. "I do believe some warm coffee and fresh gingerbread cookies would suffice."

The boys helped the servants unload the luggage while the rest of them strolled into the house. Dolley unbuttoned her cloak and slid it off, revealing a long-sleeved and high-waisted, silver muslin gown with royal-blue floral prints. Next she pulled off her turban cap. Her brown hair was crowned in a bun, loose curls lining her oval face. She looked quite elegant but simple, compared to some fancy women Ruth had witnessed in Greensborough.

"Matthew, I'll need to practice my speech tonight, right

after dinner. I hope you don't mind," James said, settling in a chair near the hearth.

Ruth took Dolley's cloak and hat, while Mother directed her to a wingback chair by the fire, across from her husband.

"Of course not. Let us know if there's anything we can help thee with," Father said.

"You're already doing plenty. You've opened your home and offered to feed us. We couldn't ask for more," Dolley said.

"I believe I remembered to make it the way thee likes it." Mother handed Dolley a steaming cup.

"Thank you." She smiled, accepting the brew. Dolley closed her eyes, sniffed, and then sipped.

"And so tomorrow is the big celebration? New Garden will finally have its very own town—Greensborough." James rubbed his hands together over the fire. "I'm honored to be speaking to the fine, upstanding citizens here. It has been a long campaign. I never imagined I'd run for president."

"Friend James, I feel I ought to at least warn thee. Not all Greensborough citizens feel the same way as we do, regarding our political allegiance," Father said.

Realizing the discussion would now turn to boring politics, Ruth stood and offered Dolley a plate of cookies. Dolley took one, and Ruth moved to James, grateful to have something to do.

"That's to be expected, Matthew. I find pockets of resistance all over my travels around the country." James bit into his cookie.

"Yes but we've our very own Federalist movement in favor of Charles Pinckney." Matthew leaned against the mantel and crossed his booted feet. "Ruth's ex-fiancé is one of the local leaders."

Ruth's hand shook as she laid the plate on the table. She'd known Josiah was part of a political group, but he never liked to talk about it since he knew how she hated politics. Now she wished she'd paid closer attention. The reminder that Josiah's loyalties went against her own family brought a fresh sting of betrayal to her scarred heart.

"Oh Ruth, I hope that isn't why you broke your engagement." Dolley lowered her coffee and sought Ruth's gaze. All eyes turned toward her, some questioning, others in sympathy.

What could she say? That she hadn't believed Josiah's political aspirations were that important? That she'd been a fool? That she was still a fool?

She opened her mouth to respond, but words of denial clogged her throat. Crossing her arms and rubbing them, Ruth felt her knees weaken. What had Josiah been planning all those times he'd left early to attend a meeting? No doubt plotting a way for her cousin to lose the presidential race. Everyone in her family knew it, but they'd said naught about it—willing to accept Josiah into their humble family—regardless of where his political loyalties lay.

Her throat stung. She swallowed with difficulty. "Please—" Ruth cleared her throat in an attempt to speak above a whisper. "Excuse me." Tears blinded her as she rushed into the foyer and up the stairs. She needed privacy. She needed to disappear.

❧

Josiah stood in the crowd beside his brothers and George, listening to Isaac Mendenhall, the new mayor of Greensborough. He hovered in his black overcoat, adjusting his top hat. If only it covered his exposed ears, perhaps his head wouldn't feel so numb.

White ribbon stretched between two trees where the new courthouse would be erected. The speakers stood on a wooden platform built for the occasion. George nudged Josiah's arm and tilted his head toward the front.

Mayor Mendenhall waved to a white-headed man, motioning him forward. He introduced him as James Madison, the 1808 presidential candidate, in their midst.

George moved with smooth caution, careful to blend in with the crowd. Josiah followed.

James Madison rose from his chair and shook Isaac's hand. He turned to address the crowd. George and Josiah slipped into the front row.

"Repeal the Embargo Act!" George called.

"The Embargo Act hurts American businesses and will cause unwanted war with Britain!" Josiah yelled above the startled and grumbling voices around them.

"No embargo!" Federalist men chanted, strategically scattered throughout the crowd, so they couldn't be assembled easily and silenced. The chants grew louder and more succinct.

James Madison smiled and raised his hands, motioning people to calm. When they didn't cease, a gun exploded. A man climbed the wooden steps to the platform with a smoking pistol in his hand. He gazed at the crowd.

The chants faded as people murmured and whispered among themselves. Silently the man stepped aside, allowing Mayor Mendenhall to face the crowd.

"I'm ashamed of you all," the mayor said. "Regardless of our political differences, we've always been a community that welcomed our visitors. This isn't a political rally. We're here to celebrate the incorporation of our new town as Greensborough. James and Dolley Madison are here visiting family. They agreed to speak today to share in this momentous occasion with us. Some of you may not know this, but Dolley was born here.

Is this how you will treat her?"

Heads bowed, and smiles faded into frowns. Conversation buzzed again as people looked at each other, and several glared at George and Josiah.

Feeling properly reprimanded, Josiah cleared his throat. "We meant no disrespect, only to exercise our rights as a democracy. How else will James Madison know our concerns if he wins? We may never get another chance to meet him again."

The mayor opened his mouth to respond but paused when James Madison lifted his hand. "I would answer, please." He met Josiah's gaze. "You're right. We're blessed to operate under a democracy, and I'll do my best to honor the integrity of it. I'll always listen to the people, but we must recognize we'll have a difference of opinions, and the majority will rule."

Several people clapped. A baby began crying from the back. Josiah could feel his toes going numb from the cold in spite of his black boots.

"Therefore if the majority elects me, I've a responsibility to them in carrying out the promises I pledged during my campaign—to support the Embargo Act that President Thomas Jefferson put into action a year ago, so we can ensure peace."

"It's causing conflict with Britain, not peace!" George blurted. A series of conversations erupted all at once. In the midst of the chaos, a shiver passed through Josiah that had naught to do with the biting temperature. With a feeling of foreboding, he glanced around, tuning out the rising voices. A pair of solid-brown eyes glared at Josiah beneath a crisp, white bonnet.

Ruth.

His heart skidded to a halt, momentarily stealing his breath. Politics forgotten, Josiah slipped around George, determined to close the distance between himself and Ruth.

Her lips thinned in obvious anger. How long would she stay angry with him? He'd never known Ruth to be a grudge holder. This wasn't like her. The image of Solomon Mendenhall escorting her from church on Sunday came to mind. Could Solomon be the reason Ruth continued to find fault with him?

Josiah braced himself to confront her. He needed to know the truth behind her behavior these last few weeks. Until he understood what motivated her, he had no idea how to defend himself and convince her to think differently.

Ruth clutched her cloak at the neck and whirled in an attempt to disappear in the crowd. He edged closer, maneuvering between people, careful to keep Ruth within sight. He wasn't about to let her go so easily—at least not without speaking to her.

She slipped by a burly man and a woman carrying a child. Another man stepped in Josiah's way, paying him no heed. Josiah pressed on around him, determined to keep Ruth in sight. Where was she going? Surely she wouldn't leave her family here and try to walk home by herself. The distance was several miles.

Josiah increased his pace. He would run if he had to and not care who witnessed his pathetic plight. Reconciling with Ruth was all that mattered.

She broke free of the crowd, lifted the hem of her dress, and ran toward a black carriage waiting by a weeping willow tree. Josiah pursued her, pumping his arms and legs.

"Ruth!" Josiah grabbed her elbow in an effort to slow her. "Please—I only want to talk."

"How could thee do it?" She turned to face him, her high-pitched voice and gasping breath surprising him. "How?" she demanded.

"How could I do what?" Josiah blinked, no longer cold. His blood flowed through him like hot lightning. "Thee will not even speak to me, so how in the world could I have done something new to upset thee?"

"Thee humiliated our family in front of everyone. Dolley and James Madison are our cousins. They're staying with us, and we're glad to have them." She looked back at the crowd. "Although now I'm not so sure they're glad to be here."

Remorse shot through Josiah as his skin crawled with prickles. Nausea swirled in the top of his stomach. "I'm sorry, Ruth. I didn't know."

"Josiah, I've never been more disappointed in thee than I am right now." She turned and left him standing in the cold wind, haunted by her words, and wrestling with self-loathing.

Chapter 7

Ruth hurried to the carriage, her heart pumping. She glanced back to see if Josiah followed. He stood where she'd left him, scratching his forehead.

If she waited in the carriage, he could still find her, but she didn't want to talk. Right now she was too angry and worried she would say something she'd later regret.

Her gaze landed on a weeping willow behind the carriage. She slipped under its limbs, which hung like swaying vines, wrapping her in its cocoon. Ruth settled herself on the opposite side of the tree trunk, out of sight. She crossed her arms, sliding her hands under them to warm them against her body.

"Ruth?" Josiah opened the carriage door then closed it. "Where is thee?"

She closed her eyes and leaned against the hard bark. At least her bonnet provided some protection and warmth.

"Ruth, please don't do this. I didn't mean to embarrass thee. Please—forgive me for everything."

She clenched her teeth. She could feel the confused tension mounting inside him. He sighed in a deep breath.

"I know thee is listening, so this may be the only chance I get to say this." Josiah's voice filled the air, each word gnawing at the defenses of her heart. "If I'd known how thee would react the second time I postponed our marriage, I promise thee, I'd have never done it." His voice cracked. He cleared this throat. "It wasn't worth this. Naught is worth losing thee." The timbre of his tone lowered.

Warm tears stung her eyes and slipped beneath her lids. She dared not sniffle aloud as her throat constricted. Should she believe him? Again?

Oh God, please help me. I don't know what to do.

"Even if thee never accepts me as thy husband, I pray thee will forgive me," Josiah continued. "And know that no matter what thee decides, I'll always love thee, Ruth Payne."

Footsteps faded. Ruth took a deep breath, now free to weep. How could Josiah love her if he was afraid to wed her? Afraid to commit his entire life to her? The man was a walking contradiction. He'd always been so sure of himself and his goals. How could she be the only thing in his life where he wavered? It didn't make sense.

"Lord, please show me what to do. I forgive him, but I don't know if I can trust him again," she whispered.

Ruth prayed until her heavy eyes closed, and she drifted to sleep. A while later someone called her name.

"Ruth?" It was Elijah's voice. "Mother and Father are worried."

"No one has seen her." Caleb ran up, breathing hard.

"I'm here." She swallowed, trying to rouse herself. "I fell asleep."

Elijah and Caleb stumbled through the weeping willow branches, their eyes wide with surprise and concern.

"Why is thee here?" Caleb raised a brown eyebrow and twisted his lips.

"Hiding," Ruth said, scrambling to her knees.

Elijah strode over and helped her up. "From Josiah, no doubt." He shook his head as they ducked to leave the cover of the tree. "He apologized to the whole family, including Dolley and James. I believe he even mentioned that thee was angry at him."

"Embarrassed and angry. Lately I don't understand him, Elijah."

"Yes thee does. He believes with all his heart that the Embargo Act will cause another senseless war. If that happens, lives will be lost over a simple disagreement. At least his heart's in the right place." Elijah looked down at her as they walked toward the two waiting carriages. "Whatever thee must think of him now, Josiah is still a man of his convictions, and I believe he still loves thee."

"Would thee keep postponing marriage to a woman thee loves, or would thee be inclined to hasten it?" Ruth's glance willed him to help her understand the mind of a man.

"I don't know." He shrugged. "I do know that I'd want to be in a position to properly take care of her and a family."

"Josiah has a whole house with plenty of rooms for our children. That's more than many other couples have starting out," she said as they walked.

"True, but every room in that house is empty. He wanted to give thee a furnished house. I can understand that, so does Mother and Father."

"Did it ever occur to anyone that I'd have enjoyed helping him furnish the house? He doesn't have to make every single piece as a wedding gift. I feel like I'm being left out of everything. Dolley ordered all the furniture in her house."

"Indeed I did." Dolley leaned out the carriage window with

a bright smile and twinkling brown eyes. "But neither of my husbands had the desire to determine the furnishings of our home. Your young man sounds like a very special gentleman. Come, Ruth." She slid over and patted the seat. "Join me on the ride home. I've been married twice now. Perhaps I can give you some insight."

Elijah opened the door and helped her inside.

"I'm so glad they found thee. I was beginning to get a little worried. It isn't like thee to go wondering off," Naomi said, sitting across from them.

Dolley slipped an arm around Ruth's shoulders like a mother, comforting her. "I imagine you had a lot to think and pray about."

"Does thee still pray, Dolley?" Naomi asked with wide, innocent eyes.

"Naomi!" Ruth admonished her sister with a stern look.

"It's all right." Dolley gave Ruth's shoulder one more squeeze and released her. "Yes, prayer will always be important in my life. I prayed a lot about my decision to marry a man outside the Quaker faith, and I believe this is how God wants to use me. Just because I've been dismissed by the Quaker church and I no longer keep the plain ways, doesn't mean I don't believe."

Elijah returned. "Now that Caleb is settled in the other carriage, there isn't enough room for me. May I ride with thee, ladies?"

"Of course," Naomi patted the seat beside her. "We've plenty of room."

Ruth tucked Dolley's words away in her heart and pondered them on the way home. Could it be that, like Dolley's faith, Josiah still loved her even though he'd acted differently than she expected?

Josiah sat by the living room fire, contemplating his choices. After his encounter with Ruth, he'd gone to the house, worked on more furniture, and prayed. Usually prayer made him feel better, but tonight restlessness still stirred in his heart.

His mother glanced at him as she took up her sewing and settled in her favorite rocking chair across from him. "Thee has that same brooding look thy father had before he left."

Josiah closed his eyes and rubbed his face, dreading the promises she would now expect from him. Their father's sudden departure brought many burdens and a deep void, but the one thing they could never escape was her fear that one of them would disappear one day as he had. She needed constant reassurance.

"Mother, Josiah has Ruth on his mind and naught else." Andrew stirred the fire and placed another log. The new bark crackled in the heat. He sat on the couch beside Josiah. "I spoke to Mayor Mendenhall today. He said they might have a place for me on the new town council, but I'd have to limit my involvement in the Federalist Party, so I don't give the perception of bias."

"Of course they're going to say that." Josiah sat back and gave his elder brother a level stare. "It's their way of controlling thee. While thee can still vote the way thee wants, their goal is to prevent thee from persuading other men to the Federalist side."

"And that would have some credit with me, if the campaigns were not over and the votes cast. In a few months, we'll know the results, and we'll have to make peace with whatever is done." Andrew shook his head as if he felt sorrowful. "Thee must learn to let things go, Josiah. What is done is done."

"Thee knows thy brother, Andrew." Mother pulled her needle through the fabric she held and tugged until satisfied it was secure. "He has a tenacious will of iron."

"And it's the very thing I'm worried might destroy him." Andrew crossed his booted ankle over his knee. "Josiah has succeeded so much that he doesn't understand failure. There comes a time when a man must give up and move on."

An image of Ruth as she ran to escape him came to mind. A gaping hole ached within him. He rubbed his chin. "Thee is no longer talking about politics, but Ruth Payne."

"Thee has taken to obsessing over her, Josiah. I'm worried. Thee isn't thyself lately."

"If this is about the store, I'm sorry I haven't been there much. I'll do better. I promise."

"No." Andrew leaned forward with his elbows on his knees, linking his fingers in the middle. "This isn't about the store. It's about the weight thee has lost. The circles under thy eyes. The other things thee has given up. Brother, thee may be present with us in body, but thy mind and spirit are far from us."

"I'm not giving up on Ruth." Josiah stood and paced around the room. "This is all a misunderstanding. I know her. She still loves me. I could tell by the way she looked at me today."

"She ran from thee!" Andrew's voice exploded. "Has thee gone daft?"

"Thee doesn't understand. Thee has never been in love like this before. Without Ruth, I'm naught. . ." Josiah couldn't go on. Frustration raced through him until his nerves itched to pound something. Instead, he forced his legs to move across the carpet, his boots clicking against the wood floor at the edge of the room.

"No, but I've been in love," Mother said, her voice calm. She lowered her sewing and stared up at him with a concerned expression. "And I've lost the one I dearly loved. It makes one feel like dying inside. The pain is so raw and fierce that I can hardly find the words to describe it. But son, I know what thee is feeling, and I want to remind thee that we are naught without God. Ruth is not thy God. Don't allow thy love for her to place her where she doesn't belong."

His heart constricted with conviction as a pain shot through him. She was right. That's why he hadn't felt the peace he'd sought after prayer earlier today.

God, please forgive me.

"When thee feels ready, go to Ruth and find some way to show her what *she* means to thee. Separate her from thy goals. Right now I suspect she feels like naught more than another goal that thee has set."

"Mother, thee is encouraging him to keep chasing after Ruth?" Andrew leaned toward her. "He must accept her decision and move on."

"He needs to know that he's tried everything before he gives up. He'll never be content if he doesn't." She turned to Josiah. "A woman senses another woman in love, and I've seen the way she looks at thee. Don't give up, son. Now is not the time. Make peace with God, and the rest of thy life will fall in place."

With hope rekindled in his heart, Josiah kissed her cheek, warmed by the heat of the fire. The room glowed in a way it hadn't before. "Thank thee. I'll repent and pray on my way to Ruth's house."

Chapter 8

Josiah needed time to think and pray as he walked to Ruth's house. When he reached the long drive leading up to the Payne house, he felt more peaceful than he had in a long time.

The late afternoon sun slanted in the sky, casting an orange halo over the land. He kept his hands buried in the pockets of his long overcoat. His warm breath blew smoke in the air each time he breathed.

The aroma of meat roasting and of gingerbread lifted the air. He ignored his rumbling stomach and watering mouth. No doubt they were preparing a nice dinner with their guests.

Guilt ripped through him at the reminder of what he'd done that morning. While the Payne family had accepted his apology, they hadn't invited him to the house as usual. Matthew Payne had turned from him as if dismissing him from their conversation.

Josiah wanted to knock on the front door as he'd done countless times before, but he wasn't sure he'd be welcome. Instead he walked around the corner and leaned against the side of the house. He wondered if anyone had seen his approach through the front window. The barn and stables were on the other side of the house. Here he had a perfect view of the well, where most of the women would go. It would be his best chance of catching Ruth. He'd wait here until nightfall if necessary.

After a while his legs grew weary. Josiah crouched into a sitting position and bent his knees. Soon the smell of pumpkin pie teased his nose. How many desserts would they make? At some point they would need water. He folded his arms around his knees and rested his chin on them.

He closed his eyes and listened to the birds chirping. The leaves rustled in the slight breeze, and his hands began to freeze. He rubbed warmth back into his fingers. The back door squeaked open and Josiah paused.

Someone stepped out onto the wooden steps. A woman laughed as a door closed on female voices. Josiah rose to his feet, careful not to give away his presence. A woman wearing a brown cloak and white bonnet descended the steps, carrying an empty bucket. Since he couldn't see her face, he could only assume it was Ruth or Naomi. He studied her walk and the way she carried herself. She walked with Ruth's confidence. Waiting until she was a good distance from the house and couldn't easily run back inside to escape him, Josiah followed.

He took a deep breath. "Ruth?"

She gasped, clutched her hand over her chest, and whirled. "Josiah, thee frightened me!"

"I'm sorry. I didn't mean to." He slipped his hands in his coat pockets, watching her pale face turn a rosy glow.

"What is thee doing out here?" Her tone changed to slight irritation as her dark eyes surveyed him.

"I wanted to talk to thee."

"Why not come into the house like normal folk, rather than hovering out here in the cold?"

"I considered it, but would thee have spoken to me?" He raised an eyebrow, daring her to deny it.

Her gaze dropped from his, and she turned toward the well. "I won't lie. Probably not."

He kept pace beside her and tried not to let her answer bother him. While it wasn't a surprise, the confirmation of what he already knew made the sting dig deeper.

She set the bucket on the stone well and cranked the handle, lowering the roped bucket, avoiding his gaze. "Now that I'm here, what does thee want?"

Josiah longed to reach out and pull her to him or tilt her face so he could see her better, but he dared not. Although he'd known Ruth all his life, this was a side of her he'd never seen. Where was the Ruth he'd come to love so much? The woman he'd always been able to persuade and tease back into his arms? A dull ache seized him, and he clenched his coat pockets to keep his hands to himself.

"I want thy forgiveness...please." The words nearly choked him, but he managed to say them anyway.

"I forgive thee." She raised the filled bucket to the surface without looking at him.

"Ruth, if thee truly forgives me then at least give me the courtesy of looking at me."

For a moment she said naught, only poured the water into the bucket she'd brought with her. Setting it aside, Ruth turned. Strands of sandy-brown hair fell across her forehead. He didn't expect her eyes to be so red and swollen. Dark circles matched her brown irises. His gut twisted.

"Josiah Wall, I forgive thee for everything. I forgive thee for postponing our wedding and for embarrassing my family at the town's celebration today." She sighed but held his gaze as moisture gathered in her eyes. "I could never stay mad at thee for long. At least that's one thing that hasn't changed."

Relief washed through him, and the burden upon his shoulders lifted with his next breath. "Thank thee. Does this mean we can resume our engagement?"

She shook her head, biting her lower lip. "I've given thee my forgiveness. That doesn't mean I'm willing to give thee my heart again."

Pain sliced through his chest as he stared at her. He gulped, clinging to the one positive thought enticing him to hope. She'd forgiven him. Wasn't that a good sign? A new beginning?

"Ruth, be honest with me. Is it Solomon Mendenhall? I saw him escort thee from church the other day."

She blinked in obvious surprise. "No, he only walked me to the carriage and came home to eat lunch with us at Father's invitation. He hasn't been back."

Josiah believed her. At least he didn't have to battle competition on top of everything else. There was only one thing that could be holding her back—she no longer trusted him. How could he win her trust back if she refused to let him? If only he hadn't been so dimwitted in trying to make their marriage perfect before there was ever a marriage, he wouldn't have hurt her so deeply, and their relationship wouldn't be at risk right now.

"Please give me one more chance."

"I've forgiven thee, Josiah. That's all I'm prepared to do at the moment. Now please excuse me before the others come find me. We're having a late Thanksgiving meal with Dolley and James Madison, before they leave in a few days."

"May I call on thee when they leave?"

"No." She shook her head. "I don't think that would be a

good idea." Ruth shoved past him, spilling water on his arm in her haste.

✺

Josiah reached up to stock the top store shelf with more chicken feed. The doorbell rang, announcing the arrival of another customer.

"Good morning!" He called over his shoulder.

"Josiah, it's me." Andrew strode toward him. "I heard some news, and I'm not sure how thee will take it."

At his brother's serious tone, Josiah paused and turned toward him, balancing himself on the ladder. As far as he was concerned, Ruth had forgiven him and the day looked bright. He was one step closer to being enveloped in her good graces again. Naught else Andrew could say would change that.

"If thee plans to tell me that George and the rest of the Federals are upset that I apologized to the Paynes, as well as to Dolley and James Madison, I'm quite aware of it. And I don't care."

"If only that were the case," Andrew said, shaking his head. "This concerns Ruth."

Josiah's chest tightened instantly. He climbed down the ladder. With his feet planted on the floor, he folded his arms and met his brother's gaze. "What about Ruth? Is she hurt?"

"No nothing like that." He gripped the ladder. "Ruth's leaving. She's decided to go back to Virginia with the Madisons."

Cold fear clenched Josiah's gut, making his stomach coil and bile rise in the back of his throat. He swallowed and shrugged, trying not to let himself grow alarmed. "I'm sure it's just a temporary visit. Naught wrong with that, since they're family." He scratched his temple. "Perhaps she's going to spend Christmas with them."

"That's what I thought at first, but then I heard that it's an indefinite trip. She and Dolley came into town this morning and Ruth's being fitted for three new gowns. At least that's what Sarah Goodson told me."

Sarah? Josiah suspected Sarah had always harbored a secret jealousy of Ruth. She pretended to be friends with Ruth by attending their quilting parties and inviting her to dinner, but she never failed to flirt with Josiah when she came to the store or when she saw him in New Garden without Ruth.

"So Sarah's the one who told thee this?" He released a relieved breath. "I think I'll wait to hear it confirmed from a more worthy source."

"I just wanted thee to be aware of what's being said in case there's any truth to it. I'd rather thee hear it from family than someone else." Andrew removed his hat and coat.

They worked for another half hour before the bell jingled and two women entered the store. Josiah glanced up from his ledgers on the counter, and his breath caught as Ruth walked over. He nodded to her and to Dolley Madison, who stood behind her in a bright red cloak and a colorful turban hat.

Even in plain gray, Ruth stood out like a canvas painting. Her sandy-brown hair curled around an oval face, ripe with cold. She must have gotten some rest last night; the dark circles under her eyes had faded, and the redness was gone. Her pink lips were prominent. Josiah swallowed, a deep ache of longing reminding him that he no longer had the right to kiss Ruth or pull her against him in a tight embrace.

"Josiah, I wanted to come by and let thee know that I will be traveling back to Virginia with Dolley and James. For the first time in years, I'll see my grandmother for Christmas."

Her soft brown eyes sparkled with excitement even as his

own gut twisted and kicked in rebellion. Had he lost her for good?

"Will thee be coming back after the New Year?" He held his breath. She dropped her gaze, and his heart thumped harder.

"Actually that's why I came by to speak to thee in person." She crossed her arms and glanced back up at him. "I need time to think and consider my future—to be alone. Every corner of New Garden reminds me of thee, and it distracts me from seeking God. I'm sorry, but I didn't make this decision until late last night."

Wasn't it only yesterday he'd come to a similar conclusion? He'd been more than distracted by placing Ruth as a higher priority in his life than God. His involvement with the Federalist movement had fallen somewhere in the middle.

He searched Ruth's dark eyes. She blinked back tears. What she'd come to tell him hadn't been easy for her. No matter what, she would do what she believed God wanted her to do. It was one of the reasons he loved her so much.

If she'd come here with any other excuse, he would have protested, but not this. He wouldn't be the right man for her if he stood between Ruth and her relationship with God.

Not my will, Lord, but Thine.

"I'd never knowingly distract thee from God. Ruth Payne, I want thee to know I'll always love thee as a man loves a wife. If God doesn't lead thee back to me, I know in time that He'll heal me, and it wasn't meant to be."

Her chin trembled, but she held it in place and continued to meet his gaze. Ruth's eyes narrowed as they filled with tears. How could she not believe that he loved her after all this time? There was naught else he could do to prove it. The rest was now in God's hands.

"May I have a good-bye hug?" he asked, aching to hold her in his arms one last time.

Ruth shook her head in denial. She turned and strode to the door with Dolley Madison taking her arm to comfort her like a mother. Josiah's world crumbled when she walked through the door.

Chapter 9

Once Ruth made it back to the carriage, she burst into tears. Dolley laid a gentle hand on her back and opened the door. Ruth wiped her cheeks as she climbed inside, eager to escape the view of passersby.

"I daresay you'll feel better soon enough," Dolley said.

"All I can say is I'm glad that's over."

How long would this gaping hole in her heart take to heal? She'd done the right thing, hadn't she?

Josiah would soon realize he didn't love her enough to commit himself to her, and he'd be grateful. Staying in New Garden held too many painful memories. It made sense to go to Virginia with Dolley. She needed a fresh new start on life with no reminders.

When they arrived home, Ruth excused herself to her chamber. She had no desire to talk to anyone. Over the next few days, she kept her mind occupied with work from the moment she rose until she rested her head on her feather pillow. When others brought up Josiah as a topic of conversation, Ruth told them she didn't want to talk about him.

She knew her behavior not only puzzled her family but also concerned them. She didn't know how else to handle the situation. Even harder to bear was that Josiah had stopped offering his help around the Payne farm, eagerly attempting to win her affections back. Ruth didn't know whether to be relieved in finally accomplishing her goal or disappointed that Josiah hadn't fought harder to save their relationship.

A week later she and Naomi returned to Greensborough to pick up Ruth's new dresses. Dolley stayed home to spend time with their mother.

As they walked by the barbershop toward the waiting carriage, George Osbourne stepped out with a new haircut and fresh shave. He stroked his jaw and nodded, his gaze glancing at Naomi and settling on Ruth. His eyes hardened as he straightened his shoulders and back.

"Well well, if it isn't Ruth Payne and her little sister." He stepped in front of them, blocking their path. In the past Ruth never had any reason to fear George since he was Josiah's best friend, but now she sensed more hostility steaming from him than ever before. He blamed her for the few times Josiah had cancelled their plans or refused to join them on one of their Federalist adventures.

Why would he have any reason to resent her, now that Josiah was free to pursue all his political interests? It didn't make sense. She gave him a polite nod.

"Good day to thee, George Osbourne."

"Is it a good day? I suppose it is when thee is planning a splendid one-way trip to Virginia with one of the most famous couples in America, while Josiah Wall nurses a broken heart in Indiana—hundreds of miles away." He shrugged. "Although I'm not surprised his brother Samuel is going with him. The boy is young and eager to discover the world. Has a little bit of his father's wanderlust about 'im." His accusing eyes met Ruth's.

"But Josiah? He's never had a desire to go anywhere—until now."

Ruth's heart thumped so hard she felt breathless. Josiah in Indiana? She'd never heard him mention it. Several Quakers had moved out that way to plant new roots and escape slavery, but since when did Josiah have a desire to go there? He'd spent the last three years consoling his mother, determined to never leave her behind as his father had done.

"What of his mother? Will she be going with them?" Ruth held her breath. If Josiah was truly going away without her, something was terribly wrong.

"I heard she has a sister living there, so I understand that she's going with them." George shook his dark head. "Josiah sold his portion of the store to Andrew. He's the only one in the family who's staying. Josiah also resigned from the Federalist Party, and now he's putting the house up for sale."

"Our house?" It was as if the blood drained from Ruth's head, numbing her down to the shoulders. An eerie sensation slithered through her spine, making her shiver.

"It isn't exactly thy house now that thee has abandoned it." George's tone sharpened. "What was Josiah to do with it?"

"I don't know, but he poured himself into that place trying to make it perfect. All his hard work and sweat can't be for naught." Tears stung her eyes, and Naomi laid a comforting hand on her arm.

"Thee still doesn't get it, does thee?" George shook his head in disbelief. His dark eyes pierced her with no understanding or compassion. "He wasn't making it perfect just to be making it perfect, Ruth Payne. He only did it for thee." He turned and strode away.

Ruth clutched her stomach and bent over. Tears blinded her. What had she done? Had she expected to run off to Virginia in a prideful rage, while Josiah waited here with open arms? Yes. She'd hoped that time would help him determine if he truly loved her and could commit to her for a lifetime. But this news changed everything.

What did it mean if he was willing to give up everything he'd ever held so dear? She never imagined he would go back on a promise he'd made to his mother. Surely Josiah wouldn't leave.

"Ruth, is thee all right?" Naomi asked, wrapping one arm around her shoulders while carrying a package in the other.

"I need to go to the store. See if this is true or all a lie." Ruth wiped at the hot tears spilling over her lids. "What if I was so hurt by Josiah postponing our wedding that I was blind to his love and everything else around me?" She looked up at her sister. "What if I've lost him because of my behavior and not because he didn't love me as I thought?" She groaned. "How could I allow that much pride to control me?"

"Come on, Ruth." Naomi guided her across the street to the carriage. "There's only one way to find out. I'll take thee to the store. Thee must find him and discover the truth for thyself."

"Yes, let's make haste. I must see Josiah Wall within the hour before he does anything else he'll regret."

❧

Josiah nailed the FOR SALE sign onto the oak tree in the front yard of the home he'd built for Ruth and their future family. His heavy chest felt like a loaded burden. He'd finally realized he couldn't force Ruth to change her mind and trust him again. In time he'd learn to live with his regrets, but until then he prayed God would make things more bearable for him.

He gripped the hammer in his hand and turned to go inside. A carriage rolled up the lane. Josiah paused. Who would be visiting him here? Everyone in New Garden knew the house was still empty, and by the end of the week, the newspaper ad would be out. Soon they would all know it was for sale.

As the carriage drew near, Josiah tensed. It looked like the Payne family. Matthew and his sons would have come by horseback or wagon. The only exception was on Sundays when they traveled to meeting. Today was Wednesday.

Hope filled his chest. Could it be Ruth? As soon as the thought crossed his mind, he squashed it. No sense in getting himself too excited. She might be coming by to congratulate him for moving on and starting over.

He walked forward as the horses slowed and the wheels crunched over graveled dirt to a complete stop. Naomi held the reins and set the break as Ruth scooted to the edge and prepared to exit. Her white bonnet concealed her gaze from him. With his heart nearly in his throat, Josiah offered his elbow to assist her.

To his surprise Ruth didn't hesitate laying a gloved hand on his arm. She gripped him tighter than he anticipated, almost as if she feared something. Ruth held her skirt with her other hand as she stepped down.

"I'll wait right here," Naomi said.

Ruth nodded and turned to glance up at Josiah. Worry filled her dark eyes as she continued to hold onto him even though she no longer needed his assistance. "I would like to talk to thee. . .alone."

Her hand trembled on his arm when he didn't answer right away. It wasn't that he wouldn't speak to her alone, but he needed a moment to calm his racing heart so he could trust his voice. A lump kept trying to form in his throat. Josiah swallowed it back several times before nodding. "Of course."

She led him toward the tree with the FOR SALE sign and

pointed to it. "So it's true? Thee plans to sell this house?" She gestured to the white two-story structure behind them, very similar to the Payne house.

He nodded but didn't offer her an explanation.

"And the store? Is it true that thee sold it to Andrew? Will thee move to Indiana?" Her hand on his arm tightened.

"Yes, it's all true."

"But why?" She tilted her head to the side and blinked up at him in obvious distress. "Thee has put so much work into everything. I heard thee also quit the Federalist group. The house, the store, the politics." She swallowed and shook her head. "I thought they meant so much to thee. I thought they were thy life. I don't understand. Josiah Wall, I don't want thee to make a mistake thee will regret."

"None of those things mean that much to me. They're not my life. God is, and next to Him, thee is." Sorrow filled Josiah's chest, and he wished he'd seen things from this perspective sooner. He covered her hand with his. "Ruth Payne, I'm so sorry." His voice cracked, but he cleared his throat and continued. "I should have shown thee how much more important thee is than all those other things. I only pursued them with such vigor to make thee happy, but I was wrong."

"And I was wrong. I see that now." Ruth stepped closer and lifted her hand to cup his cheek. "I was so blinded by hurt that thee would postpone our wedding, not once, but twice. I couldn't see beyond the pain to the truth. It took thee to give everything else up for me to realize it. Will thee please forgive me?" Tears filled her eyes, and her nose turned pink.

A huge burden lifted from Josiah's heavy chest, but he was afraid to let his guard down. "There's naught to forgive." He held himself still even though he wanted to wrap her in his arms. "Does this mean thee will still marry me?"

"Yes." She nodded as tears slipped down her cheeks. "If thee will still have me."

"Oh, make no doubt about that—ever." Josiah pulled her into his embrace and squeezed her against him. Relief gushed through him like a rushing wind, sweeping away all his concerns. Her warm body felt soft and perfect against him. He closed his eyes, savoring the moment.

All too soon she pulled back. "Would thee like to set a date?"

"No." He shook his head.

She frowned, biting her bottom lip.

"I'd like to find a preacher and marry this day. Does thee think Naomi will be a witness?"

"Indeed." She threw her arms around his neck and leaned up on her tiptoes.

Josiah could no longer resist, now that her mouth was so close. He dropped his head, allowing his lips to meld with hers. She smelled of gingerbread and felt as warm and inviting. Yes, today he would make her his. He couldn't afford to wait any longer.

When their lips parted, he leaned his forehead against hers. "What about thy trip with Dolley to Virginia?"

"Forget Virginia. I'm going with thee to Indiana or wherever thee goes."

"Let's build a fresh new start together in Indiana. We can create our own New Garden there." Josiah kissed her again. She smiled up at him, her eyes lighting with new hope.

JENNIFER HUDSON TAYLOR is an award-winning author of historical Christian fiction and a speaker on topics of faith, writing, and publishing. Jennifer graduated from Elon University with a B.A. in journalism. When she isn't writing, Jennifer enjoys spending time with her family, traveling, genealogy, and reading.

NEW GARDEN'S CROSSROADS

by Ann E. Schrock

Chapter 1

S lave hunters on horseback milled around the Coffin
family's rambling brick house, forming moving shadows
in the gloom of a stormy winter evening.

Deborah Wall shivered as she stood next to her older cousin
Katy Coffin and peered through one of the parlor windows.
Katy's husband, Levi, kept some of the soul drivers talking at
the front door.

Deborah's pa had left with the runaways only moments ago.

Deborah strode through the candlelit dining room and
looked out the window. A narrow break in the storm clouds
gave just enough light in the sunset to show that members
of the posse watched every door. Her heart thudded, and her
mouth went dry. She forgot all about being cold and wet from
the ride from home to Newport.

One of them, a tall and lean man, his shoulders broadened
by a caped riding coat, turned his horse and studied the side
door.

The horse, with its solid build and stylish head and neck,
caught Deborah's eye. A Morgan, a mighty fine animal for
someone like that.

What if that wicked man noticed Pa's wagon tracks? Her

father had figured the trees along the creek bank would hide them. They'd rushed into the night for fear the rising creek would wash out the bridge and get too deep to cross.

As if from some invisible cue, the Morgan sidestepped closer to the door. Its rider folded his arms across the saddlebow and leaned down to study the tracks.

Did he see? Did he guess who left the trail?

She heard Levi at the front door, telling the other slave hunters why—under every point of Indiana legal codes and English common law—they couldn't come in and search his house.

Cousin Katy's three daughters clustered around their mother and Deborah.

"How long does thee think they will stand and listen to Friend Coffin's message?" Deborah asked.

"I hope long enough that thy father can take those fellows clean away," Cousin Katy said. She took a deep breath and closed her eyes. Her normally cheerful face tightened with worry.

Outside, the man on the Morgan put his hand to his mouth and shouted, "Over here!"

Deborah felt blood drain from her face, leaving her dizzy. He must have seen Pa's wagon.

Time. They needed more time to get away.

The horse pivoted and took a few strides, following the wagon tracks down to the creek.

Deborah prayed for boldness then grabbed her black cloak and bonnet. "I'll try to delay them." Her mouth felt dry as sawdust and her voice cracked.

"How?" Cousin Katy gasped.

Deborah glanced over her shoulder and grinned, which lightened her fear. "As I feel led." She took a breath to steady her nerves.

Cousin Katy stepped toward her. "Truly?"

Deborah paused, her hand on the latch. What if she was wrong? No time to waste. She opened the door.

The cold wind took her breath away and sleet stung her cheeks.

The Morgan tossed its head as its rider turned toward the house and gazed up at Deborah standing in the doorway. Light from the house spilled over him. He'd be a handsome man but for his harsh countenance.

"I caution thee," Deborah said, "to beware of the water."

He stared at her. A Southern drawl slowed his voice. "Now, why would a pretty little Quaker gal be talkin' to someone like me?"

Her heart and mind raced. Were her actions so unusual that she made him suspicious? But if she kept him talking, Pa would have that much more time to get the runaways home to the farm, safely under Ma's wing.

A tart answer came to mind, and she gave him a crooked smile. "I'd given little thought to thee, neighbor. But I would hate to see any harm come to such a likely looking horse."

His quick grin showed a mouthful of white teeth, like a wolf's. "Why thank you, miss." He dropped one hand to the horse's neck and straightened its windswept mane. Then he looked into Deborah's eyes. "I know a fine filly when I see one."

Deborah ignored that. Would she be able to keep him talking about the horse? "It's a mare, then?"

"Yes, miss. In foal to—well you wouldn't—"

The storm's wind cut through her cloak, making her shiver. What else could she say? "I might, if it's from around here."

"No, miss, to a racehorse from down by Richmond."

She thought of the most notable one. "Messenger?"

"That's the one. She sure is." He studied Deborah for a long moment.

Deborah stared in awe at the mare. What a valuable foal that would be. "When does thee expect her to foal?"

"Later this spring."

Deborah edged a little farther out the door, onto the top step. She prayed for the right words. "For that reason, neighbor, thee must be careful with her. I wouldn't go any farther that direction. We just came that way, and the creek is rising fast."

"Whose tracks are these, then?"

She must keep him talking. She'd never spoken as much to a strange man, especially one of the world. "Ours. My father brought me here for another week of work. He wanted to hurry home before the creek got too high."

The stranger leaned forward and studied the mud and snow again. He raised his head and gazed into her eyes. "Lot of footprints there for just you and your dad."

Deborah inhaled sharply. "We made several trips in and out with firewood. This house uses a prodigious amount."

He glanced down at the tracks then back into her eyes. "With respect, miss, that's not what those tracks look like to me. All shapes and sizes of prints."

The front door slammed, and the mare flung up her head. The other horses and riders sloshed through the mud, joining him. The sharp smell of horse sweat made Deborah's nose wrinkle. The animals shivered and snorted.

Deborah took a shaky breath. She felt like she was on display.

The man with the Morgan smiled and took off his hat. The wind tangled his long wavy hair. "You must excuse me, miss. Business."

Before he could say more, another man, lean and predatory like a weasel, urged his horse forward. Octavian Wagner, the notorious slave hunter. He looked down at the hoofprints, tracks, and wagon ruts then turned to the group. "Well looky here. All kinds of sign."

Deborah clutched the doorframe, reminding herself to breathe. What had she done? What would they do to Pa and the runaways? Why had she said anything?

The man on the Morgan nodded at Deborah. "Little Quaker gal there made a point of sayin' not to go that way."

Another man edged his horse forward. "Wonder if we hurried, if we'd catch 'em."

Wagner grinned. "I got a better idea. What's your name, sweetheart?"

Deborah fumbled with the door latch behind her. It swung open, and warm air from the house breezed out. Cousin Katy put her hand on Deborah's shoulder. "Come inside, dear heart."

Wagner leered at Deborah. "I know you now. You're that Wall gal. Dad's the furniture maker."

"Josiah Wall," another man said.

Fear crackled through Deborah. These men recognized her? And knew of her family?

The man on the Morgan swung the horse between her and the others, almost protectively. "Go inside, miss."

Wagner got an evil grin on his face. "I believe I can make them come right to us. Thank you so much for your help, darlin'."

Such arrogance. Deborah clenched her fists.

The posse rode down the street. A few hundred feet from the house, behind the Coffins' barn, the horses splashed into the rising creek. "Josiah Wall!" Wagner called. "Friend Wall! I have a message for thee from thy daughter!"

Chapter 2

The slam of a door scared Nathaniel Fox's horse, and she leaped sideways. His body swung with the horse's motion as he tightened the reins and patted her neck to calm her. He shivered, waiting for the Quaker girl's father to answer. The wind might have carried his voice to the runaways or carried it away. While the others bet on what they'd find ahead of them, he looked back. The Quaker women and some children milled about inside the big red-brick house, and candlelight glowed warmly in the many windows.

The sound of their plain speech made his heart ache with grief and loneliness. All he'd lost—home and family among the Friends—might as well be a thousand miles away even though it was right before his eyes. One choice had led to another, and now, here he stood, in outer darkness.

"Well? Seen anything, Fox?" Wagner asked, gruff as ever. "They ain't at the house."

"Tracks are headin' out of town."

"Good enough."

The horses' hooves punched through thinly iced mud puddles, crunching and cracking. Some of the men swore as cold muddy water spurted up.

The rushing wind overhead rattled the limbs of cottonwoods and sycamores along the creek banks, and snow and sleet pelted down. Nathaniel's feet had gone numb.

They rode farther, toward the creek itself. The sound of roaring wind and water gave Nathaniel chills. The surrounding houses and barns were dark, though a few dogs barked and hens cackled. The group halted their horses. The storm and darkness upset the animals, which tried to turn back from the flood. The sudden thaw over the past couple of days, plus several inches of rain, had melted most of the snow.

Wagner leaned back in his saddle and sighed. He pointed to the dark water foaming through willow thickets. "If they drove into that, prob'ly all drowned by now."

The men murmured in agreement. Wagner motioned for them to turn around.

Nathaniel faced the water. That girl's father was out there, in danger. Nathaniel's world had ended when his pa was killed. He hated to imagine another family suffering like that. "We don't know that. We ought to try and find them."

"Bah! If slaves get clear up here to Newport, they up and disappear." Wagner sounded cross. "No sense goin' any farther. Old Man Wall took his chance."

The group turned to go, starting a long, miserable two-hour ride down to Richmond, the county seat.

Nathaniel made the restless mare stand. How could they turn their backs on someone in danger? That must be the way of the world, as he, and the Prodigal Son in the scriptures, had discovered through sad experience. "I don't know about you all, but I want to know what happened to them."

Wagner shook his head. He was just another dark blob in the whiteness of the falling snow. "Ain't ridin' into that mess in the dark," he said, nodding toward the water.

"Listen boys, I've a mind to go and see where those tracks lead," Nathaniel said. "You all going with me?"

The others shook their heads.

"You'll learn better, once you been at this trade as long as I have," Wagner said. "No night for man nor beast. You won't find nothin' tonight. Catch up with us when you can. We're headin' down the Richmond Pike."

❧

Deborah wiped up the snow she'd tracked in, wondering if that liar had tricked Pa into turning back.

When he came into the dining room, Friend Coffin folded his arms and gave her a stern look. The tall thin man in a gray suit reminded her of a great blue heron, especially when he trained his keen eyes on someone. "Thee should have left me to speak, Deborah Wall. This misadventure frightened poor Katy."

Cousin Katy put her hand over her heart and added, "That man could have grabbed thee and taken off with thee."

They were right. Deborah looked down at the floor. Mama's cousin might be upset enough to send her back home. With younger children still at home, Friend Levi's elderly mother, and so many fugitives in and out, Cousin Katy had welcomed Deborah's help. A young able-bodied woman was such a blessing, she'd often told Deborah, who began working for them after one of the Coffin girls died of a fever.

Friend Coffin sighed. "Thee has heard the saying that 'zeal without wisdom is folly.'"

Deborah nodded and glanced quickly at him.

His gray eyes twinkled. "I grant thee does have zeal. Why did thee feel led to speak out like that?"

"I thought to delay them, although I haven't had near as much practice as thee and Cousin Katy at confounding the slave hunters." She paused thoughtfully and then added, "I might have relied too much on my own understanding."

Cousin Katy breathed deeply. "Let us pray for thy father and those with him."

Deborah leaned against the fireplace mantel, closed her eyes, and prayed silently for safety for Pa and the runaways.

Sleet rattled against the windowpanes. Where were they? Crossing the flooded creek could have been a trial. Surely the bridge withstood it, but the rising water on either side might have gotten even wilder.

Did she hear voices from outside? Was that possible over the stormy winds?

Chapter 3

Nathaniel fought with the mare as she snorted and backed away from the churning water. The falling snow lightened the darkness enough to see the flooded creek rushing over its banks, already rising to the mare's knees. The bridge ahead looked to be solid, had they reached it. Sleet and snow stung his face. The wind roared through the sycamores, and water thundered at the bridge.

Mr. Wall and the wagon must be just ahead of him. If they'd wrecked, perhaps he could help them out and soothe his own soul, troubled as it was over this brutal trade. Wagner had made it sound like easy money, and Nathaniel had wanted to save for a farm of his own, make a fresh start in Indiana, somewhere other than the Friends' settlement. His relatives who'd moved up here would no doubt disown him, once they realized all the bad things he'd done since losing Pa and Ma.

He tightened his legs around the horse, urged her toward the bridge. She took a few reluctant steps. The icy water had risen to her belly and soaked through Nathaniel's boots. She reached the end of the bridge, stopped again, pawed at the swirling water. The current shoved her sideways; she lurched and stumbled to regain her footing. She put her head down for a moment then flung it up.

Nathaniel took a deep breath. "Come on, Brandy!"

A voice swirled on the wind, shouting, "Bridge out!"

Nathaniel looked over his shoulder but saw no one. "Mr. Wall?"

No answer. Must have been the wind in the trees or his imagination.

The mare tried to turn back, but Nathaniel made her face the bridge. He wouldn't rest until he knew what had happened to the other travelers. He hated to resort to spurs but touched her with them.

Brandy flung up her head, almost rearing, and then leaped forward into the surging water. She landed with a huge splash but lost her footing. Nathaniel gave her her head and knotted his hands in her mane as she struggled to stay on her feet. The horse fell. The icy water took his breath away. They slammed into the railing of the bridge. The mare crushed Nathaniel's knee into the side. With a crack, the post, rails, and floor gave way.

Nathaniel and his mare fell over the side into the flood.

Brandy would break his back or both legs, pin him under the water—not even a chance to pray. The horse's body slammed him deeper into the rushing water, which filled his nose and mouth, tore at his clothes. Trapped. The struggling horse's weight crushed him. Debris battered him. He had to breathe, had to get clear of the horse, anything to get his head above water and get some air. The flooded steam carried him away into darkness.

❧

Pounding at the door surprised Deborah. She set down her candle and turned around.

Friend Coffin strode to the door. "Yes? Who's there?"

"A Friend. . .with friends."

At the password, Friend Coffin flung open the door. "Come in, neighbors. Come to the fire."

Pa lurched in, carrying a soaked and unconscious young man in his arms.

Deborah stared at them. "Pa, what happened?"

"I had doubts about the bridge and pulled off. This man rode right past us and tried to cross, but didn't make it." The runaways behind him slammed the door, latched it, and then stood shivering.

"He might have passed away," Pa said. In a heavy voice he added, "I tried to warn him, but it was too late."

Friend Coffin picked up the slave hunter's wrist and felt it. "Still alive."

"Bring him to the fire," Cousin Katy said. "Deborah, he needs dry clothes and blankets."

Deborah hurried through the house and trotted up the curving front staircase. On the landing at the top of the stairs, she found the door that led to the attic. She opened it with a quiet click so as to not wake the girls or Grandmother Coffin. Working by feel, she located folded clothes on the attic steps. They were ice cold. Poor man. He would freeze for sure unless they let these warm up. She couldn't believe she had a shred of sympathy for that evildoer.

The commotion must have awakened the children, who rustled around in their bedroom. "Deborah? Who is here?" Little Catherine, the youngest, murmured.

"One of the slave hunters."

The girl gasped.

"He might not live the night," Deborah said. He was so alive, proud, and boastful just an hour or so ago. Where was his soul now? She shivered.

As she returned to the dining room, her father paused at the side door. "I'm going to fetch the doctor," he said.

Friend Coffin and two young black men worked over the drowned man. They'd pulled off his wet coat and waterlogged boots. Deborah handed them blankets.

One man shook his head. "I still think we should've just left him. Won't lie to you."

The other one paused for a moment. "I know, Chance, but I think the Lord would have wanted us to try."

The slave hunter coughed, making an awful noise. Was he dying, right there in front of them? What if he faced God with the blood of runaway slaves on his hands? Could the Lord save even one such as him?

She put more wood on the fire; it flared and illuminated the stranger's condition.

His paper-white face was smeared with mud, his half-opened eyes glassy, and his lips blue. He might be near her age or a few years older. Wet hair was thick and dark as an otter pelt. A full beard hid the angles of his jaw and cheekbones. Asleep or unconscious, he appeared harmless. Only the Lord knew the extent of his evil deeds.

She crossed her arms.

Cousin Katy put her hand on Deborah's shoulder. "Thee seems troubled."

She breathed deeply and let it out. "I am wondering. . . . Would the Lord redeem even someone like him?"

Cousin Katy gasped. She put her hand over her heart and stared at Deborah.

Friend Coffin glanced up from the fireside. "Tell us thy mind, Deborah."

The slave hunter's conscience must be seared as hard and black as coal. "Perhaps drowning is the Lord's judgment on him for his evil ways—and should he recover, he knows all about thy affairs."

Friend Coffin shook his head. "I'm sure the Lord would want to redeem this man, but will he accept the Lord's grace? If he lives. We should pray that the Lord's good, acceptable, and perfect will comes to pass in this young man's life." He stood and gazed into Deborah's eyes. "In all of our lives."

She looked down at the clean clothes she'd wadded into a ball. She nodded as she smoothed out the linsey-woolsey shirt and pants and hung them over the fire screen. "I'll take his wet clothes if I may."

Someone pounded at the door then opened it. "I brought the doctor," Pa said, stamping snow from his feet.

Friend Hiatt followed Pa. His brow furrowed at the sight of the injured man.

Deborah took their coats and hats then put the stranger's dripping clothes in a basket. His riding coat alone would have weighed him down. Pounds and pounds of wool soaked with water and mud made her arm ache.

The doctor got down on the floor by the victim. "Yes, yes, keep him warm." He looked up at Friend Coffin for a moment while assembling his stethoscope, a wooden trumpet-shaped instrument. "We could write an article for the medical journals about reviving patients from exposure, Friends."

"Yes indeed."

He went to work, leaning over the patient and listening. He nodded. "Wonder of wonders. Heart is still beating." He shook his head. "A great deal of fluid in the lungs." He used his thumb to gently raise one eyelid. "Ah. The pupil still contracts.

Good sign. Friend Coffin, he needs a warm bed as soon as one can be prepared. Hot water bottles, too. Does anyone know if the horse trampled him? There is something amiss with his knee."

"It's anyone's guess," one of the runaways said. "Didn't see the horse after they fell."

Deborah shivered. That beautiful mare had been swept away in the flood? And the man nearly drowned. No matter who suffered that end, it would've been cold and terrifying.

Pa took her arm. "These fellows and I want to try to cross the creek again. I expect we can cross south of town. Out of our way, but we can make it over."

Cousin Katy looked troubled. "Thee's welcome to spend the night."

Deborah hoped Pa and the others would stay here. Traveling by the morning light would be so much safer. She added up how many that would be for breakfast: Levi and Cousin Katy Coffin, their three girls, Grandmother Coffin, herself, Pa, two fugitives, and the slave hunter, if he survived. Eleven for breakfast. Cornmeal mush would work out the best.

Pa shook his head. "I have too much to do at the farm. I appreciate the offer though."

Deborah put down the clothes basket and leaned against him for a moment. "Thee has had quite a trip. Take care. Give my love to Mama."

He nodded, putting one arm around her. "I know thee likes working here. Just now is the first time thee has seemed troubled."

Deborah sighed. "I've been exercised over the wisdom of helping such a one," she admitted, nodding toward the slave catcher.

Trust Pa to simplify it. "God's will is that none should perish, but repent and live."

Deborah gazed at the young bounty hunter's face. Could someone like that repent?

Chapter 4

Warm, dry air filled Nathaniel's lungs. He was alive, still. For a long time, he didn't know any more than that.

Voices echoed then faded away. He must be in someone's house. Whose? Voices spoke of a general store, the road to Richmond, the washing for that day, mending the next, and always about the weather. Children's voices, too, came and went. From somewhere came the steamy scent of laundry. Must be daylight.

His eyelids weighed too much to open, but he could feel his heart beating, hear its slow thump in his ears. *Alive— alive—alive.* If Nathaniel had died, he would've faced God's judgment without Christ. He shivered. How would he account for himself? For all the wrong he'd done since Ma and Pa died?

But the Lord had mercy on him, and someone had rescued him. For no other reason than mercy, because Nathaniel deserved nothing from the Lord's hand.

If the Lord gave him back his life, what was Nathaniel to do? Too much to think about. His knee throbbed with every heartbeat, but the pain testified that he'd survived. He struggled to breathe. If only he could fill his lungs. His splinted leg felt heavy as a log.

Footsteps thumped on the floorboards, and someone walked over to him.

"Well, well, well. Look at that color," a man said. "Very, very encouraging."

"Indeed it is, Friend Hiatt," another man said. "Thanks be to God."

Nathaniel's eyelids felt heavy as pig iron. When he finally pried one open, he found himself on a pallet on the floor of a warm room with many windows and doors. It was a dining room, with a crane and cooking utensils in the huge brick fireplace, a table and chairs off to one side, and a braided rug on the polished floor. Not a log cabin like home, but a modern house. The blue-painted woodwork around the fireplace and chair rail looked cheerful against the white plaster walls. Nearby two middle-aged men studied him, a tall thin man with twinkling gray eyes, and a short stout man. Both wore plain clothes: white shirts, dark coats with no lapels, vests buttoned almost to the throat, and trousers of the same dark material. Nathaniel's voice sounded old, like a rusted hinge. He propped himself up on his elbows for a moment, but dizziness overtook him and he lay back down. "Why would anyone thank God for me?"

The tall man's smile showed mostly in his eyes. "For His great mercy. I am Levi Coffin, thy host, and this is Friend Hiatt, the town doctor."

Nathaniel nodded. He recognized their names. Not only had the Wagner gang spoke of them, but so had his uncle and aunt, months ago, in one of their last letters inviting Ma and him north.

The doctor asked, "What is thy name?"

He gathered his strength. "Nathaniel Fox." After taking another breath—no matter how hard he tried, he could not get enough air—he asked, "What happened to my leg, Doctor?"

Doctor Hiatt shook his head. "I believe it is not broken, but I do suspect damage to the joint."

Nathaniel's heart dropped. If he were crippled, he'd have no way to make a living. "How long will it take to heal?"

"Several weeks. Thee must give it enough time. If it heals imperfectly, thee might always have trouble with it."

Nathaniel stared in horror at his splinted leg. How could he lose weeks of work? Stranded here among the Friends meant the Wagner gang had left him behind. Some friends they were. At least his horse had some value. The mare, his pistols, and his money sewn in his coat lining—no, wait—all of those were gone, too. He sighed.

Levi Coffin watched him, tapped his forefinger over his lip. He looked off into space as though mentally going through a list of names. "Is thee related to George Fox?"

Nathaniel sighed again. His aunt and uncle now lived near Newport, but he wanted no contact with them. "Who founded the Quakers? I don't think so, Mr. Coffin."

"Who are thy people?"

"All dead, sir." He refused to use plain speech. "You wouldn't know them anyway."

Dr. Hiatt sat down by him. "May I see thy hand?"

It weighed a ton, but Nathaniel reached out to him. The doctor took his pulse then looked at Nathaniel's hand. "Thee must be a tradesman of some sort."

"Was a blacksmith for a while."

"Why did thee leave thy station to run with the Wagner gang?"

Nathaniel's eyelids felt heavier. "Money, Doctor. Each slave is worth hundreds of dollars."

The two pious old souls studied each other as though taking a moment to hide their disgust. No matter.

"The love of money is a source of great evil," Levi Coffin pointed out, as one of them was sure to do. "And so thee has pierced thyself with many sorrows."

Nathaniel shook his head. It felt as big as a pumpkin. "That's as may be. My choice."

"Let us help thee sit up to ease thy breathing," the doctor said. "He will need to put up his leg, too."

The two of them moved a couple of chairs closer to the fireplace. They each took an arm and, grunting, tried to help Nathaniel up.

Pain shot through his knee. The room tilted and whirled around him as they dropped him into the chair. The doctor propped Nathaniel's injured leg on another chair and padded it with a folded coverlet.

Light footsteps pattered, and that girl appeared in the doorway across the room. Nathaniel forgot about his knee. Even in a plain brown dress, she was the prettiest girl he'd ever seen. A white cap covered most of her shiny dark brown hair. A white cape and apron made her waist look tiny. Her eyes were dark, her face freckled from time outdoors. His heart started to race, but that made his ribs hurt.

She asked the doctor, "Does thee need anything from the kitchen, Friend Hiatt?" She glanced at Nathaniel. Even though he tried to smile, her dark eyes narrowed slightly at the sight of him. She concentrated on the other two men. Her cheeks turned pink. A moment later her glance flickered back toward him. He tried another smile. She looked wary and turned away.

"Is thee hungry or thirsty, neighbor?" Mr. Coffin asked.

Nathaniel had to pause in admiring the dark haired girl. "No thank you, sir. I want to know what happened to my horse though." Perhaps the runaways had stolen his coat and the horse. "Even if it's bad news, I wish I knew what became of her."

She looked over her shoulder at him before she slipped out the door.

Nathaniel tried to concentrate on Mr. Coffin and Dr. Hiatt, but he struggled to keep his eyes open.

Mr. Coffin shook his head. "As yet, there's no sign of the animal. I wish I had better tidings for thee."

"We should let thee rest now," the doctor said.

Nathaniel could hear them talking as they went into another room. He closed his eyes and sighed. He wasn't welcome here because of his wicked ways. He stared into the fire. Aside from his health and his money, the mare was the most valuable thing he owned. No one knew if his knee would heal. His whole future—gone. What would he do now?

If his father were alive, what would he say? Nathaniel let himself remember until sorrow overcame him. There was only one book in their log cabin, Mother's cherished copy of the Bible. Pa might have repeated a Bible verse. . . *"Let not your heart be troubled, neither let it be afraid."* From somewhere the remainder of the verse welled up. *"Peace I leave with you, my peace I give unto you: not as the world giveth, give I unto you."*

Nathaniel had tried to find peace in the world, but his wild ride ended here. He bowed his head and prayed silently. *Oh Lord, everything I have touched has turned to dust.*

Everything that Ma and Pa believed about God came back to mind. God never changes. He would be Nathaniel's unchanging Father—one who never grows old or weary, never leaves him desolate, always guides him, always with him, always knows the right way to go. Jesus came into the world to seek and save the lost, even a wretched sinner like Nathaniel, or that thief on the cross beside Jesus. He remembered a verse his mother liked—*"Come unto me, all ye that labour and are heavy laden, and I will give you rest. Take my yoke upon you, and learn of me; for I am meek and lowly in heart."*

Everything he'd depended on had been swept away—health, strength, money, and his horse. Only the Lord is forever.

Nathaniel finally knew peace, and it felt like that first breath of air after almost drowning. *Oh Father, heavenly Father, take me back. . . . But what do I do now? Will anyone ever believe I am Thine?*

❧

Downstairs, Deborah checked on the laundry.

The slave hunter's buckskin breeches were probably ruined, shrunken from getting soaked and dried. Colors from his bright-colored vest had run all over his white shirt. His wool riding coat might come out better than his other clothes. As it dried it appeared a streaky dark blue. Dye had splotched the brick floor as water dripped from his coat. It might dry better closer to the fire. She grabbed it, but it was so heavy she dropped it. The coat clinked as it hit the floor. When she picked it up, things spilled out.

What on earth? Gold coins glittered on the floor.

She hung the coat closer to the fire, put the money in her apron pockets, and trudged back up the stairs.

The slave hunter dozed in a chair with his splinted leg propped up. Deborah paused and studied him. The old clothes he wore were too short for his arms and legs, but the homespun fabric made him look more like an ordinary farmer with wide shoulders, muscular arms, and big hands. His shoulder-length wavy hair had dried to a chestnut brown. A thick brown beard and mustache framed his mouth. Frown lines still showed between his brows. Before his dissolution he might have been handsome, but his countenance was hardened, as though hunting humans like animals troubled him not. How would they see "that of God" even in one like him?

She cleared her throat and kept a wary distance. "Good morning, neighbor."

His eyes flashed open. They were a clear blue-gray. A brief smile brightened his pale, gaunt face. "Yes, miss—"

She held out the gold coins. "These fell out of thy coat."

He grabbed them and stared at them. "All there. Good."

Deborah clenched her fists and held her breath to calm herself. "Does thee think I would take anything of thine? Of that blood money?"

He closed his eyes for a moment. "I beg your pardon. I meant no offense. I feared some of it must have been lost when I fell in the creek."

Of course. Deborah felt petty and mean. If the Lord meant to redeem this man, perhaps she needed to show more of the fruits of the spirit, including patience. "Forgive me."

He smiled quickly. "Think nothing of it."

Deborah stole a glance at him from the corner of her eye and watched him run the coins through his hands. Why did he do that?

Cousin Katy and Grandmother Coffin joined them in the dining room. "Deborah, perhaps our guest would like some tea," Cousin Katy said. She focused on the stranger. "Good morning, neighbor. I am Catherine Coffin. This is my mother-in-law,

Prudence Coffin, and my cousin, Deborah Wall. Can thee tell us thy name?"

Deborah poked up the fire, lay on more wood, refilled the kettle, and swung it back into the fireplace. She watched the stranger from the corner of her eye.

He braced his arms against the chair seat and levered himself to an upright posture but winced as he disturbed his knee. "Nathaniel Fox. Thank you for taking care of me."

Deborah gave him a curious glance as she took the teapot and cups to the table. " 'An Israelite indeed, in whom there is no guile.'"

He gazed at her for a heartbeat or two, his blue eyes narrowed with a guarded expression. "Yes, at one time." He paused. "But then—" He shook his head and said no more.

Deborah pressed her lips together and tilted her head. At least he was familiar with the Bible verse. "Cousin Katy, thee must forgive me for taking so much time with the washing."

"Thee had some extra work, with the rain and all." Cousin Katy was so long-suffering, so kind with everyone.

"Mrs. Coffin," Nathaniel Fox said, the coins clinking in his hand.

"Yes, dear?"

He sighed and held out the money. "You need this. You had the doctor out on my account, and I'm another mouth to feed... and it bothers me how I came about it."

Cousin Katy took it and stared at the money in her hand. "If that is how thee feels led..."

He nodded. "I do."

Deborah stole a glance his way as she helped Cousin Katy with the tea. She hadn't expected him to give up all his money. Grandmother Coffin, tiny and drab as a sparrow in her gray dress, watched him with her bright eyes but said nothing.

Cousin Katy urged Nathaniel to have plenty of tea to help fend off illness. The mantel clock chimed nine as Deborah helped with the cups and saucers. The pink china cup looked as fragile as an eggshell in his big hand. "I thought to make potato soup for dinner."

Cousin Katy smiled and nodded. "Very good. Will thee have some soup later, Nathaniel? Our Deborah is a gifted cook."

"I'm sure she is, Mrs. Coffin." He watched Deborah. "Quaker ladies are so domestic."

Deborah wondered if he was trying to tease her. "Thee may call us Friends. Quaker is a term of mockery."

He nodded, and for some reason he chuckled. "I have heard that."

"Then why—" Perhaps he fully intended to give offense. A wise man overlooked such things. She set her jaw. "Does thee want any soup or not? I need to plan."

He shook his head. "No thank you."

Cousin Katy followed her to the basement stairs and took her arm. "I would like thee to cook it up here, my dear. The kitchen is clear full of laundry. Make some extra. I hope the scent will bring his appetite back."

"But I will have to step around him."

Cousin Katy carried the tea tray and followed Deborah down the stairs to the kitchen. As she washed the tea things, she said, "The sooner he is well, the sooner he can leave."

That did make sense. Deborah weaved in and out of the dripping laundry, gathering what she needed into a big basket. With all the rain, they had no choice about where to hang the clothes, some in the kitchen and some on the side porch. As she climbed up, to manage the sharp turn in the stairs, she put the basket on the floor above her for a moment. The angle was most unhandy for someone as tall as her. One would think the stairs could be made differently in a new house—but that might have added to the cost.

At the top of the stairs, she picked up her basket and straightened, only to find Nathaniel Fox watching her.

"I can help you peel potatoes, Miss Wall." After such a long string of words, he had to catch his breath.

"Well—all right." She sat at the dining room table, trimming eyespots from a potato and handing it to him. She glanced at him after trimming the next potato. He was almost done with the first. A thin, brown ribbon of peel spiraled away. Deborah's work looked clumsy and wasteful by comparison. "Thee must have had a great deal of practice at that."

He smiled, his face brightening. "I have."

They peeled and cut potatoes for several minutes, dropping chunks into a bowl of cold water. Every time she glanced up, she found him studying her. Even John Moore, the weaver, never more than stole a glance, never stared at her in such a forward manner. Heat rose to her face. But of course, she'd been up and down the stairs many times and had sat near the fire.

Cousin Katy came in. She must have noticed Deborah's tense posture. "My husband told me thee was a blacksmith, Nathaniel."

Deborah looked up at Cousin Katy. "If I were a man, I believe I would shoe horses."

Cousin Katy chuckled. "Thee and thy horses."

"I did enjoy it." Nathaniel smiled, his countenance softening, perhaps with happy memories.

"If thee had work that suited thee. . ." She shook her head, what a puzzle he was.

His expression hardened, his eyes narrowed, and his lips tightened. "Why did I ride with slave hunters?"

Deborah looked into his eyes and nodded.

He concentrated on a potato, elbows on the table. "Money, my dear. I was told I could get rich quick." One corner of his mouth quirked up. "No one told me what the trade was really like."

"Does thee regret it?"

"Maybe." He dropped more potato chunks in the bowl then raised his head and gazed into her eyes. She couldn't look away. "I should have counted the cost. Never reckoned on losing my horse or going lame myself."

Another coughing spell seized him; he looked miserable. She'd never seen such a worldly person, yet Christ died even for one such as him.

As Cousin Katy left them, she said over her shoulder, "Neighbor Fox, thee must rest."

He took a shaky breath. "Yes, ma'am."

Deborah slipped potato chunks into the kettle of steaming water and swung it back over the fire. She stole a glance at Nathaniel. Had she ever met someone so contradictory?

Chapter 5

Dinner with the Coffin family and Deborah was torture for Nathaniel.

Beautiful Deborah Wall helped her gray-haired cousin Katy set the table, while Mr. Coffin came into the dining room from his office in the front of the house. He helped Little Catherine wash up at the stand by the door. Grandmother Coffin came in from the parlor, where she'd been knitting. She and Mr. Coffin talked and laughed about something to do with samples for his paint business.

The Lord hadn't spared a miracle for the Coffin girl or one for Pa in his accident or Ma in her last illness. The Lord had no good reason to let good people suffer and die. The Lord also had no reason at all to save Nathaniel, just out of His great mercy. But Ma and Pa were in heaven now. Perhaps part of believing was trusting the Lord to make all those losses worthwhile somehow.

The littlest girl didn't seem to mind her condition. She stared at Nathaniel as Deborah ladled potato soup out of a large tureen. Deborah, with her long slender arms, could reach across the table and serve everyone within moments—almost as quick as a gambler stacking a deck of cards. He should tell her that sometime—when he felt well enough to enjoy seeing her dark eyes sparkle and cheeks turn pink.

Mr. and Mrs. Coffin and Grandmother Coffin talked about how soon the neighbors could rebuild the bridge. Little Catherine bumped her water cup with her shaky hands, and Nathaniel grabbed it before it spilled. The two of them smiled at each other.

"Are you home from school today?" he asked.

Little Catherine looked sad. "Maybe someday I will be strong enough to go with Sarah and Elizabeth. I pray so."

He nodded, unsure what to say next.

A moment later the little girl brightened. "In the summer Jesse and Henry might come home."

Nathaniel tried to place them.

"My older brothers," Little Catherine added.

Deborah Wall glanced at them out of the corner of her eye. When she'd served them all, they bowed their heads for a silent prayer.

How long had it been since he was in such a home? At table with a family for a meal, not having something charred over a campfire or served half raw at some tavern. So much like home in North Carolina, when Ma and Pa were still alive. Nathaniel's eyes burned, and his throat seized up. Tears? In front of these strangers? God help him. He kept his head down.

He looked up to find Mr. Coffin studying him. "I hope thy business with the Lord is profitable, Nathaniel Fox."

They all looked at him.

Should he tell them of the change in his life? Not just yet. He might give way to tears. He shook his head. "You're right. I do have business with the Lord but am not sure of His terms. I'm at a crossroads."

Mr. Coffin set his spoon down. "The Lord has said if thee loves Him, He will send the Comforter to be with thee and guide thee."

Nathaniel looked down to hide his expression. For some reason that brought him close to tears again. He nodded and cleared his throat. "I hope to be well enough to travel soon."

Mr. Coffin nodded. "Has thee anywhere to go?"

Nathaniel hesitated. How would following Christ change his plans to move on? "No, sir. Well—I don't know."

Mr. Coffin paused before speaking. "Tell us thy mind, Nathaniel." He added a pinch of salt to his soup.

He watched them eat. The soup looked and smelled better all the time. "Maybe I will have some of that soup, Miss Wall."

She nodded and smiled briefly, mostly with her dark eyes, still looking bemused by him.

The hot soup eased the congestion in his chest, and its buttery scent reminded him he hadn't eaten for almost a whole day. He'd been raised with better manners but scooped it up like a hog eating corn. He let their conversation go on without him until he'd emptied his bowl.

He gathered his nerve and glanced around at them. "About someplace to stay. . . I do have family around New Garden. Somewhere. My uncle is George Fox."

Little Catherine raised her head. "Oh. Who founded the Society of Friends? I did not guess thee was that old, neighbor."

Nathaniel had to laugh. "No dear, they have the same name. My uncle is about Friend Coffin's age."

The older man smiled slightly. "As the storekeeper of course, I know most everyone, and everyone else knows even more people. I took the liberty of inquiring of Friend Fox and his wife. They said they are missing a nephew who is a blacksmith."

Nathaniel looked up from his soup again. Telling the truth made him feel free. "That would be me."

Little Catherine had more questions. "Neighbor Fox, didn't thee say thy mare was in foal to Messenger?"

Deborah had passed bread to Nathaniel, who was mopping up the last of his soup. He paused. "You overheard?"

Little Catherine looked down, her face turning pink. "Yes I did."

He chuckled. "You must be able to hear as well as an owl. Yes, she was in foal to him. But—I have little if any hope of seeing her again."

"If the Lord wants thee to have her. . ."

"I hope so."

Mr. Coffin spread apple butter on a piece of bread. "How did thee come to own her?"

For a long moment, Nathaniel stared into his soup bowl. "I bought her after a claim race. She didn't look like anything, and no one else wanted her. Despite her bloodlines."

"At a horse race." Mr. Coffin blinked.

Nathaniel took a deep breath. Other than drinking establishments, there were probably no places more worldly. "That's not how I was raised. My parents were Friends. I fear they wouldn't be proud of me at all now."

Little Catherine and Mrs. Coffin gasped and stared at him. Deborah Wall stopped, the ladle in midair, and stared at him, too. Now that they knew some of his past, they would give up any notions that he could be civilized.

Nathaniel felt worn out and ill. "Excuse me."

Katy Coffin nodded.

He got up and hopped over to his chair by the fire. The chair creaked and cracked under his weight. He couldn't sit still as his shivering grew more pronounced.

Deborah Wall left the dining room. Her brown dress swirled around her. Watching her gliding walk was almost worth getting sick again. He would love to see her expression if he compared her to a dancer.

She fetched some quilts. He managed to catch her eye and smiled at her. Even though his teeth were chattering, he had to tease her. "I thought you might throw those coverlets at me, Miss Wall."

As he'd hoped, her cheeks colored. "The thought crossed my mind, but that is not how the Lord would want me to act."

"Of course. Do unto others."

"Not quite. Rather my kindness to thee is like heaping coals of fire on thy head."

He stared up at her. His teeth chattered. "Coals of fire sound good right now. You d–d–don't have to wait on me."

"I would do the same for anyone else." She fetched out a hot brick covered in ashes from the fire and, with a pair of tongs, carried it over to him. Muscles in her slender forearms corded from the strain. "Pick up thy feet."

She arranged it for him then stood back. "Warmer now?"

He shook his head, feeling dizzier. Shivering overtook him. The hot brick felt no better than a chunk of ice. "No, not yet." He raised his head slowly. It felt like it weighed a ton. He searched her face. What would it be like for beautiful Deborah to look kindly on him? He could start by being honest. "I don't feel well at all."

Chapter 6

Ice crunched as Deborah stepped through puddles hidden by wet snow. In these few minutes between cleaning up after dinner and starting supper, she'd begun searching the creek banks for Nathaniel's missing horse.

Every few minutes the sun broke through the torn gray clouds, their white edges glowing like molten silver against the blue sky. Red birds flitted in and out of clumps of willows. Along the creek banks, the sycamore trees' white branches contrasted with the dark clouds. The water still sped along far beyond the banks, rushing around the trees and bubbling over smaller obstacles, such as fallen limbs or the wreckage of the bridge.

Her foot slipped and went through the ice up to her ankle, over her boot top. The sting of icy water took her breath away. She was about to fall. She held on to a tree branch until she got her balance.

Perhaps that best illustrated her spiritual life: Trying to balance on her own but needing the Lord. He was the Vine; she was one of the branches.... And apart from Him, she could do nothing. If the Spirit guided her words and deeds, Nathaniel could see and respond to "that of God" in her.

The Spirit might not lead her to tell Nathaniel that he was a wicked sinner. That work most likely belonged to someone else. Strife and accusations were the products of worldly wisdom, not of the Lord. She needed so much help. *Lord, speak to my condition.*

She might have put the good work of helping runaway slaves ahead of following the Spirit. Perhaps she'd made an idol of helping the fugitives, since it took her mind off the looming possibility of never marrying for love. Who in the Bible was distracted with much serving?

She found a better place to stand, on a fallen log sprinkled with icy, half-melted snow. No sign of any animal up or down the creek, although she saw deer tracks and the paw prints of rabbits and foxes. Being outdoors helped her find peace. "*Cumbered about much serving. . .*" Mary and Martha hosted Jesus at their home, and He told Martha that.

Perhaps butting heads with Nathaniel Fox showed her where she'd gone wrong, how she'd lost sight of her first love for the Lord.

Out of the abundance of the heart the mouth speaks. Lord, I had no idea I cherished such iniquity. Lord, Thou knowest how I need Thee. Forgive me for my anger. Search me, O God. . . . Guide me in right paths. Even if that means trying to show kindness to that man. Thou hast commanded us to pray for our enemies. Precious heavenly Father, have mercy on that man. Heal his leg, so he can go away soon.

She put her hand to her eyes and studied the woods and creek banks as far as she could see. No sign of the missing horse.

❧

The creak of a door woke Nathaniel. He opened one eye as Deborah Wall came into the dining room, her cheeks rosy from the cold. "I looked for thy horse, neighbor, but found nothing."

"You went clear out to the creek? I appreciate it."

She nodded and hung up her cloak and bonnet. "Oh yes. I was glad for a chance to go outside. And I took the liberty of bringing this for thee." She held out a dripping cheesecloth bag stained from years of berry preserves. "Ice. Plenty of it, right now. If thee is going to break something, winter is a good time to do so."

He smiled. "It hurts, but I don't think it's broken." He took the bag and draped it over his swollen, throbbing knee. The splint helped to hold it in just the right place. "Thank you, Miss Wall."

"I wish only to treat thee as I would want—or how I was treated the last time I got thrown by a horse and hurt."

Nathaniel wondered if he were dreaming. She was beautiful, she liked the outdoors, and she liked horses. He had to pause and remind himself to breathe. He could foresee falling in love with Miss Wall and embarrassing himself if he wasn't careful. What had happened to the hard-drinking, gambling bounty hunter he professed to be? "You got thrown by a horse?"

She smiled ever so briefly, but a real smile it was. "Oh yes, we used to ride all the time before there were roads. When my folks came, Indians still lived around here. As long as the Friends wore their plain clothes, the Indians recognized them as peaceable people, even during the War of 1812."

"Was your family from New Garden? In North Carolina?" What if Deborah's family or the Coffins knew of his family? He could almost feel connected here.

"My family came in 1808, I think. The Coffins came later." She studied him and the ice pack. "I think thee could use a towel or two."

Someone rapped on the door that faced Mill Street. She strode across the room, her brown skirt and white apron swirling, peeked out, and then threw open the door. "Pa!"

A tall, thin, dark-haired man came in, took Deborah Wall's hands, and kissed her cheek. "Hello, dear one."

Nathaniel stared. Did he know the man?

Then he recognized the voice—one he thought he'd heard last night.

Deborah's father was purposeful. "Hello, neighbor. I'm glad to see thee looking well."

Nathaniel gripped the sides of his chair and tried to stand up, but the room slid sideways and started to go in circles. Deborah and her father lunged forward and grabbed him. They helped him back to his seat. "Not perfectly well, sir, but better than last night."

Mr. and Mrs. Coffin joined them. "Friend Wall, how good to see thee," Mrs. Coffin said.

Deborah's father smiled in return. "I brought these. We prayed thy guest would soon be well enough to use them." He held out a pair of crutches. "I trust our Deborah won't need these again for a while."

She looked down and shook her head at some memory.

"Thank you, sir." Nathaniel propped them near his chair.

Mr. Coffin cleared his throat. "The goods thee received recently, Friend Wall—"

"Oh yes. Loaned them out already." Mr. Wall smiled.

Mr. Coffin nodded as though that pleased him.

What did they mean by that?

Mr. Wall, still wearing his coat and hat, focused on Nathaniel. "I also believe I have good tidings for thee. A stray horse came to the farm—a brown mare with a star. She looks like she might be in foal. Would that be thy horse?"

Nathaniel sat up. "Must be her! How did you know?"

"I caught a glimpse of her last night."

Nathaniel put his hand over his eyes and took a deep breath. That led to a coughing spell. "Answer to prayer," he sputtered.

They all looked at him with a variety of puzzled expressions, except for Deborah Wall, who looked at him suspiciously. She must think his change of heart was an act. Maybe someday she would know that he wouldn't turn away from his heavenly Father. He'd made his decision and finally felt peace. *Thank You, Lord.*

Mr. Wall cleared his throat. "We have room in the barn and plenty of hay. I would be glad to keep her for thee until thee is more settled, neighbor."

"Thank you, sir." He smiled wryly. "I don't know how long that will take or where I'll end up."

Chapter 7

After supper Friend Coffin and Cousin Katy got ready to go to an antislavery discussion at the meetinghouse. Deborah and the girls waved to them as the horses leaned into their collars to pull the buggy through the mud. Ordinarily they would take one horse on such a short drive, but the roads were so heavy from all the rain that they needed two.

Little Catherine linked arms with her sisters, Sarah and Elizabeth. "I wish we could have gone to hear the speaker tonight."

"I do dislike having all of us scattered like this," Grandmother Coffin said. "I wish we were all under one roof. I think keeping everyone at home is best."

Deborah wondered if the older lady was thinking of the other children. The older boys had been apprenticed out.

"I am curious though, what the visitors will say," Little Catherine said.

Deborah closed the curtains. A chilly north wind rattled the windowpanes, making the gingham curtains shiver. As she put more wood on the fire, she said, "Perhaps another time when the weather is better. Come sit with Grandmother by the fire, girls."

Little Catherine glanced over her shoulder. "Nathaniel Fox, would thee like to join us in the parlor?"

The drowsy man raised his head. "I would be pleased to. Although I'm not very good company." He levered himself out of the chair, tucked his crutches under his arms, and stepped slowly toward the parlor.

Grandmother Coffin sat on the bench, her back to the window that looked onto Winchester Road, the main road through town. One pale, wintry sunbeam streamed through the window. Grandmother held her Bible up to the light. "Oh good. All these young eyes can help me read."

Nathaniel Fox limped across the room. He paused by the fireplace and ran a fingertip around the pretty woodwork. He'd never been in such a beautiful new house. "May I join you, Mrs. Coffin?"

"Of course. Would thee like to read to us?"

He set aside the crutches and hopped over to the bench. "Where does it say, 'Let not your heart be troubled'?"

"John, chapter 14. Does thee know that verse?"

Deborah arranged the wood in the fireplace, and then she and the girls sat in other chairs. She picked up her knitting— they always needed clothing to replace the rags worn by the fugitives—and glanced at Nathaniel and Grandmother Coffin. What would he answer?

He held the Bible up to the fading light and read the passage. After a moment he said, "My mother and father quoted that to each other often."

Deborah paused in her knitting. How had he lost his family? She shouldn't care. She made herself concentrate. She could knit by feel and didn't need to light a candle. Matter of fact, it was nearly time for the girls to go to bed. Such a pleasant change from yesterday's storm and the travelers.

Grandmother Coffin nodded. "Tell us about thyself, neighbor."

Nathaniel closed the Bible and gave it back to her. "My family came from New Garden, in North Carolina. Mother and I started up here after my father died, but she died on the way."

Deborah paused when she heard that. How sorrowful.

Nathaniel went on. "After that, I did blacksmithing for a while. Was told I could make more money by capturing runaway slaves. I was very useful at working with chains and shackles and such. I always meant to write to my people up here but never did."

Perhaps his conscience bothered him and he didn't want to reveal his shameful life to his relatives.

"What will thee do now?" Grandmother Coffin asked.

Nathaniel glanced over his shoulder, out the window. The Coffins' store, other buildings, and bare trees across Winchester road blocked the sunset's glow. "I don't know."

Someone tapped on the door. Deborah put down her knitting. They'd received no word of travelers tonight.

She went out to the dining room and hesitated at the door. "Yes?"

"Aunt Deborah, it's me, Tom," called one of her nephews. "Thee should know we have company coming."

"Friends?"

"Yes. I'll run back to the meeting now."

"Thanks, Tom." She went back in and picked up her knitting, trying to think what to say. She looked into Grandmother Coffin's dark eyes. "We might have company tonight."

Little Catherine understood. "Perhaps someone is coming home with Mama and Papa."

Grandmother nodded.

Deborah put away her knitting. "I should build up the fire and put the kettle on."

"We can put ourselves to bed," Little Catherine said.

"How will you get up the stairs, Little Catherine?" Nathaniel asked.

She giggled. "All kinds of ways, neighbor."

Deborah went out to the dining room, put more wood on the fire, and slipped down the stairs to refill the water pitcher from the well. She took a coal from the fireplace with tongs and lit a candle lamp. She tied back the window curtain then set the light in the window. With a sigh she looked at the roll of blankets Nathaniel had used last night. She wanted him out of the way, but where to put him?

His crutches thumped on the wooden floor. He paused in the doorway, casting a big black shadow in the firelight. "If they're going to be in the dining room and parlor, perhaps I should go somewhere else."

"There is a daybed in Friend Coffin's office." She looked over her shoulder. "It might be too short, but at least thee will be off the floor."

He chuckled. "The floor might be more comfortable." His smile softened his features. In the candlelight he looked cheerful and good natured.

She picked up the blanket roll and handed it to him. He draped it over his shoulder and hobbled out through the parlor. One of the girls pointed him to Friend Coffin's office across the entryway from the parlor, and he shuffled in there. Furniture bumped and scraped on the wooden floor as he settled in.

Deborah sighed with relief. He was out of the way. Hopefully he would sleep through any commotion.

"I will put the girls to bed, Deborah," Grandmother Coffin

said. "Good night. Thee knows it might be hours."

"I know. I will just wait up."

She gathered her knitting and sat down with it at the dining room table. Now she had too much time to think as her knitting needles clicked. The yarn and movement kept her fingers warm. Nathaniel Fox was such a puzzle. Where did he stand with the Lord? He seemed to have changed, but he also seemed so worldly with his fondness for horseracing. His recent companions were men of violence. No denying he was a handsome man, but what was he on the inside?

❧

Once again voices woke Nathaniel. He found himself in a dark room with bookcases and a big desk. The fire had gone out, and wind rattling the windows and shutters made the room more dark and cold.

Voices and footsteps echoed from the kitchen. Deborah Wall sounded upset. "Oh no—oh look at thy foot. Perhaps we need the doctor."

"Ma'am," a man's voice replied, "if we could just get the manacle off somehow." A chain clanked on the wooden floor.

Manacles and chains—must be more runaways, maybe the rest of the group the Wagner gang had pursued and lost and recaptured all the way up here from Kentucky. What would the Lord have him do? He couldn't pretend to sleep through this.

He grabbed his crutches, straightened his clothes, and limped into the dining room.

A crowd of runaways dressed in rags and covered in mud and burrs stared up at him with wild eyes. One of the men recoiled. "You!"

Nathaniel's heart dropped. "Aaron—"

Deborah Wall stared at him then at the runaway. "Thee knows him, neighbor?"

Aaron clenched his fist, took a deep breath, and then opened it. "You tell the lady what you done, soul driver. What's he doin' here?"

"He was hurt. This is the nearest house, so we brought him here." She gave Nathaniel a long look. "All God's children are welcome here."

If Aaron could've grabbed something, he would've probably hit Nathaniel over the head. Nathaniel's voice sounded unexpectedly calm. "I put that on you. I can take it off."

Aaron narrowed his eyes and stared at him. "Why would you help me now?"

"It's the right thing to do. Deborah Wall, is there a file hereabouts?"

"Out in the barn."

"Maybe we best move on. If he's here. . ." one of the others said.

Light footsteps sounded on the back stairs, and Grand-mother Coffin came into the dining room. She looked fragile. "Stay and rest, neighbors. There is nothing to fear here."

Aaron pointed at Nathaniel. "Him. You know what kind of man he is?"

Grandmother Coffin nodded. "We are all the same before God. Dreadful sinners."

Aaron looked down for a moment.

"I don't know where Neighbor Fox stands with the Lord, but we must look for 'that of God' in everyone," Grandmother said. "Have no fear, friends. He will do thee no harm."

As she put on her wraps, Deborah paused in the south door and looked over her shoulder at him, as though wanting him to hear that. She slipped out across the porch and disappeared into the night.

Nathaniel grabbed his crutches. "Aaron, sit by the fire. Let me see your leg."

"Friends, come to the kitchen," Grandmother Coffin said. "There is a good fire down there. Plenty of room. Let us find something to eat." They followed her down the stairs, several staring at Nathaniel as they passed.

Aaron limped to Nathaniel's chair and winced as he sat down. He propped up one leg and sighed.

Nathaniel stared at Aaron's leg. Swelling appeared above and below a shackle tightly clamped just above the ankle. Nathaniel had put that on Aaron only a few weeks ago, when they'd captured some of the family and tried to drag them back to Kentucky. But the runaways had escaped again. Seeing some drown in the Ohio River had sickened Nathaniel. He tried not to think about it. What to do? He lit a candle, turned a chair around, and leaned over Aaron's leg.

The other man could easily kick him in the face or hit his bad leg.

Nathaniel sat up and thought out loud. "This will be painful. I wonder if we should have the doctor out. Can you feel anything of your foot?"

Aaron's face was a study. "Little bit. Likely froze, too. Why are you helpin' me now?"

Nathaniel gazed into Aaron's narrowed dark eyes. "It's the right thing to do."

"Won't bring anybody back. Bein' kind now won't make you right with God."

Nathaniel nodded. "I know that very well. Only Christ can make someone right with God the Father."

Hoofbeats thudded outside, but Nathaniel didn't hear carriage wheels or trace chains. He turned toward the window. Someone came on horseback. He limped to the window. Outside were horses and riders, men with guns. "Wagner's gang."

⚘

In the barn Deborah gave each of the horses and the milk cow a handful of grain to keep them quiet while she searched for the tools. She found the file in the freight wagon toolbox, and when her fingers brushed the cold metal of a hammer and chisel, she decided to take those, too.

The neighbors' dogs started barking. Hoofbeats echoed.

She peeked out the barn door. The Wagner gang had returned.

Fear jolted through her. She almost couldn't breathe. The children, Grandmother Coffin, and the runaways were all in the house with no one to protect them. Nathaniel Fox might choose that moment to betray them. Such a big group must be worth thousands of dollars. Why had they trusted him? Once he let them in, they would tear through her dear ones like a pack of wolves with a flock of sheep.

She slipped out into the shadows and froze. Her pounding heart shook her whole body. If she went along the path, she could hide in the grape arbor between the house and barn, and then slip onto the porch and through the side door to the dining room. Fright sharpened her eyes. Every detail, every frosted blade of grass, and every buckle and button on the horses and riders appeared magnified in the starlight.

She leaned on the doorframe and prayed. The path looked a mile long. Her legs shook. If the gang stayed on the street, she would be safe. If the barn door made no noise, that would help, too. She slipped through and eased the barn door shut. The few yards to the grape arbor were wide open. The horses and riders clustered at the front of the house, but a few came down Mill Street. Waiting for them to turn around took forever. She strode up the path and slipped into the grape arbor, praying the tangle of vines would hide her.

She clutched the tools to her, hands trembling. If she dropped one on the brick path, the clatter would alert the slave hunters.

Finally she reached the side porch and crossed it in a few quick, quiet strides. The side door opened. Nathaniel Fox grabbed her arm and pulled her inside.

He loomed over her, his warm hand on her arm. "I started to worry, Deborah Wall."

"I brought the tools." Her voice shook.

"In a minute." He hobbled over to the other door. With a scrape he picked up the fireplace poker. "If any of them get past me, Aaron, use this."

"Thee would use violence?" Deborah's voice sounded choked.

"To protect a houseful of women and children, I would. I only wish I hadn't lost my pistols."

"Against thy friends?" What if he meant to deceive them and betray them?

He leaned forward a fraction of an inch to look into her eyes. In the dim light, his eyes looked big and dark. "They aren't my friends, Deborah Wall. I don't want them in this house. I know what kind of men they are."

Deborah gulped. He sounded so grim. *Lord, help us.*

Someone pounded on the front door. Nathaniel took the hammer from Deborah, nodded to Aaron, and then limped to the door. "Who's there?"

"Octavian Wagner. I got writs to serve here for multiple fugitive slaves."

"No slaves here," Nathaniel called as Deborah joined him at the door.

"Don't split hairs with me, Coffin."

Nathaniel laughed. "He's not here. Don't you know me, Wagner?"

Deborah put her hand on his solid arm. "What is thee about, Nathaniel Fox?"

"Not letting them in."

"Who's there?" Wagner called.

"Nathaniel Fox."

Several men swore in amazement. "We heard you was drowned," one called out.

"Not quite."

Wagner laughed. "The fox is guarding the henhouse. Open up. You'll get a double share of the money, I promise."

Deborah shivered. Nathaniel had pounced on those gold coins earlier. She stared up at him. What would he do? Was he tempted?

"Not my house. I can't do that."

"Then we're comin' in."

Deborah held her hands over her mouth, hardly breathing.

"Don't. The Friends won't put up a fight, but I will. You know I'm a pretty good shot."

Deborah's heart pounded harder and harder. He wouldn't, would he?

"You only got a couple of pistols."

"You don't know what I found in here though. Maybe a shotgun or somethin' else very useful."

"Octavian Wagner, you and your men are disturbing the

peace," a voice interrupted. "I'm ordering you to disperse."

Deborah sighed with relief. Her knees went weak for a moment.

"Who is that?" Nathaniel whispered.

"The constable."

"I got papers here—" Wagner argued.

"We'll read 'em in the morning, see if they're any good. Now go away."

Hoofbeats sloshed around outside, saddles creaked, horses snorted, and men muttered as they turned around.

Deborah took another deep breath. "Bless the constable. He needed a bank loan recently, and Friend Coffin, since he's one of the principals of the bank, helped him obtain it."

"I can't help but admire Mr. Coffin." Nathaniel chuckled.

Little Catherine called down from the girls' bedroom. "Deborah, have they gone away?"

"Yes, dear ones, everything is all right. Your mama and papa will be home soon."

They turned to go back into the parlor, but Nathaniel tripped on a rug. Deborah held his arm to steady him. "Is thee all right?"

"Yes, thank you." He organized his crutches. "I didn't mean to frighten you, Deborah, with all the talk of fighting and guns."

Deborah paused before she answered. She might have to change her mind about him. "I gather that was how thee felt led." She realized she'd left her hand on his arm and pulled away like it was red-hot iron.

"Yes it was. Now we need to tend to Aaron."

They found the black man in the dining room leaning against the window, the curtain pulled out a fraction of an inch so he could see. "They gone for sure?"

Nathaniel nodded. "They are indeed."

Aaron smiled when Nathaniel told him about the constable's bank note.

"Now let's see what can be done for you and your leg," Nathaniel said. "Deborah, what about some warm water to wash this up?"

Aaron hobbled back to his chair, dragging links of chain across the floor.

Deborah went to the fire, poured hot water from the kettle, and then added ice water from the pitcher on the washstand. She took the bowl to Nathaniel, who worked gently on the manacle.

Aaron winced, gripping the sides of the chair. She watched as Nathaniel bent over Aaron's leg. Had he changed that much? Would it last?

Chapter 8

Deborah guided Nathaniel's mare behind Ma and Pa's buggy. They were on their way to meeting at New Garden.

Nathaniel had told Deborah the mare's previous owners called her Brandy, a name he wouldn't have chosen. He hoped to open a blacksmith shop and fix up a stable and fences for the mare, as soon as his knee healed.

A dry week meant the muddy ruts of the road were frozen solid enough to travel easily. Crumbling snowdrifts lingered on the shadowed sides of trees and fences along the way, but the pale sunlight hinted that spring was coming. The road curved away from the Winchester–Richmond Pike, past the few remaining cabins of the original New Garden settlement. Most families had moved a mile or so north to Newport, once they'd discovered better water at that site.

Her brothers rode along, too. As long as the mare traveled with the herd, Deborah didn't foresee problems with her. Last week Brandy had hardly blinked when Deborah first tried Ma's old sidesaddle on her; someone might have ridden the mare aside before. An easy trip over to meeting and back would be good for the horse's health. The old saddle creaked and squeaked in rhythm to the mare's strides, but even that was enjoyable. What a merry company.

The ride buoyed her spirits, too. She'd been exercised over her attitude ever since Nathaniel Fox came to the Coffins' home. Some of her anger about the fugitives' treatment might have been righteous. But vengeance was the Lord's, not hers, and when accusations came she remembered that the Lord had forgiven her. Did she owe anything to Nathaniel since she'd wronged him?

His aunt and uncle had taken him to their home to recover, leaving Deborah to wonder what would become of him.

Her nephew Tom jogged along on his gray gelding. "She's a good mover, isn't she?"

"Yes, I like her very much."

"Too bad thee has to give her back to that Fox."

"I have been dealing with covetousness, truly." Deborah sighed. What would happen to him? She was sure she'd seen "that of God" in Nathaniel's life when he helped the runaway slave, Aaron. But had he truly changed?

Tom chuckled as they rounded the curve in the road that led to the meetinghouse. Tall trees stood around the long frame building. "Someone's bringing a farm wagon."

Deborah looked down the road toward the bridge that stood among bare trees. A team and wagon jolted over the bridge on the other side of the meetinghouse. "So they are."

She and Tom followed Ma and Pa, turned toward the hitch rack, and then greeted her older brothers and sisters. Tom reached up and helped her down. When she'd tied the mare, she looked past the animal to watch the farm wagon roll in.

A couple about her parents' age sat on the bench. A third person in a dark coat sat in the back of the wagon, sun gleaming like copper in his tousled brown hair. Deborah didn't recognize them at that distance.

Pa greeted them and helped with their team, and then walked around the back while the driver helped his wife down. Now she knew them—George and Martha Fox. They waited at the back of the wagon while the passenger scooted to the end, set down a pair of crutches, and slid out the back.

He looked up and stared at the mare then at Deborah.

She gasped. Nathaniel Fox. Clean shaven and his long hair cut. His countenance had changed. Now he looked cheerful with a quick, easy smile.

They all shook hands, and then Pa held his hand out to Deborah and the mare.

Nathaniel swung over to them on his crutches.

Deborah stared up at him. He looked so much better. The frown lines between his brows and on the sides of his mouth had eased. With all his whiskers gone, his face looked handsome as well as cheerful. Out in the pale, spring sunlight, his eyes looked sky blue, and the cold, fresh air colored his cheeks. His dark blue riding coat was unbuttoned. He wore his travel-worn plaid vest, white shirt, flowing black tie, dark trousers, and boots as though he hadn't given up his worldly and brave apparel.

Even so, she held out her hand. It trembled. He looked wonderful. "Neighbor Fox."

He took her hand. His hand made hers feel small, protected. "Hello, Deborah Wall. How is the mare working out for you?"

"We thought an outing would be good for her."

He nodded. "I'm sure you are right."

Deborah kept staring up at him. She should say something kind and encouraging. "Thee is joining us?"

He gazed into her eyes, ran a hand through his unruly,

close-cropped hair, and then smiled. "My aunt said I must or she won't feed me. Thus I cannot neglect attending meeting." He paused for a moment, still smiling at her. "I assumed you might have a comment."

Deborah tried to think of what to say. She smiled and opened her mouth. Then closed it and thought again. "I'm sure thee doesn't want to risk missing a meal. I'm glad to see thee here. And looking well."

He looked down for a moment, and instead of boldly studying her, he stole a bashful glance. Perhaps all these changes threw him off balance. Raising his gaze he asked in a low voice, "Truly glad?"

This might be the first step toward making amends. Deborah nodded then started to smile. "My integrity will not allow me to say otherwise."

He nodded and adjusted his crutches. "I'm thankful to be here. I was glad when they said unto me, let us go up to the house of the Lord."

Deborah could only stare at him. If he'd changed that much, would he join the Society?

Chapter 9

The air smelled like spring as Nathaniel drove his aunt and uncle to meeting at New Garden. Leafy trees arched over the road. Many of the fields had been plowed by now.

"I'm sure thee's thankful for the Sabbath, Nathaniel," Uncle George said. "Thee had a busy week."

He nodded as their pacing horse ambled along the road. "This ground is sure different from North Carolina. Plenty of rocks to break plow points and all. Reckon I won't run out of work anytime soon."

Uncle George chuckled. "How is thy knee? I wondered if thee was limping by the end of the day sometimes."

"It hurts once in a while, but I'm all right as long as I keep moving."

Aunt Martha cleared her throat. She was so soft spoken. "We are glad as always to have thee come with us to meeting, Nathaniel."

Nathaniel chuckled. "Given that I like to eat, I'm still very pleased to join you in exchange for room and board."

"But I'm sure thee heard something of value at the Methodist meeting."

The horse tried to swerve around a low spot, but Nathaniel made him drive straight ahead. "They do preach the Bible, but there's so much busyness about it that I was distracted." He said nothing about all the pretty girls in fancy dresses, none as appealing as Deborah Wall in her plain clothes and bonnet.

"I did hear that some of the Methodist women are also sewing things for the runaway slaves," Aunt Martha said. "In many ways we are in one accord."

"I heard that last bunch that came through needed almost everything," Uncle George said.

"All Aaron and his family wore were rags, and it still felt like winter. Town needs a shoemaker. Almost none of the travelers have shoes."

"I wonder where those people are," Uncle George said.

"I hate to ask too much when I see Friend Coffin at the shop. You never know who might be passing by. But I heard they stayed several weeks until the lame one could walk. Then someone took them to Cabin Creek. Don't know if they stayed in Randolph County or went on."

Aunt Martha breathed deeply and let it out. "I don't think we give thanks enough for having our homes and families."

"You are right." Nathaniel had to admire the Coffin family. Mr. Coffin tended to his business activities and involvement in New Garden meeting while hiding and caring for runaways. Mrs. Coffin showed each group the same calm hospitality she'd shown Nathaniel, and the runaways were probably more agreeable company than he'd been.

Nathaniel had opened a shop east of the main crossroad in Newport. Katy and Levi Coffin returned most of the money he'd given to her, providing he used it for the shop and tools, they'd said. He included a set of shoeing stocks for draft horses and oxen. Deborah Wall's father had hewn the beams and built the stocks for him.

He often saw Deborah from a distance but seldom had opportunity to speak to her, or words to say if their paths did cross. Of all people she remembered most clearly how he used to be. Some of the argumentative things he'd said to her made him wince with embarrassment now.

They pulled up near the frame building under the tall trees; only a few horses stood at the hitch rack. He looked for the Walls, but they hadn't arrived yet.

Aunt Martha liked to be early, which suited Nathaniel. He could find a seat in the back of the meetinghouse, put his leg up, and watch for the Wall family to come in. He liked to see Deborah, but did no more than nod and smile if she said hello. He knew her father, brothers, and nephews better through business.

Little Catherine Coffin was still his friend though. When the family came in, the little girl hobbled over to tell him what all had been going on. Now she could add, subtract, multiply, and divide fractions. One of the barn cats just had kittens, and as an afterthought, she told him about a group of Friends who came all the way from England. They'd stayed with her family and met a big group of runaways.

Someone like that, devoted to abolition and helping the slaves, might take Deborah Wall away. His chest tightened at the thought.

Little Catherine jumped up to join her mother and sisters. The seams of her gray dress showed her curved back. It might have gotten worse over time. He wished he could do something to help her.

Levi Coffin sat down by him. "Welcome, neighbor. How is business?"

Nathaniel smiled. "Busy right now, sir. Even shoeing some oxen."

"So the shoeing stocks were a good investment." He nodded. "I am pleased to hear thy good report."

"Thank you, sir."

The older man nodded. "I'm always glad to hear of thy progress. Excuse me—I need to move closer to the front to be sure I can hear."

Nathaniel nodded and stole a glance toward the doors as the women and men separated and went to their own sides. Their silence and dark, plain clothes helped him clear his mind and focus on the Lord.

The ministers and worthy Friends sat in benches on the platform at the front of the meetinghouse, facing the other members. Unlike the Methodist church, there was no cross, no pulpit, and no preacher in ceremonial robes. No music either. Now that was something he wished the Friends would reconsider.

Deborah Wall came in with her mother, older sisters, and nieces. Nathaniel's business with the Lord ended abruptly. Most of her family wore gray dresses, but Deborah preferred brown still. She was tall and willowy, almost as tall as her dad, and taller than her younger brothers. Her best dress was made of shiny material; her bonnet and cape were spotless.

Another man slipped into the pew beside him and blocked his view of Deborah. The man took a long look at her. Nathaniel took a deep breath. He had no claim to Deborah. Someday she was sure to marry one of the Friends. Her life was so different from his. A future with her was too much to hope for, although he knew his heavenly Father knew his heart, and Deborah's.

As she and her family found their seats, she looked his

way. Nathaniel froze and then reminded himself to smile. She glanced at her mother and nieces, and then back at him. Wonder of wonders, she smiled at him. Nathaniel's heart started racing.

The Friends settled down for several long, quiet moments. Deborah's father went to the facing benches and sat at a desk. He was the clerk for today's meeting. A minister on the platform made announcements, and another led out in prayer. Afterward they spoke of progress at the Friends' school that used the meetinghouse during the week.

Following a long, thoughtful pause, someone raised an objection to using the meetinghouse for antislavery meetings, but no one else felt led to speak one way or another. The topic died out, but the members were disquieted for several restless moments.

Friends who had called on members that needed help or spiritual guidance reported on the outcomes of their visits. One, John Moore, the weaver, was the angular man who had sat down by Nathaniel. How could he be a match for Deborah? What would they have in common?

Lord, help me listen. Several members had been appointed to attend various weddings among the young people. All the events had taken place decently and in good order.

Weddings. If he and Deborah were to marry, who would the Friends appoint—no, he couldn't think about a future with her.

Sadly some others reported that members who had broken fellowship wouldn't be reasoned with and were to be dismissed. At the mention of another girl's name, Deborah's lower lip trembled, and she blinked as though holding back tears. The girl had married someone outside the fellowship. Several people sighed and murmured among themselves at the bad news.

The members became silent for long moments after that.

Through the open windows came the sound of birds, a breeze in the trees, and water rippling through the creek bed.

Someone else felt led to speak about the dangers of being unequally yoked in marriage or in business. Nathaniel mulled that over. If both were Christians, were they truly unequally yoked?

During the next long, peaceful silence, Nathaniel recalled the previous year. Perhaps only such hard times could turn his heart and mind back to the Lord.

Finally the minister sensed that the meeting was over. He stood and shook hands with the others on the platform. Everyone else stood and shook hands all around. Nathaniel waited for the others to leave so his limping pace wouldn't delay them.

A short, stocky man with a jowly face and thick white hair spoke to Deborah's father. Nathaniel overheard Mr. Wall greet the man as Friend Smith. He was the other man who wanted to call on Deborah. Nathaniel found himself walking out with Josiah Wall, Deborah's father.

"I'm glad to see thee well, neighbor," the older man said. "Thee's moving a little more slowly today."

"Lots of plow horses and oxen to shoe this week."

"Glad of that. My family and I have a concern, Nathaniel."

"About what, sir?" He held his breath. What if he'd noticed Nathaniel staring at Deborah?

"Thy mare seems to be getting closer to foaling. We wondered if thee would like to come out and take a look at her."

"I would. When would it suit you all?"

"Even today, if thee's concerned about her. Our Deborah believed thee would be interested. She and Mother planned on one more for dinner."

Nathaniel grinned. "I'll tell my uncle and aunt."

Out by the hitch rack, he found the Walls sorting out who would ride in which of two buggies. The boys had ridden their horses over to the meeting. Nathaniel found himself in the buggy with Mr. Wall. Deborah drove the other horse, a high-spirited gelding. She managed it as well as any man, better than most.

He and Josiah Wall talked about the weather and farming as the horse trotted eagerly back home. They went north on the Winchester road through Newport, past the big, white tavern favored by the Wagner gang, past the potter's shop, harness maker's, cooper's, wagon maker's, doctor's house, and the Coffins' store. They turned east at the main crossroad. A few hundred yards from the creek stood Nathaniel's blacksmith shop. Since it opened, he'd been within sight of the Coffins' house and had even seen Deborah from a distance many times, but he didn't try to push friendship on her.

The horses and buggy clip-clopped over the new bridge. Only smears of silt on the trees showed the height of the earlier flood.

The first farm next to the creek belonged to William Smith, the widower interested in Deborah. Nathaniel studied the farm as they went by. A tall, square house stood at the end of a long lane. Behind it stood a big barn and pastures enclosed with rail fences. Milk cows and oxen lay chewing their cud among tall grass. Like every other farm here, woods edged all the fields and lined the horizons, showing where the first settlers had chopped fields out of forests.

The brick house had rows of windows and massive chimneys. Making enough money to build such a place of his own would take years, and Deborah would have married someone else by then.

"Nathaniel, I have a concern," her father said.

"What is it, Mr. Wall?"

"I hear good things about thy work and thy character. Thee attends meeting consistently. I wonder if thee has considered rejoining the Friends."

Nathaniel shook his head. "I don't feel led that way, sir. I am a Christian, but I differ from the Society's teaching on several points."

Mr. Wall nodded. After a long pause he said, "We are called to be in the world but not of it. How thee works that out in thy life is between thee and the Lord."

"I appreciate your concern, Mr. Wall. It's something I've been thinking about."

"Truly?"

"Yes, sir. If I did rejoin the Society, I'd want to be settled in my mind that it's for the right reasons."

Mr. Wall gave him a long look. "Thee's very thoughtful."

"I have a lot of time to think while I work." He didn't want to admit how much he thought about Deborah.

Chapter 10

Deborah turned the reins over to one of her brothers when they reached home. She watched Pa and Nathaniel in the open buggy. What had they talked about?

All these weeks he would only smile at her, never saying anything. He either didn't like her at all or thought she didn't like him, or he was trying to avoid giving offense. Most likely he didn't like her because of how she'd treated him while he was at the Coffins'. Every time she remembered her harsh words and cruel thoughts toward him, she felt pricked in the heart and prayed about it again.

If she'd given offense, she needed to make it right, one of the most difficult things she had to do as a Christian. Perhaps asking Nathaniel's forgiveness would give her peace.

After he'd helped Pa and the boys with the horses, Nathaniel limped into the house, the last to enter, and said hello to her mother. He turned to Pa. "I didn't see the mare. Is she out on pasture?"

"Down by the creek, most likely."

Nathaniel looked over his shoulder. "Very far?"

Deborah resisted the urge to speak up and tell him where to

find the mare. If they walked out there together, she might have a moment to apologize to him for her conduct earlier. "I can guess where she would be. After dinner we can look for her."

During the meal Deborah hardly tasted the corn dodgers Mama served. Nathaniel talked and laughed with her family as though he'd known them for years, but he barely talked to her. What if she was right and Nathaniel had been offended all these weeks? After the meal she hurried up into the loft of the double log cabin and changed into her old homespun dress and apron.

Nathaniel waited for her on the back porch. "I hope it's not too far."

"No, it will be a pleasant walk." She led the way to the gate. Nathaniel dropped the rails and put them back.

At the edge of the woods, redbud trees looked like pink clouds. The dogwoods' white blossoms glowed in the woods, and the dark shapes of the horses and cows were visible at the end of the green pasture.

Despite the soft blue sky and warm air, Deborah shivered, gathering her nerve before speaking. "Nathaniel Fox, I have something to say to thee."

His deep voice was soothing. "I'm glad. It's been a long time since we talked." He turned and gave her a hand as they picked a path around mud puddles. His hand was warm and his arm solid.

She took a deep breath and held it. Admitting to doing wrong wasn't easy. "About that—if I did anything to offend thee, with harsh words or how I acted toward thee when thee first came here. . ."

He stopped and studied her for a moment then smiled wryly. "Harsh? I think you were justified. Somewhat. Although there were times when you looked at me like I was pond scum."

She burst out laughing then gazed up into his eyes, sky blue in the spring sunshine. She had to be as direct as possible. What was she going to say? "But still—"

He put his finger over her lips. His sudden warm touch almost stopped her heart, but then it started to race. "You have done nothing to offend me."

"Thee has said nothing to me for weeks."

He looked down and started worrying a clump of grass with his boot toe. "I shouldn't speak to you. It would make you look bad, harm your reputation. People would talk."

"I have my integrity." She held out her hand and sighed. "Let's go look at the horses." Once she told him the worst of it, he might never forgive her. She hated to risk that. Her thoughts toward him startled her again. If he never forgave her, they'd have no future. She'd allowed herself to imagine too much, that this tall, handsome man who also liked horses and farming would grow into a solid Christian, diligent in business, sober in character—someone worth marrying once he rejoined the Society.

They walked a little farther. The long grass hid stumps and roots left from when Pa and the boys had cleared the field years ago. Deborah tripped and Nathaniel caught her. Both stumbled for their balance and held each other up.

She looked up into his ruddy face. His countenance had changed so much over the past several weeks. How could she have ever thought such cruel thoughts about him? "Nathaniel, there is more I need to confess."

He closed his eyes as though bracing for bad news. "Tell me, then."

"When Pa first brought thee to the Coffins, I—" She had to

take another breath to steady her nerves. "I wondered if drowning was the Lord's judgment on thee for thy wicked ways."

He breathed deeply, let it out, and then smiled.

"Nathaniel, why is thee smiling?"

"I feared worse news."

She shook her head. "What could be any worse?"

"That you planned to marry someone else."

Deborah blinked in surprise. "Marry someone? There's no one—" She cleared her throat. Her face warmed, clear up to the roots of her hair. Where did that idea come from? "Nathaniel, I wished the worst that could befall thee."

He looked down and nodded. "I'm not surprised at all. Nor offended. Tell me you haven't worried about that all this time."

"I have."

He took her hands. "Oh Deborah Wall, the Bible says if any man is in Christ, he is a new creature. But also you need to forget what lies behind."

Her voice trembled. "I was so harsh. Almost treated thee like—like—"

He kept her hands. "Like someone of the world? For all have sinned and fall short of the glory of God. You know that, as well as I do, birthright Friend or not."

She looked down and shook her head. Her voice cracked, and she paused to get it under control. "I never thought I'd act it out like that, Nathaniel."

"I never thought I'd do half the things I ended up doing either. And I was a birthright Friend, too." He held her hands then drew her after him. "We're supposed to look ahead, aren't we? I have a lot to forget, and I suppose you have an item or two you'd like to rarely recall."

She nodded. "Thee's right. Let's find the horses."

They reached the swale where a streamlet trickled toward Willow Creek. The cows were lying down chewing their cud as Deborah and Nathaniel walked up.

Two of the horses looked up then returned to grazing. The mare was missing. Deborah took a few steps farther. "I suppose, if she's off by herself, she might be foaling now."

Nathaniel nodded. "Any ideas where she might have gone?"

"There's a little clearing back here." She led him to the edge of the woods, along a muddy trail chopped with hoofprints. She glanced over her shoulder at Nathaniel. Hard to imagine he was the same person as the grim man who'd pursued fugitives to the Coffins' home.

He looked up from untangling raspberry canes from his clothes. "I wish the mare would foal about the same time as the raspberries come on."

"She's too far along. But we might see fit to invite thee back when the berries are ripe," Deborah said. She paused to study the plants, beaded with green flower buds that would yield berries in a few weeks.

"Glad of that." He smiled.

Deborah glanced back at him and smiled.

A horse snorted and a tiny voice answered. Deborah and Nathaniel exchanged glances. She took a step forward and he joined her. They pushed aside a screen of leafy branches. In the grass of the clearing, the mare stood over a tiny long-legged foal, nuzzling and licking its fuzzy coat.

Deborah looked at Nathaniel. His eyes widened and he grinned. "I thought I'd never see this. And you're here to see it with me."

She looked at him questioningly. "I'm glad thee feels that way."

He took her hand.

Deborah breathed deeply. Her hand felt so right in his—hidden, safe, protected by his strong grip. Neither John, the weaver, nor Neighbor Smith made her feel that way, because she didn't feel any closeness to them. "Nathaniel Fox, if thee has forgiven me for my harshness toward thee earlier, then do speak to me when we see each other."

He kept her hand then took her other one. Deborah's mind raced. People at weddings faced each other and held hands just like this. But wait, neither she nor anyone in her family knew him very well. "It would be my privilege."

"I think we should see if thee has a colt or filly," she added.

Chapter 11

As spring warmed into summer, Nathaniel made many calls to the Wall farm to see the mare and her filly. Sometimes when she wasn't working, he saw Deborah, too. Every time they talked about the mare and foal, he felt more drawn to her. If only he could follow his heart, pursue her, try to win her for his wife.

Whenever he imagined marrying her, he remembered how upset she'd been when one of her friends was dismissed for marrying out of unity. What would be best for Deborah? Her entire family and all of her friends were in the Society. Love was long-suffering and kind, according to the Bible, and did not seek its own way. How could marrying him be best for her?

The open secret of the Coffins' abolition work included a sigh of relief this time of year. Everyone knew most runaways arrived over the winter, when their pursuers were reluctant to go out in bad weather. As summer went on, the days grew longer and hotter.

On a drowsy afternoon, Deborah Wall led one of the Coffins' horses down to his shop.

"Hello, neighbor," she said.

Nathaniel looked up from sharpening some hand tools, easy

work in this heat. Her coarse homespun dress, sleeves pushed up on her arms, looked cool in the heat. Freckles dotted her hands, forearms, cheeks, and nose. Nathaniel had never seen such a pretty girl.

If only she hadn't seen him like this, in work clothes and in need of a shave. "Good afternoon, Miss Wall. What can I do for you?"

She tied the old gelding to the rail in front and looked around the shop. It was mostly a roof over the forge. Barn swallows darted in and out. "He has a loose shoe."

Nathaniel lifted the horse's hoof and examined the shoe. It was missing a nail. "Do you want to reset the shoes or just replace that nail?"

"Just the nail, until he needs all of them done."

"Are you in a hurry?"

She chuckled. "No, this is cheaper." She stood by the gelding and watched Nathaniel work. "I need to tell thee some other news."

He nodded.

"Neighbor Smith, outside of town, has bought a good trotting horse. Pa made bookcases for his house earlier and saw it. If thee is wondering about getting thy mare rebred, that might be a good one."

"Have you seen the horse?"

"I have. A few nights ago, I rode over with Pa."

He took a moment to gather his thoughts as well as find just the right nail. He knew Smith, a rich widower, favored Deborah. "To visit with your father or see the horse?"

She smoothed her dark hair under her bonnet. What would it look like all undone? Couldn't think like that. Or that she and her father had gone out to the Smith place. He made himself listen as she said, "Truth be told. . .a little of both."

"What do you think of that horse, Deborah Wall?"

"He's taller and has better legs than the mare. Thy mare is lovely in every way, except she toes in slightly in front. Improve that so they don't overreach or interfere at speed, and any of their foals would be even faster."

He watched, agreeing with her thoughts. "Good reason to look him over."

She nodded. "I thought thee would like to know. Good afternoon, neighbor."

Nathaniel watched her walk away. He breathed deeply and exhaled. They liked so many of the same things. They could talk about horses all day. Could he and Deborah ever have a future together? Should he even hope for that?

❧

Deborah looked over her shoulder at Nathaniel as she walked slowly back to the big brick house. As she left the shop, someone brought in a lame horse.

He worked carefully with the horse and had a long talk with the owner. The sun gleamed copper in Nathaniel's tousled chestnut hair. His face, arms, and hands were tanned. During his talk with the owner, he picked up the horse's leg and pointed to its tendons, as though those were part of the problem. The owner looked impressed. She sighed. Was she in error to hope and pray Nathaniel would rejoin the Society? She'd gotten ahead of the Spirit's leading earlier, and only the Lord's mercy had saved Pa and the runaways from the Wagner gang. She would hate to rely on her own insight again. But it was so hard to wait on the Lord's timing.

She walked up the path through the grape arbor; the fruit's

sweet scent combined with the aroma of gingerbread cooling on the dining room windowsill. She'd made the cake earlier for the sewing circle.

Inside, she helped Cousin Katy and the girls open windows on the shady side of the house. They closed other windows and curtains against the sun. The house's high ceilings, tall windows, and transoms over the doors helped capture the breeze.

She climbed the narrow, twisting stairs to the bedroom she shared with the girls. She changed into a better dress then went downstairs to help prepare for the sewing circle.

Mama and her oldest sister, Ruthanne, planned to come today. The group tried to keep ahead of clothing needed by the runaways. More women came during spring and summer when travel was easier.

She steadied Little Catherine, who'd climbed into a straight chair to get to the gingerbread. "Patience, dear, thee might fall."

The youngest Coffin girl turned her head toward Deborah, but only a little because of her curved spine. "I just wished to smell it. Perhaps someone needs to sample it?"

Deborah put her hand over her lips for a moment to hide a chuckle then looked at the mantel clock. "Not long, now, dear heart." She helped Little Catherine down.

She longed to see Mama. Sometimes the fugitives' stories made her heart ache. How blessed her family was to have each other. No one could tear them away, unlike the poor slaves.

Little Catherine looked out the window. "Deborah, here is thy mother already."

Deborah opened the door and helped Mama up the stairs.

Mama took both of her hands. "Did thee make gingerbread, dear heart? I thought I smelled it. I'm surprised the whole town isn't here."

Deborah smiled. "I hope it's like thine, Mama." She refilled the teakettle and swung it over the fire.

Cousin Katy came into the dining room and held out both hands. "I'm glad to see thee, Ruth."

"Everything worked out to come a little early, Katy," Mama said and smiled at Deborah.

Mama was so pretty, even at her age, and looked so different from Deborah. Of all her sisters, only Deborah was tall and dark like Papa.

"Come in; sit down," Cousin Katy said, and then put her hand to her forehead. "I need to ask Grandmother if she remembers what we did with those fabric samples from the store. If I can find them, we can make good use of them." She went into Friend Coffin's office.

Mama held Deborah's arm. "Come sit with me for a moment. Deborah, I felt led to come early and ask if there is anything on thy heart."

Deborah sat with Mama on the bench. The big fireplace that she'd had to fill every time she turned around last winter was empty; all the ashes swept up weeks ago. Now gingham curtains fluttered at the open windows.

Deborah nodded. The Lord knew the secrets of all hearts. And Mama wasn't far behind. She sighed. "Oh Mama, I don't know where to begin."

"I must tell thee that Friend Smith has asked Papa again if he may call on thee."

Deborah froze, and her heart dropped. She shook her head. "Mama, thee knows I don't want to marry someone so many years older than me. I do not wish to be widowed."

Mama nodded. "That does make sense." She picked up the workbasket and started sorting fabric that could be trimmed for quilt pieces. Many times, they sent things with the fugitives.

Deborah picked up her knitting basket, filled as always with walnut-dyed wool for making mittens, scarves, and socks.

Mama sorted the cloth pieces by color—gray, brown, white, black. Calico samples from the Coffins' store would make a pretty addition. "I have also noticed at meeting that Nathaniel often looks for thee."

Deborah nodded. "I look for him, too. I like him very much, but I know so little of him. Thee and Papa knew each other even as children."

"Thy situation is very different. I know this doesn't seem like much of an answer, but I'm afraid thee must be patient. See how the matter ends."

Deborah sighed. Soon she would be twenty-one. So old, so soon. She kept knitting. A step of faith would be to trust the Lord with this situation. If she had no future with Nathaniel, surely the Lord had a better plan for her life. Or perhaps she would never marry, but she believed she could trust God with this situation.

Chapter 12

On the Sabbath, Nathaniel went to the Walls' farm after meeting. Deborah let her father and brothers do all the talking with him. They talked about a neighbor boy who'd gone to a Fourth of July celebration and militia shoot. Papa and another of the worthy Friends had been appointed to call on the boy later that week and reason with him about his misconduct.

Nathaniel brought a satchel with him and after dinner told the boys it was a halter and rope to teach the filly to lead. Deborah enjoyed hearing his deep voice and hearty laugh. The boys wanted to hurry out and work with the horses. Deborah stayed back and helped Mama with the dishes.

"Is thee going to see about the filly?" Mama asked.

Deborah watched Nathaniel, the boys, and the horses out the window. "No—I would like to go for a walk." She sighed. Longing for a talk with Nathaniel had distracted her from everything that happened in meeting. Could anything clear her mind?

She went to the loft and changed into her homespun dress and apron, and then slipped down the ladder again. Outside, the grass in the cabin's shade felt wonderfully cool to her bare feet. While the boys and Nathaniel faced the other way, she slipped past the barn and into the woods.

The paths made by the cows and horses had turned to thick, warm dust that puffed up between her toes. She followed the trail to the edge of the woods and found the last of the raspberries. Couldn't let them go to waste. She plucked a few and admired the deep purple of the juice on her hands. God made such a colorful world.

Hoofbeats thudded softly on the trail behind her. She turned around. Nathaniel. The filly dawdled after him, likely out of curiosity since he'd removed the halter; she didn't see the mare.

"I thought I saw you walk out this way, Deborah. Is something on your mind? You were so quiet at dinner."

She shook her head. "It is a matter of the heart. Painful to discuss."

He nodded. "Can I ask you a question or two?"

"Of course. We should always speak the truth."

He looked down. "One of your nephews said William Smith called on your father." He took a deep breath. "This is none of my concern."

"Speak thy mind, Nathaniel." She held out some raspberries. "Perhaps this will clear thy thinking."

He chuckled as he took them.

The filly came up to them, her nose out, and snuffled at the berries. Her fuzzy tail twitched, and she stamped a tiny hoof. Nathaniel smiled and offered a berry to the creature. She mouthed it then let the pieces drop from her mouth and turned up her nose.

Out in the pasture, the mare whinnied loudly.

The foal answered in her squeaky voice. The mare galloped

past the screen of trees and brush in front of them, and then slid to a stop, neighing frantically. She ran past the end of the woods then turned and thundered down the trail.

She looked wild-eyed and blinded with fright.

Deborah stared at the animal pounding toward them. The horse would not stop for anything until she found the foal.

Nathaniel grabbed Deborah and swung her out of the way. He staggered as his knee gave out, and he lurched into a tree. Deborah caught him before he fell, wrapped her arms around his waist, and then looked past his arm to the mare and foal, whickering to each other. Deborah and Nathaniel held each other up. She imagined the mare scolding the filly for wandering off.

Nathaniel took a deep breath; she felt his ribs heave. "All's well that ends well. Are you all right?"

Her head rested against his chest; his vest felt scratchy against her cheek. "We forget how powerful they are. They seem so meek."

Nathaniel looked into her eyes. He was so warm and solid, looming over her, studying her face. Was he going to kiss her? No one ever had. It would be too much intimacy outside of marriage. Deborah barely breathed, longing for him to kiss her, but knowing it was wrong. She straightened and edged away from him.

Nathaniel let her slip from his grasp. "Like our own hearts sometimes." His face grew solemn, even sorrowful. His voice sounded choked. "Deborah, are you going to marry Friend Smith?"

Deborah shook her head. She turned and watched the mare and foal. "No, Nathaniel. He is so much older than me."

"He has a lot to offer. A big farm and a beautiful home."

She shook her head. "One of my greatest fears is to be widowed. He might have many things, but he can't turn back time. I want—if I ever marry—I want to build a life together."

He nodded again. "If we are speaking the truth, then Deborah Wall. . ." He reached out and took her hand. "I have to confess, I can hardly think of anyone or anything but you. All these weeks seeing you at meeting, the times your family invited me over, how we talked about horses—wondering if we could have a future together."

Her heart leaped, and she gazed into his face. His brows were drawn. He put one hand up and rubbed his eyes. Maybe this was the answer to her prayers for leading. She held his one hand in both of hers and looked down at his big, tanned, work-worn hand. "I've wondered the same thing. But thee has said nothing of it until now."

"I'm trying to build my business and learn to be a better Christian. I felt I had no standing, no right to speak to you."

"Thee shouldn't think so little of thyself. Thee's precious in God's eyes."

Nathaniel took a deep breath. "What about in your eyes? Deborah—" He took another breath. "Deborah, I've been falling in love with you for weeks. I never thought I'd ever feel this way for anyone, like there's a future and hope."

She touched his warm, tanned face then nodded. "I felt the same way." Was this true or a dream? The two of them together could clear new ground, build a cabin, start a farm of their own, and have a family. Tears of joy welled up in her eyes. Someday they might have a farm as beautiful as the Smith place.

He smiled, his eyes widening and his ruddy face giving his eyes a sky blue gleam. He twined his fingers through hers then raised her hand to his lips and kissed the back of it. His lips felt so warm and soft that she longed to be in his arms.

His face clouded. He looked so forlorn. "What of the Society?"

Deborah's heart raced. Surely they could work this out. "Thee only has to condemn thy misconduct."

He dropped his head. "I'm not convinced I'd be joining it for the right reasons. I question some of the Society's teachings."

She gasped. "About what?"

"Plain or lofty speech, plain dress or not, makes no difference to me." He took another deep breath. "I've been out in the world and am not convinced that a man can be completely nonviolent."

Deborah tried to understand him. "If thee trusts the Lord to keep thee—"

He nodded. "I see the logic in that. But I've seen bad things, Deborah. I wish I could trust the Lord that much."

"Perhaps such grace is given day by day, like manna in the wilderness."

"You might be right."

She took a deep breath. Her tears came from despair now. "Thee spoke the truth. I do not feel led to leave the Society."

"And I doubt my reasons for wanting to join." He rested his forehead against hers. "Oh Deborah, my hope and prayer is, someday, I'm going to marry you."

She closed her eyes, and her tears spilled over now. "But thee needs to count the cost. Both of us. I think we should speak no more of this, Nathaniel." Her breath was ragged as she shook her head. "Speak no more of this, I beg of thee."

Chapter 13

Seeing Deborah now was bittersweet for Nathaniel. On summer days when he wasn't busy, he helped some of the neighbors with wheat harvest and putting up hay. As summer faded into fall, corn ripened and dried down. The fields faded from green to gold. Sometimes the slaves fled north at times like this, when they could easily hide in the cornfields and find cover in the woods while the trees still had leaves.

Nathaniel listened intently in meeting, and as was said in the book of Acts, like the Bereans, he searched the scriptures daily to see if these things were so.

With the Lord's help—because he'd learned to lie so fluently while in the world—he always told the truth and began rebuilding his integrity. When Uncle George remarked that Nathaniel's father would have been proud of him, his encouraging words were like a stream in the desert.

The Friends made him feel welcome, and some of the older ones even knew of his parents. But how could he be sure he was joining the Society for the right reasons, not just to win Deborah?

Deborah's life seemed to go on as before. She participated in women's meetings and kept busy helping Katy Coffin and

157

her family. She was beautiful as ever. Her brown dresses along with her big dark eyes reminded him of a deer.

As soon as frosts came, the trees in New Garden blazed red, gold, yellow, and orange against the clear blue sky. When the tenth month arrived, the filly would be six months old. One First Day, after meeting, he conferred with Deborah's family about the horses. "I've finished the barn and fences at my uncle's, Friend Wall, so I can bring the mare home for weaning the filly."

Deborah remembered how frantic the mare had been for the filly earlier in the summer. Perhaps the process would be faster and easier if the two were separated.

Papa nodded. "Tonight might work, when we bring Deborah back to the Coffins'."

"I'll meet you at the shop."

❧

As soon as the sun went down, the air cooled rapidly. Deborah and Papa tried to soothe the mare as they led her out of the barn and hitched her to the back of the farm wagon loaded with wood.

Papa chirped to the team, and they rolled forward.

The filly whinnied for her mother. The mare dug in her heels. The wagon rattled to a stop, and the horses snorted with surprise. "Get up there," Pa called to the team.

Deborah turned on the seat and looked back. The mare's eyes were wild, and lather coated her neck and chest. Her nostrils flared as she snorted. She braced her legs, and the team dragged her a few steps. "Oh Pa, I don't think this is going to work."

"Try once more," Papa said. He urged the team forward.

The mare went a few steps then pulled back as hard as she could. Her halter broke, the tailgate cracked, and part of the load clattered to the ground. Just as the boys came out, she disappeared into the dark barn, whinnying for the filly.

They got down and picked up the spilled firewood. Papa sighed. "Tomorrow I'll hitch up the oxen. We can't take any more time tonight."

In town they stopped at Nathaniel's shop and told him what happened. He went around back and looked at the tailgate. "Did I mention she could be stubborn?" he said with a grin.

Deborah turned toward them, her arm over the back of the seat. He looked handsome even in his work clothes, a blue calico shirt, linsey-woolsey trousers, and tall boots. She liked his appearance better in those clothes than anything. "I have heard animals reflect their owners."

He arched his brows. "Might not be so bad." He gazed into her eyes then gave her a quick smile. "If I have my mind made up, I might be as determined as the mare."

Deborah opened her mouth but closed it again, saying nothing. He might have meant marrying her. She'd told no one, not even Mama, of his offer and her refusal. Perhaps life would be easier if he carried out his original plan and moved farther West, somewhere beyond the Friends' community. Life would be easier if she never saw him again, never saw him marry someone else.

The next day as she worked, Deborah watched for Pa, the oxcart, and the mare.

They could hear the mare before they saw her, neighing loudly for the filly every step of the way. When she tried to dig in her heels, the oxen kept going.

Deborah and Little Catherine watched from the porch.

Little Catherine studied the scene. "She has her saddle and bridle? Is Nathaniel going to ride her back to his uncle's?"

"I suppose he might." Deborah paused for a moment. What if he were hurt?

Pa and Nathaniel both took the mare's rope, fastened to her halter over her bridle. They looped it over the hitch rack and tied her. Nathaniel and Pa conferred.

The mare whinnied so loudly that she shook.

"What if they can still hear each other?" Little Catherine asked.

"Surely not."

"I believe their hearing is better than ours," Little Catherine said as the mare froze with her ears pointed to the east, toward the farm.

"Thee might be right."

Cousin Katy put her hand on Deborah's shoulder. "I know thee would like to go talk to thy papa. Why not go along now? Little Catherine can help me with a few things."

Deborah nodded. "I'll be back in a few minutes." She grabbed her wraps and darted out the door.

Both men seemed glad to see her. She held Papa's hands. "We heard thee coming."

He nodded. "She is very upset. But thee knows now, Nathaniel, she'll work out well as a broodmare for thee."

The blacksmith winced and ran his hand through his tousled hair. "If she survives weaning this one."

Pa put his arm on Deborah's shoulder. "Take care, now. I'm going to the mill to see about our corn. Soon be time to pick it. I hope all goes well for thee and the mare, Nathaniel."

He nodded. "Thank you, Friend Wall."

Deborah watched Pa as he picked up the ox goad and

ordered the team to walk on. They started up the street between the edge of town and the creek, heading to the gristmill.

The mare whinnied again, and Nathaniel stood by her and tried to soothe her. He turned to Deborah.

Deborah gazed up at Nathaniel. Over the summer he'd filled out, shoulders broadened, forearms rippled with muscles. Work had marred his hands though. They were larger and more callused, but still gentle as he took one of hers. She cleared her throat. "Does thee plan to ride her back to thy uncle's house?"

The sound of galloping horses interrupted them, and a posse rounded the corner from the main road. The dogs barked, chasing after the running horses.

"Wagner," Nathaniel said. "You run along. This is no place for a lady."

A crowd of men on lathered horses slid to a stop. The leader jumped off his horse. He reminded Deborah of a snake—lean with hard unblinking eyes. "Fox, you need to reshoe this horse quick as you can. We're in hot pursuit."

"Of what?"

"A quadroon woman worth a thousand dollars to her owner. She's a trained singer." He swung round and pointed at Deborah. "You seen anyone like that?"

Nathaniel took a half step between Deborah and Wagner.

Deborah smiled wryly at the slave hunter. "Not at my father's farm. I can't recall the last time an opera singer lodged with us."

"Never mind. Fox, put this shoe back on this horse."

"I need a dollar first."

"What? Pay you first!"

"Yep. I'm thinking of other bills left unpaid."

"All right, all right. In a hurry after all."

He nodded.

Deborah backed away. She walked up to the crossroads, thinking to go around the corner and be hidden by the buildings. There might be someone at the Coffin place who needed a hand.

Loud voices came from behind her. She looked over her shoulder.

Nathaniel set down the lame horse's foot then held up a twisted shoe. He shook his head and pointed to the horse; the horse rested the one bare foot on its toe. Even that was too much weight. It lifted its injured foot and held it in the air, trembling.

Wagner waved his hands and pointed.

Nathaniel folded his arms across his chest and shook his head.

The other men laughed and jumped back on their horses. Apparently they intended to capture the slave woman and, if they found her, cut Wagner out of the deal.

Wagner swung a punch at Nathaniel.

Deborah gasped. Would he fight back? Use violence?

He grappled with Wagner but didn't hit back. Instead he held the slave hunter at arm's length.

They thrashed through the blacksmith shop. Tools, supplies, and firewood went everywhere. Wagner flailed like a windmill but was an inch or two away from reaching Nathaniel, who kept grinning.

Men ran to the shop, including Papa, Levi Coffin, and the town constable.

Wagner grabbed a hammer off the anvil and swung it at Nathaniel's head. The blacksmith staggered and went to his knees.

Wagner untied Nathaniel's mare and jumped on her. As soon as she was free, Brandy put her head down and bolted for the farm. A cloud of dust hid them a moment later.

Deborah hitched up her skirts and raced down the hill to the blacksmith shop. She found Nathaniel sitting up, his back against one of the porch posts, his arm held over his head. With his other hand, he mashed his shirtsleeve into a cut above his eye. Despite that, blood ran down his face.

"Deborah," he said in tired voice. His eyes rolled back in his head, and he slumped over. She rushed to him. She pulled off her apron, rolled it up, and put it under his head. Perhaps he had only fainted.

He shivered. "The mare!" He tried to sit up but winced.

The constable strode after the runaway horse but turned to Levi Coffin and Deborah's father. "Men, encourage those ruffians to leave town as soon as possible. That last one though, I am taking to jail." He muttered under his breath, and his long white mustache twitched. "Can't come to my town and hit good citizens over the head and steal horses in broad daylight. That arrogant buffoon. Nathaniel Fox, are you alive or dead?"

Nathaniel groaned. "I'll be all right."

"Peace, be still," Deborah said, gripping his shoulder.

He put his bloodstained hand over hers. "I didn't hit him."

"I saw that, Nathaniel."

"Thee saw—"

"Yes. Thee did the best thee could."

"Hard not to hit him."

"I'm sure it was. Thee was sorely provoked."

"Supposed to turn the other cheek. I reckon holding him off was about the same."

The doctor arrived on his pacing horse and jumped off,

quite spry for a man his age. "Well. We meet again, neighbor. May I see him, Deborah Wall?"

She moved out of the way, but Nathaniel kept her hand.

"Scalp and facial injuries do bleed considerably," the doctor announced. "Nathaniel, did thee faint for any length of time?"

"I'm not sure."

"Did thee see, Deborah Wall?"

"Yes, he did faint."

"We will treat him as though he has a concussion. Someone needs to be with him for the next several hours, so he doesn't go to sleep and fail to wake up." The doctor looked toward the road. "Now, who's coming?"

"Some men went after that Wagner and Nathaniel's horse," Deborah said.

The doctor stood up, folded his arms, and watched horses and riders approach. "Well this doesn't look good."

Chapter 14

Nathaniel's head pounded with his heartbeat, but his double vision slowly returned to normal. He sat in the parlor with Levi Coffin. A cool autumn breeze stirred the curtains at the open windows and doors.

"I haven't had a chance to converse with thee as I would've liked, neighbor," the older man said and smiled at Nathaniel.

"We've all been quite occupied."

"The Lord works all things together for good," Friend Coffin said. "Even giving me an opportunity of operating in my gift of talkativeness."

From their chairs and benches on the other side of the room, the Coffin girls giggled.

Deborah came in with tea. Over the summer, even though she surely wore a bonnet, more freckles had appeared. They only added to her appeal. Now that he'd met all of her family over the past few months, he could see she got her height and long arms from her father but had a pretty face like her mother. Friend Coffin was saying something. Nathaniel shook his head. "I'm afraid I wasn't paying attention."

The older man chuckled then grew more solemn. "How well was thee acquainted with Octavian Wagner?"

Nathaniel sighed. "Only slightly. But to think he came to such a sudden end. . ." The mare had thrown Wagner as she bolted for the farm in search of her filly. Wagner died shortly afterward.

"Perhaps he remembered something of the Gospels at the end," Little Catherine said.

Nathaniel shook his head. "If he'd ever heard them."

The little girls grew solemn. "Could anyone have never heard?"

"I fear so," Nathaniel said. "I hope I never leave something so important unsaid again." He was silent for a long grim moment. But today's incident had cleared up something else for him. He did try to live by the Society's teaching on his own, not just when Deborah might be watching or listening. "Almost everyone in the township needs horses shod, or hinges or plow points or trammel hooks for the fireplace. In my situation I should have many opportunities to speak of our hope."

Deborah poured tea, and when she looked at him, her big eyes were solemn. But something else glimmered there. Was she proud of him?

Eventually Katy Coffin and the girls went to bed.

"Thee knows he must not sleep," Levi Coffin told Deborah. His eyes twinkled. "Perhaps thee might be troubled to talk with him until someone else can sit up with him."

She sat in the rocking bench on the other side of the parlor and picked up her knitting. "How is thee feeling, Nathaniel?"

"Tired. Head hurts. Nothing new though."

Her knitting needles clicked rapidly as mittens took shape. "I have something I need to say to thee."

Plain speech slipped out. He must be dazed still. "Please, speak thy mind. I know thee needs little encouragement."

"The Lord has made a wonderful change in thee." Her knitting needles slowed. "I have wanted to tell thee that for some time but had no opportunity."

"There's room at the other end of the bench. May I join thee?"

"Yes. Is thee using plain speech only to keep my attention?"

Nathaniel shuffled across the room. One of the Gospels talked about the Spirit giving believers words they needed. Was this situation included? "No, Deborah Wall." The bench creaked dangerously under his weight. He put his arm over the back and turned toward her. "This is how I talk. How I was raised."

He reached over and put his hand on her hands. They felt so soft compared to his. "This is how I want to live my life."

The knitting needles stilled. Deborah took a deep breath.

Here was where he needed the Lord's help. "I wonder if thee will undertake such a journey with me, Deborah Wall?" He raised her slender hand and kissed the back of it.

"I would be pleased to do so, Nathaniel," she whispered, her voice shaky.

Chapter 15

Deborah tried to remember the first time she'd seen Nathaniel as he took her hands in front of everyone at Ma and Pa's cabin. Today was fifth month, fourteenth day, 1841. Their wedding day.

His eyes were the same shade of blue, same brown lashes and brows, but today his wide grin and easy laugh made him seem like a different man. He was no longer angry and proud or pale and sick. Now he was healthy and strong, sober and honest. Deborah and her family were convinced that he would be a good husband.

All around were family and neighbors. Levi and Katy Coffin came as witnesses. They joined her parents, brothers and sisters and their families, the Coffin girls, Nathaniel's aunt and uncle, and many of Nathaniel's horse-shoeing customers in back. Some of the worldly ones stood respectfully in the very back but fidgeted and raised their heads to see to the ceremony. When they sensed it had started, the worldly men removed their hats; the Friends left theirs on.

The Friends looked sober in gray, brown, and black, but their eyes twinkled. Mama had made Deborah a new brown dress, white cape, apron, cap, and bonnet for this sunny spring day. The weather was clear and mild, an answer to many prayers.

Nathaniel repeated the words of the promises as she looked up at him. He never looked more handsome, wearing a wide-brimmed black hat, white shirt, and gray suit. His jacket had no lapels, and his waistcoat buttoned almost to his throat with plain dark buttons—so different from his brave, bright-colored apparel earlier.

"I, Nathaniel Fox, take thee, Deborah Wall, to be my wife. I promise with the Lord's help to be a loving and faithful husband until death should separate us."

She knew he meant every word. Deborah's hands trembled, and her voice shook as she repeated the same promises to him.

The ministers had the certificate ready for them to sign. Nathaniel's handwriting was neat and steady. She hardly could hold the pen as she signed her new name, Deborah Fox.

The Friends lined up to sign the declaration as witnesses.

Nathaniel pulled Deborah aside. "Tell me this is not a dream, Deborah Wall."

"Fox. Deborah Fox," she reminded him. She was still explaining when he gave her their first married kiss, wrapping his muscular arms around her, and pressing her to his warm, solid chest. His lips were soft against hers, and for a long moment, she felt like she was melting.

She stood on tiptoes and put her hand at the back of his neck. She rested her other hand on his cheek, smooth shaven and warm, then gave him a kiss in return.

ANN E. SCHROCK covered breaking news and features for local daily newspapers for ten years after graduating from Purdue University with a bachelor's degree in agricultural communication. She also has contributed devotionals for *Evangel*, a weekly paper published by the Free Methodist Church of North America. A native of Wayne County, Indiana, Ann and her husband are raising their three children on the family farm in northern Indiana.

NEW GARDEN'S INSPIRATION

by Claire Sanders

Dedication

For Tiiann, who inspires me every day.

Chapter 1

Leah Wall sat in the minister's study and gazed at the wildflowers in her hands. Young John had gathered a few yarrow and daisies, but queen anne's lace dominated the group. How had her cousin known that particular flower held a special place in Leah's heart?

"That flower is like thee," her mother had said. "Look how it stands straight on its slender body, its face pointing to the sun, praising God for giving it so much strength and purpose."

Leah ran her finger over the fragile bloom, wishing her mother had lived long enough to see her wedding day. Many farmers considered queen anne's lace a weed, and since coming to live with her aunt and uncle, Leah had felt more like a weed than a flower.

Aunt Cynthia hurried into the small room. "Is thee ready? The groom has arrived and is talking to the minister and your uncle Abram. It won't be long now."

"I'm ready," Leah answered, knowing her response was less than truthful. She was happy to be getting married, truly she was, but how she wished she could've met her future husband before today.

Uncle Abram tapped on the doorframe. "Caleb would like

to speak to thee before we begin, Leah. Is thee willing?"

Leah swallowed the lump in her throat. What would Caleb think of her? Aunt Cynthia had helped her make a new dress of pale green cotton, fashioned in the Quaker's plain style. Leah touched the brim of her white linen prayer cap. Would he think it old-fashioned of her to cover her head? So many women had given up the practice.

Uncle Abram's bushy beard twitched impatiently. "Well Leah? Shall I send him in?"

Leah took a deep breath and let it out. "Of course," she answered, wincing at the tremble in her voice.

Aunt Cynthia placed a reassuring hand on Leah's shoulder.

Uncle Abram's eyebrows drew together. "Alone, Cynthia," he clarified. "I'm sure Leah will be fine with the man she intends to marry."

"Oh," Aunt Cynthia said as her cheeks tinged pink. She turned to Leah. "I'll be right outside if thee should need me."

Her uncle closed the door, leaving Leah in anxious silence. Surely it was a good thing Caleb wanted to speak to her before the ceremony. He wouldn't have let things go this far if he planned to call it off. Of course he'd been gone for the past two weeks, settling his affairs before reporting for duty. Maybe he simply hadn't had the opportunity to tell her he'd changed his mind.

A soft knock on the door recalled Leah's wandering attention. "Come in."

The door swung open and Leah gasped. Before her stood the most beautiful man she'd ever seen. Dressed in the Union's blue uniform, Caleb was tall and well built, with a straight nose and full lips. Black brows framed piercing blue eyes. His dark hair curled around his ears and fringed the stiff white collar of his shirt. He removed his hat and stood stiffly in the doorway. "Miss Wall," he said, then swallowed and began again. "Miss Wall, I'm Caleb Whitaker."

He waited for Leah to acknowledge him, but she was dumbstruck by the man's heart-stopping presence.

Caleb cleared his throat and slid his hat's brim through his fingers. "I'd like to make sure you know what you're getting yourself into before we seal this bargain."

Bargain? Didn't he know what a great favor he was doing her?

"I have two children—a girl, twelve, and a boy of four. My wife died shortly after giving birth to Stephen, so he's never known a mother. Olivia, that's my daughter—well, Olivia is dead set against needing a new mother, so you'll probably have your hands full with her."

Leah's gaze transfixed on Caleb's hands as he continued to rotate the hat. They were so big, a farmer's hands, accustomed to hard work, and yet they gently caressed the brim.

"My aunt Rose has been helping me with the children for the last few years, but she's getting up in age and unable to take the children full time. I have eighty-three acres of good farmland. There are fruit trees—pear, cherry, and apple, of course, as well as butternut. I am to report to Evansville, but I don't expect to be gone long. I can't imagine the South lasting more than a few months, so I'll be back soon."

Caleb's gaze drifted to the small window beside the door. "In return for you doing me this honor, I promise to be responsible for your well-being for the rest of your life."

Leah tore her gaze away from Caleb's hands and looked at his profile. In her twenty-four years, she'd learned there were many kinds of men—those who couldn't be trusted, those who treated livestock better than their own wives, and those who broke their word as easily as spring ice. What kind of man was Caleb Whitaker?

"He's a good man," Uncle Abram had assured her. "It's true he's not a Friend, but he's worked with us in helping many runaway slaves on their way to freedom. Besides Leah, thee isn't likely to get another offer."

Caleb looked at her, waiting for her response. Did he really think she'd decline his proposal? He was offering her a chance to get away from Uncle Abram's constant disapproval. She'd prepared for life as a spinster, had looked into the future and seen nothing but a barren womb. Like Jephthah's daughter, she'd bewailed her virginity and resigned to life as an unwanted poor relation. But everything had changed in a scant two weeks.

She was to be married.

She was to be a mother and a wife.

Someone did want her.

Caleb's sheathed sword clattered as he shifted his weight and looked at her. "Is this arrangement agreeable to you, Miss Wall?"

Leah struggled to answer, but her mouth was as dry as an August afternoon. "I—I..."

Caleb's dark brows drew together.

She reached for the water pitcher on the minister's desk. Caleb sprang into action, pouring the water into the glass and handing it to her.

She took the glass with a shaky hand. Realizing she'd soon be drenched, she tried to steady the glass. But once free of her tight grip, her bouquet rolled off her lap and onto the canvas rug. Caleb dropped to one knee and retrieved it.

How like a suitor he looked, kneeling at her side, offering

her flowers. She almost reached out to stroke his clean-shaven cheek.

Leah smiled in spite of her trembling insides. "I thank thee," she said, taking the bouquet. "I will do all I can to be a good wife and mother."

Caleb stood. "Thank you, Miss Wall. Shall I tell the minister we're ready to begin?"

Leah nodded her assent, and Caleb stepped out of the small room. She let out the breath she'd been holding.

Uncle Abram reappeared in the doorway. "Let's go, girl. Your aunt has a wedding feast planned, and I'm hungry."

Leah rose on shaky legs, took another deep breath, and followed her uncle into the small sanctuary. Dark wooden pews lined a central aisle, and arched windows let in the afternoon sun. Caleb stood next to a portly, balding man dressed in a black frock coat, white shirt, and black bowtie. "Good morning, Miss Wall," the man said. "I'm Reverend Harrison, and I'll be conducting the service today."

In the Quaker tradition, a couple who desired to marry stood before the gathered Friends and spoke their vows to each other. Leah should have known the Methodists would be different. "Good morning," she replied.

"Is everyone ready to begin?" Reverend Harrison asked.

Uncle Abram clasped Leah by her upper arms and guided her to stand in front of the minister. "She's ready," he said for her. Caleb stood on her right side.

"Dearly beloved," the minister began.

Leah glanced at her aunt. Cynthia's hands covered her face, but Leah could see her aunt's excitement shining from her brown eyes. When Uncle Abram had told Leah about his arrangement with Caleb, Aunt Cynthia had nearly erupted with excitement. "It's too bad thee didn't bring thy wedding chest with thee," Aunt Cynthia clucked, "but we'll get some linens together quick as a wink."

Leah hadn't told her aunt she'd never begun a wedding chest. When other girls her age had begun making linens and collecting dishes, Leah's mother had directed her down another path. "It's better for thee to learn a trade than to fill a chest with dreams. I'll teach thee how to keep the bees, and thee will never want for a taste of sweetness."

"Therefore," the minister continued, "if any can show just cause why they may not lawfully be joined together, let him speak now. . . ."

No one would dare object to Leah's union with Caleb. Least not Uncle Abram. Ever since she'd shown up at the railroad station with one trunk, her box of medicinals, and two empty bee skeps, he'd let her know she was a charity case. Orphaned at seventeen, she'd had nowhere to go except to her father's brother. But every ounce of her uncle's resentment was matched by a pound of her aunt's gratitude. With four sons, Aunt Cynthia had welcomed another woman's set of hands.

The minister turned to face Caleb. "Caleb Whitaker, wilt thou have this woman to be thy wedded wife, to live together after God's ordinance, in the holy estate of matrimony? Wilt thou love her, comfort her, honor and keep her, in sickness and in health, and forsaking all others, keep thee only unto her, so long as ye both shall live?"

What sweet words. What a blessing it would be to have a man to love her, comfort her, honor and keep her. If only the women of her home village could see her now, marrying a handsome officer and taking her place among the wives of this community. Her mother's acquaintances had publicized their opinions well—plain Leah, tall as a willow and thin as its branch. Such a pretty complexion wasted on such a homely face. How she'd like to see those ladies now.

The minister cleared his throat, jerking Leah's attention from the painful memory. Reverend Harrison smiled at her and raised his eyebrows. Leah smiled back.

"Will you?" he asked.

"Will I what?"

Aunt Cynthia laughed. "Say 'I will,' Leah."

Leah looked over her shoulder at her aunt.

"Say 'I will,'" Aunt Cynthia repeated.

Her uncle sighed heavily, his very breath communicating his dwindling patience. "The man's asking if thee will take Caleb to be thy husband, Leah. Say 'I will.'"

"Oh." Leah glanced at Caleb. His left hand was on his sword, his back as straight as the ladder-back chairs of the Friends' meetinghouse, and his gaze fixed on the minister. "I will," she said finally.

Reverend Harrison nodded his approval. "Is there a ring?"

Caleb removed a small ring from his coat pocket, showed it to the minister, and reached for Leah's hand.

Leah shivered at his touch, but Caleb seemed unmoved as he slipped the gold band around her finger. The minister spoke on, but Leah's attention was riveted on the ring. It was true. She was a married woman.

Aunt Cynthia embraced her while Uncle Abram shook Caleb's hand. "Welcome to the family," he said. "My wife's prepared a fine meal for all of us. Come out to the house, and we'll celebrate. Would thee like to come, Reverend?"

"Can't make it today," Reverend Harrison answered. "I've got a funeral in a few hours. But my best to the new couple."

Aunt Cynthia took Leah's arm and pushed her toward the door. "Wasn't that just lovely? Weddings are such happy times. The boys were supposed to take thy trunk and medicinal box to Caleb's farm. Is thee excited to see thy new home?"

Leah looked back at her new husband. Caleb stood, his hands behind his back, listening to her uncle and the minister. But his eyes watched her.

Leah froze at the threshold, one foot inside the church, the other outside. Caleb's steady gaze called to her, drawing her back to his side. Wasn't that where she belonged now?

"What is it?" Aunt Cynthia asked. "Did thee forget something?"

"Is Caleb coming with us?"

"Of course he is." Aunt Cynthia laughed softly.

But Leah could neither force her feet to move nor tear her gaze away from Caleb. Every part of her being longed to return to his side, to slip her hand into his and make her allegiance clear.

As if sensing Leah's indecision, Aunt Cynthia called to her husband. "Abram, we'd best get going before the boys help themselves to Leah's wedding cake."

"On our way," Uncle Abram called back.

Leah's gaze never wavered as Caleb approached. Aunt Cynthia and Uncle Abram stepped outside, leaving the newlyweds alone in the church.

Caleb smiled at his new wife. "It's kind of your aunt to prepare a meal for us."

Leah returned his smile. "She's been preparing since Uncle Abram told us the news."

Caleb offered his arm to her. "Shall we go?"

Leah linked her arm with his and allowed him to lead her outside. This was the way it should be, walking by her husband's side for the rest of her life.

Chapter 2

L eah moved into the kitchen to help her aunt with the meal.

"No, no." Aunt Cynthia shooed her away with a dishcloth. "The bride never prepares her own wedding feast. Thee and thy husband are guests of honor today."

Thee and thy husband. Leah would never tire of hearing that.

Uncle Abram's voice sounded from just outside the open door. "Matthew! Where are thy brothers?"

"Putting the horse to pasture," Matthew called back to his father. "Mark took Leah's things to Caleb's place and let the little ones tag along. Hello, Caleb. Congratulations on thy marriage."

"Thank you," Caleb answered.

"Come in the house," Uncle Abram said, "and make thyself comfortable. The other boys will be here soon."

Leah stood in the middle of the kitchen and watched the threshold, eager to see Caleb's boot step into the house. If he came inside her uncle's house, it would somehow signal his acceptance of Quaker ways.

Young John's voice called, "Is Leah here? Did she get married? Is she back yet?"

"Slow down," Uncle Abram called to his youngest son, "before thee runs out of air and collapses like a paper lantern."

The sound of men's laughter floated through the open doorway, but still there was no black boot.

Seven-year-old John ran into the kitchen, his flushed face shining as he threw his arms around Leah's waist, turning her so quickly she almost lost her balance. "Leah! Guess what! Me and Luke carried thy trunk all by ourselves. Mr. Whitaker's house is awful big. Bigger even than ours. And Stephen's going to have a new colt."

Leah brushed the blond hair from her young cousin's forehead. John was like the wind before a spring storm, refreshing yet overwhelming. "When thee comes to visit, the colt will be there."

"Call thy brothers," Aunt Cynthia commanded him, "and tell them to wash up. It's time to eat."

John tore his arms from Leah and dashed toward the door. "Matthew! Mark! Luke! Time to eat!"

Leah chuckled at the young boy's antics, yelling his brothers' names before ever leaving the house, but when she turned back toward the door, she saw Caleb standing rigidly inside the kitchen. As soon as she'd stopped watching for him, he'd come in.

Aunt Cynthia brushed past her with a platter of meat. "Sit thee down, Caleb. Anywhere is fine. Everything's ready."

Caleb hung his hat on a peg near the door, unbuckled his sword belt, and hung it next to his hat. He drew back a chair and waited for Leah to be seated.

She smiled and moved toward him. "Thank thee," she said as she eased into the chair. Perhaps some women were accustomed to such a gentlemanly courtesy, but it was a first for Leah. Would the rest of her life be filled with such civility and consideration?

Loud voices and the stomping of boots announced the arrival of her cousins. Matthew, the eldest, was first through the door. "Congratulations, Leah," he said with a dimpled grin. "We're going to miss thee around here. Especially Mother."

Before Leah could reply, the second son, Mark, came in. "Does this mean I'll have to ride all the way to Caleb's farm if I want honey cookies?"

"There will always be honey for thee and thy family," Leah assured him.

Uncle Abram took his seat at the head of the table. "Did thee know Leah keeps bees, Caleb?"

"No I didn't."

Matthew took the seat across from Caleb and shook his dark hair out of his face. "She's got two skeps full of honeycombs and some supers beneath them. She just sold twenty jars of honey to the general store in Newport."

"Skeps?" Caleb asked.

Matthew poured milk into his younger brothers' cups. "A skep is like an upside-down bushel basket. The bees build their hives in it."

"And a super?" Caleb asked. "What's that?"

"Extra baskets," Mark continued, indicating the structure with his hands, "that sit underneath the skep. The bees store their extra honey in them. That way, Leah doesn't have to destroy the original hives when she harvests the honey."

"Sounds as though you know a lot about bees," Caleb remarked.

"Not me." Mark said. "Leah taught me everything I know. Before she came I chased away bees, but now I respect the little creatures. They work harder than my brothers and me at harvest time. Plus Leah knows all about doctoring. She's cured more than one stomachache around here with her box of medicinals."

Caleb looked at Leah. "Will you move the bees to my farm or keep them here?"

He was so close to her, she could see the small dark whiskers the razor had missed. "When I find a good spot for them on thy farm, I will move them. Does thee object?"

"Of course not. Your bees and their honey will be a good addition. Where did you learn about medicine?"

"From my mother. She knew how to mix medicinal plants with the honey and wax to treat aches and pains."

"Where's Luke?" Aunt Cynthia asked. "Has anybody seen him?"

"Want me to go look for him?" Young John asked in his high-pitched voice.

"I do not," Aunt Cynthia answered. "I want thee to stay right where thee is." She shot a glance at Caleb. "It's a wonderful thing to have four sons, but getting them all in the same place at the same time is not an easy task. Matthew, will thee—"

Before she could finish her request, Luke came into the room. Leah's heart went out to the painfully shy boy as he shuffled to his seat, his face averted from Caleb's gaze.

"Finally," Aunt Cynthia said as she took her seat opposite her husband.

Uncle Abram bowed his head. "Let us say grace."

The family sat in silence, each one giving quiet thanks. Leah adored the many moments of quiet prayer Quakers enjoyed, and after her hectic morning, she was relieved to close her eyes and reconnect her soul with God. She thanked the Lord for Aunt Cynthia, who'd welcomed her with open arms. She asked for blessings on her cousins, all healthy young men who grew stronger with each season. She thanked God for the man who sat at her side. Caleb would take her away from this house and into his own, and there they would build a life. She even gave thanks for Uncle Abram and asked the Lord again to give her a more understanding heart when it came to her uncle's harsh words.

Leah raised her head and met Uncle Abram's gaze. It was his custom to watch his family, and when the last head lifted, end the prayer. Leah looked around the table. Everyone's head had lifted except Caleb's.

They sat in respectful silence, waiting for Caleb to finish his prayer, but when the seconds stretched into minutes, and when Mark's stomach complained loudly about its emptiness, Young John dissolved into giggles.

Caleb lifted his eyes and glanced around at the others. "Aren't you going to say grace?"

"We did say it," Matthew teased. "Thee is the only one who feels the need to have such a long conversation with the Lord."

Caleb's furrowed eyebrows made it clear he was puzzled. "What?"

Aunt Cynthia chided her firstborn. "Hush, Matthew. Perhaps Caleb doesn't know our tradition of silent grace."

Leah felt obliged to stick up for her husband. "It's perfectly all right." She sent a menacing glare toward Matthew.

Aunt Cynthia passed a platter of roasted chicken. "Perhaps we should let Mark get the first bite. I don't want to hear anything else his stomach has to say."

❧

Aunt Cynthia drew Leah into a tight embrace. "Thee will be a blessing to Caleb and his children, the same as thee has been to us."

Uncle Abram cleared his throat, a sound that signaled it was time for Leah and Caleb to leave. "If thee doesn't get moving, it will be dark by the time thee get to Caleb's farm. Matthew will drive thee."

Caleb offered his hand to help Leah into the buggy. She moved to the seat's far side, expecting Caleb to join her as he had on the trip from the church to her uncle's farm, but he swung onto his horse instead.

It was natural, Leah thought. Of course he'd be more comfortable on his horse. He'd tethered the animal to the buggy after the ceremony at the church, but now he probably felt the desire to be mounted rather than squeeze his long legs into the cramped buggy.

Matthew flicked the reins, and the buggy pulled away from the place she'd called home for the last seven years. She turned to give a last wave, but her eyes filled with tears at the sight of her dear aunt crying into her apron.

Leah's heart yearned to jump from the buggy and run to her aunt, but one thought stilled her: Perhaps Aunt Cynthia's tears were tears of joy. She'd been excited about Leah's marriage, extolling Caleb's virtues, and already planning for a spring baby.

A baby. Leah's body grew warm at the thought. Tonight she'd finally discover the secret that bonded a man to a woman. Tonight would be the first of many nights she'd share a bed with her husband.

She watched Caleb as his horse cantered beside the buggy. How wonderful he looked atop his chestnut stallion. With his dark features and straight back, he reminded her of a knight, bent on accomplishing some noble deed. He held the reins loosely, confident in his equestrian skills, and kept his gaze fixed to the roadway.

How blessed she was to be married to Caleb. Uncle Abram had done her few favors since he'd grudgingly taken her in, but she'd find it easy to forget her uncle's callous remarks, now that he'd arranged a union with such a beautiful man.

Matthew turned the buggy onto a drive that bordered a small stream. How odd Leah had never come this way before. Since she'd come to live with her aunt and uncle, she'd only gone to First Day meetings and the general store.

"Here's they new home, Leah," Matthew called over his shoulder.

Leah leaned forward to get her first look at Caleb's house. Her hand flew to her open mouth as the building came into view. Two stories tall and painted a pristine white, the house sat among a cluster of towering oaks. It was double the size of other farmhouses and had one feature she'd never seen before—a wall full of windows. Glass was so expensive, no one built a house with more windows than were absolutely necessary. Caleb Whitaker certainly wasn't a poor farmer, struggling to feed his family. Only a well-to-do family could afford such a luxury.

The buggy crossed a wooden bridge over the stream and pulled to a stop in front of a wide porch. Caleb dismounted and walked to the buggy. "Welcome home, Leah. I hope you'll find everything to your liking."

Leah looked into her husband's kind eyes and smiled. "Thee has a beautiful home. How many families live here?"

"Just my two children and Aunt Rose."

Leah turned to take in the scene again. What miracle had made her the mistress of such a lovely home? Had one brief ceremony changed her from poor relation to gentry?

A dark-skinned man, dressed in work pants and a shirt, walked up to Caleb's horse. "Afternoon, ma'am," he said, tugging at the brim of his hat.

"Oh Joseph," Caleb said. "Allow me to introduce Leah Wall. She'll be staying here and helping with the children while I'm gone."

Leah cut her gaze to Caleb. That was a strange way to introduce her. It made her sound more like a servant than a wife.

"Leah, this is Joseph. He's been working here for almost ten years and will continue to run the farm while I'm away."

Leah made her way out of the buggy. "It's nice to meet thee," she said, offering her hand to Joseph.

Joseph removed his hat and took Leah's hand. "Thank you, ma'am. Anything you need, anything at all, you just let me know."

Leah returned the man's warm smile, wondering if Joseph was one of the many runaway slaves that had passed through Wayne County on their way to freedom. If Caleb was an abolitionist, it would sit well with the Friends who disapproved of her marrying outside the group.

"Where is everyone?" Caleb asked.

"Little Stephen's in the barn worrying about the mare. I imagine Olivia's inside with Miss Rose."

Caleb handed the reins of his horse to Joseph and motioned toward the barn. "Shall we check on my son?" he asked Leah.

Leah looked up at her cousin. "Thank thee for driving me, Matthew."

"Will I see thee at First Day meeting?"

"Of course."

Matthew waved farewell then drove the buggy down the drive. Leah fell into step beside Caleb. Ever since Uncle Abram had spoken to her about the Whitakers, she'd been anxious to meet Caleb's children.

The white barn stood out against the tall blue Indiana sky. The earthy smells of fresh hay and animals met Leah as she and Caleb stepped into the barn, and the chirps of swallows echoed in the rafters.

"Some say swallows bring the farmer good luck," she said, gesturing toward the roof.

"I've never understood why some farmers chase them out of their barns. The mess they make is a small price to pay for the hundreds of insects they eat."

"Papa!" A dark-haired boy straddling a stall gate jumped off and ran toward Caleb. "I think Snowdrop is ready to foal. She's been acting peculiar. Joseph says it's almost time."

Caleb placed a hand on the boy's back and squatted to his eye level. "Could be. Joseph knows more about horses than any man I know. Let's have a look at her."

Stephen ran back to the stall. The dappled gray mare lay in the hay, nickering softly. Caleb unlatched the gate and went to the horse's side. "Easy girl," he said. "Everything's going to be just fine." He placed his hands on the horse's side, pressing every few inches. "I believe Joseph's right, son. We'll have a foal by morning. But there's no need for you to be out here bothering the mother. Snowdrop needs some peace and quiet."

Stephen's shoulders slumped in obvious disappointment. "I don't want to miss it, Papa. Joseph says he's going to sleep out here tonight. May I stay with him?"

"Let me talk to Joseph," Caleb answered, "and I'll let you know before bedtime."

Stephen's glum expression changed to curiosity when he noticed Leah. "Who's that, Papa?"

"This is the lady I told you about, son. Leah's going to be your new mother."

Stephen's eyes, the same blue as his father's, widened. "It's today? Today's the day my new momma comes?"

"It's today."

Stephen left his father's side and approached Leah. "Hello."

Leah smiled. "Hello. Snowdrop is a beautiful mare. Is this her first baby?"

"It sure is." Stephen ran back to the stall. "See that white spot on her head? Olivia said it looked like the flowers that grow by the stream, so we call her Snowdrop. Do you have a horse?"

"No, but if I did, it could never be as beautiful as Snowdrop. What will thee call her foal?"

"I've been thinking about that. I like the name Star, but Olivia says we have to wait to see the foal before we name it. Have you ever seen a horse being born?"

"I certainly have. Horses make great mothers."

Caleb put a hand on his son's shoulder. "Where is your sister, Stephen?"

"In the house with Aunt Rose. She made a cherry pie. I begged her for a slice, but she said she put frog guts in it." Stephen turned to Leah. "Don't worry. She just said that so I wouldn't sneak a piece."

Leah hid her smile behind her fingers. What an adorable child. So full of life and love and already wise to the scheming of big sisters.

"I'm sure Olivia will share the pie now that we're home," Caleb assured him. He winked conspiratorially at Leah and walked toward the house.

She'd already made an ally, Leah thought as she walked beside Caleb. Stephen had accepted her easily. But earlier that morning Caleb had warned her about Olivia. The girl had been eight years old when her mother died, old enough to remember her mother's loving touch and old enough to feel the dreadful pain of loss.

Stephen ran through an open doorway at the side of the house. "Olivia! Papa's home, and he brought our new mother! Where are you, Olivia?"

Leah followed the boy through the doorway and stepped into a spacious kitchen. A large wood-burning iron stove took up most of one wall, and cupboards lined another. Pink-tinted light from the setting sun streamed through the large windows.

"Papa," Stephen said, "don't forget about the pie."

"I won't forget. Run upstairs and clean up."

"And then we'll have pie?"

"Do what I said. Then we'll talk about pie."

"If I'm going to spend the night in the barn, why should I clean up?"

"No clean hands, no pie."

Stephen grinned at his father and ran upstairs.

"Caleb, is that you?" A lady's voice called from another room.

"Yes, Aunt Rose."

"Come into the parlor."

Caleb turned to Leah. "My aunt is most anxious to meet you."

She nodded to Caleb and followed him into the parlor. A gray-haired woman, dressed in a dark blue skirt and white lacy blouse, sat on an upholstered settee. A wooden cane was propped against the edge of a nearby table.

"Good evening." The woman smiled warmly. "I am Rose Martin, Caleb's aunt. Won't you have a seat?"

"Thank thee," Leah answered as she moved to a matching chair near the fireplace.

Caleb stood near Rose, his hands behind his back. "How are you feeling today, Rose?"

"Fine, Caleb, just fine. Stop worrying." Rose turned her gaze on Leah. "Rheumatism. It gets worse with each birthday, but I still get around." She gestured to the cane. "Are you hungry? We've had our dinner, but I can prepare a plate for you."

"Please don't go to the trouble," Leah answered. "Caleb and I ate at my aunt and uncle's house."

"How nice," Rose replied. "Have you met the children?"

"I met Stephen," Leah answered.

Rose's smile widened. "I'm heartened to learn you met our whirlwind of a boy and lived to tell the tale. The only time that boy is quiet is when he's sleeping. Caleb, Olivia's in her room. Will you call her?"

"Of course," Caleb answered, but before he'd taken two steps a young girl appeared in the doorway.

There was no rough-and-tumble play dress for this girl. Olivia sported a blue hooped skirt with red piping, a matching jacket, and a white blouse with a lacy collar. The girl's glossy black shoes reflected the white lace around the hem of her drawers.

"Good evening, Papa," Olivia said and curtsied.

The girl looked like a fine porcelain doll, her clothing fancier than anything Leah had ever owned. Was this normal dress for the Whitaker household? Leah looked at Rose, but when she caught the older woman's gaze, Rose covered her lips with a handkerchief and looked out the window.

Caleb stepped back, a frown on his face. "Why, Olivia. What's this all about? Your Sunday best on a Friday?"

"I simply wanted to look nice. Isn't that all right?"

Caleb tilted his head. "I suppose so."

Olivia moved closer to Leah's chair, her hooped skirt swaying back and forth like the bell it was designed to imitate. "How do you do?"

"I am pleased to meet thee," Leah answered in the same formal tone Olivia had used. "Thee looks lovely."

"Thank you." Olivia touched the long curls of her auburn hair. "Why do you wear a cap? Not even Aunt Rose still wears a cap."

"Olivia," Caleb said in a warning tone.

"It's all right," Leah said. "I don't mind Olivia's curiosity." She turned her attention back to the child. "I am a member of the Society of Friends. Perhaps thee has heard our sect referred to as Quakers."

"Oh." Olivia's mouth turned down in a sullen frown. "I know some Quaker girls who attend my school. They're awfully plain."

"They would be proud to hear thee describe them that way. We Friends believe plain dress is part of our testimony of equality. If we dress simply, all Friends can afford the clothing, and no one is tempted to be wasteful or self-seeking. We Friends focus on simplicity and the important things in life. Fashion isn't nearly as important as seeking the Lord's will in our life or giving our funds to worthy causes rather than for the latest fashions."

Olivia pursed her lips as though deep in thought and then pivoted to return to her father's side. "I made a cherry pie all by myself. I used the preserves Aunt Rose and I made last spring. I know cherry is your favorite."

Caleb placed a hand on his daughter's shoulder. "Thank you, Olivia. But I think you should go upstairs and get ready for bed. We'll have the pie before you and Stephen go to sleep."

"But Papa—" Olivia glanced at Leah from the corner of her eye. "Very well, Papa. I'll go and change now."

After another curtsy, the girl strode from the room. The grown-ups listened to her footsteps as she made her way upstairs and closed a door.

Rose let out a noisy breath. "Oh my word, Caleb. I told you Olivia would be a problem."

Caleb rubbed the back of his neck. "Olivia never has adjusted well to change."

Rose shifted in her seat and addressed Leah. "You'll have your hands full with that one, my dear. Olivia's trying to show her father she's old enough to be the lady of the house."

Leah's heart went out to the girl. Of course she'd see a new mother as a threat to her place in the family. "A way will open."

Caleb studied her. "A way will open?"

"It's a saying we have in meeting when we're faced with a problem," Leah said. "The Lord's way often starts with great difficulty but then eases as He shows us the right path."

Rose looked at Caleb, and Caleb returned her gaze. Leah smiled and relaxed in the chair. Of course the Lord would open a way. He wouldn't have blessed her with a husband, a home, and children unless He had a plan.

❧

At last the pie was eaten and complimented, the dishes washed, and Stephen allowed to spend the night in the barn. Olivia bade them all a polite good night, and Rose retired to her room for the evening. Caleb and Leah were finally alone.

A balmy summer breeze fluttered the white lace curtains in the parlor, and the night sounds of insects and a nearby bullfrog filled the awkward silence.

Caleb cleared his throat. "It seems as though everyone has gone to bed except us and the crickets."

Leah's chest was tight with nerves. Should she take the lead, indicating to her new husband she was ready for her wedding night, or should she wait for him to direct her? She tucked her hands under her legs. "It has been a long day," she said, forcing the words out of her constricted throat.

"You must be tired." Caleb took an oil lamp from the table. "If you'll follow me, I'll show you the upstairs bedrooms."

Leah's heart raced as she followed Caleb up the narrow steps to the second floor. It wasn't fear that made her breaths shallow or panic that made her stomach tighten. It was excitement. In a few minutes, she would finally know the joy of a man's lips on hers. Before morning, she would be joined to a man in the manner God intended.

Caleb held the lamp higher to show her the layout of the upstairs rooms. "This is Stephen's room," he said, gesturing to a closed door in the middle of the hall. "Olivia's is directly across. Because of her rheumatism, Aunt Rose's room is on the ground floor. My room is at the end of the hall, and this will be your room." He opened a door and set the lamp on a chest of drawers. "Feel free to make any changes. I'm leaving before sunup tomorrow. Rose will explain everything that needs to be done."

Leah's mind raced to understand what Caleb was saying. Her room? His room? Leaving tomorrow?

"Well," Caleb said, "if that's all, I'll say good night."

He was halfway through the door before Leah found her voice. "Wait Caleb, wait."

He turned, his eyebrows raised in question.

"What— Where— I don't understand, Caleb. I thought. . ."

Leah swallowed hard. "We were married today. Are we not to act as man and wife?"

Leah knew the moment Caleb understood her question. His gaze dropped to the floor, and his weight shifted from one foot to another. "I thought your uncle... That is, I explained to him I wouldn't take advantage of the situation. Didn't either he or your aunt explain the arrangement?"

"I was told thee needed a wife and that thee found me to be a suitable candidate. Was there more?"

"No. Not exactly. But, Leah, I never intended to—to—"

A cold hand of disappointment wrapped around Leah's heart as she absorbed the reality of the situation. Traitorous tears filled her eyes, and she turned her back to him. "I understand. Thee never intended to make me a real wife. I'm to keep thy house and care for thy family, but I shouldn't expect more. Is that what thee meant when thee asked me if I agreed to thy bargain?"

She waited for him to deny it, to explain how she'd misunderstood, but all she heard was the click of the door and his footsteps as he walked down the hall to his room.

Leah sank onto the bed and gave in to tears. What a fool she'd been to think someone had wanted her for anything more than free labor. She was no better off in Caleb's house than she'd been at her uncle's. In fact, now that she was legally married, she was bound to stay.

She was a fool.

A silly, lonely fool.

Chapter 3

Leah awoke the next morning to the sight of Stephen sitting cross-legged on her bed.

"Finally," the boy said. "Aunt Rose said I couldn't disturb you, and I've been waiting and waiting for you to wake up!"

Leah raised a hand to her aching head, a result of her tear-filled night. "What time is it?"

"I don't know. I can't tell time yet. But we've all had breakfast, and Rose is making meat pies for lunch. Do Quakers always sleep in their clothes?"

Leah sat up and realized she was still wearing her wedding dress. She'd cried herself to sleep, like some fussy baby, rather than undressing to her muslin shift. "Where's thy sister?"

"In her room. Rose says she's sulking. What does that mean?"

Leah wasn't up to a vocabulary lesson. She made her way to the washstand and poured water into the basin. "Does thee have a new foal?"

Stephen's eyes shone. "Sure do! A filly. She doesn't look like her momma though. She's mostly black, but she's got a few white spots."

The cool water soothed Leah's swollen eyes. "And how's Snowdrop?"

"Joseph says she's doing great. She was out in the pasture with her baby when I left."

"Does thy foal have a name yet?"

"Nope. Olivia gets to name all the horses and dogs and cats on this farm."

That didn't sound fair, but perhaps Olivia had that privilege since she was older. Leah dried her face with a towel. "After I change my clothes and speak to Rose, I'll come out to the barn to see the foal. All right?"

Stephen hopped off the bed. "Sure! Aunt Rose," he shouted as he ran through the doorway, "she's awake!"

Leah listened to the boy's footsteps as he tramped down the stairs. It didn't take much to make Stephen happy. Olivia, however, presented a greater challenge. If Caleb had truly left before sunrise, no one had had a chance to say good-bye or to wish him a safe return. Perhaps Caleb had thought his departure would cause the children pain, but Olivia may have been hurt by what she considered her father's disregard. Leah found a gray dress in her trunk, changed out of her wedding dress, pinned her hair into a bun, and tied her prayer cap into place. Then she donned a clean apron and made her way to the kitchen.

Rose sat at the table, rolling out small circles of piecrust. "Good morning, Leah. I hope you got some rest."

"I'm sorry to be so late in rising. It's not like me to sleep the day away."

"New brides are allowed to sleep late after their wedding night."

Warmth rushed into Leah's cheeks, and she knew she was blushing. She covered her face with her hands and turned away from the older woman.

"I told Stephen to leave you alone," Rose continued. "I hope he didn't wake you."

"No. I didn't even know he was there until I opened my eyes."

"Thank goodness. That boy has the patience of a chicken at feeding time." Rose took her cane and struggled to stand. "Would you like something to eat?"

"Don't trouble thyself. It's time I learned the layout of this kitchen. What can I do to help thee finish lunch?"

"The pastry is finished. Just spoon in the meat mixture, and I'll seal the pies."

Leah retrieved an iron pot from the stove. "What time did Caleb leave?"

"Before dawn. I heard the horses, but he was gone by the time I got outside. Deciding to leave almost tore Caleb in two. No wonder he didn't want any tearful good-byes."

Her new husband was such a puzzle. If he hadn't wanted to leave, why had he volunteered? "Why did Caleb join the militia?"

"He felt it was his duty. I tried to talk him out of it, but Caleb said he couldn't sit by and do nothing. Especially after his friend, Conrad Baker, recruited him. Caleb signed on for six months. He'll be home soon enough."

And then what? Would her new husband return and take up where they'd left off? He in one room and she in another? Leah filled the last meat pie and returned the pot to the stove. "It seems as though Olivia is taking it hard."

Rose clucked her tongue and shook her head. "That girl's got a lot of growing up to do. One day she acts like the queen of the castle, and the next she's pouting like a two-year-old. My advice is to leave her alone until she comes out of her bad temper."

Maybe Rose was right. Leah had learned that leaving a beehive alone was often the best strategy when the colony was under stress, and Olivia's sting was probably worse than a bee's.

"Leah! Where are you?" Stephen ran into the kitchen, his face red from the exertion. "Are you coming or not?"

"I promised to see the new foal," she explained to Rose.

"Then off you go," the older woman said. "Lunch will keep until you get back."

Stephen pulled Leah's hand. "Come on."

If she'd a fraction of the boy's enthusiasm, it'd be easier to get through the day. Leah allowed Stephen to lead her through the side door.

"There she is!" Stephen said.

The gray mare browsed placidly in knee-high grass, and insects flitted around her new foal, causing it to flick its tail and twitch its ears.

Leah smiled at the sight. "She's lovely, Stephen. All fresh and new and ready to discover the world. Thee didn't tell me she had a white spot under her ear. It looks like she's wearing a pearl earring."

Stephen perched on top of the split rail fence. "Pearl. That'd be a good name, don't you think?"

Olivia wouldn't like that. Leah was already treading on thin ice, and usurping the girl's naming rights would send her straight into frigid water. "I think thee should ask thy sister before settling on a name."

A man's deep voice sounded behind her. "Morning, ma'am."

Leah turned to see Joseph's kind face smiling at her. "Good morning, Joseph."

"Look Joseph," Stephen said. "The baby's drinking milk from Snowdrop."

Joseph leaned against the fence and looked at the horses. "That's right. Snowdrop's going to need extra feed for the next few months. Got to keep the momma healthy so the baby will grow up to be strong."

"I'll get it!" Stephen ran into the barn.

Leah glanced at Joseph, and they both chuckled. "Did Stephen keep thee up all night?"

"No, ma'am. I made him a pallet on the straw, and he fell asleep right away. I woke him shortly after the foal was born."

"He slept through the birth?"

"Sure did. I thought about waking him, but I decided things would be calmer for both Snowdrop and me if I let the boy sleep."

From what she'd seen of Stephen, Joseph had made the right choice. "Is it possible for me to use a wagon today?"

"Sure. What did you have in mind?"

"I'd like to find a good spot to set up my bee hives. Caleb told me there were fruit trees nearby. That would probably be the best site, but I also need a way to keep the hives dry."

"Why not let me show you around this afternoon? I'll take you to the orchard, and we'll scout a good location."

"That would be wonderful, Joseph."

"Joseph!" Stephen called from the barn's open doorway.

"What is it, Stephen?"

"Should I bring some grain out to Pearl?"

Joseph turned to Leah. "Pearl? Did *he* name the foal?"

What had Leah stumbled into? "I told him he'd best talk it over with Olivia."

Joseph nodded solemnly. "Yes, ma'am. Olivia will be mighty put out if she's not consulted first."

❧

Leah sat beside Joseph as he maneuvered the wagon along a dirt trail. The fruit trees stood in straight ranks. Many years ago, one of Caleb's ancestors had planted saplings that had grown into a beautiful and productive orchard. Leah gestured to a stand of tall, leafy trees. "Those are pear trees, aren't they?"

"That's right. See the tiny green fruit growing amid the leaves?"

"Oh yes. Now I do."

"Cherries in April, pears in September, and apples after that. Yes, ma'am, you've arrived just in time for picking season."

"The orchard would be a wonderful site for my hives. But the skeps will be ruined if they get too wet. Uncle Abram built a small shelter for them. Would it be all right if I asked him to build one here?"

"I'm sure it would be fine, ma'am, but I'll be happy to take care of it for you. Just tell me how big you want it, and I'll get to building."

"Would it be possible to go to my uncle's farm now? Thee could see the shelter and the skeps."

"This is as good a time as any." Joseph turned the wagon in a broad arc and headed it toward the road.

"I thank thee, Joseph. My hives are important to me."

"No need for thanks, ma'am. Not after what you and the other Quakers did for me."

Leah smiled to hear the Friends complimented. "Will thee tell me thy story?"

"It'll be ten years come September. Ten years since I made my way from Kentucky to Ohio, and then to Newport. Quakers helped me every step of the way. I love to hear you speak, ma'am.

Thee and thy—every time I hear somebody talking like that, I remember the safe hands that led me from slavery to freedom. There's no finer people than the Quakers. I put my very life in their hands and they delivered me."

Slavery. One of the world's worst evils. How awful for Joseph and for all the other human beings held in bondage. "Does thee have any family?"

"No, ma'am." Joseph smiled broadly and cut his gaze to Leah. "But I've been thinking about taking a wife."

"A wife? Thee has plans to marry?"

"I'm thinking on it. There's a fine lady in Henry County I'd like to court, but. . . Well, it'll have to wait until Mr. Caleb gets home. I have to ask his permission."

"Permission? Why should thee need Caleb's permission to marry?"

"He's my boss, ma'am. Don't you think it'd be a good idea to get his consent before I bring a woman to live on the farm?"

"I see thy point. But don't put off thy own happiness until Caleb returns. Couldn't Rose give her consent? Or me?"

"I hadn't thought about that, ma'am. I suppose it'd be all right."

Joseph's tone didn't sound as though he believed his own words. But in Caleb's absence, surely Rose would be the person to ask. Yet something made Joseph hesitate. "Would thee like me to speak to Rose?"

Joseph turned toward her. "Would you?" His voice was ripe with excitement. "That'd be mighty kind of you."

Leah had guessed right. "Of course I will. Perhaps thee would like to bring thy lady to see the farm and to meet us."

Joseph tilted his head back and laughed loudly. "I'll do that, ma'am. You talk to Rose, and I'll talk to Delia."

❧

Matthew was in the barnyard when Joseph stopped the wagon at the Walls' farm. "And who's this come to call?" Matthew asked, smiling broadly. "I do believe it's Mrs. Whitaker."

Leah stopped her descent from the wagon and looked at her cousin. "If thee calls me by that name, I'm not likely to answer."

Matthew reached up to help her. "Fair enough. Thee will always be Leah, my cousin who knows how to charm delicious honey out of bees."

Leah smiled at his good-natured teasing. "Speaking of bees, Joseph has agreed to build a bee shelter. Will thee show him the one thy father built while I visit Aunt Cynthia?"

"Of course. Hello, Joseph," Matthew said as he shook hands with the man. "Nice to see thee again."

"Nice to see you, too," Joseph replied. "Hope you won't mind Miss Leah taking the hives to her new home. Sounds as though you're a might partial to the honey."

Matthew climbed up the wagon and took the seat Leah had vacated. "I plead guilty to the charge, but Leah has promised to keep us supplied, so I don't mind sharing."

Joseph passed the reins to Matthew, and the younger man drove toward the squash arbor, where Leah had situated her hives seven years earlier. She loved all of her cousins, but she had to admit that, as the eldest, Matthew held a special place in her heart. He'd turned nineteen the previous spring and would leave his boyhood behind any day now, but she hoped he'd never lose his easygoing nature. Matthew was like the rainbow after the storm, always looking on the bright side of whatever problem beset him.

Leah walked into the house and found her aunt in the kitchen. "What a nice surprise," Aunt Cynthia said, holding her arms open to embrace Leah. "How does thee like thy new home?"

Leah removed her bonnet and hung it on its usual peg near the back door. "Caleb's house is a fine place, Aunt Cynthia. And I'm already in love with his boy, Stephen."

"And Rose? Surely thee met her."

"Oh yes. She's been most kind. It's the other lady of the house that gives me the most concern."

Cynthia frowned. "Not little Olivia. She's just a child."

"A child who's sulking because her father left her with a stranger for a mother."

"But a child, nonetheless. Give it time, Leah. She'll come around." Cynthia poured coffee into two cups and set them on the kitchen table. "Now it's time for we two married women to talk. Does thee have any concerns or questions about thy wedding night?"

Leah felt heat climb her neck and settle into her cheeks. No doubt her face was the color of ripe apples. "Oh Aunt Cynthia." Leah sank into a chair. "I can't. . .I mean. . ."

Cynthia settled herself in a chair and reached for Leah's hand. "Who else is there to speak to? I remember my wedding night quite well, and I would've given anything to speak plainly to my mother about what happened. I'm only giving thee that opportunity."

Leah closed her eyes and drank deeply from the cup. Her aunt's curiosity felt like a colony of ants marching across her chest. What should she say? How could she explain? She forced herself to meet her aunt's expectant gaze. "I don't have any questions."

"No? But how did thee know what to expect?" Cynthia patted Leah's hand. "Was there pain?"

Where were Matthew, Mark, Luke, and John? Any other time, the boys would be tramping through the kitchen asking for a taste of this or a bite of that, but the one time she needed them to divert her aunt's attention, her cousins were in the fields.

"Thee has nothing to be embarrassed about," Cynthia said. "It is the Lord's will for husbands and wives to love each other with their hearts as well as their bodies. Was Caleb patient with thee?"

There was no escaping. Unless she chose to be rude, Leah would have to admit everything to her aunt. "I didn't have a wedding night."

"No wedding night? Didn't Caleb leave for Evansville this morning?"

Leah's throat closed around her voice. "Yes," she whispered hoarsely.

"He left without. . ." For all her boldness, not even Aunt Cynthia could say the words.

"Yes," Leah whispered.

Cynthia propped her elbow on the table and rested her cheek in her hand. "Did thee say something, Leah? Did thee ask Caleb to wait?"

"It's not like that, Aunt Cynthia. The thing is. . ." There was only one way to tell her aunt. Leah took a deep breath and let the story fall out of her mouth like rocks tumbling down the side of a hill. "I suspect Caleb never told Uncle Abram he wanted a wife," she said in conclusion. "All he needed was someone for his children, someone who was able to care for them until he could return."

Aunt Cynthia shook her head slowly. "I don't believe it."

Leah used the hem of her apron to wipe away the tears that threatened to embarrass her. Why couldn't Cynthia leave well enough alone? Being rejected by her husband had been bad enough.

Hoofbeats sounded outside, and Uncle Abram's voice called to his son. "Mark, take my horse. I'll be back in a few minutes."

Cynthia's gaze met Leah's.

"No, Aunt Cynthia, please don't—"

"This is between me and my husband, Leah. Thee shouldn't interfere." Cynthia stood, her hands on her hips, and waited for her husband to enter.

Abram came through the door, removed his hat, and turned to his wife. "Thee looks as though a summer storm is brewing in thy stomach. What's happened?"

"Thee." Cynthia pointed her index finger at her husband. "What has thee done to Leah?"

"To Leah? What is thee talking about?"

"When Caleb Whitaker approached thee about Leah, what did he ask for?"

Abram looked out the open kitchen door, probably wishing he could escape through it. "Caleb told me about his decision to join the Army. He was worried about his aunt being able to care for the children."

Cynthia crossed her arms in front of her chest. Her foot tapped a warning rhythm. "And?"

"And he wanted to know if I knew a woman who could live in the house and care for his children while he was gone."

Cynthia's foot kept pace. "And?"

"And I told him about Leah."

"Leah had a home. She didn't need a job."

"She needed a home of her own. So I made a deal."

"A deal? Just what kind of deal did thee make?"

"He could have Leah, but he had to marry her."

Cynthia dropped her arms and fisted her hands at her side. "I don't believe it. Did thee give so little thought to Leah that thee bartered her away like a horse?"

"I found someone who would take care of her for the rest of her life."

"She already had that with us."

"But now she's off my—"

Abram didn't need to finish the sentence. Leah knew exactly what he'd meant to say—off his hands. She'd heard him say it time and time again during the seven years she'd lived in his house. She'd slept in a tiny room off the kitchen. She'd cleaned and cooked and shared the profits she'd made from the sale of honey. Nothing had ever been enough.

Leah wouldn't let him see her grief. She stood, straightened her back, and lifted her chin. "I'll be taking the bees soon, Uncle Abram." She turned to her aunt. "I hope thee will pay me a visit."

Cynthia reached out a hand to Leah, but Leah stepped away. One touch of sympathy would be her undoing. She took her bonnet from the peg and stepped outside. There was no going back to her aunt and uncle. There was no way to go except forward.

Chapter 4

"Are you coming to church with us, Leah?"

Leah looked at Rose and Olivia, decked out in brightly colored dresses with matching bonnets. "I prefer to attend the Friends' First Day meeting," she answered, tying her plain black bonnet over her prayer cap. "Is that all right?"

"Of course, dear," Rose assured her. "You are free to attend whichever service you prefer. I'll ask Joseph to hitch a horse to the buggy for you."

Stephen, dressed in a brown jacket and pants, left his sister's side and took Leah's hand. "I want to go with Leah."

Leah smiled down at the boy. With so much rejection in her life, it was nice to have an ally.

"Is it all right with you, Leah?" Rose asked.

"Of course. Stephen will be most welcome." Leah glanced at Olivia. The girl hadn't spoken a word to Leah since her first night at the Whitaker's. "Would thee like to join us, Olivia?"

The girl's eyes widened. "No thank you." Olivia's incredulous voice sounded as though Leah had asked her if she'd like to swim in a river with alligators.

Leah decided to ignore Olivia's conceited tone. "Then it's

just us," Leah said to Stephen. "Shall we go?"

The boy didn't bother to answer. He sped through the doorway, yelling for Joseph.

"That boy," Rose grumbled. "The only time I see him slow down is when it's bath time."

Leah laughed at Rose's comment and followed Stephen outside. The boy was sitting in the front seat of a surrey while Joseph hitched a two-horse team. "There's just Stephen and myself, Joseph. The buggy will be fine."

Joseph removed his straw hat and wiped his forehead with a kerchief. "Well ma'am, I hoped you'd let me join you this morning."

Leah bit her bottom lip. How shortsighted of her not to realize Joseph had no place to worship. "Of course. Thee is always welcome."

"Thank you, ma'am." Joseph returned his hat to his head and called up to Stephen. "Are you planning on driving Miss Leah to church this morning?"

"I'm big enough," the boy answered. "I'll be five years old in two months."

"Is that right?" Joseph said. "I hadn't realized you were so close to being grown."

Leah grinned at Joseph and climbed into the seat behind the boy. "I'm glad to know I'm in such capable hands."

A few moments later, the three of them were on their way to the meetinghouse in Newport. "Like this?" Stephen asked as Joseph examined the boy's grip.

"You're doing just fine," Joseph replied.

"Do you think Pearl will pull a surrey one day?"

"Pearl?" Leah asked from the back seat. "Did Olivia agree to that name?"

Stephen looked over his shoulder. "She said she didn't care what we called a stupid old horse. Can you believe she said Pearl was stupid? Why, Pearl's going to be the smartest horse ever born on this farm."

Leah bit her bottom lip. Olivia was like an unwatched pot of milk on a hot stove. She was sure to boil over, eventually, and scald anyone near her. Leah lifted up a prayer for the girl. She knew the Lord would open a way to Olivia's heart, but the girl's bad humor made everyone walk as though the floor were made of porcelain.

When they arrived at the unadorned frame building that served as the gathering place for the Friends of Wayne County, Young John ran to her side. "Leah!" She opened her arms to embrace her young cousin, but he stopped before reaching her side. "Stephen! Thee came to meeting? Come on, I want to show thee something."

Stephen bounced on the balls of his feet. "May I, Leah? May I go with John?"

"Of course," she answered. "But don't go too far."

"We won't!" the boys answered simultaneously before running toward the back of the meetinghouse.

Joseph tied the reins to a hitching post, chuckling. "Think we'll see Stephen before it's time to go home?"

"John knows he must attend meeting. Uncle Abram can be a stern master if the boys step too far out of line. I'm sure Stephen will find us."

Joseph looked toward the meetinghouse then back at Leah. "Should I wait out here? Or maybe sit in the back?"

"Thee is welcome to sit anywhere thee feels comfortable. However, it is our custom for women to sit separately from men."

Joseph didn't appear to be convinced. His gaze darted from the meetinghouse to Leah, to the ground, and back to her.

Leah searched for Uncle Abram but found his eldest son instead. "Matthew!"

"Morning, Leah," Matthew called, walking toward her. "I was hoping to see thee this morning. When would thee like me to bring the bee skeps?"

"Joseph is building a bee shelter," Leah explained. "I'll get the bees once the shelter is finished."

"You can bring them later in the week," Joseph said. "I ought to be finished in a few days."

"Good enough," Matthew said.

Leah laid a hand on Matthew's arm. "Joseph has come to meeting today. Will thee see that he finds a comfortable spot?"

"Of course. Would thee like to sit with me and my brothers? Perhaps thee could help keep them in line."

Joseph returned Matthew's warm smile. "I'll do my best. Thank you."

Leah noticed her aunt talking to a group of women. "If thee will excuse me, I'd like to speak to Aunt Cynthia."

"Thee go on," Matthew said. "Joseph and I will find the boys."

Leah watched the women's faces as she approached. Sister Greenwood smiled at her, but Sister Haines cupped a hand around her mouth and said something to Sister Letts. Sister Letts glanced at Leah then quickly looked away.

Gossip. Leah had no doubt the women spoke of her. She lifted her chin and squared her shoulders as she joined the women. "Good morning, Friends."

Aunt Cynthia embraced her and kissed her on the cheek. "Good morning, Leah. I'm so glad thee made it this morning.

Was that Stephen I saw with Young John?"

"Yes. I asked Matthew to take charge of them."

Sister Greenwood, a white-haired woman with a round, kind face, patted Leah's back. "Cynthia told us about thy marriage to Caleb Whitaker. Blessings on thee and thy new family."

"Thank thee, Sister."

Sister Letts wrinkled her jet-black brow. "How many children does Mr. Whitaker have?"

"Two," Leah answered. "A girl and a boy."

Sister Haines straightened her starched apron. "I know the Whitakers," she said. "My girl goes to school with Olivia."

"Does Mr. Whitaker plan on joining the Society of Friends?" Sister Letts's black brows seemed to rise to her hairline.

"I'm not sure," Leah answered. "We haven't talked about it."

Sister Haines reached out to straighten Leah's apron. "It's a shame thee couldn't find a better match, but I suppose it's better than never being chosen."

Leah winced at the veiled insult. How casually Sister Haines spoke the cruelest of words. But it was true, wasn't it? Leah hadn't been chosen before her marriage to Caleb. Some would say she still hadn't been chosen.

Sister Letts scanned the groups of men who stood nearby. "Where is thy husband this morning?"

"He went to Evansville to report for duty."

"A soldier?" Sister Letts's bony hand splayed across her bosom. "Thee married a man who left his family to go to war? How awful!"

A pain shot through Leah's clenched jaw. Sister Letts knew nothing about Caleb or his family, and her words hadn't been voiced in sympathy. Ten unkind retorts sprang to Leah's mind, but her aunt saved her from the sin of voicing them.

"Come with me," Aunt Cynthia said. "Meeting will be starting soon." They stepped away from the other ladies, and Cynthia bent her head close to Leah's. "Thee has surely earned a blessing today," she said in a low voice. "Thee held thy tongue even though those two gossips baited thee."

"If I have earned a blessing, it's only because thee saw my temptation and rescued me."

Cynthia smiled and entered the silent meetinghouse with Leah at her side. Leah scanned the benches and saw Joseph seated next to Matthew and the younger boys. Stephen removed his hat but quickly put it back on when he noticed all the other men and boys kept theirs firmly in place.

A great calm settled over the gathering. Leah breathed deeply and invited the Holy Spirit to touch her soul. She closed her eyes and gave thanks for all the Lord had provided, the bounty of the farm, and the beauty of the land. She asked God to keep Caleb safe and to return him to his family, and she prayed for Olivia and Stephen, asking the Lord to show her how to best help the children. She opened her eyes and found Uncle Abram watching her. A familiar hardness touched her heart, and she closed her eyes again. She'd spent many years asking God to help her understand her uncle, but she still found it difficult to forgive the man who'd always treated her like a burden.

Before she could renew her prayer, a man cleared his throat. Leah opened her eyes. Brother Greenwood stood in the men's section, his beard streaked with silver, and his gaze dark with serious intent.

"Friends," he began, and then cleared his throat a second time. "Friends, I wish to speak this morning on the subject of the governor's call for volunteers."

A murmur passed through the crowd. First Day meeting was a time for members to share thoughts put on their hearts by the Holy Spirit, not to discuss contentious political issues.

"We all know the Friends' testimony of peace," Brother Greenwood continued. "We know we have done everything in our power to avoid war, but many men of our community wish to answer the call. Are we to turn our backs on those who love their country? Are we to cast them out of meeting because they fight for a just cause?"

Brother Haines stood. "We all know why thee brings up this question. Thee has two sons, one of whom has already turned his back on the testimony of peace."

Low voices of dissension sounded through the congregation.

"Brother Haines speaks the truth," Brother Greenwood replied. "My son traveled to the capital to join the militia, but I speak of other Friends as well. Each person must answer his own conscience, and we can't cast out Friends. When the insurrection has been put down and our sons and brothers return, will we gather them back to our bosom or send them on their way?"

Brother Letts, an elder, raised his hands in a placating gesture. "The time may come for us to discuss this matter, but so far, only one of our congregation has volunteered. Surely this question can wait until a later time. Thee may be worried about something that will never happen."

Aunt Cynthia gasped loudly. Leah looked at her aunt then followed her gaze to where Matthew stood.

"I plan to join the militia when the harvest is in," Matthew said.

Aunt Cynthia moaned. "No, son," she whispered.

"Sit thee down," Uncle Abram commanded in a gruff voice.

Matthew looked down at his father and then returned his gaze to the congregation. He wasn't yet twenty, but he stood with the confidence of a man. "I have helped many of thee fight against slavery. I will not sit by now and let other men do my duty."

Heads shook from side to side as the Friends talked among themselves. Uncle Abram's features looked darker than usual.

Brother Letts spoke again. "Matthew Wall, is thee willing to sacrifice thy membership in the Society of Friends in order to fight thy fellow man? Would thee turn thy back on thy family and thy beliefs in order to kill?"

Matthew looked at his mother. "I don't believe my family would disown me for following my conscience. I can't know if service to my country will require me to kill another. But when I return to Wayne County, I would hope to be welcomed back."

"I will hear no more of this." Brother Letts waved his arm as if to brush away the argumentative words. "Let us consider this matter in silent worship. The answer will come from our Lord. Let no other voice be heard except His."

The men returned to their seats, and a hush fell over the congregation, but it wasn't the usual tranquil silence of the First Day meeting. Instead a current of unease slipped through the crowd like a frigid wind.

Leah bowed her head, closed her eyes, and prepared her heart to listen. Her new husband had gone to fight; her cousin was set to do the same. Turmoil and upheaval seemed to be in every part of her life. At times like these, she needed the comfort that only the Holy Spirit could provide.

✌

A week later, Leah removed the last skep from the wagon and gingerly placed it in the compartment of the bee shelter Joseph had built. Uncle Abram's structure had been little more than old boards loosely nailed together, but Joseph had constructed columns of five-sided sturdy boxes, topped with a pitched roof. He'd even provided empty alcoves for future skeps. Perhaps Leah would be able to divide the hive and increase honey production. The bees were sure to thrive in their new home.

She stepped back and listened to the bees' constant hum inside the skep. They'd settle down soon and begin exploring their new home, just in time for the autumn honey harvest. She'd have to make a trip to Newport to order jars from the general store.

The sound of a horse called Leah's attention to an approaching rider. It was Joseph, with Stephen perched in front of him.

"What brings the two of thee out to the orchard?" she asked.

"Aunt Rose sent me to get you." Stephen slid off the saddle. "We got a letter from Papa."

"That's wonderful. Is thy papa well?"

Stephen picked up a stick and used it to brush the top of the tall grass. "I guess so. I sure wish I could be with him, fighting those Rebs and showing them what's what."

"The Confederate soldiers are men, just like thy papa. Thee wouldn't hurt thy father; why then would thee hurt another boy's father?"

Stephen squinted his eyes and cocked his head like a curious puppy. "What?"

Joseph chuckled low and tied his horse to the wagon's side rail. "That's a lot for a little head to take in, Miss Leah. Everything all right with your bees?"

"They are sure to flourish here, Joseph. The extra cubicles were a good idea."

"When can I chew the honeycomb?" Stephen asked.

"In a few weeks."

Stephen climbed into the back of the wagon while Joseph helped Leah up to the bench. "Olivia said your bees are stupid," the boy said. "She said anybody who likes insects must be stupid, too."

Leah caught Joseph's glance as he drove the wagon out of the orchard. Two weeks had passed without Olivia speaking to Leah, but obviously the girl had spoken many cruel words about her.

"Many people fear what they don't understand," Leah said. "Perhaps Olivia will change her mind when she tastes the honey."

"Miss Rose sure likes your bees," Joseph said. "She told me you were doctoring her with a honey balm."

"It's not honey, but a sticky substance the bees make to protect the hive. My mother taught me to mix it with ginger and arnica as a remedy for sore joints."

"Ginger I've heard of, but what in the world is arnica?"

"It's a flower, actually. I have a good supply of it in my medicinals box."

"Whatever it is, Miss Rose swears her old joints are growing younger every day."

"Maybe," Stephen said, "but everything else on Aunt Rose is growing older."

Joseph threw back his head and laughed loudly, but Leah hid her smile behind her apron. If Stephen knew he'd made an impression, he was likely to repeat his opinion to Rose.

When they reached the house, Rose and Olivia sat in the garden, their heads bent over sheets of paper.

"There you are," Rose said. "Caleb has sent us each a letter."

"Where's my letter?" Stephen asked.

"Olivia has it," Rose answered.

"I want to see it," Stephen said.

"Papa wrote it to both of us, and I'm keeping it," Olivia said. "You can't read, anyway."

"But it's my letter, too. Come on, Olivia, give me my letter."

"No." Olivia pushed the paper into the sash of her dress. "It's for me, and I'm keeping it." The girl turned on her heel and dashed into the house, with Stephen chasing after her, screaming her name.

Rose propped her head in her hand and sighed loudly. "I don't know whether to be proud of Caleb for answering the call of duty or to be angry at him for leaving me with those two."

"How is Caleb?" Leah asked. "Is he well?"

"Oh yes. He's in Missouri." Rose passed a small folded paper to Leah then turned to Joseph. "Caleb sent instructions for the farm. Let's go inside, and I'll relay everything to you."

"Yes, ma'am," Joseph said.

Leah watched them leave then sat on the bench and examined the letter. It was small and innocuous, a simple piece of folded paper with her name written in black ink. Why then did her chest ache at the prospect of reading it? She took a deep breath and untucked the flap that held the letter closed.

Dear Leah,

It is my fervent hope this letter finds you well and adjusting to life with my family. I wish to convey my regret for having to leave so quickly after our wedding and for not having time to help you settle in. I trust my aunt has made you feel welcome. When I return, I hope we may

become better acquainted. Until that time I invite you to
write me and to tell me more about yourself.

It was hardly a love letter. It was hardly anything at all. Leah refolded the paper and slid it into the pocket of her apron.

Stephen stomped out of the house, his head hanging, and his eyes shining with tears.

"Why Stephen, what is it?"

The boy collapsed beside her and laid his head against her side. "My letter," he said between sniffles. "Olivia won't let me see my letter from Papa."

Leah wrapped her arm around the boy's shoulders and felt a tremor of sadness pass through his small body. "Thee may have my letter, and we will write to thy father. Won't he be surprised when he sees a letter from thee?"

Stephen turned his sorrowful gaze toward her. "But Leah, I can't write. And I can't learn until I go to school next year."

"Says who? There's no law that says children can only learn at school. I will teach thee to read and write."

Stephen wiped away a tear. "You?"

"Me. Shall we have our first lesson now?"

Stephen's sadness vanished as he smiled. "Wait till I tell Olivia I'm going to learn to read and write. She thinks she's better than me 'cause she knows how and I don't. But after you teach me, she'll never be able to say that again." The boy ran back into the house, yelling his sister's name.

Leah shook her head slowly. She'd meant to help Stephen, but somehow she'd given Olivia another reason to dislike her.

Chapter 5

Although it was an uneasy peace, the mere routine of daily life forged a type of harmony at the Whitaker farm. In September Olivia returned to school, Joseph prepared for the apple harvest, and Leah took on more and more household duties. As the oak trees changed from green to gold, she immersed herself in the everyday chores of all farm wives. In the mornings, she cooked and cleaned; afternoons she spent in lessons with Stephen and tending the kitchen garden, and evenings, sewing and writing letters. Despite Caleb's invitation, Leah had declined to write, focusing instead on helping Stephen compose notes and drawings to send to his father.

She was an in-between woman. She was married, but she was not a wife. She'd come to love Stephen, but she was not a mother. And as far as Olivia was concerned, she was little more than a live-in housekeeper.

The girl rarely spoke to Leah. She ate the food Leah prepared, but during meals, she spoke only to her aunt and brother. Olivia handed her dirty laundry to Leah, accepted freshly starched and ironed clothes in return, but still frowned at Leah's plain brown dress and severe black bonnet.

Near the end of September, Leah entered the house from

the kitchen garden, her basket full of freshly picked yellow squash, and heard Olivia speaking to Rose.

"When Papa comes home, will he send Leah back to the Quakers?" the twelve-year-old asked.

"Of course not," Rose said, disapproval evident in her voice. "Leah is your father's new wife, and the sooner you accept that, the sooner you'll be happy."

"I'll never be happy again," Olivia protested. "Not until that ugly woman leaves this house. She's much too tall, and she's skinny as a blade of grass."

Although she understood the reasons behind Olivia's unkind words, Leah's heart ached to hear the old slights. Too tall. Too skinny. Not pretty enough.

"That's enough," Rose said harshly. "Leah has done nothing to deserve such cruel words from you."

"We don't need her," Olivia continued. "I can do everything she does, and I'm ten times prettier. When Papa comes home I'll show him."

The tone of Rose's voice grew sterner. "I won't listen to another word of this nonsense, Olivia Louise Whitaker. Even if you continue to refuse Leah as your stepmother, you will respect her as your father's wife."

"I'll never—"

"Not another word, Olivia."

Olivia ran through the back door, tears flowing down her blotched face. She brushed past Leah as though she were invisible and ran toward the orchard. Rose appeared in the doorway, one hand covering her mouth.

"Oh Leah," Rose said. "I hope you didn't. . ."

"Olivia is hurt and confused," Leah replied. "I know what it's like to lose a parent, and if my mother had remarried,

I probably would have felt the same way."

Rose clucked her tongue. "You're too kind. If we give in to Olivia's selfish ways, we'll have a brat on our hands. Caleb babied the girl when her mother died, and look at her now. If Olivia is to grow into a respectable woman, I must put a stop to her bad behavior."

"Perhaps if we give her more time—" Leah's words died in her throat.

A peculiar, high-pitched sound traveled on the wind. "What in the world?" Rose asked.

The noise grew louder, and a spark of fear flared in Leah's chest. Olivia was screaming. Screaming and running toward the house.

Leah dropped her basket, picked up her skirt, and ran toward the orchard. She recognized the noise that accompanied Olivia's panicked shrieks. The humming wings of hundreds of bees, swarming around the girl.

"Get a blanket!" Leah called over her shoulder.

Rose disappeared into the house just as Olivia came into sight. Furious bees bore down on her as she tore through the brush, swatting the insects as they buried their barbs into her tender skin.

"Stop running!" Leah called.

Olivia screamed, stumbled, and fell face-first.

Leah untied her apron and threw it over the girl's head. "Calm down, Olivia. The bees will leave once they no longer feel threatened."

Rose hobbled toward the pair, a woolen blanket clutched to her chest. Leah took the blanket and spread it over the sobbing girl's body. "Easy now. The bees are leaving. Take a deep breath. Let it out. Take another breath. Let it out. Nice and slow."

Olivia's sobs slowly receded. The bees' constant humming subsided as they abandoned their pursuit and returned to the orchard.

Leah removed the cover and brushed away the few trapped bees that clung to the blanket. "Sit up, Olivia, and let me see if thee is stung."

"Of course I'm stung," the girl shouted. "Those awful bees attacked me! You brought them here, and now they've attacked me!"

Leah removed her prayer cap and used it to brush away the stingers. "Let's go into the house, Olivia. I'll make a poultice to draw out the pain."

Olivia pushed to her feet and ran to Rose's side. "Aunt Rose, make her take those horrible bees away. They attacked me for no reason."

Rose lifted the girl's hair and inspected her neck. "I don't believe that, Olivia."

Olivia's blotched face turned a deeper shade of red. "Didn't you see how those awful bees attacked me?"

"Perhaps we should talk about this after we care for your stings."

Olivia stamped her foot. "But surely you don't believe I did something to those bees."

Rose's gaze connected with Leah's. With those words, Olivia had inadvertently admitted her guilt.

But the girl hadn't noticed the silent communication that passed between Rose and Leah. She flung her arm toward the orchard. "I was just walking down the path that leads through the orchard when all of a sudden, for no reason at all, those terrible bees attacked me."

Rose stepped away from the girl, as though trying to distance herself from the lies. "What did you do, Olivia?"

Olivia's hands fisted at her sides. "I didn't do anything. It's Leah who should be in trouble. She's the one who brought bee hives to our farm."

Rose put a hand on her forehead and spoke in a voice ripe with exhaustion and frustration. "What did you do, Olivia?"

"I told you what happened!" she yelled. "Why do you keep asking me?"

Rose kept her voice calm. "Because I'm hoping you'll find your way to the truth. Leah, perhaps you should go and check on your bees."

Leah stepped closer to the pair. "The bees will wait. I'd like to take care of Olivia's stings first."

Rose put a hand on Olivia's shoulder. "Did you hear that, Olivia? Leah knows you've done something to her bee hives, yet she wants to take care of you. That, young lady, is Christian love. Leah is putting you before herself. I can only hope that someday you will grow into such a fine woman."

Olivia froze like a threatened rabbit. Her bottom lip quivered, and her chest heaved with uneven breaths. She covered her face with her hands and turned her back to Leah and Rose.

Leah held her breath in anticipation of Olivia's next move. Would the girl bend, or would she hold on to her painful anger? If she could put aside her wounded pride, love would find its way into her young heart.

Olivia's slender shoulders shook with silent sobs. Leah walked quietly to the girl's side. "Come inside, and let me tend to thy injuries."

Olivia leaned toward Leah, and Leah slid her arm around the girl's shoulders. "I will mix a paste of bicarbonate and water. It draws out the pain of a bee sting and reduces the redness.

Thee will be good as new in just a little while."

"I'm sorry," Olivia said, sobbing. "I didn't mean to... If you'll show me how to repair them—"

"*Shh.* Calm thyself, Olivia." Leah guided the girl into the kitchen, settled her into a chair, and went to the cabinet. "I'll see to the hives when I'm sure thee is all right."

Rose joined Leah at the counter. "I'll leave the two of you alone for now. Call me if I'm needed."

Leah nodded to the older woman and mixed the paste while Olivia's sobs abated.

"I found a big stick and knocked the skeps over," Olivia said. "I wanted to smash them and make the bees fly away."

Leah dampened a cloth and used it to clean the girl's face. "I know thee is angry, Olivia. But taking out thy anger on bees wasn't a smart thing to do."

Olivia smiled for the first time. "I know that now. But I thought if the bees left, you'd leave, too."

Leah dabbed the paste on the girl's many stings. "I have nowhere to go, Olivia. My aunt would take me back, but my uncle wouldn't. Plus I made a vow before God that I would be thy father's wife until the day I died."

Olivia sniffed loudly. "Where are your parents?"

"With the Lord."

Olivia sighed, as though exhaling all the anger and bitterness she'd been carrying inside since her father left. "I'm sorry, Leah."

"I know, Olivia. I know what it's like to be left behind. I was angry, too."

"You were angry when your parents died?"

"Oh yes."

"Are you angry at me?"

"Do I seem angry?"

"No. But I destroyed your bee hives."

"Bees are more resilient than thee thinks. When I finish here, I'll go to the orchard and check on them."

"May I come with you?"

Leah smiled at her stepdaughter. "Next time. Thee needs to rest, and the bees may need special attention. Now go upstairs and change thy clothes, and if thee finds any more stingers or swollen spots, let me know."

"I will." Olivia threw her arms around Leah's neck. "Thank you, Leah."

Leah's heart warmed as she returned the girl's embrace. She laid her cheek atop Olivia's silky hair. "It will be all right. 'All things work together for good to them that love God.'"

Olivia sniffed one last time, smiled at Leah, and ran up the stairs.

" 'All things work together for good to them that love God,'" Leah repeated. "But only thee, Lord, would use bee stings to open a way to Olivia's heart."

Chapter 6

Leah retied her apron and entered the barn. Without the swallows' constant chattering, the barn was as quiet as the meetinghouse on First Day. The little travelers had left just after the apple harvest, a sure sign the first snowfall couldn't be far away. It was past time to harvest the honey.

Joseph carried the last box of jars into the barn and set it on the workbench next to Leah. "It's hard to believe your bees made enough honey to fill all these jars."

Leah cut off a small piece of the wax honeycomb and gave it to Joseph. "The bees love their new home in the orchard. Just taste how sweet this year's honey is."

Joseph put the honeycomb into his mouth and smiled. "Mmm-hmm. I bet you make a heap of money. What will you do with it all?"

"I haven't given that much thought. Save it, I suppose, and buy something nice for thy new bride."

A deep chuckle sounded in Joseph's throat. "Delia wants to get married on Christmas Day, but that's almost six weeks from now. I'm going to have to think of a way to hurry her up."

"You certainly won't hear any of the Whitakers object. They can't wait until Delia takes over the cooking. Apparently my cooking is acceptable but not actually desirable."

"You never heard me complain, did you?"

"No but thee rarely asked for seconds."

The rap of Rose's cane on the doorway caught their attention, but it was her pale face and trembling hands that alarmed Leah. "What is it, Rose?"

"A letter from the War Department," Rose answered in a shaky voice.

An invisible fist of dread clutched Leah's heart. *Not Caleb. Please, Lord. Not Caleb.*

Rose dabbed at her nose with a handkerchief. "Caleb's been wounded and is in a hospital in Washington. They've asked for a family member to come and care for him."

A breath forced itself into Leah's lungs. Caleb was injured, perhaps sick, but alive.

"You must leave right away," Rose said. "I'll go to the railroad office this afternoon and arrange your passage."

"Me?" Leah asked.

"Of course. I'd never survive such a trip, especially now that the weather has turned colder."

"But, the children. Who will take care of them?"

"We'll manage until you return."

"But I can't go alone. I'll need a companion of some sort."

Rose held the fisted handkerchief to her forehead. "Perhaps one of your older cousins could accompany you, but if not, you'll have to go alone. We can't leave Caleb in the hands of strangers."

Leah's heart winced. The image of her husband, wounded and lying in a hospital bed, seeped into her mind. "I'll go straightaway to Uncle Abram's farm. Perhaps Matthew or Mark will be able to accompany me."

✳

Leah had spent many years caring for bees, but it wasn't until she arrived in Washington that she had an idea what it felt like to be one of the insects. The throngs of people entering and exiting the Baltimore and Ohio Railroad Station reminded her of bees leaving the hive to forage and returning with their treasured pollen.

Matthew squeezed Leah's arm and spoke into her ear. "Wait here. I'll hire a carriage and driver."

Leah nodded her consent and clutched her reticule closer to her body. Rose had given her hundreds of dollars, more money than Leah had ever seen, and although she'd hidden most of it in a secret pocket she'd sewn to her petticoat, she worried about losing even a dime of the Whitakers' money.

A small carriage pulled by a single horse stopped nearby, and Matthew jumped out. After handing her up to the seat, he gathered their bags and tossed them in beside her. "Shall we go to the hospital or find a hotel?"

"It's almost dark, and I doubt the hospital would allow us to visit so late in the day. Let's find a hotel."

Matthew climbed up the wheel, spoke to the driver, and then joined Leah on the hard seat. "The driver says our best bet is the Willard Hotel."

"Thank goodness thee is with me, Matthew. I don't know how I'd manage alone."

"Oh thee would do just fine. Thee has always been resourceful. But I'm glad to have this opportunity to see the capital."

As the hired carriage lumbered along the rough road, Leah had to remind herself to keep her mouth closed. For a woman who'd never seen a building higher than two stories, the capital city was astonishing. Huge stone buildings stood beside crowded streets, and people hurried and shouted as though their business was more urgent than their neighbor's. In the distance she could see the Capitol's unfinished dome, the dying sunlight glinting off the building's white walls. It would be magnificent once it was finished.

But for all its grand buildings, Washington was a noisy, dirty place. Carriages and men on horseback vied for the right-of-way, and more than once she overheard rude words shouted by unruly men. The houses were small and packed closely together, like odd-sized books forced onto a small shelf.

At last the cab pulled to a stop in front of a six-story white building. On the roof a pennant with the name WILLARD flew beside the US flag. "Is this the hotel?" Leah asked.

"It must be," Matthew answered. He climbed down from the carriage, paid the driver, and helped her alight.

Leah held fast to her cousin's arm as he wove through the crowded lobby. While Matthew spoke to the desk clerk, Leah stared in astonishment at the many uniformed men who chatted in small groups. So many uniforms, some with stars on their collars, others with clusters of leaves. There were only a few women, but all of them dressed in elegant clothing. Leah smoothed her plain gray skirt and examined her ungloved hands. Among the farmers of Newport, dressing plainly had never been difficult, but here she looked like a crow amid peacocks. Leah shook her head in silent chastisement. How quickly she'd let the world's ways influence her.

Matthew returned with two keys. "The rooms are on the top floor, but I said they'd be fine. Thee looks exhausted, Leah."

"I am tired," Leah agreed, "but I don't know what's worn me

out the most. The three-day train ride from Newport or the one hour I've been in Washington."

Matthew smiled and picked up her bag. "Let's hope it's nothing a good night's rest won't cure."

The next morning dawned cold and dreary as a November rain beat steadily against Leah's window. After a quick breakfast in the hotel's dining room, Leah and Matthew hired a carriage to take them to Seminary Hospital. The three-story red-brick building had black shutters and dormer windows peeking out from its steep roof. Such a large building could hold hundreds of sick and injured soldiers.

Matthew opened the door, and Leah passed through. Blue-uniformed men lounged on the first floor, and although some were missing limbs, others seemed healthy. They were all young, some with scraggly beards and others clean shaven, but hunger shadowed each of them. Whether they craved food, home, or simply something to do wasn't clear to Leah, but she easily recognized the look of yearning that hovered around their eyes.

Matthew approached the nearest soldier, a blond-haired boy who was unsuccessfully trying to grow a beard. "Good morning."

"Morning," the soldier replied.

"Who's in charge of the patients?"

It seemed like an innocent question, but a low sardonic chuckle passed among the soldiers. "Don't know that anyone's in charge," the blond boy replied, "but the devil himself has hold of most of us."

Leah gasped at the boy's bold irreverence, but his compatriots only laughed louder.

Matthew didn't appear to be fazed. "We're here to see my cousin's husband, Captain Caleb Whitaker of Indiana. Is there someone we should check with?"

An older soldier with an empty right sleeve spoke up. "Go up to the third floor and turn left. That's where they keep the officers."

"Thank thee." Matthew took Leah's arm and escorted her toward the staircase.

On the second floor, Leah passed through an open doorway. On either side of her, rows of cots stretched from one end of the room to the other, each cot occupied by a wounded man. Uniformed men and white-aproned nurses moved among the cots, seeing to the men's needs. Without warning the vilest odor she'd ever experienced took Leah's breath. Mingled scents of unwashed bodies, unemptied bedpans, and putrefying flesh made her long to throw open the nearest window. Surely the patients would appreciate the fresh air, even if it did come with a dose of chilly rain.

A young man carrying linen stopped long enough to address Matthew. "Good morning, Friend. May I help thee?"

Leah relaxed upon hearing the familiar salutation. It was easy to identify a member of the Society of Friends. Their plain dress and speech singled them out.

"Thee is a Friend?" Matthew asked.

"I am Joshua Anderson from Salem Meeting, in Ohio. And thee?"

"Matthew Wall. We're from Newport, in Eastern Indiana. Allow me to introduce my cousin, Leah Whitaker."

Leah nodded to the young man. "Does thee work here? Is thee in the army?"

"I serve as an orderly here. I wanted to do something but couldn't bring myself to join a fighting unit. What brings thee to Seminary Hospital?"

"I'm looking for my husband, Captain Caleb Whitaker. He may be with the soldiers from Indiana."

"I know Captain Whitaker. This way." Joshua pointed to the right.

Matthew and Leah trailed him through the maze of cots. The men's pale faces drew Leah's attention. Some wore stained bandages in need of changing; others moaned in obvious pain. What could she do to help the injured? What comfort could she provide?

None. The soldiers' wounds were more than her box of medicinals could treat, and although she longed to clean the hospital from top to bottom, it was clear the need was greater than any one woman could fulfill.

The orderly stopped in front of a cot near the window. "Here's Captain Whitaker. I didn't know he was a Friend."

"He's not," Matthew said.

Leah stood at the cot's foot and stared at the sleeping man. The orderly had made a mistake. The gaunt man had a full beard. His skin had a yellowish tinge, and his hair was gray at the temples. "This isn't my husband."

Joshua picked up the card tied to the cot's leg. "Captain Caleb Whitaker, First Indiana Cavalry."

Leah shook her head in disbelief. Perhaps the soldier had the same name as her husband, but he wasn't her husband.

"Well there's one way to find out for sure," Joshua said. "Let's wake him up."

Leah started to object, but the orderly was too quick. "Captain Whitaker?" He shook the soldier's upper arm. "Captain Whitaker, you've got guests."

The soldier opened his eyes slowly. "Water, please," he said softly.

Joshua filled a tin cup from a nearby bucket and helped the soldier drink deeply.

"Thank you." He passed a hand over his face and squinted at Matthew. "Matthew Wall, as I live and breathe. Is that really you?"

Leah gasped. It *was* Caleb.

Matthew squatted next to the cot and took Caleb's hand. "It's good to see thee, but I'm sorry to find thee like this. What happened?"

Before Caleb could answer, the orderly interrupted. "I need to get this linen to Ward B, but if thee needs anything more, just say the word, and I'll do my best to help."

"Thank thee for thy help," Matthew replied. The orderly nodded and left. Matthew repeated his question to Caleb. "What happened to thee?"

A long sigh escaped Caleb's lips. "A Confederate minié ball, that's what happened. Hit me right here." Caleb touched his left rib. "The doctor said it most likely took out a piece of my liver before it went out my back."

Matthew whistled softly. "Thee is lucky to still be breathing. Where did thee see action?"

"Missouri. I was wounded at Fredericktown, trying to capture a twelve pounder. We lost only seven men, but many more were wounded. You wouldn't believe the number of prisoners we took. At least eighty, if not more. But enough talk of battles. Why are you here?"

"To escort Leah, of course."

Matthew stood, and Caleb looked at Leah for the first time. "Leah?"

She opened her mouth to answer him, but no sound escaped her lips. Where was her voice when she needed it?

She remembered her wedding day, how he'd poured her a glass of water and gone down on one knee to offer it to her. Had that really been only ten weeks ago? Leah cleared her throat, struggling to make her voice heard. "Yes, Caleb. Matthew escorted me here so that I may take care of thee."

As though he couldn't believe his eyes or his ears, Caleb repeated her name. "Leah." He rubbed his eyes then returned his attention to Matthew. "Can you get me out of this place?"

"Is it safe for thee to leave?" Matthew asked. "If thee hasn't recovered from thy wounds, surely the hospital is the best place for thee."

"Lying in this cot hour after hour, day after day, with nothing to do except remember the battle and wish for home? I'll never recover here. The nurses have their hands full with men in worse shape than I. All I need is some fresh air, good food, and to get away from this pestilence."

Leah couldn't argue with that opinion. From what she'd seen, the hospital offered little in the way of healing. "Matthew and I have rooms in the Willard Hotel. Perhaps thee would like to go there until thee feels ready to make the journey to Newport."

"It was a difficult trip," Matthew said. "The railroad companies may boast of the speed of train travel, but they're mute on the subject of comfort. Poor Leah had the worst of it. There are scarce facilities for ladies, and we spent one night in an unheated, dark car waiting for a locomotive to take us into Washington."

Caleb looked at Leah again. "It was good of you to come. The hotel is a fine suggestion. If Matthew will help me dress and gather my things, I'll be ready to leave." Caleb rubbed his bearded cheek. "And I'd love a shave, if Matthew will help me hold a razor."

Matthew smiled. "I've never barbered another man, but I'll do my best to not cut thy throat."

Both men looked at Leah. Her gaze traveled from her cousin to her husband and back again. What were they trying to tell her? "What is it?"

"Well Leah," Matthew answered, "thee might want to return to the hotel and wait for us there."

"Why?" she asked.

Matthew grinned at Caleb. Caleb returned the smile. It was obvious Leah didn't understand their unspoken message, but what were they trying to say?

"Privacy, Leah," Matthew explained. "Thee is not a nurse, and what we need to do is best done without thy watchful eyes."

"Oh!" Leah felt the warmth in her face and knew she was blushing. She started to remind her cousin she was Caleb's wife then thought better of it. Caleb would be more comfortable without her, and he was the one she'd come to care for. "I'll find the orderly and tell him thee is leaving."

"Good," Caleb said.

"And I'll wait for thee at the hotel."

"Good," Matthew repeated.

Since it was obvious neither man wanted her there, and feeling very much like the runt in a litter of piglets, she turned and marched out of the hospital.

❧

"We've got a problem."

Leah stood in the hallway outside her hotel room and looked at her cousin. "Is something wrong with Caleb?"

"He will never make it up the stairs. He nearly passed out walking from the carriage. Six flights of steps will kill him."

"Where is he now?"

"In the lobby. I told him I'd fetch thee, and we'd all have dinner in the hotel's dining room. But Leah, he's much sicker than he led us to believe."

"I'll go downstairs and meet him. Will thee explain the problem to the desk clerk? Perhaps something can be done for Caleb. All he needs is a quiet room with a bed."

"Of course."

Leah retrieved her reticule and hurried down the stairs. She found Caleb leaning against a wall near the back of the crowded lobby. His eyes were closed, as though he tried to conserve every ounce of unnecessary energy, and his uniform so loose he looked like a well-dressed scarecrow. Without the beard, she could see clearly the hollows of his cheeks and the dark circles under his eyes. God only knew what illnesses circulated within his emaciated body, but with the Lord's help, Leah would make her husband well again.

She scanned the lobby for an empty seat where he could rest, but blue-coated officers occupied each couch and chair. Couldn't they see their comrade in arms needed help? She moved to a couch where two men lounged while smoking their cigars. "Excuse me, sirs."

The two officers stood and smiled at her. "Well what do we have here?" the taller man said. "A little Quaker dove in the midst of war hawks?"

The shorter man chuckled at his friend's joke. "What can we do for you, ma'am?"

"My husband is recovering from injuries he received at the Battle of Fredericktown." Leah gestured to Caleb. "Would thee be kind enough to allow him to rest on this couch while his room is being readied?"

The two men studied Caleb then looked back at Leah. "I see he's with the First Cavalry of Indiana," the taller one said. "First time I've heard of a Quaker captain."

Leah didn't want to waste time explaining the circumstances. "As soon as I settle my husband into a room, I will return the couch to thee. However, I can't say how long that may take."

The shorter man moved away from the couch. "Of course you may have our seats, little Quaker. Despite what the Rebs say about us, chivalry is alive and well among the Union officer corps."

The two men laughed and moved away. Leah returned to Caleb and touched his shoulder. "Caleb?"

His eyes flew open, and he straightened. "Yes, Leah?"

"Come and sit down." She gestured to the empty couch. "Matthew will be with us soon."

Caleb offered his arm, and she placed her hand on it. But a few steps later, it was clear Caleb needed her assistance more than she needed his. She slid her arm under his shoulder and across his back in order to bear his weight. He collapsed onto the couch.

"Thank you," he said.

"I'm not sure thee should have left the hospital."

"The place was driving me mad. So many men were in worse condition than I, it was difficult to get care. The doctor said there was nothing they could do for me that couldn't be done by my own family. But I never expected to see you."

"Who did thee expect would come?"

"Rose or perhaps my brother."

"Thee has a brother?"

"Yes. He lives in Randolph County. Didn't Rose tell you?"

There was so much about her husband she didn't know,

but before she could ask any questions, Matthew joined them. "Good news. There's a large suite on the second floor that's come available." Matthew held up a key. "Shall we go?"

Leah bent to help Caleb.

"I don't need any help," he said, pushing her arms away.

But it was clear he did need help. He moved to the couch's edge and tried to lever himself up with his arms, but he was too weak to do such a mundane task. Caleb's gaze met Leah's.

He didn't want her help. He didn't want her at all.

She walked away from the couch and turned her back. She could hear Caleb's labored breathing and the grunts of effort that standing and walking cost both Caleb and Matthew.

After several long minutes, Caleb was at her side. "Why don't you go into the dining room and arrange a lunch to be delivered to our suite?"

"They do that?" She immediately regretted her words. Caleb would probably find her ignorance of such things laughable.

"Yes," he replied. "Especially if one is paying for a suite. I assume Rose sent some cash with you?"

Leah nodded.

"Good. Order whatever you'd like."

Leah turned and walked toward the dining room. How she'd like to be back in Newport at this moment, tending her bees. Alone.

Chapter 7

The suite was much too elegant for Leah's comfort. Yards of brocade covered the windows, and plush carpet softened her footsteps. An upholstered settee and chairs furnished the sitting room, and the two bedrooms on either side had spacious beds dressed with linen sheets and silk coverings.

Matthew disappeared after lunch, saying he wanted to see the sights of Washington, leaving Leah alone with Caleb.

Her husband sat by the window looking out at the rain, his head resting on his hand. Leah searched Caleb's face for signs of discomfort but found only fatigue. "Would thee like to lie down?"

"I'm tired of beds and sickness. If the weather were better, we'd go for a ride in the country. Fresh air and sunshine would do me good."

He could barely sit erect. How did he think he could manage a ride in the country? "The kitchen staff gave me radish leaves. The juice, mixed with honey, will be good for thy liver." Leah dipped a large spoon into the pitcher of mixture and held it to Caleb's mouth.

He frowned suspiciously at the spoon. "How do you know I suffer from problems of the liver?"

"The whites of thine eyes are yellow as well as thy skin. And thee told Matthew the shot damaged thy liver. I can also see thee has a fever. I don't have to be a physician to diagnose what is so plainly evident."

"You and your box of medicinals. Do you think honey will cure everything?"

"Not everything, but neither will it hurt. Now, will thee take the medicine, or will thee continue to scowl like a four-year-old?"

Caleb's eyebrows shot up in obvious surprise at her forceful tone. Leah grinned at him. Despite the times her voice had refused to show itself, and despite her husband's poor condition, her position as wife and caregiver empowered her. She knew what to do for him, and she intended to do it. Caleb opened his mouth, and Leah slipped the spoon between his teeth. "Four times a day, I think. Until thy skin and eyes return to their normal color."

"At least the honey masks the taste." Caleb shifted in his chair so that he faced the sitting room rather than the window. "Tell me about my family."

"Everyone is well," Leah answered, lowering herself onto the settee. "Stephen spends every day with his colt and is learning his letters. Olivia does well in school and has begun to accept me. Rose is healthy. Joseph intends to marry and bring his wife to live on the farm."

Caleb stared at her for a few moments, as though disbelieving so much could have happened in the short time he'd been gone. "I believe you are leaving out a lot of details. Who is teaching Stephen?"

"I am," she said.

"I wondered if you could read and write."

"Of course I can. We Friends believe strongly in education.

Why did thee doubt my ability to read and write?"

"Because you never wrote to me. I assume you received my letter."

The letter. The one that said so little. "Yes."

"You had no interest in writing me?"

Leah shrugged one shoulder. "I didn't know what to write."

Caleb watched her as though she would suddenly erupt with all the unspoken feelings she'd been guarding. But Leah wasn't about to tell him how disappointed she'd been with his curt message.

Caleb cleared his throat. "I don't believe Olivia simply woke up one morning and decided to start calling you mother. Did she give you any problems?"

Leah turned her head. Olivia would consider it a breach of trust if Leah told Caleb about the beehives. "She took it very hard when thee left. Olivia wants to please thee. She wants to earn thy esteem and be treated with respect, but thee thinks of her as a little girl."

"She is a little girl."

"She is a young woman."

Caleb's dark brows drew together. "You're dodging the question. Did she give you any problems?"

She should tell her husband the truth, but how could she do that and keep Olivia's trust? "Does thee remember when I told thee God would open a way?"

"I remember."

"He did indeed open a way to Olivia's heart. It involved bee stings and broken honeycombs, but the outcome was forgiveness and redemption. Olivia and I get along fine now."

Caleb leaned forward. "You're not going to tell me more, are you?"

Leah smoothed her skirt then folded her hands in her lap.

Caleb leaned back. "Very well. Who gave Joseph permission to bring a woman to the farm?"

"Your aunt. Delia, that's Joseph's intended, is a wonderful cook, and Rose offered her a position."

"When's the wedding?"

"Christmas Day, I believe, although it may be earlier. Joseph and Delia plan to be married during a First Day meeting."

"Joseph is going to the Quaker meetings?"

"He is. Stephen goes with us, too."

Caleb leaned forward, his hands gripping the chair's arms. "My son is becoming a Quaker?" he asked, his surprise evident in his voice.

"No, although I don't think that would be a bad thing. He comes to play with my youngest cousin, John."

"Hmm." Caleb relaxed in his chair and turned his gaze to the window once again. "How much money did Rose send?"

Leah thought about the bulging pocket underneath her skirt. "Hundreds of dollars. Shall I give it to thee now?"

"Is it in your reticule?"

Leah looked at her small bag. "No. I'll go into the bedroom and get it." She stepped into a bedroom, closed the door, and lifted the hem of her skirt. She'd just begun to unbutton the secret pocket when she heard the door swing open.

"Aren't you the smart one?" Caleb asked. "Surely there's no place more secure than a Quaker's petticoat."

Leah dropped her skirt and whirled toward the door. Her husband stood in the doorway, a look of amusement on his face.

Leah smoothed her skirt. "Doesn't thee knock before entering a lady's room?"

Caleb bowed. "My apologies. I thought you'd come in here

to get your traveling bag, and I wanted to tell you Matthew had put it in the other bedroom."

Leah tucked wisps of hair under her prayer cap. Then, aware that her hands were flying around her face like moths to a lantern, she clasped her hands behind her back. "I was afraid to leave such a large sum of money unguarded."

"So I see. Will you give it to me now?"

"Will thee please wait in the other room?"

Caleb crossed his arms in front of his chest and leaned on the bureau. "I don't think so."

Leah narrowed her eyes. What game was he playing? She had no reason to be modest around her husband, and yet he wasn't her husband. Not really. She turned her back to him, reached under her skirt, and retrieved the money. She placed it on the bureau and stepped back.

Caleb took the money and counted it. "This should be enough to last us several weeks if we choose to stay at the hotel. But I have been given medical leave and am anxious to return home."

Leah thought of how difficult the trip to Washington had been. "I'm concerned about thy ability to make the journey. Would thee consider waiting until thy strength returns?"

"Perhaps. But if I have to sit in this hotel room with nothing to do but worry about my family and wonder about my regiment, I'll be as miserable as I was in the hospital."

"Does thee enjoy reading? There's a stationer's shop nearby. I could buy some books for thee."

"That would be a good start. And while you're out, see if you can find information about concerts or lectures or plays in the city. Anything to break the monotony of being in the same room, hour after hour."

Leah brushed past Caleb, returned to the sitting room, and retrieved her bonnet and cape. "I understand thee is tired of bed, but try to rest until I return. There are worse treatments than radish leaves, and I'm not above trying them on thee."

For the first time that day, Caleb smiled. "Did my Quaker wife make a joke? Why Leah Wall, I didn't know you had a sense of humor."

There was a lot her husband didn't know about her, but Leah declined the opportunity to point that out. She smiled and walked out of the room. Concerts, lectures, and plays. Life in the capital certainly was different from Newport.

⁘

Caleb closed the novel and looked over at the park bench where Leah sat with her sewing. "I believe this is my favorite of Mr. Dickens's novels. I've read them all, you know."

"What is it thee likes so much about *Great Expectations*?"

"The main character, Pip, is a fine fellow. He's been mistreated, as all of Mr. Dickens's characters seem to be, and I fear love will play him for a fool. But he's got a brave heart, and that will most likely see him through to the end."

Leah looked at the book on Caleb's knee. "I'd like to read it when thee has finished, but thee mustn't spoil the ending for me."

"Have you read any of Mr. Dickens's stories?"

"None. Reading novels was considered a waste of time in Uncle Abram's house."

"I have several of Mr. Dickens's books at home. I'll gladly lend them to you." Caleb covered his mouth with his hand and yawned, leaned his head against the back of the bench, and closed his eyes.

Leah waited for the steady breathing she'd come to recognize as sleep. During the first nights at the hotel, she'd sat by his bedside and nursed him through feverish dreams, but bit by bit, the fever had left his body, and peaceful slumber had done its part to restore his health.

Matthew took over the nursing duties in the daylight hours, allowing Leah a chance to sleep on the sitting room settee. But as Caleb's health improved, the sleeping arrangements had become more awkward. Husbands and wives slept together. That was the way Leah had been raised, and that was what Matthew had expected when he'd placed Leah's traveling bag in Caleb's bedroom. But once Caleb began sleeping through the night, there was no reason for Leah to keep vigil.

One night after Matthew bade them good night, Caleb asked Leah to join him in the sitting room. "You've been a most attentive nurse," he said, "but your eyes are showing the effects of sleepless nights."

Leah's fingers had automatically gone to the dark circles she knew were shadowing her eyes, but she said nothing.

"You will take the bed from now on, and I'll sleep on the floor."

"No," Leah protested. "Thee needs rest and the cold floor will do thee no good. I can continue to sleep on the settee."

Caleb's frown communicated his disdain for her idea. "You're too tall for that tiny settee. How you've curved your body to fit into it is a mystery. If you don't get real rest soon, our roles as patient and nurse will be reversed. And I warn you, I do not make a good nurse. Would you prefer me to speak to Matthew? He could share my room, or I could rent a room for you."

"No," she answered, more forcefully than she intended.

Caleb raised an eyebrow in question, and Leah hurried

to explain. "Matthew doesn't need to know the details of thy agreement with my uncle."

"I see. You've spoken with your uncle about that agreement?"

"Yes," she said.

"And what did you think about it?"

Leah felt her heart shutter itself against the pain of her uncle's bargain. She'd been so foolish on her wedding day, secretly rejoicing to be a wife. Who had she been to think a man like Caleb had truly desired her? "Does it matter?" Leah said in what she hoped was a casual tone. "I am married. I made a vow before God to love, honor, and obey thee until death parts us. I will do my best to fulfill those vows."

"To love, honor, and obey me."

"Yes."

"Well I certainly have no complaints about your obedience, and your behavior has honored my name, but how can you vow to love me? You don't love me, do you Leah?"

How could she answer such a question? She loved his family, she loved her new home, but she didn't know her husband. "I could ask the same question of thee, Caleb Whitaker. Thee vowed to love, honor, and comfort me. How does thee plan to fulfill thy vows?"

Caleb couldn't meet her gaze, and Leah knew her words had hit a sore spot. "I'm sorry," she said in a low voice. "Perhaps it's best if we don't speak of such matters. I confess my pride took a beating when Uncle Abram told me he'd bartered me away like a bondservant, but the Bible teaches us pride is a barrier to the Lord's will. I've tried to humble myself and listen for the Holy Spirit's guidance."

"And what has the Holy Spirit told you so far?"

"That perhaps I am of use to thee and thy family." Leah

smiled as images of Stephen and Olivia formed in her mind. "Thy children have captured my heart. Stephen's mind is open to all the wondrous things of God's universe. He marvels at the wings of dragonflies and the swiftness of squirrels, and his questions never, never stop. Thy beautiful daughter is like a young bird, perched on the precipice of adulthood. One day she is eager to try her wings and fly toward independence; the next day she clings to her girlhood, fussing with her dolls or playing make-believe with school friends."

Caleb held out his hands, palms up. "You have indeed been of use to me and my family, and I thank you for it."

Leah looked at her husband's hands. He was clearly waiting for her to place her hands in his. "It's hardly necessary to thank me."

"And yet I do."

Leah's heart warmed at his words. She gently laid her hands on top of his, and he closed his fingers around them.

"But we still have the issue of beds to solve," Caleb said. "If you do not wish Matthew to know of our arrangement, we'll share the bed. You have no need to fear any unwanted actions on my part."

How Leah wanted to tell him she'd never been afraid of him. How she yearned to tell him she longed to be a true wife. But she couldn't. The gift of bold speech had never been one of her talents, and her tongue failed her once again. "Very well," she said meekly.

She'd gone into the bedroom, undressed, and pulled the wrapper tight against her shift. She slid under the covers and lay on her side, her face to the wall, and her muscles taut. Caleb followed a few minutes later and dimmed the oil lamp on the bedside table. As she listened to him undress in the semidarkness, her mind filled with questions she'd never ask. Did he regret marrying her? Were his few months of military service worth the sacrifice he'd made?

Caleb eased into the bed beside her, and Leah's breath caught in her throat. Every nerve stretched to feel his presence beside her.

They lay in silence, side by side, for several minutes, until Caleb whispered her name. "Leah?"

"Yes?" she whispered.

"Tell me about the farm."

She turned over and studied his profile. He lay on his back, one arm at his side, the other resting on his stomach. Neither darkness nor illness could diminish his handsomeness. His dark brows framed eyes that glistened in the soft moonlight, and his breath passed through his perfectly formed lips. He was homesick, she realized. Wistful for his family and home. She paused to gather her thoughts and sent a quick prayer heavenward. She needed the right words to comfort him.

"My favorite spot is the orchard," she began. "I put my beehives there in a shelter Joseph built, and I often go to tend the bees when they don't really need my attention."

"What is it about the orchard that attracts you?"

"The active stillness of the place."

A glint of moonlight shone on Caleb's teeth as he smiled. "What does that mean?"

"The orchard pretends to be a peaceful place, but it isn't. At dawn the birds sing a raucous chorus as they flutter through the trees, quarreling over which tree belongs to whom. In the evening, it's the insects' turn to chirp and whirr as they fight over the last scraps of food, and at night, the trees are limned in silver as they dance at the wind's command. Thy orchard is a place of promise. After the first snowfall, the trees will go dormant, protecting the forthcoming fruit as though it were King Solomon's treasure. But spring always comes. No matter how bitter the winter, spring always comes."

"And my children? Tell me more about them."

Leah conveyed a second quick prayer, waiting for the words to form in her mind before answering. "In a few years, Olivia will undoubtedly marry and begin a family of her own, but her heart will always belong to thee. How she loves thee, Caleb. 'My father is fighting in the cavalry,' she tells her friends. 'He rides better than any man in the county, and he knows everything about horses.' She yearns for thy approval as she leaves her childhood behind and becomes a woman. Stephen, however, has no such qualms. He seldom pauses to consider our approval before acting. Joseph caught him climbing the barn rafters one day, and when I asked Stephen what he'd been doing, he simply answered, 'Looking for bats.' Such curiosity and adventurousness is a blessing, I think. Thy son's bravery will serve him well as he grows into manhood."

Caleb closed his eyes and moved his hand toward Leah. Leah's heart quickened as she placed her hand in his. "Thank you, Leah." Then he rested their hands on the bed and surrendered to sleep.

Leah let happy tears fall onto her pillow. Holding her hand was such a small thing, but Leah's heart sang with hope.

Chapter 8

Leah sat at Caleb's side, counting the hours until the train pulled into Newport Station. Caleb was not yet the healthy, robust man she'd met on her wedding day, but the combination of fresh air, good food, and her honey concoctions had restored some of his strength and vigor.

She longed to see Olivia and Stephen. How their faces would glow when they saw their father again. But she dreaded giving Uncle Abram and Aunt Cynthia the news that Matthew had stayed in Washington. He'd chosen to work as an orderly at the same hospital where Caleb had convalesced, and although she carried a letter he'd written to his mother and father explaining his need to do something to help the cause, Leah knew it would be little comfort to her aunt Cynthia.

Caleb closed the book he'd been reading for the last hour and passed it to Leah.

"Finally finished?" she asked. "How was it?"

"Very good. There's an unexpected twist in the story and redemption in the end, but I'll say no more, lest I spoil it for you."

"Redemption in the end? That's a worthwhile promise. I'll start on it tonight."

Caleb stretched his arms above his head. "We'll be pulling into the Newport depot in less than an hour. I can smell it."

Leah grinned. "I didn't know thy nose had such power."

"It's the smell of rich Indiana farm land. Makes me eager to get back to the fields. I've missed the apple harvest, but there's still plenty of work that needs doing."

"I hope thee doesn't push thyself too much. Thee doesn't make a good patient."

Caleb returned her smile. "I don't?"

"No thee doesn't. Cranky. That's the word for thee."

"Humph." Caleb's mouth drew downward, as though he was considering her words. "There are worse affronts. Besides I would find it difficult to refute that description."

Leah threw her head back with laughter, and Caleb joined her.

"But didn't you enjoy some part of your trip to our nation's capital?" he asked.

"It was an adventure, I have to admit. I can't wait to tell the children we saw President Lincoln's pet goats."

Caleb shook his head slowly. "One has to wonder at the nature of our president. What type of man is prepared to wage war to keep the Union together, and yet is tenderhearted enough to keep goats as pets?"

"Does thee really believe this fighting will continue?"

"Who knows? But the Southern states show no sign of coming to their senses, so I fear our nation is headed for a true civil war."

"I'm glad thee is finished with fighting."

"Don't be so sure, Leah. I'll go back if my regiment calls me."

Leah's chest hurt with the thought of Caleb leaving again. During the past three weeks, she'd come to care for him, to appreciate his kindness, and to tolerate his impatient nature.

She placed a hand over her aching heart. "But how can thee? Thee knows what battle is like, I heard thee shouting during thy fevered dreams, yelling orders to invisible soldiers, and cursing the death of thy comrades. And thee would go back to that?"

"If I'm needed, I'll go back. I know we differ on this, Leah. Quakers are well known for their pacifist beliefs. But I'm not a Quaker."

But he was her husband, and she'd vowed to obey him. She had many more arguments against war stored in her mind, but she'd keep quiet for now. Keep quiet and pray for Caleb.

Caleb nudged her with his shoulder. "Was there anything else you enjoyed about Washington? Other than the president's goats, that is."

"The hotel was an eye-opener. So many people! The chambermaid told me the Willard had space for a thousand guests. Can thee imagine it? A thousand people in one place?" Leah shuddered at the thought.

Caleb chuckled and slid his arm across her shoulders. "Anything else, Leah?"

What was he hinting at? "The food was very good. I'd never eaten at a hotel before, but it was very appetizing."

Caleb moved closer, until his chest nudged her arm. "Wasn't there anything else you liked?" He pulled the strings of her prayer cap. "Maybe in the evenings?"

"Is thee referring to the concert we attended? That was most interesting. We Friends avoid music since it is a worldly pursuit, but I have to admit the concert was a wonderful experience."

Caleb frowned. "I'm glad you enjoyed the orchestra, but I wasn't referring to the concert." He moved closer.

What did Caleb want from her? "No?" she whispered.

"No." He caressed her jaw. "I was thinking about the nights, Leah. Lying side-by-side, whispering in the dark. Did being near me please you?"

Leah straightened her body and took a deep breath. What should she say? How could she answer him? Should she admit how difficult it'd been to stay on her side of the bed? Could she tell him she'd longed to lay her head on his shoulder and feel his arms around her?

Caleb's finger brushed her lips. "Must I speak to your uncle if I wish to renegotiate the agreement, or may I discuss the matter directly with you?"

Leah looked at him out of the corner of her eye. Did he want her to be a true wife? Was that what he meant? He was so close she could barely think. "There's no need to speak to Uncle Abram. I can speak for myself."

Caleb touched her cheek with the back of his finger. "And what do you say, Leah?"

She turned her head to look at him, but his lips were on hers before she knew what was happening. His mouth, soft and warm and tender, touched hers with exquisite gentleness, and her body sang in response. She relaxed into his embrace, and the rest of the world disappeared. There was nothing except this man, his lips and his arms, and his desire for her.

How could it be true?

Caleb pulled away, and the world rushed in where his lips had been. The matron seated behind them cleared her throat, and a wide-eyed young girl watched with interest. No one kissed in public, not even couples who'd been married for decades. What had Caleb been thinking?

Leah covered her mouth with the tips of her fingers and looked at Caleb. He was waiting for an answer. Was she ready to be a real wife? She opened her mouth to speak, but could only produce the barest of whispers. "I—"

Why had her voice failed her now?

"I—" Why could she never say the important things that needed to be said?

Caleb slid away from her. "I trust you'll let me know your answer when you have one." He removed a watch from his pocket. "We should be home in an hour or so. I think I'll stretch my legs and get some fresh air."

Leah watched him walk to the back of the car and step out onto the observation platform. Her lips still tickled from the kiss, and her heart still danced with joy, but her mind feared to believe. He hadn't wanted to marry her, but now he wanted to change their arrangement. What did that mean? She'd been wrong on her wedding day. Did she dare to hope now?

❧

Happiness surged through Leah's heart when she spotted Rose and the children at the station. Thank goodness the telegram Caleb sent from Columbus had reached them. Caleb stepped off the car and turned to help Leah do the same, but she held back. Stephen spotted his father, and she wanted to watch the reunion.

"Papa!" Stephen yelled as he tore through the crowd and threw himself around Caleb's legs.

Caleb lowered to one knee and embraced the boy.

"Oh Papa," Olivia cried as she reached the pair. "What's happened to you?"

Caleb held out one arm to include his daughter in the embrace. "I'm fine, Olivia. Just fine. Nothing a few weeks at home won't cure."

Rose came up behind the children, her hand over her mouth in obvious shock at Caleb's altered appearance. Rose's gaze found Leah. "Oh my dear," she said, holding out her arms to Leah. "Thank you for bringing our Caleb home where he belongs."

Leah descended the steps and returned the older woman's embrace. "I'm glad to be home."

"Even though you wrote of Caleb's injury and illness, I admit I'm taken aback," Rose said. "He's lost so much weight. And his beautiful black hair has begun to turn gray."

Caleb stood and embraced his aunt. "I don't want to hear another word of concern about me. I'm home, and before you know it, I'll be starting the spring planting."

Rose dabbed at her eyes with a handkerchief. "Thank the Lord for your safe return."

A woman's voice called above the crowd. "Leah?"

Leah turned to see Aunt Cynthia standing on the platform.

"Oh yes," Rose said. "I sent word to your aunt and uncle that you and Caleb would be home today."

Leah rushed into her aunt's embrace. "Oh Aunt Cynthia. It's so good to see thee."

Happy relief shone from her aunt's kind face. "Thanks be to the Lord thee has returned safely. Where is Matthew?"

Leah stepped back and looked into her aunt's eyes. "He decided to stay in the capital." Leah removed her cousin's letter from her reticule and placed it in her aunt's hand. "He's working at Seminary Hospital."

Aunt Cynthia clutched the letter to her chest and gazed questioningly at Leah. "Has he joined the army?"

"No. Fear not." Leah felt a tug on her skirt and looked down to see Stephen's ecstatic face.

"Let's go home, Leah!" Stephen said. "Joseph says he'll come back and get the baggage. Let's go!"

Leah turned to her aunt. "Matthew is fine, Aunt Cynthia. He said he'd found a way to serve his country without raising a weapon to his fellow man."

Stephen interrupted the women again. "Let's go, Leah! Papa is waiting for you."

"Thee should go with thy family," Aunt Cynthia said. "I will read my letter. No doubt I'll need time to pray about my son's decision."

Leah squeezed her aunt's hand. "Come to the house soon. I've missed thee, and I have much to talk to thee about."

Cynthia nodded and turned away while Stephen continued to tug on Leah. "I'm coming, Stephen. My goodness, thee pulls like a mule."

"Aunt Rose said the same thing," Stephen replied. "Except she said I kicked like a mule."

How like Stephen to consider the comparison a compliment. Leah laughed, took the boy's hand, and joined Caleb and the others in the surrey. As Joseph drove away from the station, Leah looked for Aunt Cynthia. She would need time to accept Matthew's decision, but at least he hadn't broken the Friends' Testament of Peace. Leah prayed he never would.

Chapter 9

Caleb's first days at home were busy ones. Well-wishers kept the parlor full from afternoon to evening, each visitor curious about Caleb's experiences. He surveyed the farm, studied the accounts, and pronounced everything better than he'd left it.

Leah hadn't missed the tinge of injured pride in his voice, but it was Rose who'd rushed to reassure him. "We managed," Rose said, "but just barely. You are needed here, Caleb, and you were sorely missed."

Upon hearing her aunt's statement, Olivia had wrapped her arms around her father's neck. "I hope you never leave again, Papa."

Caleb smiled and hugged his daughter. "Thank you, Olivia. You are growing into a beautiful young woman. The man who claims you for his wife will be most fortunate indeed."

Olivia's face had shone with pleasure. She hugged her father again and then walked to Leah's side and hugged her. "Thank you," she whispered into Leah's ear.

Leah smiled and nodded, accepting the girl's affection. Once free of her anger and pain, Olivia had become a loving child, generous and eager to please.

On Sunday Leah hurried to get the children ready to attend worship services with their father. As the children and Rose climbed into the surrey, Leah joined Joseph in the buggy.

"Where are you going?" Caleb called to her.

"To First Day meeting."

Caleb walked to the buggy. "Why not join us at our church today? It is my first Sunday back, and I'd like for all of us to go to services together."

"But Joseph and I always go to meeting together."

"Can't you miss one Sunday? Come with us, Leah. I'd like you to come."

Leah looked at Joseph. "Does thee mind?"

Joseph smiled amiably. "Course not, Miss Leah. I know the Friends will welcome me whether you're there or not."

Leah looked down at Caleb. "Thee knew I was a Friend when thee married me."

Caleb rolled his eyes, a sure sign his patience was wearing. "I'm not trying to convert you, Leah. I'd just like it if the whole family went to church together."

Why was she hesitating? There was no reason she couldn't go to the Methodist church with her new family. The Friends wouldn't criticize her, and Caleb wanted it. "All right," she said, taking the hand he offered and climbing down from the buggy.

An hour later the Whitakers arrived at the same brick building where she'd been married. The sound of singing met her ears as she climbed down from the surrey, and she realized the services had already started.

"Are we late?" she asked Caleb.

"Nothing to worry about," he answered dismissively. "There's no penalty for tardiness."

Olivia took one of Caleb's hands, and Stephen the other.

Leah and Rose walked side-by-side behind them.

How strange the service was with its music and gaily dressed women. But she was a Whitaker now, and even though she'd never discard her membership in the Society of Friends, she could find a place in her heart for Caleb's church. She missed the Quaker's silent worship and wished for a longer moment of prayer so she could quiet her mind and communicate with the Holy Spirit, but there was no denying the joy she saw on the faces of the congregation as they praised the Lord.

When the service ended, many of Caleb's friends crowded around him. "Good to have you home," a bald man said, shaking Caleb's hand so vigorously Leah was sure she saw Caleb wince. "You showed those Rebs," another man said, clapping Caleb on the back. An older woman wearing a tiny bonnet with an enormous feather pulled Caleb's head to her bosom. "Oh my word, Caleb Whitaker. I thank the good Lord every day for your safe return." At least Caleb had the good manners to blush as he pulled away from her improper embrace.

Leah watched the exchanges with patient forbearance until a younger woman dressed in black approached. Her pale complexion and graceful manner reminded Leah of a swan on a placid lake. Her blond hair curled under a beribboned velvet cap.

Caleb bowed slightly as he took the hand she offered. "Good morning, Lucinda."

"It is a good morning now that I see you," the woman answered, "but no day is good since I lost my Richard."

"My deepest sympathy for your loss," Caleb said, "but you are looking well."

The petite woman stepped closer to Caleb, dipped her head, and looked up at him with wide green eyes. "Thank you. Your family is so fortunate to have you back. I am quite alone now, with no one to look after me."

An invisible hand tightened around Leah's throat. Was that woman actually flirting with Caleb? Leah crossed her arms in front of her chest and narrowed her eyes.

"I am always at your service, Lucinda. You merely need to call, and I will come."

Had she heard correctly? Had Caleb responded with his own flirtation? Acid rose in Leah's throat.

Lucinda's voice was soft and feminine, with a musical lilt women usually reserved for talking to babies. "How gallant you are, Caleb. I heard you were wounded, but I don't see any change in you at all. You're still as handsome and fit as ever."

Caleb smiled politely. "Thank you, Lucinda."

That was too much. Leah wouldn't stand by while her husband spoke so inappropriately to another woman! But before she could break up the pair, Reverend Harrison interrupted them.

"Caleb Whitaker, finally home and back in the bosom of your loving family," the minister said. "Thank the Lord."

Caleb shook the minister's hand. "Thank you, Reverend Harrison. It's good to be home. I was just telling Lucinda how nice it is to see her again."

Leah could stand no more. She turned away from the crowd and marched out of the church. Anger lurched in her stomach as she recalled Caleb's words. "All she has to do is call, and he'll come running," she muttered through clenched teeth, "like a puppy to a bowl of milk."

Had Caleb forgotten he was a married man? It might not be much of a marriage, but he had freely spoken the vows. He was bound to her. He had no right to engage in such talk with another woman.

"Leah!" Stephen ran to her side. "What are you doing out here by yourself? Mrs. Harrison has invited us for coffee and cake. I'm supposed to bring you back."

The anger jumped from her stomach to her chest, causing Leah to fight for breath. "Thee should go back inside," she instructed the boy. "I'll be there shortly."

Stephen squinted at Leah, as though he sensed something was wrong. But Leah knew where the five-year-old's loyalties lay. "Thy cake is waiting."

Stephen ran back toward the church. "Hurry up, Leah," he called over his shoulder, "or there might not be a piece for you."

If only Leah could calm herself, she'd be able to join the family. But how did one calm the kind of anger Leah felt? It was a once-in-a-lifetime kind of anger, the type that erupted from deep wells of disappointment and rejection. Leah's outrage was hot with spite and prickly with indignation.

Leah paced the length of the walkway in front of the church, trying to soothe her anger. But the rage wouldn't subside.

She was the one who'd traveled to Washington to rescue Caleb from that horrible hospital. She was the one who'd stayed up night after night to nurse him. And yet all of Caleb's attention had been for the beautiful Lucinda. He hadn't even bothered to introduce his wife to the woman.

Beauty. Leah wanted to spit the word into the dusty road. Lucinda had it. Blond ringlets and moss-green eyes, porcelain skin and peony-pink lips. Leah imagined rubbing mud into the woman's perfect face.

What was wrong with her? She knew what the Bible said about anger: "The wrath of man worketh not the righteousness of God." Yet there she was, allowing rage to blind her.

Leah looked at the church and pictured Caleb and the children enjoying a cozy repast with Lucinda. Caleb probably wished he hadn't rushed to marry Leah, now that the lovely Lucinda was available. Olivia would have certainly preferred the fancy Lucinda to plain Leah.

Perhaps Leah should march into that church and make it clear Caleb belonged to her. She was his wife whether he liked it or not.

Sharp pain pierced Leah's heart as that thought took root. She was Caleb's wife whether he liked it or not.

And he probably didn't like it.

Like a swollen stream seeping its way upward, Leah's anger finally reached her eyes. Hot tears of fury streamed down her face. She'd never be able to calm herself now. It would be better for everyone if she simply left.

Without another thought, she turned on her heel and marched down the dirt road away from Caleb Whitaker and his family.

With each step her anger vacillated between righteous indignation and self-censure. Who was she to rage against her circumstances? She'd agreed to the marriage, hadn't she? And it wasn't a bad life. She had a home and children who loved her. Some women had much less.

But hadn't she earned her keep? She'd cooked and cleaned, mended Stephen's clothing and sewn new dresses for Olivia, and once the honey harvest was complete, she'd add to her new family's finances. Hadn't she earned even a little respect?

Apparently not. All it had taken was a wink from a pretty woman, and Caleb had discounted everything she'd done. Well fine. Leah wouldn't beg for his esteem.

A horse approached her from behind, and Leah moved to

the edge of the roadside to give the rider space to pass, but the hoofbeats slowed to a stop.

A familiar voice called to her. "Leah, where are you going?"

She whirled. Caleb sat atop a bay horse, a puzzled look on his face. "Whose horse is that?"

"Reverend Harrison's." Caleb twisted in the saddle so that he could see her better. "I repeat, where are you going?"

Leah wiped the tears from her face. "Home."

"That's over five miles from here. Awfully far to walk when there's a perfectly good surrey waiting for you."

As if she'd simply sit in his surrey and wait for him to finish his coffee and cake. "Won't Lucinda be missing thee about now? Hurry back, Caleb, and perhaps she'll let thee drive her home."

Caleb dismounted and stood in front of her, frowning. "Lucinda's not at the church. She went home with her parents."

"Oh really? Is she waiting for thee there?"

"I don't think so." Caleb cocked his head, as though trying to solve a particularly onerous problem, and then smiled broadly. "Why, Leah Wall. You're jealous."

"My name is Leah Whitaker!" she shouted. "Whitaker! In case thee has forgotten, thee is a married man!"

Caleb drew back, as though slapped by her words. "I know I'm a married man. I'm here at your side, aren't I?"

"But thee doesn't want to be, does thee? Thee would rather be at Lucinda's side."

"That silly girl? I'd sooner spend the day having a tea party with Olivia's dolls than spend an hour with Lucinda."

"Thee said, 'Call me, and I'll be there.'"

Caleb shrugged one shoulder. "What else was I supposed to say? Don't call on me?"

Leah blew out a breath and considered Caleb's words.

Lucinda had been flirting. There was no denying it. But maybe Leah had overreacted to Caleb's words. She eyed her husband with guarded relief. "She is a beautiful woman."

"She's pretty enough, but she's not a woman. She'll always be a needy little girl who gets what she wants through trickery and flirtation. I've never been interested in her."

"Never?"

"Never. Lucinda's older sister was a friend to my late wife, and I know firsthand just how devious Lucinda can be. What I want in a wife is someone I can rely on. Not someone I have to rescue every day."

Leah looked at the dirt road. Confusion mixed with shame as she considered the words she'd shouted at her husband. She'd been taught God's holy light lived within her, but where was her inner light now? Buried under anger and resentment.

Caleb shifted his weight and glanced down the road. "Now, if you're feeling better, will you return to the church so we can all drive home together?"

She should accept Caleb's invitation. He wasn't an insincere man and wouldn't have offered unless he truly wanted her to return with him. But Leah's anger emboldened her. It was time to raise the question she'd been afraid to ask. "If thee wishes it, I'll agree to an annulment. We haven't consummated our marriage, and I won't hold thee to the agreement thee made with my uncle. Since thee returned much sooner than originally planned, I'll understand if thee wishes to put our marriage aside."

Caleb took a few steps away from her, stared at the ground, and returned. "What about you? Will you return to your uncle's farm?"

"I wasn't wanted there. I'll find a place to work, perhaps as a nurse to a widow, or as a housekeeper. I will make my way."

Caleb stepped closer to Leah. "Do you want to end our marriage?"

Her tears flowed again as Leah considered the pain of leaving Caleb and his children. She shook her head. "No, but I don't want to be pitied. I know I'm not pretty. I know I'm not what a man wants."

"Why do you think that, Leah?"

Leah's voice broke as she revealed her long-hidden sorrow. "No one has ever wanted me. My mother loved me, but even she knew I was too plain to be chosen as a bride."

"Did she say that to you?"

"She didn't have to. When other girls planned for marriage, my mother taught me how to keep bees. She knew I'd have to make my own way in the world."

Caleb retrieved a handkerchief from his breast pocket. "Wipe your eyes, Leah."

She took it from him and did as he instructed.

Caleb stood beside her until her sobs abated. "There's a stream just beyond that rise," he said. "Let's go and sit awhile."

"Why?"

"Because I have some things to say to you, and I don't want to say them in the middle of the road."

Here it comes, Leah thought as she trudged behind Caleb, her head hanging down like a withered tulip. *My day of reckoning has finally arrived.*

Caleb tied the horse to a branch, took the handkerchief from Leah, and wet it in the stream. "Sit down," he said. "The bank is dry."

Leah lowered herself to the leaf-covered slope and wiped her face on her sleeve.

"Here," Caleb said, "let me clean your face."

A gasp of surprise escaped Leah's lips as he gently applied the cool, damp handkerchief to her cheeks. "Take a deep breath, and let it out."

She did as he asked, but her breath caught on sobs.

"Again." He sat beside her, his arms resting on his knees.

She breathed deeply and looked at her surroundings. The autumn sun shone through scarlet-leaved maples, illuminating the bank with dappled light.

"You are quieter now," Caleb said. "There's nothing scares me more than an angry woman."

Leah smiled in spite of her distress. "Thee has battled Confederate soldiers, but an angry woman scares thee?"

"Oh yes. You see, I don't care what a Reb thinks of me, but I do care what you think of me." Caleb watched her for a few seconds then ran his hand through his hair and turned to face her. "It's true I didn't have marriage in mind when I spoke to your uncle. But when he suggested it, I saw no reason to object."

"Thee didn't want a wife."

"Not then." Caleb must have seen the pain that flit through Leah's heart, because he hastily added, "But I changed my mind."

Leah's breath eased. "Thee did? When?"

"The first time I saw you. I don't know who told you that you were plain, Leah, but they lied."

Leah's eyes widened with disbelief. Everyone had remarked on her plain looks. Everyone.

"You have a lovely face," Caleb said. "Deep brown eyes that twinkle with good humor and intelligence, and wide lips that are quick to smile. Your body puts me in mind of a young doe, eager to spring into action at the slightest sign of danger. You're strong in both body and mind. A woman like you is equal to any task."

How could it be true? Caleb actually thought her pretty.

"I walked into Reverend Harrison's study that morning expecting to see a timid spinster. Instead I found a strikingly beautiful woman whose bravery matched my own."

The ache beneath Leah's heart subsided. "Why—why didn't thee consummate our marriage?"

"I told you. It was my agreement with your uncle not to take advantage of you. But as you may recall, I recently requested a change to that arrangement."

On the train, Leah recalled. He'd kissed her and asked permission to share the marriage bed. "I forgot," Leah murmured.

"Forgot?" Caleb's voice was ripe with disbelief. "You forgot?"

Leah smiled at his exasperated tone. "I mean, I didn't forget thy kiss. But when I got so angry, I forgot thee had made that request."

"I assume you're still considering it," Caleb said.

Leah nodded and smiled at her husband. Of course she'd take him as her husband. It was what she'd wanted from the day Uncle Abram had told her of her marriage. But her answer could wait until tonight. Leah rested her head on her knees, suddenly exhausted by her fluctuating emotions. Caleb's words had dissolved her anger and sorrow. Now joyous hope began to grow in her heart.

"Many years ago," Caleb said, "when arranged marriages were typical, the honeymoon was a time when the newly married couple would get to know one another. In a strange way, I think my convalescence in Washington was our honeymoon."

"We certainly spent a lot of time together."

"You were a wonderful nurse. If you hadn't come, who

knows what would have happened to me."

"It was the juice from the radish leaves," Leah said. "Plus the honey."

"If you say so," Caleb allowed. "But it was much more than your medicinals that made me well, Leah. It was you."

Leah raised her eyebrows in question.

"You talked to me," Caleb explained, "and sustained me. I was lonely, and you kept me company. I was fretful, and you eased my worry. Even if you don't love me, you treat me in a very loving way. I am most fortunate to have you in my life."

Tears formed in her eyes once again.

"My word, woman," Caleb said as he passed the damp handkerchief to her. "What have I said to upset you?"

"Nothing," Leah said between sniffles. "Nothing at all." She sprang from her position, wrapped her arms around her husband's neck, and kissed his mouth as the salty tears fell down her cheeks.

Caleb drew her closer and returned her kiss. "Being married to you is more than just a stroke of luck, Leah. The Lord blessed me when He arranged for you to be my wife. I've come to love you very much."

Leah laid her head on his shoulder, enjoying the strength of his embrace. "I love thee, Caleb. Thank thee for choosing me."

Caleb kissed her again. "If I weren't already married to you, I'd propose."

Leah kissed him. "If I weren't already married, I'd accept."

Caleb gently placed his hands on her cheeks and looked into her eyes. "Leah Wall, will you marry me? Will you give me more children and live with me until the Lord calls us home?"

Leah's soul overflowed with joy. Her years of aching

emptiness faded as Caleb's words sank into her heart. "I'll marry thee, Caleb Whitaker, and I'll be a mother to thy children. All of them. I may not have loved thee when we married, but I do so love thee now."

Epilogue

Caleb smiled down at Leah from the cherry tree. "Ready for another basket?"

Leah shielded her eyes from the April sun and looked up at her husband. "Send it down, and I'll add it to the others."

A basket tied to a rope descended from the branches. Leah untied the knot and set the basket on the ground. "That's two bushels of cherries from this one tree."

"And more to come," Caleb said, climbing down the ladder. "It's been a good year for cherries." A bee flew lazily around Caleb's head; he swatted it away.

"Don't hurt my bee," Leah scolded, reaching for his hand. "Thee wouldn't have so many cherries if my bees hadn't done their job."

"Not to mention the honey I enjoy every morning on Delia's biscuits." Caleb laid a hand on Leah's rounded abdomen. "How's my son today?"

Leah covered his hand with hers. "Thy daughter is doing quite well. She's pushing against my ribs with the strength of an ox."

Caleb kissed her forehead. "No daughter would be so strong. It must be a boy."

Leah wrapped her arms around his waist and nestled her head on his chest. "Thee doesn't really care if it's a girl, does thee?"

Caleb pulled her closer. "Of course not. But think of poor Stephen. Two sisters to boss him around hardly seems fair." The baby pushed against Leah's ribs with such force that Caleb felt it. "I see what you mean about the little ox," he said. "Stay in your warm cocoon, little one," he said to Leah's stomach. "It's not yet time to greet the world."

Leah ran her hand through her husband's dark hair. "I love thee."

Caleb straightened and held Leah's face in his calloused hands. "And I love you." He kissed her brow. "I will love you until my dying day." He kissed her cheek. "And I will kiss you until all my kisses have been used up." He kissed her lips.

Leah's heart soared as she sent up another prayer of gratitude, her fourth one that day. The Lord had made her wait, preparing her to be a wife and mother, but at last, the secret desires of her heart had been fulfilled.

After many years of writing and publishing in the nonfiction world of academia, CLAIRE SANDERS turned her energy, humor, and creativity toward the production of compelling romantic fiction. Claire lives in the greater Houston area with her daughter and two well-loved dogs. When she isn't writing, you'll find her cooking, gardening, and dreaming of places to travel.

NEW GARDEN'S CONVERSION

by Susette Williams

Dedication

I can't thank God enough for blessing me with such a
wonderful, supportive family, and for allowing me to
pursue the gifts He has given me. I also want to thank
my agent, Terry Burns, and Becky for giving me the
opportunity to work with Barbour. My copyeditor, Vicki,
was fabulous to work with. Special thanks to my friends
and family who offered input, the critique partners who
helped along the way, and to you, the reader,
for continuing to support Christian authors.
May God bless each and every one of you.

Chapter 1

Present Day
Porter County, Indiana

Jaidon Taylor's heart pounded in his chest as he briskly strode into the hospital. Concern coursed through his veins to his inner being. *Lord, please don't let him be dead.* The fluorescent lights brightened the ER waiting room but did nothing to lift the spirits of those within the four walls. A frail, elderly woman coughed violently. Jaidon tensed at the hacking sound she made. He glanced around the room, looking for a familiar face that could give him answers. Numerous family members and friends of D–Dog filled a third of the room.

Why would anyone shoot D–Dog? Could it have been a random act of violence? Or was it someone from the gang D–Dog ran with before? Jaidon tried to do all he could to keep things like this from happening. It was why he got involved with the Porter County Youth Center. He spotted his friend, Kacey Carpenter, the director from the youth center, heading toward him. "Is he alive?"

Kacey nodded. "Yes." He gripped Jaidon's shoulder reassuringly as he shook his hand. "Thanks for coming. He just came out of surgery. The doctor said D–Dog is going to be fine," Kacey said. "It wasn't as bad as the kids made it out to be. They saw all the blood and panicked."

Before he could respond, D–Dog's ex-girlfriend Tanesha ran up and threw her arms around Jaidon. Tears streamed down her cheeks. Her short, coarse curls brushed against his chin. "Mr. Taylor, I told D–Dog to stay away—I told him Bruno would kill him."

Jaidon embraced the teen. "You need to stay away from Bruno, too."

"I know, Mr. Taylor." Tanesha sniffed. "But getting away from Bruno ain't as easy as it seems."

How could he console and guide the teenage girl? Jaidon wished they had more women working at the youth center. Unfortunately most women didn't want to go into the area where the center was located. However, right now Tanesha and the other girls needed a woman to talk with to help them see that gangs and gang leaders like Bruno were a bad choice of friends. True friends didn't ask you to go with them when they shot or robbed someone. That's the kind of "friend" you could expect to find in a gang. He'd been trying to help teach the youth that Jesus would be their friend and go with them. He would guide them on their way and help them avoid temptation. He would also help them find peace and a life away from drugs and violence.

"You know D–Dog has made an effort to change. You can, too," Jaidon said. D–Dog had started coming to the youth center a little over a month ago. Tanesha came a couple times, but couldn't resist the pull of the gang. She broke up with D–Dog. Shortly afterward Bruno chose her to be his girl. It rivaled the equivalent of being chosen as Prom Queen—for the girls who actually stayed in school. The only reason some of the kids in gangs went to high school was to access their market— other youth to sell drugs to.

"I want to, but Bruno won't let me." Fresh tears rolled down Tanesha's cheeks.

"If you want to get away from Bruno, we'll help you," Jaidon said. How, he didn't know.

"You can't help me. No one can." Tanesha shook her head violently. "You see what Bruno did to D–Dog when he tried to get out of the gang. I'm Bruno's girl whether or not I want to be." Tanesha pushed away from Jaidon. Fresh tears streamed down her face. She ran toward the doors and out of the hospital.

⁓

Catherine Wall helped Daryl Jones get situated in his hospital bed after they brought him up from the operating room. She placed a pillow behind his head and another one behind his injured shoulder to make him more comfortable. "If you need pain medication you can push this button." She showed him the button in question and clipped it close enough for him to reach.

A pleasantly plump, dark-skinned woman with tear-stained cheeks bustled into the room, three small children in tow. "Daryl, you know I told you to avoid that gang."

"I know, but—"

"But nothin'." The woman's hands went to her hips, and her head bobbed from side to side as she spoke. "You had me worried. Here I thought my baby was lying dead in the streets. You wanna worry your momma like that?" She didn't give him time to respond. "You stay away from Bruno and that Jezebel, Tanesha. She ain't gonna do nothin' but get you in trouble, boy."

Catherine hooked up Daryl's new IV and checked his pulse. The muscles in his forearm were tense. "Ma'am, we need to keep the patient calm. He's still recovering from surgery." His mother nodded and drew the smallest of the three children with her closer to her side.

Catherine offered a faint, reassuring smile as she laid Daryl's arm back down on the bed. "If you need anything, just press the call button on the remote."

Daryl nodded briefly.

She hated violence. It went against everything her Quaker heritage taught her. Catherine wished she could share more of her faith with her patients. Didn't they see how they were harming others and themselves? She glanced at Daryl as she left his hospital room—and collided with something solid—another visitor. His arms steadied her.

"I'm sorry." Catherine inhaled a woodsy, exotic scent. Her arms pressed against his medium-blue dress shirt. Her eyes focused on his striped, color-coordinated tie. He was clean shaven, obviously a professional. What kind, she couldn't surmise. Not the type of person she would have expected to be coming to see a gang member. She looked up and peered into the depths of the bluest eyes she'd ever seen. "I'm. . .sorry." She gently pushed away from him.

He continued to hold on to her right arm. "Excuse me, Miss—" He glanced at her name tag. "Catherine. A friend of ours just came from surgery. I think this may be his room."

"What is your friend's name?"

"D–Dog," the man holding her arm said.

"Daryl Jones," someone else replied.

Catherine looked over at the other two men standing nearby. She'd been so distracted by the man next to her that she hadn't noticed them. She glanced back at the man holding her arm. He released his grip. The other two wore workout clothing. All three of them appeared to be harmless. Given that the patient they were inquiring about had just been shot, the hospital stayed on high alert in case someone wanted to come and finish the job.

"This is his room. His family is in with him right now." She moved aside.

"Thank you." He continued to stare at her; neither of them had moved more than a foot apart. "My name is Jaidon Taylor."

Catherine shook his extended hand. "Nice to meet you."

"We work at the youth center. That's where we met Daryl," Jaidon said.

Catherine nodded. "Doesn't seem he's made some very good friends."

Jaidon laughed and ran a hand through his nicely trimmed brown hair. "No it doesn't."

Her cheeks warmed. "I'm sorry. That didn't sound right. What I meant was, it would be good if the youth center could help."

Jaidon smiled. "That's why we've been trying to get him and other youth involved in the center. We want to give them positive role models and help keep them off the street and out of gangs."

❧

Two days later Jaidon stood in front of a group of around two dozen youth at the old, dilapidated center. "Violence has never solved anything. In Psalms it says, 'His mischief shall return upon his own head, and his violent dealing shall come down upon his own pate.' And in Romans 12:19, it says, 'Dearly beloved, avenge not yourselves, but rather give place unto wrath: for it is written, Vengeance is mine; I will repay, saith the Lord.'"

"You trying to tell us we ain't got any right to settle the score?" Romeo, D–Dog's friend, asked.

Light blue hospital attire moving toward the group caught

Jaidon's attention. Wavy brunette hair and a gentle smile. Catherine. The nurse from the hospital. His heart raced. What was she doing here? Jaidon couldn't stop and ask her. He needed to finish speaking to the youth. The center's staff needed to squelch any acts of retaliation before they happened. "No, trying to settle the score will only escalate matters, and next time instead of someone ending up in the hospital, we'll be attending a funeral."

"Yeah, Bruno's," a youth said.

"So you shoot Bruno, and then members of his gang come after you, but instead of getting you, they shoot up your home, and your mother or your little sister gets killed." Jaidon clenched his fist. "Do you really think it's going to just end there?"

They were silent. He could see the frustration in their eyes, the pursed lips and agitation in each kid's stance.

"Trust God to take care of things. He can handle this situation better than any of us can. He can calm the anxiousness you feel." Jaidon ushered up a silent prayer to calm his own anxiety. "Why don't we take a few moments and pray?"

The volunteers helped to split up the teens into small groups and prayed with them. For the next half hour, as he talked and prayed with his group, he forgot about Catherine until he looked around to see how the other groups were doing. He spotted Catherine with a group of girls and the youth pastor's wife, Josephina. Their group was still chatting. Should he join them? Or would he be a distraction?

Catherine smiled, her hazel eyes glistening, when she talked with the girls. She listened and interacted intently, readily engaging in conversation with the group. Josephina and the girls included her in their conversation. Who would have guessed this was the first time Catherine had ever been to the center? Was it possible she was an answer to his prayer?

Chapter 2

After the prayer groups broke up, the youth joined in their regular activities—playing basketball, socializing, or taking advantage of the tutoring assistance available to them at the center. While the youth gravitated toward their own cliques or activities, Jaidon took the opportunity to introduce Catherine to the staff. "This is Josephina's husband, Roberto."

Roberto shook hands with Catherine. "It's nice to meet you."

"Likewise." Catherine's genuine smile captivated Jaidon.

"He's also the youth pastor at the church several of us attend." Jaidon directed his attention to the other three people standing around in the circle with them. "This is Nathan and Ariannah. They are both youth sponsors at our church. You may remember seeing Kacey at the hospital. He is the director of the youth center."

Ariannah tilted her head and studied Catherine. "So what brings you to the center?" Jaidon thought her tone of voice and pursed lips belied a teenaged attitude. But why? Maybe Ariannah was tired or had a paper due the next day. He knew college demanded a lot of effort, especially if students like Ariannah wanted to keep up their grades and maintain their honors scholarships.

Catherine's eyes glimmered when she smiled wider. She didn't seem the least bit taken aback by Ariannah's straightforwardness. "Daryl told me great things about the program and all the people that have been helped through peer mentoring. It sounds like an organization that I want to be part of."

Roberto and Kacey's eyes lit up as smiles creased their faces. Jaidon couldn't deny part of him was equally happy, if not happier, as the others were to have another woman come to help at the center. Ariannah had recently turned twenty, and while she was a sponsor, she served as a peer mentor since she wasn't much older than the girls or youth at the center. She wasn't someone who'd yet garnished enough life lessons to counsel teens on a deeper level. This left Josephina as the only experienced woman who could offer sound advice. As much as he wanted Catherine there, one thought plagued him. "You do realize this is. . .um, not as safe an area as it should be? Perhaps on days you are available, you could ride with me—or our church group?"

Way to go, Taylor, he mentally chastised himself. *Now scuff your sneaker tip across the floor while you talk, and you could be back in high school again asking Suzie out on a date.* Jaidon had dated several women since then, but none, other than Catherine, made him feel like an awkward teenager with a crush. Although his stomach skittered with excitement, he liked feeling the heady emotions.

"Jaidon?" Roberto backslapped his arm playfully. "You listening?"

"Huh?" Jaidon looked at Roberto and then the others. He hadn't realized he'd been staring at Catherine, lost in his thoughts. His cheeks warmed. "I'm sorry."

Roberto chuckled. "I said at first I thought you were trying to discourage Catherine from coming to help. We didn't want you to run her off."

Catherine laughed. "I don't scare that easily. And yes, I would like to ride with your group if it isn't an inconvenience."

"No inconvenience at all." Jaidon would gladly bring her himself if they didn't have room in the car. That way they'd have time alone together and could get to know each other.

"What church do you go to?" Ariannah asked.

Catherine's eyes narrowed momentarily. Was she hesitant to answer? Maybe she didn't go to church. His heart sank.

"I go to. . .New Garden Fellowship." Catherine's chin jutted up a fraction.

"So you're a Christian?" Relief flooded Jaidon.

"A Quaker," Catherine said. "As was my father, and his father before him, and so forth. Dating back a couple hundred years."

Jaidon perused her attire. She didn't dress weird. Although the only clothes he'd seen her in were hospital or medical-office-type attire. Maybe she dressed differently in her free time. Her wavy brunette hair flowed just beneath her shoulders. She didn't wear it in a bun. "Aren't Quakers Christians?"

Catherine shrugged. "That depends on who you ask. Not all Quakers consider themselves Christians."

Weren't Quakers up there with the Amish? More devout, didn't have TVs and such, focused more on spirituality and less on worldly things? Jaidon could deal with that. Catherine would be less likely to want to rush home to watch her favorite sitcoms—or expect him to watch them with her—like Kaeli. Chick flicks and reality shows hadn't ruined their relationship. Kaeli didn't share in his desire to help others. Her outlook on doing things for the needy or reaching out to underprivileged children could be summed up: God helps those who help themselves.

Catherine possessed a giving and caring heart, which was

evident by the profession she'd chosen and by the fact that she showed up at the youth center to volunteer all because a patient had told her about their work.

"We're very fortunate to have you," Jaidon said.

❦

While the other volunteers mingled with the youth, Josephina talked with Catherine longer and explained more about the center and when their church group came together to the center to volunteer. She liked the thought of riding with them, if for nothing else, for the companionship.

Catherine wanted to get to know some of the youth at the center. After all, she was there to help. So far she'd interacted most with the sponsors, though she'd had some insight into a few of the teens during prayer-group time. She'd felt their angst, fear, and frustration at having a friend shot. She wanted to help them find peace and an alternative to a violent lifestyle.

Catherine drew closer to a group gathered on the bleachers next to the basketball court and overheard Rosie say, "I had Quaker cereal for breakfast this morning."

She hadn't told Rosie she was a Quaker. Why would a teen be discussing their breakfast when it was way past dinnertime? Ariannah had obviously said something. What was it with youth and drama? Was Ariannah trying to get under Catherine's skin on purpose? She learned a long time ago that getting upset or offended at the jokes people made didn't help. Catherine took offhanded comments in stride and tried to use the opportunity to her advantage. "That's funny. I'm a Quaker and ate cereal this morning, too."

All except Ariannah laughed; her cheeks flushed. Catherine sighed. Ariannah was a Christian. Why would she talk about her, and obviously in an unflattering way? Didn't Christians profess to show the love of God?

"Exactly what is a Quaker?" Rosie asked. "The only thing I've ever seen was the guy in the funny hat on the box." Rosie gave her a quick once-over glance. "You don't dress like him, do you?"

Catherine couldn't help but smile. "No, but his clothing was fashioned after early Quaker attire. Some Quakers still dress that way. But the reason the company decided to use the Quaker garb and name was because it symbolized good quality and honest value."

More youth began to gather around them. One of the guys said, "I still don't understand what a Quaker is."

"Do you ride in a horse and buggy?" another guy asked.

A girl standing next to him jabbed him in the side with her elbow and rolled her eyes at him. "You got here *after* she did? Did you see a horse and buggy outside when you came in?"

He rubbed his side and shook his head.

"You're thinking of the Amish," she said.

"Oh," he replied.

Their inquisitiveness was refreshing. It was definitely a better alternative to the raised eyebrows and standoffish behavior she normally encountered when she shared her beliefs with others. "Maybe this will help you. Think of different denominations of religions. For example, you have Catholic, Baptist, Methodist, or even other faiths." Catherine could tell they were following along by the nods of heads. It was hard for her to explain how different their beliefs were. It was part of her heritage. Not something she could ever deny. Thus far she'd only found one way to explain it to non-Quakers to help them to somewhat understand. "A Quaker is more like a different denomination or belief. Ours is more of a spiritual search in order to connect with God and follow His leading."

"So you felt *led* to come here?" Ariannah frowned.

"Yes." Catherine didn't know why, but she sensed the young woman didn't like her by her tone and the way she'd looked at her all evening. "We believe all humans are inherently good." Catherine reminded herself that included Ariannah, no matter what ill feelings Ariannah harbored toward her.

Ariannah glanced over at Rosie, rolled her eyes, and flipped a couple strands of long blond hair over her shoulder.

"Therefore everyone should be given a chance." If lucky, Ariannah would give her a chance as well. Catherine took a deep breath to relax. She would never reach the youth if she let frustration get the best of her. She continued, "William Penn wrote, 'True godliness does not turn men out of the world, but enables them to live better in it and excites their endeavors to mend it.' We can do that by reaching out and helping others."

Somehow she would find a way to help Ariannah as well. Whatever the reason the younger youth sponsor didn't like her, she'd try and make a friend of her.

"You don't have to be a Quaker to help others," Ariannah said. "This center is here because of Christians reaching out to help youth find alternatives to gang violence."

"Yeah, thanks for giving your time," one of the guys said to Ariannah. "If you really want to help, you could go out with me Friday night."

"I'm not even going to dignify that with a response." Ariannah crossed her arms in front of her. The movement effectively blocked the text on her black T-shirt that reflected, REACHING THE LOST.

Catherine debated telling Ariannah that Christianity wasn't the only religion to want to bring about peace. Quakers had won the Nobel Peace Prize, but chances were that telling her would only lead to more confrontation.

"We're very thankful to have all the volunteers we can get," Kacey said.

Catherine almost jumped. She hadn't realized Kacey and Jaidon had joined their group, or that they were standing so close behind her. How much of the conversation had they heard? If the scrunched eyebrows and frown on Jaidon's face were any indication, he'd heard enough. Hopefully he hadn't misinterpreted her comments. She in no way meant to sound like Quakers were better. The youth were inquisitive, and her only desire was to enlighten them.

"It's getting late. Time for us to wrap things up for the night. How about you guys put away the gym equipment, and you girls can help Josephina." Jaidon motioned Catherine in the direction away from the others. "Come on. I'll walk you out."

Catherine swallowed the lump in her throat as she walked outside with Jaidon. Did this mean they didn't need her help? Kasey had said they were thankful for all the volunteers they could get, so maybe they weren't dismissing her. Maybe they were giving her a warning. "I'm sorry. I shouldn't have—"

"What are you sorry for?" The street light barely illuminated Jaidon's face. She couldn't read his expression. "Ariannah is. . .a zealous youth. She means well." Jaidon sighed. "Don't let her get under your skin."

"I won't." Which was a lie. She already had. Catherine wished she knew how to convince Ariannah they were on the same side. They both wanted to help at the center and make a difference in other people's lives.

"So—you'll be back?"

Catherine thought about it a moment. Spending her

evenings with her Siamese cat held some appeal, but not on a routine basis. She liked helping others. The youth seemed interested in hearing what she had to say. Giving up before she really got started wouldn't help anyone. "Yes. I'll be back."

"Excellent. How about I pick you up Thursday evening, if you're available, and we can ride together," Jaidon said. "That way I make sure you get home safely."

"Sounds good." Catherine smiled. "What about the rest of the group?"

"They'll ride together in another car." Jaidon had a welcoming air about him. Perhaps it was his sincere blue eyes, his easygoing attitude, or maybe even his reassuring smile. It was nice that he was considerate enough to want to look out for her.

She gave Jaidon her phone number. When she started toward her car, he reached for her arm to stop her. "Did you need something else?"

"About earlier tonight." Jaidon let go of her arm. "I just wanted to say thank you again, and tell you not to mind Ariannah. It doesn't matter that you're a Quaker. Actually if you think about it, we're a lot alike."

Catherine shook her head. "Not really."

Jaidon frowned. "What do you mean?"

"We both come from very different upbringings. My beliefs are an integral part of my life and a big determinant in the decisions I make for my future." Catherine sighed. "But aside from our religious beliefs, yes, I guess we are a lot alike. We both want to help youth stay out of trouble and make better decisions for their lives."

Chapter 3

Jaidon pulled into the parking lot at the newer apartment complex that Catherine lived in. He scrolled through his text messages to find her text so he could verify her address and apartment number.

He'd given their previous conversation a lot of thought. Thought that kept him up the last two nights. How could he help Catherine see they weren't that different? He needed to give her time to get to know him, see their similarities, and realize they both loved the Lord. The desire to help youth was only one of the *evident* things they shared in common. With time and patience, she would come to see his convictions. Now if only he could be patient.

Jaidon climbed out of his yellow Hummer. Catherine came down the sidewalk. It was refreshing to see her in street clothes. She wore a dark blue T-shirt under her light jacket, and sweats. Her hair pulled back in a ponytail looked practical, but he preferred it cascading down over her shoulders.

So much for being the gentleman and meeting her at the door. He opened the passenger door for her to climb in. "It's nice to see you again."

"You, too." Catherine smiled, climbed in, and buckled up

as he closed the car door. He slid into the driver's seat and did the same.

"I'm curious," Catherine said. "You have a really nice vehicle. Aren't you afraid someone will steal your Hummer when you're at the youth center?"

"I debated whether or not to buy an older, less expensive vehicle, but then it's almost pointless to leave the Hummer sitting idle while I drive the other one. Unfortunately I bought this one previous to volunteering at the center, and definitely before gas prices skyrocketed." Jaidon laughed. "And to be honest, why do you think I got a bright yellow one? If anybody steals it, it's kind of hard to miss going down the road."

"I guess it would be." Catherine chuckled.

His heart quickened at the tune of her laughter. He had so many things to learn and discover about the woman sitting next to him. "Tell me about yourself."

She blinked a couple times. Catherine opened her mouth and then closed it, almost as if she didn't know what to say. Her expression grew somewhat reserved. "What do you want to know?"

"Everything—nothing. I don't know." Jaidon shrugged. Did all her relatives have beautiful hazel eyes like magnets that had the ability to captivate you without warning? He cleared his throat. "Tell me about your family." After all, he hoped to meet them one day, and with any luck, it would be soon.

"Well I have an older brother who is married. They are expecting their third child in June. My mother is a junior high math teacher." A smile creased her lips when she talked about her family. That was a good sign—happy memories associated with them. "I take after her more than my father."

"What does your father do?" Jaidon asked. When Catherine

didn't answer immediately, he glanced back at her. She was the one who'd brought her father up in the first place. Her tone didn't sound negative when she compared herself to either parent.

Catherine wrung her hands together and stared at them before she finally looked back at Jaidon. "He passed away when I was fourteen. Cancer."

"I'm sorry." Jaidon reached over and clasped her hands in his free one. "I didn't mean to upset you."

"It's not your fault. His birthday is this weekend. I always get a bit sentimental." Catherine sighed. "This is the first year since he passed away that I don't have to do something to keep my mother occupied."

How does one respond? Or should he? He continued to hold her hands in his right one and let the silence linger until she was ready to talk.

❧

"My mother recently started dating someone." There. She said it. "After twelve years of her being without a mate, I know my mother deserves to find happiness again. But preferably with someone more suitable."

Catherine never expected that letting go would be harder for her than her mother. Her father had meant the world to her. He'd shared stories about her grandfather and great-grandfather. Stories about their faith, their trials and struggles.

"More suitable?" Jaidon frowned. "What's wrong with him?"

"Alex, the gym teacher my mother is dating, doesn't share our faith. Although he did say he is willing to go to meetings with my mother." Jaidon reminded her of a younger version of Alex, except Jaidon was handsome and in better shape. They both loved working with youth. Jaidon showed more spiritual commitment. He was also strongly connected with his church—not likely to make compromises either. This was another reason an intimate relationship between them wouldn't work.

"Why is it so important that he goes to your church?" Jaidon asked. "If he loves the Lord, that should be enough, shouldn't it?"

"Because it's part of our heritage. My father grew up in a long line of Quakers. I can already tell my mother's convictions have weakened since my father passed away. Dad would be *very* disappointed." Since her mother had begun dating Alex, Catherine wondered about her parents' varying differences of commitment to their faith. But who was she to judge anyone's relationship with God? Even Jaidon's? Or the other volunteers? They were free to worship God how they chose. Her choice was made. . .albeit, made somewhat for her by her father. How did you deny your father's dying request?

"Why would he be disappointed?"

Catherine blinked and shrugged her shoulders. The answer should be obvious, but by the puzzled look on his face, it wasn't. "My father would expect my mother to set the example for my brother and me. Dad had a great-great-uncle who turned away from the faith, and it was strongly frowned upon. My father, and his father before him, were so concerned it might happen again that they made their children promise to only marry Quakers and never leave the faith."

"Ah," Jaidon said.

"Anyhow I know it's silly to get upset after so many years. I guess I've just gotten used to doing something with my mother for Dad's birthday, and now she doesn't need me to keep her company."

"It's not silly." Jaidon squeezed her hands reassuringly. "So, what are *we* going to do this weekend?"

"Uh—" Catherine blinked several times then smiled. He wanted to keep her company? That was sweet of him. Her girlfriends hadn't even offered to keep her occupied. "I don't know. What are we going to do?"

"Tell you what. Why don't I make it a surprise?"

"Sounds intriguing." Catherine wiggled her eyebrows. The anticipation of the unknown sounded fun. Although his version of *fun* and hers could be two very different things. "Just promise me it doesn't involve jumping out of a perfectly good airplane."

Jaidon smiled. "What about one that isn't perfectly good?"

Catherine's eyes widened as she shook her head vehemently. "N–o, thanks!"

He laughed at the way she over-exaggerated her words. "Don't worry. No airplanes. I promise."

Jaidon pulled his hand back in order to parallel park the Hummer, and she experienced an instantaneous sense of loss. Catherine mentally shook herself. She valued the blooming friendship developing between her and Jaidon. His reassuring touch had offered much needed comfort—that's all.

Throughout the evening Jaidon seemed to keep an eye on her. His protectiveness touched her, but it confused her as well. He needn't feel obligated to look out for her just because he gave her a ride. It wasn't as if she'd been delivered into a den of thieves. The youth at the center wanted to feel safe also.

Roberto and Jaidon chose teams for a basketball game. For his fourth pick, Jaidon motioned for her. "Catherine, come on. You're on my team."

Her cheeks warmed. When they'd begun choosing, she thought it was going to be just the guys playing. She looked around then half jogged to line up with the rest of Jaidon's team.

She was the first female chosen for either team. Roberto added a woman to his team.

By the time both teams finished choosing, Ariannah and Rosie ended up on the same team as Catherine. She silently hoped it would give the three of them a chance to bond. Thankfully Rosie never displayed an attitude toward her. Perhaps she would be an ally in winning over Ariannah.

Twenty minutes into the game, Ariannah dribbled the ball halfway down the court. Catherine made her way farther down, positioning herself for the set up. "Pass me the ball."

Ariannah was boxed in. She glanced at Catherine then looked around for other teammates. Even though Catherine was the clear shot, Ariannah threw the ball to Jaidon, who struggled to reach around a guy four inches taller than him. The other team intercepted the ball, headed down the court toward their net, and scored.

"What's up with that?" Rosie shook her head in disgust. "You cost us points."

"Yeah," a couple of the guys said, grunting.

Romeo brushed by Ariannah, bumping her shoulder roughly. "Doesn't look like you're playing on the same team."

Ariannah glared at Catherine as if it were her fault. The urge to roll her eyes and shake her head was overwhelming, but she sighed as she headed down the court to get back into the action. She snatched the ball from one of the guys on the other team, dribbled down to the top of the key and made a three-point jump shot, draining it straight through the hoop.

"Girl got game," Romeo said and high-fived her.

Catherine felt a sense of redemption. Her shot tied the game. To top off her jubilation, a few minutes later Jaidon scored the winning basket. Romeo patted him on the back. Ariannah gave him a sideways hug. Jaidon slipped away from Ariannah, Romeo, and the others who were still congratulating him and made his way to her, throwing his arms around her. "We did it."

"We sure did." The moistness from Jaidon's sweaty T-shirt made her cringe. She preferred his normal woodsy-exotic scent—and a dry shirt. She patted his back and moved away slightly.

"Why don't we celebrate on the way home? We can stop and get a pizza with the works," Jaidon suggested.

"I think that would be great," Ariannah said cheerfully. Before Jaidon could utter another word, she turned and called out, "Pastor Martinez, Jaidon suggested we stop and get a pizza on the way home."

Jaidon closed his mouth. Whatever he was about to say, he'd apparently decided against it, and none too happily by the scowl on his face. Maybe he wanted to invite the others himself. Then again maybe he didn't intend to invite the teens from the center. Wouldn't they need parental permission slips to take them anywhere? Ariannah's presumptuous attitude might inadvertently cause a rift between the youth and the sponsors.

Maybe she could help him out. Catherine whispered, "If you'd like to get out of going, I can make an excuse and say I have to work early tomorrow."

Jaidon shook his head and smiled when his eyes met hers. His expression softened. "No that's okay. I'd rather go out with you—and the others."

He kept one arm around her as they walked the ten or so feet to where the bulk of their team stood talking.

An idea came to Catherine. "Why don't we pick up some pizzas next week and bring them?"

"Then we can have a rematch," Rosie said.

Catherine giggled. "You do realize we won?"

Rosie chuckled. "Girl, I'm just playin' with you. I figured if we win again, we might get another pizza."

"I hear that." Romeo high-fived Rosie.

Jaidon laughed. "We'll see what we can do. But first we have to win again."

"Oh, we will." Romeo leaned his forearm on Catherine's shoulder. "We got Miss Hoops on our side."

Catherine blushed as her teammates cheered.

Before they left the center, Catherine decided to freshen up. Kristen and Gabby were lingering in the bathroom, talking while they messed with their hair. Catherine smiled at them. She'd only talked with them a little since she'd started volunteering. Both girls had cheered their friends from the sidelines during the basketball game. Catherine washed her face with a damp paper towel and finger-combed her hair back into a ponytail.

"Are you and Jaidon going out now?" Gabby asked.

Perhaps they'd seen Catherine get out of Jaidon's Hummer. Catherine smiled and shook her head. "No. He was just being nice and giving me a ride."

"Yeah right." Kristen laughed. "He's got it for you bad."

Gabby nodded in agreement. "He's got a dopey grin and practically drools when he's watching you."

Drools? That didn't create a very good visual. Jaidon couldn't like her. He already knew her dilemma—she couldn't consider dating someone who wasn't a Quaker. She'd made that clear to him on the way to the center.

Catching the frown on her face in the mirror, Catherine changed her expression to one she hoped conveyed light-hearted nonchalance. "We're just friends. That's all."

When they left to get pizzas, a twinge of guilt still plagued

Catherine. She wished their teenage teammates could have joined them for a victory pizza. But she reminded herself that the rest of the group from Jaidon's church was going and only Ariannah was on their team, so it barely constituted a victory pizza. Although Ariannah had used that fact as leverage to join them on the car ride to the pizza parlor. Catherine didn't mind totally. It meant she wouldn't have to be alone with Jaidon again. Hopefully by the time they left the restaurant, she'd think of how to confront him concerning Kristen and Gabby's accusations.

Chapter 4

"You're awfully quiet." Jaidon glanced over at Catherine on the drive home from the pizza parlor. The smell of the restaurant still lingered on their clothing. She didn't know whether or not to be thankful that Ariannah hadn't come with them this time.

Her tumultuous thoughts remained below the surface, threatening to wreak havoc with everything she held dear. Catherine didn't want to lose her newfound friendship with Jaidon. Yet she had a promise to fulfill to her father. She didn't want to mislead Jaidon. How should she broach the subject? Her stomach knotted. She opted for the chicken way out. "I'm not sure hanging out this weekend is a good idea."

"Why?" Jaidon stared at her. If the frown on his face was any indication, he wasn't happy. "Did Ariannah say something to you?"

Catherine shook her head. "I really don't know her that well. What would she have to say to me?"

"I don't know. She's been acting weird for a while. Normally she's a nice kid, but lately—" Jaidon shrugged. "I don't know what her problem is."

Catherine's lips pursed. What could she say? She didn't

know how the other youth sponsor used to act. Adding a comment would only contribute to gossip or speaking ill of someone when they didn't have a chance to defend themselves. She couldn't think of any reason she'd given the woman to dislike her. She didn't want to start now.

When Catherine didn't speak, Jaidon continued, "Anyhow. What's wrong with this weekend?"

"It's just—" How could she make him see the futility of even trying to have an intimate relationship? She'd never been able to get other guys to understand. They didn't want to be *just* friends. She'd made a promise to her father. A promise she couldn't break. "I come from a long line of Quakers."

"I know. That doesn't bother me." Jaidon shrugged. He glanced at her a couple times. His eyes widened. "But it bothers you."

"I don't want it to bother me." And she didn't want it to. "But like I explained earlier, I'm stuck. I promised my father on his deathbed that I would marry a Quaker."

Jaidon's brows furrowed. He nodded. "Hmm. So you can't hang out with non-Quakers either?"

Hang out? "I thought you *liked* me?"

"I do. You're fun to be around, and I had a blast playing basketball tonight," Jaidon said. "I thought it'd be great to hang out this weekend and help get your mind off things, like your father's birthday and your mother dating another man."

Catherine's cheeks warmed. Jaidon was only trying to be a good friend. She'd let Gabby and Kristen's assumptions put her in an awkward situation. "I'm sorry, Jaidon. I'd really like to go, if you are still interested in going—as friends."

Jaidon reached over, cupped her hands with his right hand, and smiled. "Friends."

❧

When Jaidon picked Catherine up Saturday morning, he *almost* felt guilty. One look into her beautiful hazel eyes and he squelched the niggling feeling. He'd already had the last couple of days to bolster his confidence, knowing Catherine had considered him as a possible suitor. He couldn't help grinning every time he thought about it.

The fact that he wasn't a Quaker was an obstacle they could get over. With time, either he could get her to at least consider going to his church to visit so she could see for herself that his church really wasn't so different from hers or—but *or* wasn't something he wanted to think about right now. It meant either he would have to convert or their *friendship* would be over. He swallowed hard. That definitely wasn't something he wanted to contemplate at the moment.

"I haven't been here in a long time," Catherine said as Jaidon drove into the parking lot of Taltree Arboretum and Gardens. "Didn't they open a new garden?"

Jaidon smiled at her enthusiasm. She sounded like a kid who'd just pulled up to an amusement park. It made his day knowing he'd chosen well. "Yes. The Railway Garden is open."

"Oh goodie."

Jaidon laughed at her enthusiasm. "I even packed a picnic lunch."

"You thought of everything." She returned his smile.

Almost everything, Jaidon thought to himself. Now if only he could find the magic ingredient to make her feel the same way about him that he felt for her—hopelessly in love.

During the next couple of hours, Jaidon walked along Railway Garden's beautiful landscaped paths, enjoying the lovely scenery that also included his delightful companion. He should have brought a camera. That way he'd have more than just his memories to capture the moment.

At lunch Jaidon laid down an old quilt he had from his youth for them to sit on the grass beneath the shade of a bur oak tree. While they ate their sandwiches and chips, they sipped on bottled tea and chatted about the scenery. Jaidon stuffed their trash back into the picnic basket then lay on his left side, arm crooked to lean against his knuckles in order to better observe his lovely companion's beautiful face—the cute way her nose tipped up slightly on the end. She was beautiful, both inside and out.

Catherine lay on her stomach, arms crossed in front of her and head resting on her forearms. "You know, it occurred to me that I really don't know much about you."

"I'm an open book." Jaidon laughed. "Read me."

"Read you?" Catherine raised her head and chuckled. "That sounds like a bad pickup line or something."

"No not a line." Jaidon shrugged. "You've been around me three times in the last week. What have you ascertained since we met?"

"You're going to make this hard on me, aren't you?"

"Is it that hard?" Maybe she hadn't paid any attention to him since they ran into each other at the hospital. Had he only been getting his hopes up?

Her expression grew solemn. "Your sea-blue eyes convey genuine sincerity. And you have a very caring nature, which is evident in your love for working with youth. You light up around them at the center." Catherine pretended to clear her throat. "Mind you, I've only observed you around youth at the center."

"So you were observing me?"

"No." Catherine's eyes widened. Her cheeks blushed. She play-slapped him and laughed. "You have a deviant side, my friend."

"Is that another observation?"

"Yes." She chuckled. "So tell me what I don't know. For example, we've never talked about what you do for a living. For all I know you may be a vagabond."

"Really? Do I look like one?" Jaidon smiled.

Her expression grew stern, but a hint of playfulness danced in her eyes. "I thought we'd completed the obvious observations." Catherine shrugged, a smile creasing her lips. "Besides I've never met a vagabond"—she wiggled her eyebrows—"that I know of. I wouldn't know how they dressed."

"Oh no you didn't." Jaidon reached over and tickled Catherine's sides until she laughed uncontrollably. "I'm not a vagabond, and you know it. Take it back."

"All right. All right," she gasped between giggles. "I take it back."

As their laughter subsided, they lay side-by-side on their backs. Jaidon clasped his hands together on his stomach, resisting the urge to reach over and hold her hand. "I'm a workers' comp lawyer."

She turned her head and studied him. "Hmm. I can actually see that."

"Oh?" Jaidon smiled. "You can?"

Catherine nodded. "It fits with your caring nature." She glanced at him, and he lost all train of thought, hypnotized by the warmth of her hazel eyes. "This is where you say something."

"Huh?" Jaidon blinked. "Sorry." He rolled to his side and smiled. "What are you doing tomorrow?"

Chapter 5

Catherine, following Jaidon through his church, bumped into a teenager. She looked over her shoulder as she continued walking in the direction she was being led. "I'm sorry," she whispered.

Part of her wanted to turn around and follow the teenager out of the sanctuary, but Jaidon had a secure hold on her hand, guiding her toward their seats. When Jaidon asked her what she was doing Sunday, she had no idea he was going to ask her to go to church. Not even in the building ten minutes, and it was already proving to be the cultural learning experience he'd told her it would be, and not just because his church didn't have hard wooden pews facing each other.

Taking a Sunday off from her church to visit another church couldn't hurt. After all it was only *one* day. She hadn't missed a Sunday since last summer, when she went to visit a college friend in California.

Catherine gripped his hand tighter as they maneuvered through the crowd. She silently prayed they wouldn't get separated. She wanted to whisper, but Jaidon wouldn't be able to hear her. Other people were talking; perhaps it was acceptable at this church. "There must be at least two hundred people here."

"Closer to six if you count the kids in children's services and nursery. Plus there are a couple adult Sunday school classes that take place during second service." Jaidon pulled her closer to him, slowing his pace, and she followed toward the direction he pointed. "We can sit over here."

They edged in front of two couples, passed down the aisle, and sat toward the middle of the row. She leaned over to whisper in Jaidon's ear. "Why is everyone still talking? Shouldn't they be quiet in the sanctuary?"

Jaidon smiled. "Because service hasn't started yet."

Catherine looked around at people greeting others on their way to their seats; some stopped to converse longer. How did they know when service started?

Jaidon nudged her gently with his shoulder. "Why are you frowning?"

"I'm sorry." Catherine sighed. "I'm just used to my church. We always begin worship as soon as we come into the sanctuary."

"It'll begin shortly." Jaidon opened his church bulletin, something her church didn't have.

Catherine wanted to close her eyes and worship but found the chatter around her distracting. She couldn't wait for church to begin.

"Hello," Roberto said and extended his hand for Catherine to shake. "It's good to see you again."

"Likewise." Catherine smiled and shook his hand; then he shook hands with Jaidon. "Where is Josephina?"

Roberto nodded toward the first row of chairs in front of the sanctuary. "She's sitting up front with the youth." He pointed to the next row over. "That's our senior pastor and his wife. Jaidon will have to introduce you after church." He smiled and nodded toward Jaidon. "I'll catch you later."

Jaidon smiled and nodded back. "Will do."

Catherine felt like she missed some kind of unspoken exchange between the two men. Probably a guy thing. She shrugged it off and sat back, quietly observing. A few plants and flowers decorated the platform. While they were pretty, they could serve as a distraction. A piano, drum set, and a couple guitars were on stage. This must be one of those *programmed* churches she'd heard about. She could visualize some of the elders' eyes widening if they caught sight of instruments in a sanctuary. She did find the padded chairs comfortable; they would be a welcome addition to her church.

Catherine leaned closer to Jaidon. "Some people are getting on the stage. Does that mean it's about to begin?"

Jaidon laughed. "You'd think you've never been to church before."

"I have." Catherine turned her attention to the front of the sanctuary and crossed her arms. "Next week you have to come to my church."

"Oh do I?" Jaidon said. Amusement made his blue eyes glisten.

"Yes. As you said, it's a great cultural learning experience." Catherine smiled sweetly as she used his argument against him.

"It's a date." Jaidon stood and Catherine followed suit as the musicians began to play. "I'd be happy to go to your church with you."

Her heart skipped a beat even though Jaidon didn't mean it was an *actual* date. But if he did become a Friend. . . Catherine glanced at him from the corner of her eye. Wishful thinking. That's all it was.

As the service proceeded, Catherine tried to process everything. The members of the church came in and sat down before church started. They stood for music, which was another thing her church didn't have. They began with prayer, standing, and then they sat. They finished, on their feet again, before they sat for announcements and for the pastor to deliver the Word. No one who shared in the Quaker meetings spoke as long as Jaidon's pastor did. And apparently, he was the only one allowed to speak—though Jaidon's pastor said some interesting things.

According to the pastor, anyone who believed the Bible verse John 3:16 and accepted Jesus Christ as Savior became a Christian. That would make her one. Catherine smiled. For some reason that knowledge made her feel warm inside. Her father had never considered his family to be Christian. Perhaps because he'd been brought up more strictly, based on older traditions and his family's heritage.

When service was over, Jaidon introduced Catherine to the senior pastor, Thomas Burnside, and his wife, Natalie. Catherine was surprised to learn that Nathan was the youngest of their three children. Especially since neither Roberto nor Jaidon had mentioned he was their pastor's son when they'd introduced him to her at the center. He hadn't said much, if anything, to her. She hoped she could remember everyone since these were Jaidon's friends.

"I hope you've enjoyed visiting our church today," Thomas said, "and you'll come back again soon."

"I'd like that." Catherine smiled politely. She glanced from the pastor to Jaidon, who looked somewhat like a cat with a canary in its mouth and wasn't quite sure if it should swallow or not. Obviously the pastor was trying to gain a new convert. Why not have a little fun, make him sweat that he could be losing one? *If only*, she wished silently. "However, I do have a church I attend regularly. Jaidon is coming with me next week."

"He is?" Thomas's eyebrows raised a fraction before he quickly regained his composure. "That's nice of him."

"Well we really should get going if we want to beat others in line at the restaurant." Jaidon shook the pastor's hand and said good-bye to Natalie before leading Catherine outside. "I'm sorry."

Catherine laughed. "Maybe if our church was a little less subtle we'd have more members."

Jaidon ran a hand through his hair. "It was that obvious, huh?"

Catherine nodded. "Do you think he's afraid I'll persuade you to become a Quaker?"

Jaidon stopped and stood close to her instead of opening the car door. The heat of his breath warmed her and yet sent a chill down her spine. "I don't know. What does your church have to offer?"

"What—" Catherine swallowed hard, hoping to keep her voice from cracking further. "What were you hoping for?"

His eyebrows rose slightly, and his head tilted. He eyed her lips before staring into her eyes. "Besides the spiritual aspect of it, I'd like to meet a nice Christian woman that I could date and possibly marry one day."

"Maybe you could expand a bit on your preferences." The thought of Jaidon pursuing one of the women from her church made her stomach turn. Okay, so she was attracted to him. What woman in her right mind, and who still had breath in her, wouldn't be? Not only was he sweet and kind and caring, but he also served as delicious eye candy she was finding hard to resist. "There aren't a lot of single women at my church."

"Hmm. . ." Jaidon moved closer. "But you go there?"

She nodded.

"And you're single?"

Her heart beat faster. She looked from his eyes to his lips and closed her eyes in anticipation. She felt his arm brush hers, and then he stepped back.

"If you think of anyone who'd like to go out on a *real* date with me, and work on a lasting relationship, let me know." Jaidon leaned against the door of the Hummer, waiting for her to get in. "Because changing churches is a big commitment."

Chapter 6

Maybe he shouldn't have put so much pressure on Catherine. He hoped he hadn't scared her off. Jaidon resisted the urge to look at his watch again while he shot hoops with Nathan and a couple youth at the center. She said she'd be there. She would. Part of him wondered if the real reason she wanted to drive separately tonight had something to do with Sunday, not with having to work late. Especially since she'd turned down his offer to pick her up from work.

The phone in his pocket vibrated. "Hold on, guys."

He reached in his pocket to retrieve the phone. Noticing it was Catherine, he motioned to the guys he'd be a second and walked off the court to take the call. "Hello. I was beginning to worry about you."

Catherine laughed. "No need to worry. I'll be there in less than ten minutes."

"Good." He breathed a sigh of relief. "I can't wait to see you."

"Me either."

His heart skipped a beat; she couldn't wait to see him. He hung up the phone. Nathan zinged a basketball toward him. He barely had time to jump out of the way before it grazed past him. "Hey. What are you guys grinning about? You missed me."

"We were going to ask you the same thing," Nathan said. "Have anything to do with a certain someone you brought to church Sunday?"

"It might." Heat rose to his cheeks. Okay, so his grin gave him away. It wasn't like he had anything to hide.

❧

Catherine looked at the time on her cell phone. She'd gotten to the center quicker than expected. Good. She could surprise Jaidon by being a couple minutes early. Pulling the key out of the ignition, she grabbed her purse and climbed out of her car.

She collided with a solid object then swayed back against her car.

Even though he wore a hoodie, she recognized his face. "I'm sorry, Daryl. I wasn't expecting someone to be standing there."

"Just give me your purse, and nobody gets hurt."

She felt something against her stomach and looked down. She swallowed hard at the sight of the gun. "Daryl, why are you doing this?"

"I got to." Daryl glanced over his shoulder at an older black Ford Explorer. She could see hesitancy in his eyes and pain. "If I don't, I'm dead, and so are you."

"D–Dog!" Jaidon's panicked shout rang out from the distance.

There was nothing he could do, and nowhere she could go. She'd had to park down the street from the center. Even if he could reach her, what could he do, especially with the menacing guy in the black vehicle across the street from her?

"Sorry." Daryl yanked her purse out of her hands then hit her in the head with the butt of his gun before he took off on foot.

Catherine staggered. She shook her head to try and clear it

but was rewarded with pain and a wave of dizziness. Her knees buckled, and she fell, struggling to focus her eyes so she could identify the dark-skinned driver of the Explorer. The driver pointed at her, index finger and thumb poised, as if he were holding a gun and pulling the trigger. A cold chill went up her spine, and she shivered.

Jaidon rounded her vehicle and grabbed hold of her. She collapsed in his arms. Unable to resist, she gave way to the darkness that engulfed her.

❧

Although the other volunteers came with him to the hospital, Jaidon hadn't felt like talking to any of them at the moment. He let the police officers interview them first while he tried to calm down. The waiting room may have been large, but to Jaidon it felt like a cage as he paced, waiting to find out how Catherine was doing. He wasn't family, so they hadn't allowed him to go back with her. If it had been an accident and not a crime, they might have let him stay with her.

"Excuse me." An officer paused near Jaidon. "Someone said you saw what happened."

Jaidon nodded. He wanted to throw up every time he recalled the scene, D–Dog hitting Catherine with the gun and the look on her face as she collapsed into his arms. "Yeah, I saw what happened."

"Do you mind having a seat so I can take your statement?" The officer motioned toward a couple of vacant chairs. They both took a seat. "Can you give me your name?"

"Jaidon Taylor. I'm a lawyer and do volunteer work at the Porter County Youth Center." Jaidon folded his hands and leaned against his thighs, nervously jiggling his right leg. He should have insisted on picking Catherine up, and then this wouldn't have happened.

"Please tell me what you saw of the incident. Start from the beginning," the officer said.

"Catherine Wall, the victim—" Jaidon swallowed hard. His stomach turned. "Called and told me she would be at the center shortly. I came outside to wait, and she was already there. I saw a young man in a hoodie approach her and recognized him. It was Daryl Jones."

"And you're positive?" the officer asked.

"Yes." Jaidon nodded. "He used to come to the center. In fact, only a couple weeks ago he'd been shot—a flesh wound. Miss Wall was his nurse."

"So they had previous contact with each other?"

"Yes." Jaidon sighed and sat back in his chair. It took every ounce of self-control not to track Daryl down himself and pulverize him for what he did to Catherine. How dare he hold her at gunpoint and rob her!

"Any chance Mr. Jones could be retaliating for something that happened between them?" The officer's expression was hard to read, but Jaidon didn't like his implication.

"No. Miss Wall is a very caring individual. She was inspired to work with inner-city youth after she helped care for Daryl during his recovery."

The other officer who'd been questioning Ariannah came over to them. He stopped a few feet away and motioned for his partner to join him. After a couple moments, the officer who was taking his statement returned. "Thanks to a couple witnesses at the location of the incident, Mr. Jones has already been apprehended. Would it be possible for you to bring Miss Wall by the station when she's released to make a positive ID?"

"If she's up to it I'll bring her by later. If not, I'll bring her by tomorrow."

The officer nodded and handed Jaidon his business card. "Thank you, Mr. Taylor."

"You're welcome." As soon as the officer walked away, Jaidon sprang out of his chair and began pacing.

An hour and a half later, a nurse came out and called his name. "Catherine Wall asked if you could come back."

"How is she?" Jaidon asked.

"I'm afraid you'll have to ask her yourself," the nurse said. "HIPAA laws and all, we're not allowed to disclose patient information."

"I understand." Jaidon's heart pounded in his chest as he followed the nurse back to Catherine's room. The nurse left him at the doorway.

Catherine looked pale. She had a couple stitches on the left side of her forehead; it looked swollen and purplish. Jaidon clenched his fists. Part of him wanted to run over and hug her; the other part wanted to make a beeline for the police station and crucify Daryl.

At her lopsided grin, he edged closer and gently kissed her on the uninjured side of her forehead. "You don't know how worried I've been about you."

With her left hand, she reached up and grabbed his arm, while continuing to hold him to her with the other hand. "Thank you for being there for me."

"Always." And he meant it.

"They're keeping me overnight for observation." Her voice was barely louder than a whisper. "Apparently I have a concussion and the knot to prove it."

"I'd be happy to stay." He didn't care if it looked inappropriate to the others from his church. Right now he didn't want to leave Catherine's side.

"That's not necessary." She nodded and then moaned. Several of her friends were scheduled to work the night shift; they'd check in on her often. "I'll be okay."

He wasn't so sure of her assessment. "I'll pick you up tomorrow when they're ready to release you. I told the police officer I'd take you by the police station when you're able so you can identify your attacker. In fact you can rest easy. They have Daryl in custody."

Catherine struggled to sit up.

"Whoa. Relax. It's okay." Jaidon tried to ease her back against the mattress amid her protest.

"No." Catherine swallowed hard. "You've got to help him."

"Help who?"

"Daryl." Catherine's eyes were pleading.

"How can you ask me to do that?" Obviously she was disoriented. "You realize he was the one who attacked you?"

Catherine shook her head slightly. Crease lines marred her face as she winced. "He had to. He didn't have a choice. There was—"

"He had a choice." Jaidon gritted his teeth. "He figured you were a vulnerable target and attacked you. You're lucky he didn't kill you."

Jaidon might as well have been the one with the concussion. He was nauseated and felt light-headed. What if Catherine had been killed?

"Jaidon," Catherine mumbled as tears brimmed her eyes. "He apologized. Bad guys don't say they're sorry when they're committing a crime."

Jaidon clenched his jaw. There was a first time for everything. Maybe D–Dog hadn't realized he knew his victim when he approached her.

"Someone was watching him." Catherine moistened her lips and swallowed. "Jaidon, please. Just go talk to him. I think he needs help."

If Jaidon went to talk to him, he *would* need help.

"Please?" Catherine pleaded. "Take his case. . .for me."

He groaned. For her? "How can you ask me to help the man who hurt the woman I love?"

"Love?" Catherine blinked several times.

"From the moment we met, I knew you were the one." Jaidon ran a hand through his hair. "I know you made your father a promise, and I'm willing to try going to your church and seeing if we can make this work. If you'll give me a chance."

Tears trickled down her cheeks. "You would consider changing churches for me?"

Jaidon nodded. "Just please don't ask me to help the man who hurt you. I can't do it."

Catherine reached for his hand and brought it to her lips, gently kissing the back of his hand before she clutched it to her chest. "I need you to do this for me. At least talk to him. Find out what really happened."

Jaidon ran the fingers of his free hand through her hair and then stroked her cheek gently with his thumb. The smell of lavender and lilacs teased his senses. Her hazel eyes drew him closer to her like magnets. When her lips parted a fraction, his pulse raced, and he closed the remaining distance between them to claim her lips.

A moan escaped her that only increased his hunger and he deepened the kiss. When he drew back, they were both breathless.

"Wow."

He nodded in agreement and gently kissed her again.

"I have another favor." Her breath was still ragged. "Ask Daryl who the man was that wanted me dead—the one in the black Ford Explorer."

Chapter 7

H ere are the spare keys to your car." Catherine's mother handed the key ring back to her. "Your brother asked a friend to go with him to pick it up. He dropped your car off at my house." Her mother laid a fresh change of clothes on the foot of Catherine's hospital bed. "I want you to stay with me until we know you're safe."

Catherine couldn't argue with her mother. She was too much like her to deny, in both physical appearance and personality type. Catherine was a slender version of her mother, brunette instead of blond, interspersed with minor strands of gray, and both with that same determined streak. She wasn't afraid of Daryl, but the other guy—it wouldn't do any good to mention him and concern her mother. A shiver ran down her spine and up her arms just thinking about the look in the man's eyes—pure evil. "Thanks for letting me stay with you."

"You're welcome, dear. You know I'm always glad to have you around." Her mother smiled.

Catherine forced herself to focus on brighter things while she dressed, thankful to be getting out of the hospital. It was one thing to work there and another to stay as a patient. "Can I ask you something, Mom?"

Her mother paused from gathering Catherine's belongings. "Sure, sweetheart."

"I met someone."

Her mother smiled.

"Before you say anything or read anything into it, let me finish."

Her mother grinned wider and nodded. Guilty as charged. She could tell by the look on her mother's face she was already making assumptions.

"Jaidon, the man who is picking me up, isn't just a volunteer at the center. We've been getting to know each other on a personal level and…he said he was willing to consider becoming a Quaker." Catherine swallowed hard. She watched her mother's expression change from a huge smile to contemplative. She didn't know if that was a good thing or not.

"I wondered why you only needed me to bring you a change of clothing and not to take you home." She grinned. "I assume he is only contemplating changing for you. Not because he has any personal conviction to change."

"Does it matter?" She realized how shallow she sounded. "I really like him a lot, Mom. If he doesn't change, we can't be together."

Her mother sighed. "I know you made a promise to your father. One he should have never asked you to make."

"It's not like I can go back on my promise. Plus, how would it be for our children if we didn't go to the same church?" Catherine sighed. She didn't want to think of a life without Jaidon. She enjoyed his company and friendship. He was kind and caring, putting the needs of others ahead of his own. The way his kiss had the ability to make her toes curl was a perk to the overall package. There was no denying that she loved him. Every day they were around each other, her feelings for him grew deeper. No one had ever made her heart soar like this. It raced just thinking about Jaidon. "I know we can make this work."

"I'm sure you both can, but it's not me you need to convince." Her mother placed Catherine's clothes from the previous day in a plastic bag and handed a pair of tennis shoes to her. "You'll have to get approval from the meeting."

Catherine's breath caught. They were stricter than the other two meetings she attended when out of town on vacation or visiting. Her family had always attended. That didn't necessarily mean she would be shown any special favor, but she had to try. "I know. I was hoping you would help to put in a good word."

Her mother shrugged. "I'll do what I can, but you know I don't have as much influence, especially since I've been seeing Alex."

Would they allow Jaidon to join the church if they found out it was for possibly getting married? Perhaps they should try membership first. After all, he'd only implied he was thinking of marriage. He hadn't actually asked her. Her head hurt thinking about it. What if she couldn't get Jaidon read into meeting? Then there was little hope of getting their approval for ever marrying either.

❧

Jaidon knocked on Catherine's hospital door. "Is it safe to come in?"

A middle-aged blond opened the door and grinned. Her facial features, even the cute upturned nose, resembled Catherine's. "You must be Jaidon."

"Yes." He extended his hand. Instead of shaking it, she hugged him.

"I'm Evelyn." She laughed and moved away to allow him to enter. "My daughter was just telling me about you."

"Nothing bad I hope." Especially after the kiss they'd shared last night. He hoped that part, of an otherwise horrific evening, wasn't a dream.

"Not terribly." The smile on her face and gleam in her eyes hinted that Evelyn was teasing. At least he hoped so. "Listen, since we've got midweek service tonight and Catherine isn't working, why not stay for dinner when you drop her off and go to meeting with us?"

He did say he was willing to go to her church, but he thought he still had several days to build up the courage. The sooner he started, the quicker they could be together—nothing coming between them. Excitement bubbled inside him, in spite of the next task that lay before them. "I'd love to. I'm not sure how long it will take at the precinct. We can call if you'd like."

"I like this boy already," Evelyn said.

"He's not a boy, Mom. He's a man." Catherine rolled her eyes and sighed.

"I'm glad you noticed." Her mother laughed.

"Mom," Catherine squealed. She grabbed the pillow and hit her mother with it. "Behave yourself, or I'm going home—to my house."

Jaidon frowned. Was it safe for her to go home? Her address had to have been on her license. Was Daryl the only one who knew where she lived? Or did other gang members know, too? Where else could Catherine go?

Catherine obviously recognized the look of concern on his face. It wasn't something he could hide. "Mom wants me to stay at her place for a while. Until she's sure I'm okay."

"And this way I don't have to worry about anyone else

coming after her either," her mother said sternly.

"Thank you. I agree wholeheartedly." If he couldn't watch after her twenty-four-seven, at least her mother could. He was glad she was protective—and insistent.

After Catherine checked out of the hospital, her mother waited with her at the curb while Jaidon pulled the Hummer around to pick her up. Evelyn hugged Catherine then hugged Jaidon. "Take care of my baby."

"Will do," he promised and waved to Evelyn before pulling off. His stomach knotted as he drove toward their destination. He'd waited to go see Daryl, hoping Catherine would change her mind, and giving himself time to cool off. "Are you sure you're up to going by the police station?"

"Yes." Catherine nodded. "I'm anxious to get this cleared up and make sure Daryl is safe."

Was she crazy? He looked at her a long moment. No crease lines on her face, she looked at peace. His eyes focused on the road while his mind struggled to comprehend her attitude. "Why are you so concerned about Daryl after what he did to you?"

Catherine glanced at him and smiled. "God wants us to turn the other cheek, forgive others as He has forgiven us. I believe Daryl deserves a chance, and I don't believe he really wanted to hurt me."

"Well he had a funny way of showing it." Jaidon gritted his teeth.

"Please, Jaidon. Just give him a chance to explain." Catherine reached over and touched his arm.

Jaidon relaxed a fraction, lowered his arm so they could hold hands, and stroked the back of her hand with his thumb. Her dainty hand felt right in his. He closed his hand tighter around hers and took a deep breath to calm himself. All he wanted to do was protect her.

"I'll talk to him," Jaidon said. And if he didn't like Daryl's answers. . .

Half an hour later, Jaidon sat in a room at the police station, waiting for his *client*. It was a choice he was greatly regretting, especially after learning the gun the police had confiscated when they arrested him had been used in a homicide. Jaidon stood and put his hands in his pockets as they brought Daryl in and sat him down at the table.

"I'm sorry about what happened, Mr. T." Daryl's head hung low.

Jaidon hadn't realized he'd clenched his fists in his pockets. He forced himself to relax and leaned against the wall.

"Tell me what happened." He couldn't curb the edge in his tone.

Daryl sighed, his fists balled on the table. "It all started 'cause I wanted out." There was pain in Daryl's eyes when he looked up at Jaidon. "Once I got involved with the center, and Bruno saw that it was changing me and Tanesha, he laid claim on Tanesha, even though we belonged together.

"So Bruno gets himself a new girl and decides I gotta pay for leaving the gang. He gives me an out. Says unless I want to get shot by him at point-blank range, I need to sever my ties with you all at the center."

"Why?" It didn't make sense to Jaidon. What did Bruno care about any of them? They'd never even met him.

"Bruno knew if I hurt one of you guys, you all would never forgive me, and then you wouldn't let me back in the center." Daryl shrugged. "He figured then I'd have nowhere to go but back to him."

"Hmm." In a weird way, it made sense to Jaidon.

"I saw that nice nurse, figured I could just take her purse and run off, but Bruno put a gun in my hand and told me to take care of things or he would. I didn't know what to do. When you came out, I grabbed her purse and hit her." A tear strolled down Daryl's cheek. "Tell me she's okay."

Jaidon swallowed hard and clenched his fists again. "She spent the night in the hospital with a concussion and had to get stitches."

"I'm sorry," Daryl pleaded. "Bruno was watching. If I didn't do something, he would've."

Jaidon stiffened. He didn't recall seeing anyone in particular that stood out. Of course his focus had been on Catherine. He faintly recalled a vehicle driving by. It might have been the one Catherine told him about. "Where was Bruno?"

"Across the street in a black Ford Explorer."

The blood drained from Jaidon's face, and he felt faint. "Catherine said he made a gun with his hand and pretended to shoot her. Would he?"

"I—I don't know." Daryl ran his hand through his hair. "He might've done it just to scare her so she wouldn't talk."

"Even if Catherine doesn't file charges against you, the prosecutor in Indiana will. And by the sound of it, they're looking to add homicide to the charges."

Daryl's dark skin paled noticeably. "You said she was released from the hospital."

"She was." Jaidon nodded. "The gun was used in another crime. Yours aren't the only fingerprints on it. If you testify to where you got the gun and the fingerprints match Bruno's, then the police can arrest him."

"What about me? I go to prison, get a shorter sentence that ends in a casket?"

"I want to help you." Jaidon was surprised at how much he actually meant his words. If not for Daryl choosing the lesser of two evils, Catherine might be dead right now. "I have a friend who is a criminal attorney. He's better equipped to handle your case. I'll give him a call. Perhaps he can work out a deal with the prosecutor if you promise to cooperate."

Chapter 8

P erhaps I should warn you before we go inside," Catherine
said. "Our worship meetings aren't the same as your
church services."

"Okay." Jaidon leaned back against the driver's seat, his left
wrist resting on the steering wheel. How different could their
service be that she felt the need to warn him? Perhaps that was
why she was persistent in having her mom drive separately.
And to think he'd hoped it was because she wanted him to kiss
her again. The possibility still existed—as long as he drove her
home. He smiled. "Okay, fill me in on what I should expect."

"You know how when you go into your sanctuary and
everyone is talking and greeting?"

Jaidon nodded.

"We don't do that."

"You don't talk to each other or greet anyone?" He pictured
them to be friendlier, like Catherine and her mother.

"No—I mean yes. We do that, but not until service is over."
Catherine sighed. "I mean our service begins the moment the
first person walks through the doors. Everyone sits down and
meditates or prays. It gives us a chance to listen to the voice of
God within," she said. "We don't have music or a pastor who

preaches. But if someone feels led to offer vocal ministry then they speak."

"How do you know when service is over?" With all the questions he had, it was likely to be over before they got inside. Making a good impression meant a lot to him; not to mention their future together hung in the balance.

"A designated person stands and begins shaking hands with his neighbors." Catherine bent to grab something from the floorboard then straightened, empty handed. She sighed. "I'm so used to grabbing my purse. At least I called and canceled my debit card and stuff this afternoon. Unless the police find my wallet, I'll have to get my driver's license renewed as well."

The police had found Catherine's purse in a dumpster, but her wallet was missing. Jaidon hadn't thought to ask Daryl about it when he was at the precinct questioning him. He made a mental note to call the lawyer he'd referred him to. "I'll try to find out what Daryl did with it tomorrow."

Catherine took a deep breath. "Thank you. You're too good to me." She leaned over and kissed him on the cheek. "We'd better go in now."

As much as he would have liked to kiss her back, he knew she was right. Several people had already gone inside. The last person he noticed entering the building had been at least five minutes earlier. Hopefully he and Catherine wouldn't be the last ones to go into the service.

He opened the Hummer door for her. The outside of the two-story building had plain white siding with black shutters. Inside her church, he felt like he stepped back in time. Three rows of wooden pews lined each wall and faced toward the center of the room; there was no stage or platform where a preacher might speak, just an empty space in the center.

A couple of children watched as they made their way to a pew with empty seats. Thankfully they wouldn't have to edge in front of anyone and disturb them. Jaidon was glad he'd chosen casual dress instead of a suit since several others were dressed casually, many in jeans, even some of the women. Perhaps their midweek service was more casual than their Sunday service, like at his church.

Most of the congregation had their eyes closed and heads bowed. He looked at Catherine. She was already praying quietly. Normally the singing and music helped him unwind and focus on God. Jaidon closed his eyes and began giving thanks as he entered into prayer. God had kept Catherine safe, wounded but alive, and had blessed him by bringing her into his life.

As the minutes ticked by, Jaidon relaxed and forgot about everyone else around him. A deep sense of peace engulfed him, like nothing he'd ever felt before.

He wiped at a stray tear. When Catherine touched his arm, he opened his eyes and looked at her. A nonverbal connection passed between them as they stared into the depths of each other's soul. Catherine's peace came from her time of truly focusing on God, something that was missing in his life. He prayed daily, went to church regularly, volunteered, participated in some of the church plays, and was even a member of the deacon board. Yet he'd let busyness keep him from quiet time with the Lord.

An older gentleman stood and shook hands with another person who sat on a pew three feet from him. This was the sign Catherine had mentioned that signified church was over. Time had passed quicker than Jaidon expected. It wasn't like the services he was accustomed to attending. Even without a minister preaching, he felt a closer connection to God than he had in a while. Jaidon remained seated, waiting for the others to get up before he did. Yet no one moved.

The man directed his attention to Jaidon and asked, "Would you please stand and introduce yourself?"

Jaidon swallowed hard, rubbed the palms of his hands on his thighs, and stood. "My name is Jaidon Taylor. I want to thank Catherine Wall for inviting me here today. I hope that you'll give me the opportunity to join your church."

❧

What? Catherine stared at Jaidon and tried to contain her shock. It was too soon for him to ask about joining their church. The elders might contemplate his motives, especially since he came with a woman who was single. It wouldn't take much to put two and two together and come up with the obvious conclusion.

"You're interested in joining our church?" Matthew Payne, the elder who stood to conclude services, asked gruffly.

Jaidon nodded.

"Hmm." Matthew's brows furrowed. He glanced from Jaidon to Catherine and back again. "And what is your sudden interest in joining?"

Catherine swallowed hard, wishing she could shrivel down in her seat, away from watchful eyes. This was not how she expected this to go. She hadn't even discussed Jaidon with any of her friends from church.

"To be honest," Jaidon said, "I had invited Catherine to my church in the hope of showing her how much we were alike, that it didn't matter what church we went to. I silently hoped I could convince her to come to my church instead of me having to come to hers."

Catherine glared at Jaidon. Her cheeks warmed as his words simmered like coal in a fire. She wanted to get up and run so she wouldn't have to face her family and friends after his humiliating revelation.

"But then I learned of her family's heritage and her promise to her father. After I got to know Catherine," Jaidon continued, "I saw such a peaceful and forgiving spirit in her. I can't expect her to change for me. She exudes the Christian faith in everything she does. It makes me hunger for the relationship she has with God.

"I've grown up in church. Learned all the Bible stories and studied God's Word. But when I came here tonight, for the first time ever, I felt such peace wash over me." Jaidon looked away from Thomas momentarily and focused his attention on Catherine.

She felt speechless. One minute she wanted to ream him about trying to get her to join his church, and then after his confession, she wanted to reach out and hold his hand.

"I want more, and I don't only mean an everlasting relationship with you. I want that, too." Jaidon smiled sheepishly. "I can appreciate and understand your family heritage. It's not something I can ask you to change, nor do I want you to. You are who you are, and that is good enough for me."

Catherine reached out and took his hand. Jaidon was kind and loving. He cared about others and was concerned about how she felt. Enough so he was willing to change churches for her. She loved him and wanted the opportunity to spend a lifetime getting to know everything about him. She stood next to him and leaned close, offering moral support.

Jaidon turned to address Matthew. "Your church has helped contribute to the fine upbringing of this wonderful woman, and the peace I have felt here is something I have longed for and didn't even know I was missing. I would very much like to be a part of your church."

"That is something we'll have to think upon and take up at the monthly meeting." Matthew's expression didn't betray what he may have been thinking or feeling. "Should you be considering marriage with Ms. Wall, you would also need to write a letter of intent, and then we will appoint the clearness committee to review your request and make a decision at the following monthly meeting."

What if they didn't approve Jaidon to join their church? Things were happening so fast. Did he even want to consider marriage? He did say an everlasting relationship. That meant marriage. Didn't it? Catherine exhaled a deep breath.

Jaidon squeezed her hand and smiled down at her. "Sounds good."

Catherine's heart fluttered like a flock of wild geese let loose inside her chest. Her eyes were still locked with Jaidon's. She hadn't realized everyone had gotten up and started to mingle until people came to greet Jaidon and shake his hand.

Her mother knelt on the pew in front of Catherine, leaned over, and hugged her. "Congratulations, sweetheart. Looks like you've got a keeper," her mother whispered in her ear.

"You're blushing." Jaidon grinned. "Your cheeks always turn so rosy. I like it." He kissed her forehead.

Her mother went around to the edge of the pew. "Come on, you get a hug, too."

Catherine would have loved to hear what her mother whispered in Jaidon's ear. He laughed and nodded in agreement. "Thank you."

When her mother went to greet one of her friends, Catherine nudged Jaidon. "Are you going to tell me what she said?"

His grin widened. "No."

Chapter 9

"Hey Jaidon. You made it, amigo." Roberto greeted Jaidon with a hug when he joined Roberto's small group at the center. "Where were you last night? We missed you at church."

Nathan and Ariannah joined the men. Jaidon was a little hesitant to answer the youth pastor's question. He normally didn't miss Wednesday night service. "I went to church with Catherine last night."

"How is she?" Roberto stood with his arms folded across his chest. "I would've gone to the hospital to see her if I'd known they were going to keep her overnight."

"That's okay." Jaidon was glad his friend cared enough to follow up on Catherine's progress. "She's doing better. She really wanted to come, but I persuaded her to stay home tonight. I didn't think it was safe. Not after what happened."

"I understand," Roberto said.

"What's her church like?" Ariannah rolled her eyes. "Bet you're glad that's over with."

Jaidon was beginning to understand why Catherine seemed a little defensive when she first came to the center and everyone questioned her about her beliefs. Was she always met with negative attitudes? "It was wonderful. I liked it so much I'm considering joining."

"You're what?" Ariannah squeaked.

"No way." Nathan, who was normally reserved, shook his head vehemently. "You belong at our church. There's no way Dad's going to let you leave."

It was hard not to laugh. He knew Nathan meant his father would do everything he could to persuade Jaidon to stay. . .by friendly persuasion. While Nathan's father may have been the senior pastor, he didn't have the ability to keep Jaidon from changing churches. Only one person had that ability, and she was the reason he was willing to change. If he planned to marry her, their children needed to be brought up in the church they attended, and if they attended different churches. . .

Right now the only thing that was important was getting the clearness committee to approve his membership and marriage to Catherine. Then the two of them could work out their plans from there together.

"I appreciate all of your concerns." Jaidon could tell by the strained look on Roberto's face that he wasn't happy with his revelation either. "But it's my decision. And it's not like you won't ever see me again. I'll still volunteer at the center, and I'm sure Catherine would agree to visiting our church from time to time."

Ariannah pointed a finger at him and glared. "See. You still consider it your church. You're only changing because that no good—"

"That's enough, Ariannah," Jaidon said sternly. "It's obvious you never liked her from the beginning, but stooping to name calling is way out of line."

"Mr. Taylor." Jaidon turned when he heard his name shouted.

Tanesha.

She hadn't been to the center in at least a month. The last time he saw her was at the hospital when Daryl had been shot. She ran over to him. "Bruno's going after that woman to make sure she doesn't say nothin' about him."

"That woman? Do you mean Catherine?" Jaidon stammered.

"I don't know her name," Tanesha said. "That woman." She shook her hands frantically. "The one D–Dog robbed. Bruno has her wallet. He knows where she lives."

"Thanks, Tanesha." Jaidon fumbled for his cell phone and dialed.

"Hey, how are you?" Catherine's melodic voice rang out.

She was safe. For now. "Sweetheart, listen. You need to make sure all the doors and windows are locked. I'm calling the police. I'll see if they'll send a squad car by your mom's."

"What's wrong?" He heard the panic in her voice, mirroring his own.

"Bruno has your wallet. Was there any information in it, or in your purse, that might give away your mom's location?"

There was a pause.

His heart quickened. "Catherine?"

"No," she replied. "Not that I can think of."

"Good." Jaidon breathed a sigh of relief as he headed toward the door. "I'll be there in a few minutes."

"We'll be praying for you," Roberto called.

He glanced over his shoulder. "Thanks," he said and jogged toward his vehicle while he dialed 911.

❧

Catherine paced, peered out the blinds, and paced again. She didn't know whether or not to be glad her mother wasn't home.

Being alone right now scared her, but she didn't want anyone else to get hurt either.

"*For God hath not given us the spirit of fear; but of power, and of love, and of a sound mind,*" she reminded herself then flopped down in the recliner and started to pray.

The doorbell rang and she jumped. She heard loud voices before she reached the door; more than one person was outside her house. She peeked through the living room blinds. Jaidon stood on the porch with his hands raised in the air. Flashing lights flickered. An officer was pointing a gun. Her heart pounded in her chest. Jaidon wasn't the bad guy. The police must have confused Jaidon for Bruno—the last thing she needed was for them to shoot him. She opened the door.

"Close the door!" Jaidon shouted over his shoulder. "And lock it!"

She stood dazed a brief second before doing as instructed. Catherine ran into her old bedroom that faced the front of the house and peered through the blinds. She caught a glimpse of a dark-skinned man holding a gun, pointed at one of the officers. She glanced at the commotion on the curb and in the street. Her breath caught when she noticed the black Ford Explorer. Bruno. He really was after her. And for what? Catherine shook her head and sighed. Violence was senseless. *Lord, please help them to settle this peacefully.*

"Put down the weapon!" the police yelled.

Bruno hesitated then relented. His odds weren't good if he put up a fight. He might be able to shoot one of the officers, but the other one would take him down. Chances were the police officers had backup on the way. As soon as the thought passed through her head, Catherine heard sirens.

She rushed back to the living room and opened the door.

This time she was greeted by Jaidon's smiling face. She flung her arms around his neck. "My hero."

Jaidon squeezed her tight. "Don't I wish."

"But you are." She leaned her head back and looked at him. Pain etched his eyes. "What's wrong?"

"He followed me here." Jaidon ran a hand along the side of her face, staring at her as if he'd never seen her before. "You could have been killed because of me."

"I wasn't. God is faithful. He kept us safe." Catherine kissed him on the cheek.

"Amen," Jaidon said and nuzzled her close. He lifted her chin and stared into her eyes then claimed her lips in a breathtaking kiss.

❧

The next morning Jaidon called his friend Harvey. "I wanted to thank you for taking Daryl Jones's case. Any chance you've heard anything from the police about Bruno's arrest?"

"For a workers' comp lawyer, you sure get mixed in with the wrong element," Harvey said. "Are you sure volunteering your time at that center is worth all the hassle? You could've gotten yourself killed."

Or someone else. Jaidon closed his eyes. He'd talked with Catherine last night after the police left. She'd insisted she still wanted to volunteer at the center, even when he offered to quit and suggested they do something else together.

Catherine was right. They were making a difference. Even though Daryl had messed up, he tried to do the right thing. Tanesha had even warned him. She'd cared enough to reach out and let them know Catherine was in danger. "It's a thankless job, but somebody has to do it."

"Better you than me," Harvey said. "Anyhow, the short of it is, I've gotten Daryl a deal in exchange for his testimony. Come to find out he witnessed several drug deals and can name some key players. Plus he saw Bruno kill a rival gang member who was trying to sell drugs in his territory. Bruno isn't going to see the light of day for a long time."

"That's good to know." Jaidon exhaled a deep breath. That was one load off his mind.

He just had to figure out how to transition his life to the upcoming changes. With time he knew his friends would be happy for him. Right now. . . He had to prepare Catherine for the resistance they might encounter in the meantime.

He also needed to write a letter.

Chapter 10

Three weeks later
New Garden Fellowship Monthly Meeting

We have a couple of things to review today," Matthew Payne announced to the clearness committee and to the congregation's members who'd chosen to stay for the meeting.

Jaidon took a deep breath and rubbed his palms against his thighs, the fabric of his khakis absorbing the sweat. He'd never proposed before. Should he get down on one knee or stand to propose after the church gave its approval?

"We have a request from someone to join the church." Matthew unfolded Jaidon's letter.

Evelyn looked at Jaidon from her seat across the room and winked. Her smile offered him some reassurance. Not that her confidence helped to bolster his. He was more nervous than waiting for a jury to deliberate a court case. He would breathe better once Catherine accepted his proposal.

"Allow me to read the letter we received before I give the decision of the clearness committee," Matthew said.

Dear New Garden Fellowship,
I want to thank you for the opportunity to worship
with you and get to know you. I have learned to take

quiet time to focus more on God. Having grown up in
a fairly large church, I had become so busy that I forgot
this simple truth. Your church has helped me get back to
the basics and deepen my faith and commitment. It is my
desire to join your church, where I know I will continue
to grow as I seek Him.

It is also my desire to pursue marriage to Catherine
Wall. She has exemplified the Christian faith and proven
what a Godly woman and wonderful wife she will make.
Upon your approval of membership, I wish to propose in
the near future, so that Catherine and I may begin to make
plans for our life together.

Sincerely,
Jaidon Taylor

Matthew folded the letter and laid it on the pew. "After carefully discussing these matters with the clearness committee, it is our decision that Mr. Taylor's request be denied."

Jaidon turned to Catherine in horror. Her hand flew to her mouth and she gasped. Tears brimmed her eyes. Her shock reflected his own.

"I don't understand," Jaidon mumbled. He stared blindly at Matthew. "Why?"

"It is our feeling," Matthew said, "that your motives for wanting to join the church are self-serving."

"What?" Jaidon flew to his feet. Anger bubbled up inside his chest. "Because I want to go to the same church as the woman I intend to marry?"

"That request has also been denied." Matthew looked at him sternly, but his tone remained level. "You two have only known each other a little over a month. Certainly not long enough to contemplate marriage. I knew Catherine's father for years and can assure you he would not want his daughter to act rashly and marry someone who converted for his own personal agenda."

His own personal agenda? This was ridiculous. His chest tightened. Unless he convinced the committee otherwise, he wouldn't be able to marry Catherine. "Since you knew her father, I'm sure you know of the promise he made his daughter make. It's this promise that prompted me to convert but not the only reason I'm willing to do so. Seeking the church's approval is important for us to move forward in our relationship. It's not like we plan to marry in the next couple months. We would just like to have your approval and know we are working toward a common goal."

"I'm sorry, Mr. Taylor," Matthew said. "You have our decision." A couple of the men sitting near where Matthew stood nodded in agreement.

Matthew made it sound so final. Like there was nothing more that could be done. Their minds couldn't be changed. "How can you stand there and dictate who can marry and who can't? That should be a decision between us."

Jaidon glanced at Catherine. No doubt the look of shock on her face mirrored his own disbelief. What right did they have to choose whether or not they could be together? This had to be a bad dream. Without their approval, Catherine would never agree to marry him. He felt like a failure. His shoulders slumped.

"It's obvious you aren't willing to accept our ways, which only serves as evidence that you do not hold the same convictions as we do or support the committee's authority and final decision." Matthew folded his hands in front of him.

⊷

Catherine saw Jaidon's face turn pale. He stormed out of the pew and headed for the door.

It wasn't fair. She didn't want to date someone else, or marry anyone else either. Jaidon loved her—enough that he was willing to change—for her. If her father were alive, surely he could see that Jaidon was good for her, made her complete.

She stood abruptly. "Please don't do this," Catherine pleaded. "We love each other and want to be together. What's wrong with us wanting to belong to the same church? After all, marriage is about two fleshes becoming one."

"We feel that you are both acting on physical attraction, which is a bad way to begin a relationship," Matthew said. "There are plenty of eligible men to choose from. You need to find someone, like my nephew Michael, who already shares your faith and isn't making a halfhearted attempt to become something he's not."

"Something he's not?" Catherine glared at Matthew. She'd gone out on one date with Michael in high school. She wouldn't have even done that if Matthew hadn't pressed her mother, trying to encourage her to be nice to his nephew when they'd moved to the area. Michael, or any other man she'd met, could never stack up to Jaidon. "I can tell you something he is—he's kind-hearted and giving. Jaidon lives out his faith in the love and dedication he shows to others. He didn't think anything of putting himself in harm's way to protect me—"

"Which only shows he has a violent side," Matthew contested. "He stood up to someone who was violent and possibly deadly. Was he going to talk his way out of it?" He didn't wait for Catherine to respond. "We are peaceful, and we avoid violence."

"He—" Catherine stammered.

"Enough!" Catherine's mother stood. Everyone stared at her. Normally her mother was very docile. . .unless her feathers were ruffled enough. The look on her face was one her mother wore when she'd been pushed to her limits. Growing up, when Catherine got in trouble, she knew that look meant don't press your luck or you'd find out the hard way she's not the pushover people often mistook her for. Her mother's eyes had focused on something behind Catherine.

When Catherine turned to follow her mother's gaze, she saw Jaidon. He hadn't left; his angry glare remained focused on Matthew. She didn't blame him for being upset. The committee members didn't care how she and Jaidon felt. They hadn't talked with either of them; how could they know their hearts?

Catherine looked back at her mother, silently pleading for her to help.

"You asked Jaidon what I told him that night in church, when he declared before everyone that he wanted to convert." Her mother smiled. "I told him that no matter what they decide, you have my blessing."

"Our decision is final," Matthew said.

"And you're entitled to your opinion, but in the life of my daughter, I'm the one who can give her my blessing." Catherine had never seen her mother take such a stand. Not even against her father. "You were only twelve when your father passed away. Way too young to know what love is. Your father should have never made you make that promise to him. It was unfair. You have the power to choose for yourself."

Catherine nodded. She felt as if a weight had been lifted from her. Her heart soared like a feather, floating in peace. She turned back to Matthew. "I will always cherish my heritage.

But I can't believe that God would be so stringent to not allow me to follow my heart, or His leading. I choose the love of my heavenly Father and the man He has placed in my life. The man that I want to spend the rest of my life with."

"If you do this," Matthew said sternly, "you will force us to read you out of meeting."

"Do what you must." She didn't want to live without Jaidon. Even if she had to suffer the consequences—it was better than giving up love. Catherine turned to step out of the pew, intent on leaving, when she collided with Jaidon. She smiled. "Déjà vu," she whispered. "Like the first time we met."

Jaidon laughed. He took a step back, held out a small velveteen box, and opened it. "They can't stop us from being together. No matter what they or their committee decides."

A woman who sat nearby gasped, and Catherine's mother clapped.

With shaking fingers, Catherine traced her finger over the large beautiful diamond, gleaming in its halo setting, and inhaled deeply. It was unbelievable. He'd even chosen white gold, which she preferred. "It's beautiful."

"What do you say?" Jaidon grinned, the most adorable sheepish grin she'd ever seen. "Will you marry me?"

Catherine didn't need to look at Matthew, the Friends around them, or the clearness committee to answer. "Yes."

Chapter 11

Three months later

"Let's sit somewhere else today." Catherine held Jaidon's hand as he guided her to *their* nicely padded sanctuary seats. She couldn't believe she was already a member of his church, and before long, she would be part of his family. "We've sat in the same general area for months. I'm starting to feel like we're in high school again and have assigned seats."

"Fine. We'll move." Jaidon chuckled. He changed directions and headed for several empty seats to the left of the section they normally sat in. He scooted down to leave a couple empty seats on the end of the row. "If your mom and Alex don't find us, it's your fault."

"Church isn't that big." Catherine nudged him playfully. "And she knows I'm wearing this bright floral sundress. She'll find us."

"You're both here early as usual." Thomas stopped to greet them. "How is everything going?"

"Fine," Jaidon said and shook his hand.

"Are you excited about the wedding next week?" he asked Catherine.

Her mother and Alex approached them. "She's not as excited as I am," she said and hugged Pastor Burnside. "Thank you for performing the ceremony."

"It'll be my pleasure." The pastor's smile was sincere. "Good to see you again, Alex. I'm looking forward to officiating your wedding next week."

"Thank you." Alex nodded. A rare smile crossed his face. No matter how tough he acted on the outside, Catherine knew he was a softie and adored her mother.

As soon as the pastor moved on, her mother hugged Catherine and sat next to her.

"Hey, kiddo. Jaidon." Alex winked at her and nodded toward Jaidon. "We going out for lunch later?"

"Sure thing," Jaidon said.

Catherine watched as their senior pastor went on to greet others. The more she'd gotten to know Thomas, the more she liked him. He watched over the congregation and offered sound spiritual advice. She enjoyed the Bible study she and Jaidon attended on Monday nights. Not only did she take quiet time for God, but she also felt she was learning more of the Word and growing as a Christian.

Her outlook on life had changed so much in the last few months, and it all started when she walked into the center. It was exciting to see other lives changed as well. Tanesha and Daryl not only went to the center regularly but were also attending a local church. The change in their lives had inspired other youth to become involved with the center.

Catherine couldn't wait to begin premarital counseling classes in a couple weeks. Life with Jaidon, working and ministering by his side, held so much promise. Catherine sighed.

"I know that sound." Her mother linked her arm through hers. "You've got that dreamy look on your face. Whatcha thinkin' about, kiddo?"

"Marriage." Catherine nodded toward the front of the sanctuary. "You and Alex are getting married next week."

"And you wish it were you." Her mother giggled. "See that engagement ring on your finger?"

Catherine nodded.

"Every time you look at it, just keep reminding yourself that you only have four months until you are Mrs. Jaidon Taylor. And with each new day, you are one day closer to the blessed event." Her mother kissed her cheek. "I'll be back from my honeymoon in plenty of time to help you plan your wedding."

"Are you two supposed to be talking in church?" Jaidon whispered, leaning closer.

"*Shh*." Catherine let go of her mother's arm and put an index finger to her lips while trying to contain a laugh. She remembered when she first came to this church and the people were talking before service. It wasn't the bad thing she'd thought it was, just as long as they didn't talk *during* service.

"I'm going to *shh* you." Jaidon leaned against her, giving her a small nudge. "And don't I get any say in our wedding plans?"

"We agreed that you can plan the honeymoon," Catherine said, "because I'm not having a sports-themed wedding.... And if you plan a honeymoon that includes any sports events, you can count me out."

"So you won't mind if I take Alex then?"

Catherine's mouth flew open.

He laughed.

She jabbed Jaidon in the ribs.

"If we were alone, I'd kiss you."

She closed her mouth. The smoldering look in his eyes reflected the truth in his words. Catherine licked her lips as she stared at his. Her breath caught. She almost tasted the sweetness of his lips as she thought about his kiss.

"You temptress," Jaidon said in a breathy tone. "I've half a mind to drag you out of here and kiss you anyway."

"And you call me a temptress?" Catherine turned her nose up at Jaidon as she twisted her head toward her mother. "We'll be back in a moment, Mom."

"Make that a couple minutes." Jaidon laughed. Taking her by the hand, he got to his feet and tugged her swiftly behind him. She followed him to a secluded area outside beneath the shade trees. "Now aren't you glad I insisted on coming to church early? Or we wouldn't have time to do this."

Without giving her time to respond, Jaidon cupped the back of her neck, tilted her head for his lips to claim hers, and closed the gap between them.

She savored the warmth of his kiss. "Mmm. I will never get tired of kissing you."

"I hope not." Jaidon laughed and gave her a peck. "Now let's get back in service. You're always making me late."

Epilogue

Four months later

E verything is in place," Ariannah said. Her peach bridesmaid dress complimented her skin tone and slender figure. "You look gorgeous."

"Thank you. So do you." Catherine hugged her. Now that Ariannah had found a guy her own age, she'd given up her school-girl crush on Jaidon. It allowed peace to settle between them, which budded into a fast-growing friendship, one Catherine deeply treasured. "I couldn't have done this without you."

"I'm glad I could help." Ariannah moved behind Catherine to straighten her fish-tail train. Catherine loved the wedding dress Ariannah had helped her choose. The sleeveless peach bodice added a flare of elegance yet remained simple in design. She'd opted not to wear a veil but allowed Ariannah to apply makeup, something she normally didn't wear.

Catherine fanned her face with her hand as they lined up in the order they would walk down the aisle. She placed a delicate, manicured hand in the crook of Alex's arm and smiled. "Thank you for giving me away."

"My pleasure." He kissed her cheek and patted her hand.

The wedding march began to play. Catherine lifted her flowers, white stephanotis with peach spray rose bouquet, to her chest and breathed deeply. Ariannah, and then her other bridesmaid, a friend from work, walked slowly down the aisle. Catherine's stomach fluttered like hummingbird wings. She straightened, squared her shoulders, and smiled as they slowly made their way to the front of the church.

A flurry of excitement coursed through her when she glanced at Jaidon. He looked dashing in his black tuxedo with coordinating peach tie and vest. Kacey and Roberto stood next to him.

She winked at her mother and smiled at Jaidon's parents. Jaidon stepped forward as she approached him.

"Who gives this woman in marriage to this man?" Thomas asked.

"Her mother and I do." Alex took her hand and gave it to Jaidon, who kissed it, placed it in the crook of his arm, and walked with her the few remaining feet to stand before the pastor.

As they faced each other, Catherine looked into the depths of Jaidon's sea-blue eyes, drawn by the purity and love shining in them. The pastor allowed them to exchange the vows they'd written.

"I, Jaidon Taylor, promise to live each day serving Him, so that I can better serve you. I promise to be faithful and love you all the days of our lives. May God grant us many," he said and smiled, "because forever could never be long enough with you."

She desired nothing more than to enter into marriage in the sight of God with the man she loved with all of her heart... surrounded by family and friends.

SUSETTE WILLIAMS lives in Missouri with her husband and six children. Her family is very competitive and enjoys playing games together, which sometimes can be classified as "contact sports" at her house. She loves to write, scrapbook, sew, and share tips with family and friends on saving money. Visit her online at www.SusetteWilliams.com.